'Tess Little is a modern Aga— —— —— ——r nine suspects, locking them in a spr—— Los Angeles mansion, and knocking them down one by one over the course of a decadent, stomach-turning dinner party . . . *The Ninth Guest* kept me guessing until the very last'

Tanen Jones, author of *The Better Liar*

'Dark, compelling Hollywood intrigue and a diverse cast of well-drawn characters make *The Ninth Guest* a unique locked-room mystery that readers will simply devour! It's perfect for fans of Lucy Foley'

Wendy Walker, bestselling author of *Don't Look for Me*

'With a knowing satirical eye, Tess Little skilfully weaves a page-turner full of satisfying twists and turns. What starts as a murder mystery soon turns into a carnival of LA parties, blending and bleeding into each other, as time doubles over on itself. Ultimately, *The Ninth Guest* is the moving story of power, cruelty, and one woman's quest to reclaim her daughter, her past, and ultimately, herself'

**Kyle McCarthy,
author of *Everyone Knows How Much I Love You***

Tess Little is a writer and historian. She was born in Norwich and studied history at the Universities of Oxford and Cambridge. At the age of 22 she was elected as a Fellow of All Souls College, University of Oxford, where she completed a doctorate on 1970s feminist activism in the UK, France, and the US. Her short stories and non-fiction have appeared in *Words and Women: Two*, *The Mays Anthology*, *The Belleville Park Pages*, *The White Review*, and on posters outside a London tube station. This is her first novel.

TESS LITTLE

The Ninth Guest

HODDER

First published in Great Britain in 2020 as *The Octopus* by Hodder & Stoughton
An Hachette UK company

This paperback edition published in 2021

1

A CIP catalogue record for this title is available from the British Library

Paperback ISBN 978 1 529 35884 1
eBook ISBN 978 1 529 35882 7

Typeset in Plantin by Palimpsest Book Production Ltd, Falkirk, Stirlingshire

Printed and bound in Great Britain by Clays Ltd, Elcograf S.p.A.

Hodder & Stoughton policy is to use papers that are natural, renewable and
recyclable products and made from wood grown in sustainable forests. The
logging and manufacturing processes are expected to conform to the
environmental regulations of the country of origin.

Hodder & Stoughton Ltd
Carmelite House
50 Victoria Embankment
London EC4Y 0DZ

www.hodder.co.uk

For A.S. & I.L.

We believed he had died from an overdose. There was no reason to suspect otherwise: limbs limp on the couch; pink vomit splattered across his shirt, dribbling from the corners of his mouth; the Gucci belt, the residue-stained needles – our own memories, in flashes and throbs and waves. We did not call an ambulance. The flesh was cold to the touch.

It had been my fingers stroking his stony neck for a pulse. With none to be found I looked up, caught Honey's eye, gave the nod. The others were lifting their heads. I would have to tell them, I realised, as Honey crept over their stretching arms, slipped the cell phone from his back pocket, and disappeared around the corner.

I shut my eyes, let the morning light glow through, as it had for a few moments upon waking. There were yawns and groans, and then a gasp. I steeled for the chaos.

ACT I

'Elspeth,' he said.

His eyes were tired but his teeth were whiter than before. He held open the door to the house.

'Richard,' I replied. 'Happy birthday.'

We leaned towards each other for a kiss of each cheek. His stubble pricked. One hand on my inner elbow pulled me close – his other, still on the door. He pushed back to regard me once more. I told myself not to tuck the hair behind my ear again, not to smooth my skirt or run my finger beneath the gold band on my wrist, tried to calm the cells of my body. Let him look at me; let him see what I had become.

'And what a fabulous present you are.' He grinned. 'I'm so glad you came.'

Laughter echoed from the belly of the house.

'Here,' Richard said, twitching to action with a wave down the corridor. 'Come in. I can't wait to introduce you to everyone.'

Entering the building, I found I had been deceived. From the driveway, its façade loomed large: two colossal cubes atop a thin rectangle, all in a smooth, pale concrete. Its angular grey assaulted the eyes, accustomed, as they had grown on the drive up, to the thick, hatching branches of the pines, the swells of the landscape. This was not our family home – sold, immediately, to pay the settlement. This was a fortress. As I had stood in its shadow, tugging my skirt before ringing the doorbell, I had tried to imagine the harsh surfaces, the darkness within.

Instead, I followed Richard into brightness.

'Welcome,' he said, 'to Sedgwick.'

He watched for my reaction to the name, but he would find

no trace of surprise. I had seen the sign, driving in, and I refused to acknowledge it.

'How long have you been . . . ?' I asked, eyes skittering over the bare grey walls, the cold marble and clean glass. All were flooded with natural light, but from where, I could not tell: each room we passed seemed a floor of its own, overlapping and overlaid. To draw a map of the place would be impossible.

'Living at Sedgwick? Five years now and it does feel like home.' He walked three feet ahead of me, spoke without turning. 'And yet every time I welcome a new guest, when I see their expression as I open the door, I'm reminded of its beauty all over again. Classical in its modernity. Sparse, but with a flourish.'

I hummed my agreement, concentrating on the placement of my stilettos. My stomach was acid. My tongue was dry. And I was here, with Richard, a decade to the day since we had last spoken, unaccompanied, in the flesh.

As we continued through the corridors Richard asked about my trip, asked if he could put anything in the cloakroom. I declined, clutching my purse close, regretting, not for the first time, that I had been forced into arriving alone. Perhaps it could have been interesting, peering into Richard's new life with Lillie on my arm. Facing him by myself, I could barely muster a sentence. I let him tell me about the architect, who had lived in the home until his death, which occurred, so *fortunately*, a month before Richard had begun his property search. I let him recount his first visit, how it had been love at first sight. I let him talk about the origin of the materials; the trajectory of the sun; refittings, renovations.

They were nothing but boasts: a spiel he had presumably recited to his other guests. It was only when he mentioned the interior – 'the vision isn't mine, of course; I'm not the aesthetic genius' – that I bristled, knowing who that true visionary was.

The voices grew louder – my heartbeat faster – as we passed into a darkening area of the corridor, illuminated cool by a wall of water. It was exquisitely blue, perfectly clear.

'How unique,' I said to Richard, who turned to me, shadows tracing the contours of his blue face, and smiled. I noted his lingering scent, still Eau Sauvage, of course, of course. 'Some kind of contemporary sculpture?'

Richard laughed. I waited, uncertain and unsmiling, for him to finish.

'Yes, I can see it. A slice of the sea, a light installation,' he said and laughed again, one staccato: *Hah*. 'What a marvellous notion. But no, it's not artwork. I had to find somewhere to show off Persephone, and this was the only suitable space.'

'Persephone?'

The wall was empty. I would have thought the water motionless were it not for dancing rays of light.

'You'll meet her soon enough,' he answered, continuing along the passage.

And then we emerged to sunlight and sound. Richard threw out his arms and announced: 'The atrium.'

It was magnificent. If the façade of the house had concealed a secret, then this was its dazzling conclusion. The corridor opened onto a vast, vaulted room, which, I realised as we entered, was only a mezzanine, overlooking another floor below. But these shifting perspectives were not the showstopper. For, where a wall should have faced us, at the far end of this concrete cathedral, there towered instead a window, stretching all the way across and up.

There it was, the sloping vista I had avoided until now. There, in the pit of my throat – the sudden drop, the return of those hills.

Richard called my name. I pried my fingers, knuckle-white, from the balcony wall and turned to catch him disappear down a spiral staircase.

However unexpected this architectural drama, none of it surprised me. Instead, I was surprised by the lack of faces that now tilted upwards to register my arrival, examine my appearance. Seven faces: two known, the rest perhaps familiar – from the pages of a magazine, pixels, or parties, I could not say. Lillie was not among them. Lillie had not arrived. My hands trembled, my nerves thrummed, at this terrible realisation.

I neatened my skirt, my hair, my bracelet. I followed Richard down.

Picking my way, I told myself to calm. I had spotted Jerry and Tommo, two old friends. They would look after me until Lillie arrived. Which would surely be soon. Everything would be fine. The group of guests, sitting on couches at the centre of the cavernous room, was surrounded by twice as many champagne-bearers; I was simply early. Lillie would arrive, the house would fill with people, and everything would be fine.

My heels clanged the metal steps. I winced with each ringing note.

Three staff, solemn in head-to-toe black, awaited me at the bottom of the stairs: one with a tray of full flutes, one with a dish towel and frosty bottle, one to ask, 'Champagne?' and hand me the stem.

Richard lifted a glass from the tray for himself.

'You're drinking these days?' I asked, and took a mouthful. The fizz stung; the gulp was harsh. I blinked back the tears in my eyes.

He laughed, like the question had been ridiculous. 'For a once-in-a-lifetime occasion, darling, yes.'

I pursed my lips, but he could do whatever he wanted. Richard was no longer my responsibility.

As we neared the little gathering, the room fell silent. There were smiles both warm and empty – and, I noticed, a smatter of annoyance at my presence interrupting talk.

'So,' I looked around the guests, at the staff lined up behind them, 'am I early?'

Jerry winked, approaching me for a kiss, and added, 'Yeah, Rich, where are all your friends? Interstate bumper-to-bumper?'

'Fuck off,' said Richard. Then, to me, gently, 'I felt an intimate gathering would be more . . .'

'Manageable?' said Jerry.

'Fitting.'

Conversation had bubbled back on the couches. I could now see that it was not simply a wall of water we had passed in the corridor upstairs, but an enormous aquarium spanning both floors. Above and beneath the blue, the shape of the tank continued in concrete, smoothed seamlessly into ceiling and floor. But it was so luminous, so alive with dancing sunlight and swaying plants – so antithetical to the surroundings.

The nearest waitress, a woman with sunny hair slicked into a ponytail, replenished the sips I'd taken from my glass.

'Thank you,' I said.

She beamed at me, replied, 'Of course,' then let her face fall back to blank.

'Let me check something with the caterers,' said Richard, touching my back. 'And after that I can introduce you around properly.'

'Caterers?' I turned to Jerry. He was dressed in characteristically hopeless clothes: a suit both over- and undersized. The shoulders were wrinkling, belly pushing at the shirt. 'Is this a dinner party? I hadn't – I didn't expect any of this.'

'Tell me about it. And when he says intimate,' Jerry lowered his voice, 'I don't know. I've been here for an hour now and you're the only person that's arrived.'

'You've been here an hour? He told Lillie things weren't starting till six-thirty, so I thought seven—'

'Rich told me five-thirty. But I got the impression, when I came in, that some of the others might have been here for a while. They were surprised when I showed up.'

We examined the group. Only four discussions were taking place, including ours. Tommo smiled at me, nodded, over the shoulder of a short dark-haired woman. To their left were two men: one older, sitting with his legs spread wide, dominating conversation; the younger barely listening, eyes blandly roaming the room. An actor, almost certainly: he had a striking, yet forgettable face – the kind of face one could mould into any thick-necked, all-American, Wonder Bread hero. I wasn't sure whether I recognised him or not.

And there, on the other couch sat Richard's partner, speaking with a woman whose face I could not see. I did not let my eyes linger in that direction; I couldn't be caught staring.

'Wonder what's on the menu,' said Jerry.

'This is ridiculous,' I said. Then, pathetically, 'I've already eaten.'

Jerry chuckled. 'I don't know, I gotta tell you, I can't see Rich accepting that excuse.'

'Well maybe he should let people know what they're getting into.'

'Elsie,' he said, 'come on, you know that's not his style.'

'So he can accept the consequences,' I said. 'I'll stay for one more drink after Lillie arrives and then I'm leaving. It's lovely to see you, of course, but I didn't fly across the country to spend time with' – I whispered – 'whoever these people are. Not for an unexpected, *intimate*, whatever-he-wants-to-call-it dinner party.'

Jerry clasped his chest. 'You mean you didn't schlep all that way for me? Because you missed this beautiful face?'

'If I could spend all evening with your beautiful face, Jerry, I'd be thrilled, believe me. It's the prospect of spending hours with a handful of strangers that concerns me.'

I had expected a large, bursting party – one of the sprawling carnivals Richard usually held in his own honour – and on the flight I'd comforted myself with the thought that I could tuck into a corner, avoid uncomfortable encounters, cling to Lillie's side. I had not prepared for this claustrophobic, unnatural scene. It was a movie set. The cast, costumed, at the centre; the staff circling the periphery, ensuring everything would unfold as planned. Constructed scenery, the carefully placed furniture, the champagne and glasses as props. And there was Richard, slipping between the two worlds, ready to direct the dialogue between guests, to task his crew, here and there.

What did that make me? I felt I belonged to neither role, but I was not like Richard – I was not in among it all. I wouldn't perform. I was passive. Maybe the camera, or the audience.

I sipped again; the woman standing at my shoulder filled my glass again; I thanked her again.

'Of course,' she said.

It was a chirpy response, I thought, but not one that entirely made sense.

'Glad to hear Lillie's coming,' said Jerry. 'Oh,' he added, as the woman moved to refill his champagne, 'no, thanks. Actually, you know if there's any Scotch?'

'Of course,' said the woman. 'We've got a Macallan – would that be okay, sir?'

I studied the aquarium while they talked. The rocks and plants – purple, green and red – were hypnotic. Enough to distract my stare from the couch on the right, where Richard's partner sat. The stalks were rippling; the water almost glowed. It was a splendid display, but for what? 'Persephone' must have been there, among the crags and fronds. Yet the luscious foliage appeared unoccupied from where I stood. The blue stretched empty above.

'Very nice,' said Jerry. 'Sure. Neat, but I can get it myself if you—'

'No, please, allow me, sir. Macallan, neat.'

'Thanks,' said Jerry.

'Of course,' repeated the woman. The emptiness of the phrase, her enthusiasm, was grating. What did it mean? That we should, *of course*, be thankful?

'Lillie, yeah – what was I saying?' said Jerry. 'Yeah, it'll be good to see her. Finally emailed my pal Bob, like she asked, and he's fine with her getting in touch. Guess I'll give her his details when she gets here.'

I nodded like I knew who Jerry was talking about, like my daughter let me in on the details of her life, her career. Jerry was Richard's manager, so I imagined this Bob was a casting director, maybe an agent or manager.

'How is she?' Jerry said.

'Lillie? She seems to be doing great. New house, new life. I'm staying with her. Over on Cahuenga.'

'You must be so proud of her.'

'I am,' I said, 'I am.'

The waitress returned with Jerry's Scotch, presented on a black square napkin. He thanked her.

'Of course.' She took up the champagne bottle and resumed her position, just a foot behind us. Would the little group be waited upon like this all night?

Jerry held the napkin in a pinch to inspect it – then scrunched the thing into his pocket.

'Anyhow,' he said, 'I gotta say it's nice to have you in town again. *Long* time no see.'

'Not since Richard's fortieth,' I replied.

'Was it really ten years ago? Fuck. Ten years. But you look great.'

And I did, following a weekly facial and the extra half-hour added to my daily schedule for moisturising, for smudging Touche Éclat, for taming flyaways. Had Jerry become as paranoid about ageing as I had over the last decade? Or was it simply a new item to add to my never-ending checklist: wipe the lipstick from your champagne glass; cross your legs; lift your chin to hide the budding jowl?

'You look like shit,' I said, touching his arm. And he did – hair thinning, withered. His hopeless suit.

Jerry laughed. The laugh was the same, as was his voice. Thick, a little throaty: peanut butter scooped straight from the jar. 'Been keeping busy?'

It was the question I dreaded the most. There were different ways to answer. I could invoke my investment portfolio, my charity work – but this was Jerry. I opted instead for honesty.

'No, I haven't – but tell me, how's Judy doing these days? Still no divorce?'

'Oh jeez, not for lack of trying,' Jerry said. 'But I love her, separation threats and all. She's great. How about you, anyone special?'

'There have been one or two men in my life, but not currently, no.'

Richard was making his way back across the room, directing staff to fill glasses as he went.

I moved closer to Jerry, whispered, 'So Richard's drinking now?'

Jerry sighed. 'I don't know. I've given up on telling the guy what to do. He said it was for his birthday, but come on, I know how he is. You and I both know. I was like, fine, whatever, long as you don't give me these bullshit excuses. I just figure . . . I mean, with everyone else here, it's not my place, you know? Like when you were around. I took a back seat then. Not my place, not my problem.'

Jerry watched Richard for a moment, then added, 'He seems to have a handle on it. Just two champagnes, I've counted. But it's – I mean, he's always in control, until suddenly he isn't. You know?'

I did.

I let my gaze drift back to the aquarium, to the motion of the fronds, the back and forth . . . and then I caught it – bright and red – snaking out from the rocks at the bottom of the tank. A tentacle: the ninth guest.

Richard noted my stare, sidled back to us.

'Persephone, Elspeth,' he said. 'Elspeth, Persephone.'

Only a sliver of the creature was visible – two limbs now and part of the head were spilling out of the crevice. Nevertheless, there was something about the fluid mass that raised the hairs at the back of my neck. It was mesmerising. It was grotesque.

Richard watched me, a smirk dancing around the edges of my mouth.

I tried to appear nonchalant as I said: 'And we'll be spending the night with that creature watching over us?'

Richard nudged Jerry. 'You see, this is why we divorced – now I can buy all the pretty presents I desire.'

I laughed with the men, but it came out plastic: hard and fake.

'That's funny,' I said, to Jerry. '*I* thought we had divorced so he could *fuck* all the things he desired.'

I hadn't thought it would carry over the chatter.

There was silence until Richard laughed, then a couple of his friends, three seconds behind.

Jerry threw up his hands and cried indignantly: 'Am I the only one here who hasn't slept with Rich?'

Richard stole me from Persephone and Jerry, introduced me to each cluster of guests.

'Charlie, Miguel, this is my ex-wife, Elspeth,' he said, as both rose to their feet to kiss my cheeks. 'Charlie you'll recognise as the star of *Dominus*. Miguel, my dearest fat cat.' Richard gestured towards the two men as he spoke. They had already resumed their private conversation – Charlie, vacant and gorgeous, reclining on the cushions, fiddling with his hair; Miguel emphasising each syllable with a thrust of his hand. I didn't recognise the former from *Dominus* – I hadn't seen it yet – but maybe from posters, the trailer; maybe I'd driven past his billboard-stretched face.

Richard added: 'I don't think I was working with Miguel's studio back when you and I were together, but he's the man to thank for my last few films. Perfect producer. As you know, Ellie darling,' he flashed me a grin, 'a good exec should be seen and not heard.'

I recognised both inhabitants of the next couch, now that I was closer: the woman who'd had her back turned to me was Sabine Selmi, Richard's latest leading lady, and there, beside her, was Honey, whose bleach-blond hair was shaved close to his head. His shirt was bright white, crisp against his mahogany skin.

Neither looked up until Richard said their names, choosing Sabine first – 'my Gallic muse' – then, without pause: 'and this, of course, is Honey.'

I watched Honey tug one sleeve an inch to the left, so the obsidian cuff link lay perfectly over his outer wristbone. The gesture was somehow youthful – discomfort at all the formality – which he certainly was. Younger than me, much younger than Richard. I knew that Richard was back with Honey – this was why Lillie had asked me to attend the party; she hadn't wanted to face her father's boyfriend alone – yet nothing could have prepared me for that moment.

A heat was building in my chest: the need to escape their

beautiful stares, their judgement. Neither Sabine nor Honey stood to greet me; no fake kisses, just a polite pause, nods.

Then they looked away, unimpressed. Sabine continued talking; Honey ran a hand over his golden hair. I turned to find Richard already moving on to the final pair.

'Now this scoundrel, you know all too well,' he said.

Tommo, an old schoolfriend of Richard's, squeezed my shoulder as he kissed my cheeks. 'Elspeth, what a delightful surprise.'

'And Kei,' Richard continued, 'you might remember, is my favourite cinematographer.'

I could recall neither the face nor the name. She was small but well built; tattoos studded up her arms, down her neck. A short back and sides, a thick, silver watch.

We locked eyes, she smiled, as Richard went on: 'You've been my DP for how long, Kei?'

'*One Hundred Years* was our first real project together,' she said.

'So that must have been . . .'

I remembered exactly when it was released: as our divorce was finalised. The making of the movie was carved into my past: how the filming trip had lengthened the distance between us; how the wrap party had exposed our lies and our apathy; how, finally, I had left with Lillie and Richard had let me. I'd never managed to sit through the film – Richard's third studio-backed feature; a surreal, anthological exploration of the Battle of Agincourt. But I had idly wondered whether our divorce's boosting of the box-office figures, with all the TMZ articles and E! segments, should have factored into the final settlement.

'A decade?' said Kei.

Yes, a decade. The film had been released eight years, nine months, two weeks ago. Give or take.

'Thereabouts,' said Richard. 'Anyway, I'll leave you in these capable hands, while I check everything backstage.'

'Where on earth does he keep dashing off to?' asked Tommo.

He was taller than I remembered, with an Adam's apple that bobbed as he spoke and that hearty British look. I could picture him with a newspaper rolled under his long arm, striding in his Monday-morning work suit – though he was dressed, that night, in a cream shirt unbuttoned at the neck and pants too bright blue for finance.

'I heard something about caterers,' I said.

'Caterers? Bloody hell. Is this a dinner party now? I did wonder about the numbers. A little unconventional for Dicky.' Tommo looked at Kei. 'Did you hear anything about this?'

'I'm as clueless as you, dude,' she said. Kei held herself awkwardly, one hand in pocket – the stem of her glass in a fist. 'So, uh, Elspeth. Did you have far to travel? Or are you local?'

Tommo scoffed before I could answer. 'Oh no, look at her. She's far too pale for California. No offence intended, darling. You're the purest porcelain.'

'None taken,' I said. And then to Kei: 'New York City.'

'Cool,' she said. 'Whereabouts?'

'Manhattan. Upper East Side.'

Kei nodded and nodded, like she was searching for something to say. I looked to the aquarium – I was curious to see what the others thought of Persephone – but she had disappeared again, and I couldn't quite phrase the question.

Tommo stepped in. 'And how's Lillie?'

'She's great, yes, she'll be arriving any minute now, so you can ask her yourself.'

My words had come out too cheery and my facial expression, I was certain, was verging on sarcastic. I was happy to see Tommo again, really, and the cinematographer seemed nice enough, but I felt too aware of myself in this three-way conversation, too preoccupied with my daughter's absence.

I tried to relax my shoulders. Put down my champagne glass and found a bottle of water I had thrown into my purse on my way out of Lillie's house. Acqua Panna – still cold, condensation on the glass.

'I didn't know Lillie was coming.' Kei seemed genuinely pleased. 'Are you staying with her? When we were working on *Dominus*, she was telling me about all of that shit with the realtors, and I was like: Welcome to the real world, my friend. From here on out everything is admin, your hangovers are gonna suck ass, and everyone will let you down. Especially LA realtors. Especially.'

'Oh she moved, did she?' Tommo said. 'Where to?'

I opened my mouth to answer, but was interrupted by the silver-sounding ring of metal on glass.

'Now that we are all, at last, gathered together,' called Richard. 'I'd like you to join me in the dining area. Our dinner is served. This way.'

My gaze followed the shaft of light down to the couch. I could have been a young woman in morning sun, slowly opening my eyes to the face of my lover. I might have discovered something beautiful in his lazy posture. I might have seen something fragile in his exposed neck.

But the spell of sleep could not last.

Stale cigarette smoke lingered in the air. Empty bottles, concrete floor. I was awake. My arm was cold and wet. My body ached.

And his elbow was bent. And his fingers were splayed. And his head was thrown back.

I pushed myself up from the floor, shaking, wiped the hairs caught in my saliva, smeared across my cheek. I sat down beside him. I looked. My breath caught, my heart clenched—

The wet 'O' of the mouth, the stare of the eyes, the stench of vomit.

I did not think; I reached forwards.

The flesh was cold to the touch.

As I rounded the aquarium to find the dining area, the bursting detail that met me felt like a reflection of the tank, with its colourful weeds and rockery: a contained chaos. The table, at first glance, was beautifully laid: pink, blue, yellow wax candles, dribbling down their sticks; lilac wisteria tumbling from bowls; blue glass plates; dishes piled heavy with food. It was busy and bright, vivid against the stark room.

At second glance, the dishes were anarchy. Sugared doughnuts battling lobster; strawberries and cream almost escaping to the sushi platter below; a whole roast turkey kicking tiramisu. The other guests laughed, exclaimed with delight.

'Yes, yes,' Richard called, 'it's eccentric, I know. Take your seats and I'll explain.'

I was silent. We were not all gathered. Not yet. But there were only nine places: no chair for Lillie. I circled the table, reading the little hand-painted cards on each plate, hoping I had miscounted. I had not: my daughter's name was absent. So Lillie would not arrive until after the meal. Could I survive another hour or so without her?

I slipped my cell from my purse to text her, but Tommo held my arm. Murmured: 'Didn't you get the lecture on the way in? Dicky said no phones tonight. I mean, he didn't go so far as to confiscate them at the door, but I got the impression he'd try if we pushed it.'

Another ridiculous demand. I would message her, surreptitiously, when attention was directed elsewhere.

I found my own name last, between Charlie on one side and an empty end at the foot of the table. Why hadn't the chairs been pulled around? Maybe the space had been saved in case Lillie arrived in time – or maybe Richard, at the head of the table, wanted all attention on him.

The waiters stood behind us. White-gloved, now. I took my seat, placed my bottled water on the table, and turned to Charlie. He was talking with Sabine, and so I picked up my place card. Stared at the name until its cursive gold letters became almost unrecognisable. It was surrounded by a burst of dark-blue lines. I turned over the card, found one word: *Soul*.

Charlie was inspecting his card as well. It was bordered with yellow and gold constellations.

'*Ether*?' he read from the reverse. 'What the hell is that supposed to mean?'

'Aren't they gorgeous?' said Richard. 'It's all Honey's work. The flowers and the candles too. But those place cards, I absolutely adore.'

'Did you paint them?' Charlie asked. 'Why does mine say *Ether*?'

Honey smiled to himself. 'It's not – I just kind of got carried away.'

'Don't be modest,' said Richard. 'It's unbecoming.'

Honey mock scowled at him, then turned back to the table to explain. 'I wanted a theme,' he said, 'so I decided that each of us would be an element. In one branch of Hindu philosophy there are nine—'

'I'm Time,' said Jerry. 'Why am I Time? You think I'm getting old? Shouldn't that be Rich?'

'Richard is Space,' said Honey. 'I'm Earth.' He pointed at each of us in turn. 'Sabine, Water. Elspeth, Soul or Self. Kei is Fire, Tommo is Mind and Miguel is . . .'

'I'm Air,' declared Miguel.

'Air, yeah, that's it.' Honey cleared his throat. 'But it's not like it's significant or anything, I just – I was interested in the concepts, so I thought—'

'But, like, what does it *mean*?' said Charlie. 'I still don't understand why I'm Ether.'

'It's not important,' said Richard. 'They're just place cards. A pretty bit of fun. Please. The food is getting cold.'

Honey looked down at his plate, straightened his knife and fork.

'Well, I think they're thoughtful,' said Kei. 'And I like mine. Fire. I'm gonna keep it.'

Richard tapped his glass again, though no one else was talking. The head of the table was nearest to the towering window, and so he was silhouetted against the sky, which blushed with the setting sun. 'I'm sure you're all wondering about this eclectic feast before you. I do hope you can forgive an old man his whims. Please, start tucking in while I explain.'

The guests passed the dishes back and forth, ladling cream, drizzling sauce, dipping fries in tiramisu. Tommo waved a waiter away so he could carve the turkey himself. He draped slices on the others' plates, over cream and sushi and coffee-soaked ladyfingers. Kei was passing out steaks with a pair of tongs. I declined. Took one small doughnut instead. Placed it on my plate, licked the powdered sugar from my fingertips.

'When I was a young boy,' Richard began, raising his voice over the crockery, the clatters and the scrapes, 'I had a sweet tooth and a very old-fashioned nanny – an unfortunate combination. She'd engineer the most foul concoctions for supper. Dry mutton, glutinous kidneys, and I'd only be allowed the saving grace of custard for pudding if I finished every last mouthful.'

I watched as Jerry held a lobster's head in one hand and tail in the other – twisted and tore them apart with a crunch. Each claw was snapped off; he split the shell of the tail, freed the meat with his bare fingers and ripped it apart. Dipped each piece into a bowl of butter, sucked each finger. Then Jerry paused, wiped his hands, picked up his cutlery, and sliced into his steak. He groaned as he removed the knife, as the flesh settled into shape. Pink and red and glistening.

'Well,' Richard continued, 'I swore that when I was old enough to decide for myself, I'd start with pudding every night. And although we don't quite do that every night – do we, baby?' He looked to Honey. 'I nonetheless wanted to give it a go for this special occasion. And who can deny the delicious taste of salty with sweet? Perhaps we'll discover a new culinary combination tonight.'

'Turkey and tiramisu?' said Jerry, still working his way through the pile of meat. 'I don't think so.'

'But,' Richard went on, 'I didn't want this to be just a treat for me. The staff have been working incredibly hard tonight to create dishes that I know you'll all enjoy. They've had to suffer some quite strange requests. Now, what do we have? Nine dishes, one indulgence for each of my guests.'

If there were nine, then maybe one had been created for Lillie. I could only hope. I brought my purse to my lap so I could compose my text to her while pretending to look for something.

'Ah yes,' said Richard. 'Here's the surf and turf for Jerry, which we have a long tradition of ordering when we have something to celebrate.'

I waited till I could see that the message had been delivered. 'Been getting it for years,' said Jerry through a mouthful.

'Decades! But somehow I'm the only one who piles on the pounds.'

'It's not from our usual place – a little Scottish tavern in Atwater Village. My chef has made his own version. Then what else? Tiramisu for Charlie because I know how much you love coffee.'

'Yes sir, I do,' said Charlie. He laughed, like it was a private joke, though I noticed he hadn't spooned any onto his plate.

'Miguel,' Richard continued, 'yours is particularly special.'

'Rich,' the producer grinned, 'don't tell me this is actually from Nozawa.'

'It is, it is. Nozawa Bar created these sushi items just for you – jellyfish, I think, maybe eel too. They're not even on the menu at the restaurant tonight. Let me tell you, that was no mean feat.'

'Unbelievable. You know me too well, buddy.'

'I won't reveal which organ I had to sell on the black market to pay for that. What else? Doughnuts for Kei, who always brings a colossal batch for the cast and crew on the last day of shooting. Strawberries and cream for Tommo, his childhood favourite—'

'Will I find vinegar in this one?' asked Tommo. He addressed the rest of us: 'Dicky pranked me with this dish in school. Said I was a philistine for never having tried strawberries with vinegar, and after much, much provoking, I finally gave in.'

'It's true,' said Richard. 'Vinegar and strawberries are a match made in heaven.'

'Didn't explain that strawberries work best with balsamic, though, did you, Dicky? For the record, malt vinegar and curdled cream are a terrible, terrible match.'

Richard laughed. 'No vinegar this time. And finally we have: some pastries, some asparagus, and Thanksgiving turkey with all the trimmings. I'll let you talk among yourselves to work out which is for whom and the reasons why – it can be a fun little ice-breaker, can't it? Ah yes, I almost forgot the ninth dish! My own.'

So the ninth was not for Lillie. Then it was certain: she wouldn't be arriving for a while. I checked my phone.

'Hot cross buns,' Richard was saying. 'A reminder of my childhood – Elspeth?'

I looked up, tried to recompose my expression as though I'd been listening.

'Is that a phone?' he said.

'I was just checking when—'

'No excuses, Elspeth. Rules are rules. And what's that bottle doing?' He gestured at the water I had placed on the table.

'Put it away,' Richard scolded. 'This is strictly a champagne moment. And if you insist on drinking anything else, we have the waiters for that.'

The others were watching. Their knives and forks hovered. For a moment, I wondered whether this was worth an argument – to show he held no sway over me. But Richard was smiling. He wanted a challenge. I couldn't be bothered to fight him. There was no response from Lillie anyway. And how would it have looked, if Richard was the one to tell me, in front of everyone, where our daughter was? He would love that.

I put away my phone and the bottled water. Tore the doughnut in two and took a bite. It was dry. It stuck to the roof of my mouth.

'As I was saying,' Richard continued, 'a reminder of my childhood. Toasted, with butter. Anyway, I'll leave it there. Bon appétit, bon appétit. May you feast till your bellies burst. And no phones. Please. It's for your own good.'

The guests were still eating but had settled down – no more plates travelling across the table. In their wake, the tablecloth was a mess: dollops of cream, the grease of the meaty knives and tongs, and was that a pool of egg yolk or candle wax crusting into the linen?

I sipped at my water. I was not hungry. Wondered, lazily, which dish was mine. None of the unclaimed plates was recognisable. Was it the Thanksgiving turkey? It hadn't been a huge celebration in our house, but the triangular pastries were entirely alien, and I'd never cooked asparagus before.

'Who's left?' said Tommo.

'These are mine.' Sabine pointed to the pastries. '*Brik*. My mother's is best, but these are not so bad. Try, try. But there is raw egg inside, so you must be careful when you bite.'

'*Now* you tell me,' said Jerry. Yolk had dripped down his shirt.

'And this turkey,' Sabine said, holding her champagne glass out to a waiter for a refill. 'Very American. I think I will guess: is it for Charlie?'

'No, he's the tiramisu,' said Tommo.

'Then we say . . . Ah, for Honey? Is it you?'

He nodded.

'You are patriotic?' Sabine said.

His mouth was full; he smiled, bashful. Waited until he had swallowed before saying: 'No, it's – I had this religious upbringing, where we didn't celebrate any secular holidays. And when Richard found that out, right at the start of our relationship, he surprised me with a Thanksgiving meal the next day. For breakfast.'

'The whole shebang,' said Richard. 'And you know what he said? *I'd have been happy with turkey sandwiches.*'

The group laughed. Richard reached across the table to kiss Honey's cheek.

'Very romantic, I'm sure,' said Tommo. 'But we've got a game to win. Who's the asparagus?'

'The asparagus . . .' Sabine bit into a strawberry as she looked around the group. 'But no, we have already guessed everyone.'

I had finished my glass of water and was having trouble signalling to the waiter facing me. He was enamoured with Sabine. I waited for him to break his stare for just one moment, but it was hopeless.

Sabine took another forkful, slid the fruit off the prongs with her teeth. 'I know,' she said. 'It is a trick.'

Another waiter noticed me, nudged Sabine's admirer. He jumped to refill my glass.

'No, you're wrong,' said Tommo. 'There's one more person left.'

He waited for a moment to build the suspense, then turned his head, sharp. Almost an accusation. 'Elspeth – are you the asparagus?'

I froze under their stare. 'I don't know,' I stuttered. 'I don't think that—'

'Come on, Ellie,' said Richard. 'Don't tell me you've forgotten?'

He smiled strangely: with his mouth, not his eyes. The table was silent. The guests were watching.

'Our honeymoon,' he said. 'Norfolk asparagus, remember? That picnic?'

That picnic.

'You remember, don't you, Ellie?'

I hadn't remembered before, but I did now. I nodded. Tried to smile. Raised my glass to Tommo.

'Congratulations,' I said, 'you got me.'

'Well, there we are,' said Tommo. Then to Sabine: 'Tough luck.'

Kei was sobbing. 'How could we—'

Tommo, eyes wide open, was shaking his head.

'He must have taken more after we went to sleep,' said Jerry. 'Did anyone see? What do you remember? He must have done more while we were sleeping, right?'

'When was he—' Kei said. 'How could we – how could we—'

'Should we clean up this shit before the cops arrive?' Miguel, lurching towards the table, seemed to be directing this at me – but I could not think, I could not talk.

'My manager's going to fucking kill me,' said Charlie, shaking his head. 'Why the fuck am I here? There's no way this won't get out. No way. Fuck. Fuck. I can't be here.'

Sabine pulled Kei out to the lawn.

'Fuck,' cried Charlie. 'Fuck.'

Needles and spoons clattered back onto the marble as Miguel tried to gather them.

'Hey,' shouted Jerry. 'Don't touch that, don't fucking touch that. We leave everything as it is. Nobody leaves. Nothing covered up or we're looking at jail. Hey. Hey!'

He slapped Miguel's wrist, pulled him up by the collar.

'You want the lead role in San Quentin's Christmas cabaret?' He spat. 'Calm the fuck down.'

The sirens were low in the distance. Jerry dropped Miguel, who crumpled to the floor, trembling.

'A mess, a fucking mess,' he seemed to be saying. 'A mess.'

Jerry looked at Charlie, at Miguel. 'Okay,' he said slowly. Voice lowered. 'Okay. We wait until the cops arrive and then we explain everything. Richard overdosed while we were asleep. Nobody needs to *lie* about anything, nobody needs to *cover up* the drugs – we can't change that now. It's all here. We're here. Richard overdosed. Those are the facts. We just explain everything to the cops when they arrive. Richard overdosed while we were asleep.'

Honey returned to the room in silence, perched on the arm of the couch, inches from the body. I was horrified to see it loll, ever so slightly, with this movement. It was too much.

'Fucking look at him,' said Charlie, eyes on Richard.

The sun was coming clean through the window. Sabine, just beyond the glass, was stroking Kei's hair, whispering into her ear.

We sat in silence till the sirens were upon us. Only then did I think of Lillie – that I would have to reach her before the paparazzi captured the yellow-taped mansion.

'Richard,' said Tommo, dropped his head into his big hands, and wept.

'I'd like to say a few words,' said Richard.

'Speech,' shouted Jerry. 'Shut the fuck up, the old man wants to speak.'

Conversation crumbled away as Richard cleared his throat.

'First of all,' he said, 'I'd like to take this opportunity to thank the chefs and the wait staff for looking after us so well tonight.'

As we applauded, the chefs trailed into the room in a long line. Stood awkwardly, the four of them, with hands behind their backs – apart from one, who was wiping his palms on his apron.

'I have to say,' continued Richard, 'they really have performed feats of magic tonight. Chef Brady even baked authentic hot cross buns from scratch after I discovered that the locals add icing sugar – sacrilege. Thank you, again. Thank you to all of you.'

The tallest chef nodded, and they filed out.

'That was . . .' Jerry, patted his belly, exhaled. 'That was phenomenal.'

'I don't think I'll need to eat again for a week,' said Tommo.

Richard waited until the plates were gone before clearing his throat again. I checked my phone quickly. Nothing from Lillie. I would have to pull Richard aside and ask what was happening. But not now: he was engrossed in his hosting theatrics.

'Well,' he said, beaming, surveying the room, 'who can believe we're here? Half a century, gosh . . .'

He looked wistfully to the window, as if lost for words. I knew this was not the case, knew he would have been rewriting and rehearsing this speech for months: recitations to the bathroom mirror, tears welling as he waited for his espresso to dribble from the machine.

'. . . what a thing to behold. There are many celebrations that might befit an ageing man's birthday, and I so wanted to make this year's festivities special. I mulled over the possibilities: another large party full of characters I can't even name? A retreat to the other side of the world? Put on a show at Grauman's?'

Richard stood up. The candlelight flickered his face golden as he picked up his glass, taking his time to drink – to force a pause on the room.

'But then I considered the cast of my entire life.' He wandered to Miguel's chair. Rested one hand on his shoulder. 'The people who had shaped me into the round-bellied, cynical fool that stands here before you. And I thought: the celebration for this milestone should not be a celebration of me. It should be a celebration of each and every one of you.'

A moment of silence for this perfect performance.

'So, dearly beloved,' Richard strolled back to stand behind his own seat, 'we are gathered here today to honour the memories of the last fifty years . . .'

Titters of laughter sprinkled here and there.

'. . . as tonight, I celebrate you and your lives, friends and loves, old and new. Let us begin with a little toast.'

We lifted our glasses from the stained tablecloth.

'To Miguel,' he said, 'who fights for my dream every day. The man to whom I owe the last few years of my professional life, whom I've entrusted with my most important work. Sometimes, Miguel, I think you're the only person who truly understands my vision.'

The producer wiped the corner of his eye with a knuckle, as Richard moved on.

'To Tommo – my oldest, dearest friend. My brother.'

Tommo raised his glass to Richard, nodded.

'To Jerry, without whom I'd have no career at all. And to Kei, who weaves my ideas into being.'

I braced myself as he turned to our half of the table.

'To Ellie,' he said, 'who raised my wonderful Lillie into a bright young woman.'

I smiled back at Richard, but my foot was tapping under the table. I wanted this lengthy toast to end so I could ask him when our *bright young woman* would arrive. I must have suffered nearly two hours without her already. When we'd discussed arriving separately, Lillie had said nothing about coming this late. She needed to visit a friend beforehand, but she would get to the party at six-thirty, and I'd been careful to arrive half an hour after that. Now the clock on my phone had crept past eight-thirty. I could feel the worry encroaching – had something happened to her on the drive? – but Richard seemed not to have noticed, seemed relaxed, which made me think he knew exactly where she was.

'To Charlie: a talented young man at the very start of a dazzling career. To Sabine – a star, an artist, an icon. And to Honey, to Honey . . .'

Richard paused.

'To Honey, my love, beside whom I know, I *know*, I want to spend every day of the rest of my life.'

Honey kissed two fingers, held them up to Richard, in some kind of secret gesture. Richard took the hand and squeezed it. Turned back to his audience.

'To each and every one of you.' His voice was booming now.

'To each and every year. To all days of glory, joy and happiness.'

Had his eyes deliberately fallen upon me with those words?

But no, of course not: they were sweeping back across the room again, to rest on Honey, sitting by his side.

They held each other's gaze. I knew that look of love. How Richard could kiss you with his eyes, adorn you with his words, lift you up before a crowd and say: *this is special, this one is mine*. I held my breath, felt the air press down upon me, averted my eyes to the aquarium in case anyone looked on.

And then the moment passed.

'To love,' Richard croaked.

'To love!' the guests cheered, each raising a glass.

We sipped, some applauded; Jerry slapped his thigh. Richard took Honey's chin in one hand and pulled him close for a kiss.

As toasting slid back to talk, I pushed my chair from the table. Approached my ex-husband. Leaned in, discreetly, taking in the familiar aftershave – a familiar look of guilt.

'Earlier,' I whispered, 'you said we were all here. But where's Lillie? Isn't she supposed to have arrived by now? Has something happened?'

To my alarm, Richard grabbed my hand.

'Apologies, Miguel,' he said to the producer. And then, to me: 'Let's talk in the corridor.'

As Sedgwick was taped off and the uniforms swarmed, we were each taken aside and asked some simple questions: when the body had been found, whether anybody else had been in the house, whether we would remain in the city and pass on our contact details. Tommo cancelled his flight back to London, and Sabine hers to Paris. There would be a routine inquest; the death was not being treated as suspicious.

I was only supposed to be staying with Lillie for a couple of nights, to spend some time together and attend Richard's party. With his death, my return to New York had been postponed indefinitely. The police needed me present, yes, but my daughter needed me more. To keep her company, hold her tight, tell her it would all be okay. She hadn't asked, we hadn't discussed it. I had, simply, not left.

I was making Lillie a breakfast I knew she would not eat when the phone call came, three days later – I was required at the station. The scrambled eggs, still half raw, were scraped straight from pan to bin. But I knocked on her door lightly, set a steaming coffee and some water on the bedside table.

'I have to leave,' I told Lillie, sitting down on her quilt.

She was lying on her side, facing the wall. The sun seeped through her curtains.

'They want me at the station,' I said. 'I don't know when I'll be back. Will you be okay by yourself?'

I tucked her hair behind an ear.

Lillie blinked, glassy. 'What did you say?'

'The police called – I need to answer some questions for them. Are you going to be okay staying here alone?'

She nodded, just.

'Did you get some sleep? How are you doing today?'

'I don't know,' she said.

There was a humming and a tapping at the window – an insect hurtling into the pane. I could make out its shadow, every now and then, a smudge behind the curtain.

'Do you need me to get you anything while I'm out?'

'I don't know,' she said. I put a hand on her forehead: hot.

'Have you been drinking water?' I asked, but Lillie seemed not to hear me.

She murmured: 'It keeps going through my mind.'

'What does?'

'The sentence. It's only words and nothing else.'

The insect paused for a moment – maybe resting, maybe crawling on the glass.

'He's dead,' she said. 'That's the sentence: *He's dead.* It's only the words and they're not stopping and I can't figure out what they mean so I just keep saying them to myself. He's dead.'

The window-tapping resumed.

'Sometimes,' she said, staring at the wall, 'I'll think about something else. Like maybe I taste my breath and I think: *I should brush my teeth.* Then it hits me again: *he's dead.* And I can't move.' Her voice was flat; her lips were white. She mouthed the phrase, slowly: 'He's dead,' she said. 'He's dead.'

Lillie closed her eyes, wrinkled her forehead. 'But it's not – they aren't making sense to me.'

The air conditioner woke up. Its airy white noise, the click as the slats angled up and down, made the room quieter, emptier, somehow.

Each time I'd slipped into her room over the past couple of days, to check how she was doing, I had expected to find chaos: soccer gear and socks strewn, books spilling from strange corners, maybe crumb-scattered plates and at least fifteen mugs. That chaos had been the source of many arguments back home – there were months when I could barely wedge open her door, the floor was so buried in junk.

When she had shown me around her pristine house that first afternoon, I'd smugly told myself that the polished surfaces wouldn't last. Lillie had obviously set the stage for my arrival and I almost laughed: I knew my nineteen-year-old daughter didn't live like this. She didn't regularly refill the dish-soap dispenser; she didn't have a closet of spare towels; she certainly didn't sift utility bills from the post, slip each stack into a different drawer.

No, I had been wrong. Everything had remained untouched since that evening. Of course, Lillie had barely moved from her bed, and I had been tiptoeing around, carefully returning each item to its designated home. But that wasn't it – increasingly, as I haunted her house, I had the feeling it would have stayed pristine regardless. Something about the way her shoes were paired up beneath the coat rack, the way the books were arranged to a rainbow on each shelf. When Lillie was little, no matter how messy everything else, her pots of nail polish would be lined up in height order. If I asked her to tidy her bedroom on a Saturday morning, that was how she whiled away the hours. Shifting her dollhouse couch an inch to the left, straightening the nail polishes – the muddy soccer gear remained.

Lillie's new house, I realised, was not an adaptation of her bedroom back home: it was hers, each inch, even the dish soap and the cloths. The mugs here deserved as much consideration as her nine-year-old self had given those tiny glass bottles of polish, with their sparkling lilacs and blues.

And yet this realisation had done little, over the past few days, to change my expectations. The shock was still there, opening this bedroom door to find that expanse of carpet. To see my daughter in the bed in the corner, surrounded by very little at all.

'I hate leaving you like this,' I told her. 'Do you want me to call a friend?'

'No,' she said. Her eyes were still shut. 'Don't.'

'Can I open the curtains?'

She didn't answer.

On that terrible morning, I had reached Lillie before the news broke. Drove as fast as I could. She was in the kitchen, still wearing pyjamas, cutting strawberries for her breakfast. I took the knife out of her hand, made her sit down.

'I don't understand,' she kept repeating, after I had told her. 'I don't understand.'

She was shaking, unblinking. There was a smear of red juice on her cheek.

'I don't understand,' she said. 'Dad?' And that was when she cried out. Not a sob but one choke – a strange, strangled sound.

It was all I could do, whisper, 'I'm sorry, I'm sorry, I'm sorry,' into her hair, hug her as she rocked back and forth.

'I'm sorry,' I said, and I could not rinse Richard's image from my mind: the wet 'O' of his mouth, the stare of his eyes.

Perching on Lillie's bed, thinking of that moment, I was not sure which hurt the most: the violent wrench I had felt in my chest that morning; or this drawn-out ache, watching her lying limp, only a husk of herself. I had known that first scream would end and I had known how to hold her then. But this?

Lillie's phone drilled violently – once, twice – somewhere on the other side of the room.

'Do you want me to get that for you?'

'No,' she said.

There was nothing I could do.

'Drink some water.' I bent down to kiss her cheek. 'It's there, next to you, with some coffee. I'll be back as fast as I can. And you can call me. Call me, if you need anything. Will you call?'

She didn't answer, so I kissed her again. Tried to not look back at her, bundled in the covers, as I gently closed the door.

This time the police needed a detailed timeline:

When had I been invited to the party?

When had I arrived?

Who was there?

Which of the other guests had I known before that night?

Did I remember how the night proceeded?

And then, who did I talk to?

What did I eat, drink?

And then?

And did I remember how Richard was behaving? Did he seem anxious?

And at what point were drugs consumed?

Did I consume any drugs?

And then I just fell asleep?

On the floor?

But – they wanted to get this straight – I hadn't consumed any drugs?

I had missed the two detectives' names when first introduced; my mind was still with Lillie. As this dawned on me, I studied their faces, tried to find solid footing in the blinks and freckles of the male officer, in the frizz and fidgeting of his colleague.

She had been staring into her mug while he questioned, repositioning it on the table with an audible scrape every now and then. There was something coming, I knew.

When her colleague was done, she raised her head and said, quite slowly and deliberately: 'Ms Bryant Bell, you were the one who found your ex-husband's body.'

The fluorescent lighting buzzed overhead. She did not continue.

'Sorry,' I said, 'is there a question?'

She took her hands from the mug, clasped them together.
'Can you recall that discovery for us?'

'When did Lillie say she would arrive?'

The music tinkled over the sound system in the hallway, but even there it was nothing more than an accompaniment to the voices from the party, which doubled, tripled over themselves as they ricocheted off the cavernous walls.

I moved out of the way as the blonde waitress passed with an ice bucket.

Richard's lips pursed for a few moments before he replied.

'She won't be coming tonight.'

I frowned. He took a step forwards, placed a hand on my lower back, continued speaking before I could gather myself to sentences.

'Something came up, a premiere, and we both agreed it would be better for her to attend that than my birthday – she and I can celebrate another time. Now, darling . . .'

My skin prickled at this intimacy.

'. . . please, darling, do try not to—'

'I saw her today,' I was saying, measured, 'and she told me when she'd get here, and what she would wear, and . . .' It fell together in my mind. 'She lied to me?'

Lillie had told me she would only attend with me by her side and I had leapt at the chance to support her – despite the distance, despite the fact that I would see my ex-husband again. Our first party, together, as two adults. The first evening we would spend together in months.

But no, my daughter had never wanted me. How could I have been so naive? How could I have let Richard dupe me so easily?

'Don't blame Lilliput, please, Ellie.' I felt his hand pressing harder. 'I put her in the most awful position, I know, and she was loath to lie to you, but I asked her not to mention her cancellation because—'

'No.' I threw down his hand, stepped away. Let pleasantries die. 'There is absolutely no excuse for asking my daughter to lie to me. How dare she – and *you*. *You*. How dare you both.'

The waitress dashed past us again, ice bucket full. Richard did not pause: 'Elspeth, Ellie, darling. I so terribly wanted you to attend and I knew you wouldn't without her, but—'

'No excuses, Richard,' I said. My words were clipped; I was trying to stop my voice breaking. I would not cry, nor shout. 'No excuses for either of you. Of course I wouldn't have come. After everything, Richard. How dare you ask Lillie to lie to me.'

I flinched as he reached for me again.

'Don't fucking touch me,' I hissed.

A waiter – the one who had been staring at Sabine – walked past us with a tray of fresh glasses. I held my tongue until he had rounded the corner.

Was Richard smirking? Was this funny? The bastard. I felt sick. The air in the corridor was thick with kitchen smells: deep-fat-frying and meats.

'I've spent hours here, already,' I said, 'under a completely false impression. I don't know why you want me here; I don't know what kind of game you're playing. This feast, your toasts, and you were . . .'

I fell to a whisper as the waiter came back the other way.

'. . . you were lying the entire time? I'm going to get my bag and then I'm leaving. I don't care what your friends think – tell them what you like.'

Before I could escape, Tommo appeared behind me, holding up his hands as if he was hiding.

'Looking for the loo, sorry, don't mind me . . .'

'It's fine.' I tried to smile, cheeks still hot. 'We were just finishing our conversation.'

'Oh great, excellent – let me catch you when I come back?' He brushed my arm. 'We haven't had a chance to catch up properly yet and it's been so long.'

'Actually, Tom, I'm thinking of leaving.' I put a hand to my forehead. 'I'm really exhausted from the flight, and I was waiting for Lillie to get here but Richard just told me she won't make it, so I think I should get back and—'

'Come on, no, don't be ridiculous, Elspeth,' he pleaded. 'Don't leave me with these LA types.'

'I can't, Tom, I'm so sorry.'

'Take some ibuprofen . . .'

'Tom, I really—'

'Drink some coffee, do some coke. I don't give a fuck. Just stay, please. Elspeth.'

I looked from Richard – the dashes of grey in his hair, the slight slump of his shoulders – to his school friend. Tommo had always been my favourite. He was softer around the mouth and far better dressed than he had been at our first meeting. But that earnestness in his eyes was untainted; it was an earnestness that broke my heart.

I realised, with surprise, that I had missed him. We could have one conversation and then I would leave.

'She'll stay,' said Richard.

And I did.

'I don't remember waking up,' I told them. 'Only that he was the first thing I saw.'

(The sleeping lover.)

'And you were the first guest to wake?' asked the female officer.

'I couldn't say. I hadn't looked around the room yet.'

(The exposed neck.)

'Could you please describe the scene for us?'

'It was bright. But it wasn't the light that had woken me, it was . . . My arm was in a puddle of cold water, and I rolled over to dry it off. That's when I opened my eyes and I saw how Richard was lying.'

(And his elbow was bent. And his fingers were splayed.)

I added: 'It seemed unnatural . . .'

(And my heart was clenched and my breath was catching and so—)

'. . . so I sat up. The others were asleep. I went over to feel his pulse . . .'

(The wet 'O' of the mouth, the staring eyes, the stench of—)

'But there was nothing there?' The female officer clicked her fingernails against her mug.

I shook my head.

'And then?' she asked.

'And then I saw that Honey was awake and he saw in my face that . . . there wasn't a pulse.' I inhaled shakily. 'He understood me. I don't think . . . We didn't say a word to each other, but he understood. He went out to make the call. Then the others were waking and I had to tell them what had happened – that Richard had overdosed in the night.'

The light flickered with a clink.

'But I wouldn't want you to rely on my impressions too much. It was all . . .' I rubbed an eyelid. 'I was confused when I woke up, and maybe I'm not remembering right.'

'You believe you were still under the influence?' asked the male officer.

'I couldn't say. I was confused. My head was throbbing.'

'And your immediate conclusion was that he had died from an overdose.' The female cop had stopped moving her mug.

'Yes, the others – we all thought so, yes,' I said. 'He shot up the night before. He was covered in vomit.'

Her nails tapped on the china again. Something about the rhythm took me back to Lillie's room – that insect against the glass.

'Ms Bryant Bell.' The detective's voice was measured. Her nails clacked, one after the other. 'Following the initial forensic examination results, we have significant reason to believe your ex-husband's death was not caused by a drug overdose.'

(The sleeping lover.)

I frowned.

'The autopsy revealed wounds running along the inside of Mr Bryant's throat. Bruises,' her fingers froze, 'which seem to have been caused by a long, blunt object.'

(The exposed neck.)

She took a gulp of her coffee, not breaking eye contact. Her colleague said: 'The official cause of death is suffocation.'

'The external security-camera footage shows that, after catering staff left at approximately 10pm,' she interjected, 'nobody else either entered or exited the property. Not until 9:05 the following morning, when police arrived at the scene to find your ex-husband's body. What that means, Ms Bryant Bell, is that there were eight people present when somebody forced something down your unconscious ex-husband's throat until he choked to death.'

My hand reached for my necklace.

'Ms Bryant Bell, your ex-husband was murdered, and the only people currently under investigation are the eight attendees of the party: Anton Carlisle, Thomas Coates, Jerry Debrowski, Miguel Montana, Keiko Nakamura, Charles Pace, Sabine Selmi – and you.'

I asked for my lawyer.

'Lime, lime, he must have lime somewhere,' Tommo muttered from the depths of the fridge. 'Why are other people's kitchens always so enigmatic?'

'Can't we just have it without?'

He emerged, pink, brandishing his citrus trophy. 'Absolutely not, you perverse Yank.' And then to a waiter carrying a tray of dirty glasses: 'Oh, sorry, yes, of course. You first.'

Tommo carried the fruit to a quiet corner. He had insisted, against the forceful protests of the sunshine waitress, that he wanted to make the drinks himself. And so we were there in the kitchen, amid the dishwashing, the uncorking of more bottles, the wrapping of the leftovers.

I made myself as small as possible; watched as he counted four cubes of ice, squeezed one wedge of lime, rubbed it along the rim, dropped it in, then measured an inch of gin to three of tonic – into one glass and then the other – all with a painstaking precision.

We smiled over our first sips, licked the sour from our lips.

Tommo sighed. 'I hadn't realised how much I needed a good slug of gin.'

'Difficult week at work?'

'I wouldn't say difficult, but challenging. Full on. And it has been for the last five years. Not easy being your own boss.'

He dodged as two waiters passed him with a long platter: the stringed and sinewed turkey carcass.

'So you finally struck out on your own? Good for you,' I said, rubbing his shoulder. 'It was just a sparkle in your eye when I saw you last.'

'And who knew giving birth engendered so much stress?'

'Ha, well, it's the following years that are the hardest.'

'I'll drink to that,' Tommo said, knocking his glass against mine. 'But it's true, it is. The first stage was nowhere near as difficult as this – we just opened a New York office.'

'Oh you did? Oh, congratulations. Why didn't you tell me? We'll have to get dinner next time you're in town.'

'God, if only I could.' Tommo smiled, shook his head. 'I can't remember the last time I socialised outside of work. Speaking of which, I hear you're seeing Julian Schwarz – now that is a coup. You'll have to pass on my details; it would be great to connect.'

'Unfortunately, you'll have to forge your connection through someone else, Tom. We've broken things off.'

I watched a group of chefs goofing around outside: a cigarette break. One of them was dancing; the others clapped their hands. I wanted to laugh with them but the sight only filled me with dread: dancing chefs were not part of Richard's vision. They had been hired to set the scene – his laden table, his gift for each guest – and as extras, trotted out to be thanked on cue. Not to improvise, not for comic relief. What would Richard do if he spied them through the window?

'Ah well,' said Tommo. 'Poor chap. Biggest bank balance in the world couldn't compensate for such a colossal loss. I never did forgive Dicky for letting you walk away.'

He took my hand in his. 'Look, darling, I meant what I said earlier. Please do stay with me. I know you have every right to leave, but I've got a thirty-seven-year-old duty. I'm stuck here.'

I smiled sympathetically, but gave no answer.

'What's he doing, Tom? Inviting us – only us. Are we really the most important people in his life? This eight? This hodge-podge? Some of the other guests are half our age. And that feast? What was that?'

'Perhaps he wants to bring his worlds together.'

The sunshine-blonde waitress approached. 'Excuse me, can I get to the shelf behind you for a second?'

I shifted aside, apologised.

'Of course,' she replied, reaching up for another champagne bucket. She took it to the freezer, filled it with crushed ice.

'Please,' I whispered to Tommo, when I was sure she was out of earshot. 'Don't tell me you fell for his little performance out there. Forgoing an enormous party? No, he's up to something.'

Tommo considered this, crushing an ice cube between his molars.

'And the name of the house? Sedgwick?' I added, frowning. 'I didn't want to say anything about it, but I find it quite alarming, given—'

'Oh, it's just a joke of his,' he said. 'I'm sure it goes over most people's heads; they'll think it's Edie or Edward, won't they? Does anyone even pay attention to house names? I never do, they're always so boring. The Old Rectory, Post Office Mews. As a matter of fact, I hardly even notice the name of this house nowadays. Background noise.'

'I don't think Richard intended it as background noise,' I said, remembering that pause, that stare, as my ex-husband had welcomed me to Sedgwick. 'Didn't you notice it when you first visited? Didn't you ask him why he—'

'Of course not, that's just what he wants.' Tommo waved this suggestion away. Then said: 'You know, I learned to stop guessing Dicky's motives the day of the river incident.'

'The river incident?'

'Wait – you haven't heard this? Christ.' Tommo pulled himself onto the counter. 'How have we never told you before?'

He began the tale: how the two boys had been walking through the school grounds one November morning on the way to their first lesson. I had seen one of Richard's class photos, and I could picture them now: little men in their uniform suits, black leather shoes crunching frosty grass. I had not forgotten Richard's most recent deception – the co-opting of Lillie into his master plan – but it was difficult to hate this child, abandoned at boarding school by heartless parents, tufts of chestnut hair and a skip in his step.

'We were messing around,' Tommo continued. 'We were always seeing who could run the fastest, arguing about who was better at cricket . . .'

Yes, I could see it. The boyish bragging and gap-toothed grins – the cold, red noses.

'. . . and then Dicky threw his weight sideways, plunging me into icy water.'

I gasped. 'What did you do?'

'Clambered out,' said Tommo, grinning. 'Made my way back to our dorms so I could change my uniform. Unfortunately I was caught by a prefect and marched to the headmaster in my frozen clothes.'

'My god, you poor thing.'

'I had to write a five-page essay on Hardy's poetic exploration of nature, which cost me hours of homework time and dashed my grades in several subjects. It became school legend. The other boys swapped my pillows for inflated armbands and put river water in the glass I kept by my bed. Thankfully I noticed the stench before I took a sip – and it was all good fun, all jokes. Never did tell on Dicky.'

'You should have.'

'Call it an Englishman's honour.'

My stomach sank as I remembered Richard's earlier lie. I would have to talk with Lillie in the morning. I pushed her from my mind and asked: 'Do you know why he did it?'

'I kept trying to rationalise his actions,' began Tommo. 'Had I said something to offend him? Had I taken our schoolboy rivalry too far?'

He took the drink from my hand and began mixing another

before I could protest. I hadn't planned on drinking much, but I could always call a taxi.

'I couldn't recall anything. Nothing that would justify his actions. After the event he acted as if it had never happened at all. So I was left to wonder. Maybe it was a random, uncontrollable impulse. Maybe it had been a test – to find out whether he had gained my loyalty – or maybe he simply wanted to assert his dominance.'

Tommo handed back the replenished drink.

'Perhaps he just thought it was funny,' he said.

'You could have died.'

Tommo shrugged.

The kitchen flurry had died down – leftovers piled neatly, clean glasses on one side and dirty on the other.

The waitress was outside now, joining the chefs for a cigarette. There was something jarring about the scene. I didn't know her at all and yet I was certain the habit didn't suit her. Smoke soaking her ponytail, tar yellowing her teeth: it seemed wrong.

'*Of course*,' I imagined her saying, as she lent a lighter to one of the chefs. '*Of course*.'

Tommo was watching the group too.

He said: 'We did a lot of stupid things, Elspeth. We were schoolboys.'

'There's stupid and there's spiteful,' I said. 'Why on earth would you remain friends with him?'

'You know as well as I, that Dicky's far too charismatic to abandon. We've had a lot of fun together. Cheers.' He clinked my glass. 'And he never pushed me into a fast-running body of water again, so . . .'

A peal of laughter snatched our attention.

'We should probably return to the atrium,' said Tommo. 'But we'll make a pact. If either of us needs rescuing, sneeze, then scratch your right ear twice.'

He looked at me, hopeful, desperate. How could I have left, at that exact moment, after hearing his story?

We shook on it.

I left the police station, trembling – abandoned my car and called a cab. When the driver asked for my destination, I told him I had none, that I wanted him to drive and drive until I needed to stop. His brow furrowed in the rear-view mirror, but he asked no further questions. The car rumbled into action. I let my head fall against the vibrating window.

I will admit that since that terrible morning, I had entertained an involuntary thought on more than one occasion: that Richard had known exactly what he was doing. That if his death was not planned, then it was also not prevented. Either he had deliberately overdosed, or he had measured out the powder with reckless abandon. If true, I wasn't sure what it would mean – to imagine Richard carefully orchestrating his last night on earth, selecting me for a front-row-and-centre seat. And the other guests – why those seven? Had he chosen us for a loving farewell? Or did he detest us, blame us, all?

But now . . . the notion that this was an act committed by another – moreover, someone at the party – this was unthinkable.

As I watched stores and motels and apartment buildings glide by, the words of the female officer dripped incessantly.

(The wounds; the bruises; a long, blunt object.)

I pinched my left forearm again and again: foolish, foolish woman. I should have called my lawyer as soon as I discovered the body. And now I was embroiled in this mess, an investigation into the murder of my ex-husband, when I needed to be caring for our grieving child.

My Lillie. How would I tell her when I barely understood it myself? How would I string the words to an explanation? How could I say that I was there, right beside her father, as somebody suffocated him to—

I could not breathe. I could not breathe.

A mall materialised in the distance. I asked the driver to pull over. I needed the noise and the lights and all the ugliness. I unclipped myself as fast as I could, pushed a twenty into the driver's hand. Threw open the door, gasping.

It was a 1970s abomination of mirrored escalators and flecked linoleum floors. Mobility scooters cruised by, their drivers barely visible beneath plastic bags on handlebars. The echoes of misbehaving children; riffs of chart-topping pop. I busied my mind as best I could, browsed the colourful bottles in Sephora, tried to anchor myself in the world. I tried on shades at an illuminated kiosk and settled on a blue pair, Chanel. And then I found myself on the fourth floor, where the scent of buttered popcorn lured me to a movie theatre.

I waited in line for a ticket with white-haired seniors and kids cutting class, but then Richard's movie was still showing – of course it was – and a glimpse of Sabine's face on the poster, Charlie in her shadow, warned me away at the last minute. My dread was a sickness. I needed to scream it, vomit it out. I wanted to claw it from my stomach.

I breathed.

(To each and every one of you. To each and every year.)

My fingers trembled.

(To all days of glory, joy, and happiness.)

My head was aching. I entered the nearest store to distract myself again.

This was impossible. The officer's words had lodged a cold blade of suspicion into my heart. I couldn't help but run over my memories of that night again, again and again, with a growing sense of unease, as I moved the plastic limbs of baby dolls in Target and fingered the cheap fabrics of last season's coats.

A silent spectacle had seized the crowd. Even the staff were staring.

Persephone was crawling across the aquarium on the tips of her tentacles. The white suckers moved rhythmically with each twist and wave, bulbous head dragging behind.

'She looks like an alien,' said Kei.

'Well,' Sabine raised an eyebrow, 'she belongs to another realm, no?'

The creature's skin was a bright, brickish red, luminous against the blue.

'It's funny you should say that,' Richard was standing behind them, arms resting on the back of the couch, 'because zoologists describe them as aliens. They evolved in an entirely different way to other intelligent animals. Fascinating beasts.'

Her limbs were continuously unfurling and curling as slowly, as delicately, as silk tumbling through water.

'They can navigate mazes,' Richard continued, 'recognise individuals, use tools, camouflage their skin. You should watch her hunt. Majestic. She might look gentle, but her soft flesh conceals a sharp, bony beak.'

'What does she eat?' asked Sabine.

'She's a carnivore.' He downed his champagne and placed it on the table. 'Her favourite's crab. You should have seen her as a baby. She was smaller than a saucer, but she could calmly wrap her arms—'

'Her tentacles?' asked Miguel.

'Her *arms*, they have *arms*, not tentacles – wrap her arms around the shell until it stopped struggling. And she has a paralysing venom. Countless weapons in her arsenal. She's the largest species of octopus. Possibly one of the most intelligent, too.'

'Octopi—' began Miguel.

'Octopuses,' corrected Richard.

'Keeps me on my toes,' Miguel laughed. 'Always the intellectual. As I was saying, *octopuses* can escape through the smallest gaps. I swear, it's like nothing you've seen. So last summer one of my golf buddies caught one – like, fifty pounds – on his yacht in Cabo, but it squeezed itself through a pipe this big,' Miguel held up forefinger and thumb in a neat little ring, '*this big*, back to freedom. I watched the video on his cell. Unbelievable.'

'Spineless.' Richard was nodding.

'All I can say,' Jerry said, 'is they taste fucking delicious. Calamari? Yes. Carpaccio? Fuck yes.'

'Calamari is squid, you cretin,' Richard said.

Sabine tapped the glass of the aquarium. 'Can you eat this one?'

Kei shuddered.

'You can, actually.' Richard became animated. 'I found this oyster farm—'

'No,' Kei said. 'No, you fucking didn't.'

'I found this oyster farm in Washington State that does tinned—'

'No, no, please.' She covered her face with her hands.

'—tinned giant Pacific. In organic olive oil. I could get some from the kitchen if you just hold tight for one minute.'

He was already leaving the room.

'This is disgusting, I can't.' Kei looked to Sabine. 'You're not going to eat it, are you? I mean, I've had octopus before, but fucking look at it. It's right there. It can *see* us.'

Sabine shrugged.

'I'll try,' piped Charlie. 'I don't care.'

Kei scowled at him. 'It's fucked up.'

He shrugged, pouted.

'Come on,' she said. 'Like you're not full after that meal? Don't do it, Charlie. It's sick.'

A strange quiet settled on the rest of the room as we considered the creature before us. Her skin was suede-like beneath the water, but on land I could imagine it slick, mucous. Who would eat such a thing? I couldn't fathom holding an animal's gaze whilst chewing on its flesh.

'Ma'am?' A waiter was holding out another glass of champagne.

I declined. 'Thank you, I already have a—' I looked for my gin and tonic; it had disappeared from the table beside me.

'I can get you another. What was it?'

'Actually, I'm fine for now, thank you.'

'Bon appétit.' Richard had returned, open can in palm. He flashed a grin at Kei.

Charlie looked at her, then leapt up. 'I'll go first.'

Nobody raced him.

There was something about Charlie that unnerved me. I didn't like him – he'd clearly thought himself too important to speak to me throughout the meal – but that wasn't it. I think it was the eyes. Although his features were perfect, magnetic, and although he smiled and laughed and joked with the other guests, his eyes seemed expressionless: always a little too serious, a little too composed. As though there was nothing behind them, as though he was never himself.

When Charlie was bored, that lack of life had only made him seem more indifferent – a blankness that I'd suffered each time I tried to converse with him. But when I watched him smiling with the others, the effect was disconcerting, somewhat incongruous – verging on sinister, in fact, as he contemplated the can, looked back up at Richard, and grinned.

'Would you like a fork, sir?' asked the waitress beside him.

Charlie ignored her. Delicately pinched out a piece of the meat, held it aloft for us to inspect. I was not too near – and unlike Sabine and Jerry, did not creep closer to peer – but I could see it was almost cylindrical. A cross-section of limb, pinkish tinged. He squeezed it between his fingers; the oil dripped down.

Charlie held Richard's gaze as he opened his mouth, wide, and dropped the pink flesh in.

Another car was pulling away from Lillie's house as my cab turned in, but I could not glimpse the driver. As I unlocked the front door, my cell vibrated – two missed calls from friends. Three messages. Ten emails. So news of the death must have finally broken, but was the murder public knowledge? I should have come straight back from the police station. What the fuck was I doing wandering around a fucking mall? I threw my phone back in my purse, praying to god Lillie had stayed away from the internet.

She did not greet me.

'Who was that I just saw leaving?' I asked.

She was rinsing two cups in the sink.

'Did you have a visitor?'

'A friend.'

'Well, that's nice, sweetie.' My voice was too high; I was sweating. I put down my bag on the counter. 'I'm glad people are looking out for you. I know you don't always like to talk about things, but it can be good . . .'

Her shoulders tensed.

'. . . to share.'

I was irritating myself with this blithering – but how to begin?

Lillie stopped the water and placed the cups on the draining board. She did not face me.

'Have you eaten anything today?'

No answer.

'Sweetheart, you need to eat something. How about a—'

'I'm not hungry.'

She turned around, crossed her arms. Her eyes were puffy and raw but stony, dulled to my words. She wiped her nose on the palm of her hand.

'Lillie . . .'

I tried to hug her. She pulled away.

'We need to talk,' I said.

Lillie shut her eyes. Sighed. Whispered, with great effort: 'Please. I can't talk now. I can't talk.'

'You need to hear this.' I sounded too desperate. I slowed my words, chose them carefully: 'There's something the police have just told me and it's going to be out there, in the public, soon. I think you should hear it from me. Your father—'

'I know, Mom,' she said, beaten. 'I know somebody killed him.'

I was so shocked I did not pause to wonder how she knew – I just pulled her in tight. This time she let me. Her body was stiff, neither of us spoke.

My cell buzzed again. I let it ring.

When I called my lawyer back, there was no hint of exasperation in his voice; Scott was far too professional for that. But with the firm and swift directions he gave, it was clear he believed someone needed to take control of the situation.

'Elspeth,' he said before hanging up, 'in future, please don't hesitate to call. I can only take care of your interests when I'm aware of those interests and you do, after all, pay me a handsome retainer for that very purpose.'

Yes, I had chastised myself many times for not calling Scott sooner. In hindsight, I could tell that the other guests had been phoning their lawyers as soon as the cops descended on Sedgwick, but I hadn't been paying attention at the time. I had been trying to get through to Lillie. And then I had been cooperating with what I thought would be a straightforward investigation. It was foolish. It was reckless. What kind of person, possessing the means, ever entered a police station without their lawyer? When illegal substances were involved? When they were present as their ex-husband lay dying?

Scott liaised with the police, and then reported back: I wasn't needed at the station for another week; he'd fly in from the East Coast the day before. In the meantime, he wanted me to document my memories from that night, as well as my communications with Richard and general activities in the preceding months. And how well did I know the other guests?

A little, some of them, I told him. Old friends.

He was unflinching in his response: 'Okay, here's what I want you to do, Elspeth: don't see them, don't speak to them. No contact at all. Don't even read their messages, if possible.'

This was no challenge: neither Jerry nor Tommo had tried to get in touch. They had probably received the same advice from their own lawyers.

I barely noticed this, however. I wasn't thinking of the other guests at all and for the first few days forgot Scott's instructions entirely: taking care of Lillie was far more important than reconstructing my recollections of that night. If I ever thought of Richard – if I saw his limp body, if I recalled the detectives' words – that memory would be swiftly followed by concern for Lillie. The murder was horrific, yes – and how could my daughter cope?

She had begun to lock her bedroom door, was ignoring my tentative knocks. I'd hear TV shows faintly, through the wall, for hours, for entire days.

Sometimes I paused by my bedroom door for the sound of her emergence. I would wait two seconds, then walk down the corridor casually, carrying an empty glass to refill.

'How are you doing today?' I asked, having cornered her in the kitchen a couple of nights after we'd learned of the autopsy report.

Lillie was holding the refrigerator door open, staring into the light. Her hair was wet and she was dressed in sweats. She did not answer.

'Are you going to eat something? I could make you a grilled cheese, or . . .'

'I don't think I want anything; I'm not sure what I'm doing.'

She shut the fridge but did not turn to face me.

'Do you remember when you were little,' I said, 'and you woke up with a nightmare? I used to make bread pizza for a midnight snack. Your favourite toppings were canned corn and ketchup, but we'd have to make it with whatever was in the cupboard. Olives, anchovies . . .

'There was one time,' I continued, 'you must've been about four, when we'd run out of toppings but you refused to have it with just the cheese and tomato. Then I found a packet of beef jerky. I cut it up small so you could sprinkle it over. It wasn't too bad, once you could finally chew through it.'

Lillie turned and looked at me as if I were a stranger – not a hint of recollection.

'Have you had trouble sleeping?' I asked. 'I know you always used to when you were worried about tests. We could watch some TV together? What was the name of that show you liked?'

'No,' she said. 'I think I should go back to bed.'

'Lillie,' I said quickly, before she could leave, 'I know it's difficult to—'

'Do you, though?'

I didn't know what she meant.

'Do you know?' she said. 'Because I'm not sure I know. I don't know what to think, Mom. I don't know what I'm supposed to do. What am I supposed to do?'

How could I answer that?

'I think,' I said, 'we've just got to get through it. You've just got to look after yourself, that's all you can do.'

She nodded, but I wasn't sure she had heard. I wasn't sure

that mattered. I didn't know what I was saying. I tried a different approach.

'I was just thinking,' I told her, 'I'm going to need some more things. Because Scott said the investigation might take a while and if I'm going to be staying with you, I'll need . . . Do you want to come shopping with me tomorrow? It might be good to get out.'

Lillie's head dropped. Her shoulders were shaking – was she crying?

And then I heard it: a mechanical laughter.

'Go out?' she said, hysterically. 'You want me to go out? You want – should I wear a Day-Glo T-shirt as well? So that the camera lenses can pick me out?'

'I'm sorry,' I said. 'I didn't think.'

Lillie stopped laughing abruptly.

She sniffed, crossed her arms. Traced her slipper along the groove of a kitchen tile.

'I know,' she said. 'I'm sorry. I'm not mad. I'm just – tired.'

The ice-maker in the fridge hummed and clattered.

'I keep picking up my phone,' Lillie said. 'It's like this habit. Because I always check social media when I'm bored, and I don't think sometimes, I just pick up the phone. And then I suddenly remember, as the apps are opening. I close them as fast as I can.'

The fridge fell silent.

'I don't want to see what people are saying,' she said.

'So you haven't spoken to your friends?'

Lillie looked up. 'I meant people on social media. But my friends . . . To be honest, I haven't heard much from them. When the news broke about Dad's death, people kind of knew what to say. I mean, they didn't always say the right thing, but at least they were reaching out. Since the media heard about his . . .'

'The investigation,' I offered.

'The investigation,' she said carefully. 'Over the past few days, I don't think anyone – I mean, I wouldn't know what to say to me either.'

'You have to give them time,' I said.

'But,' Lillie said, 'if they find it difficult now, what about when more details come out? What about when the media reports that it happened at his house, or that drugs were involved, or they start to speculate about who was there? What about when they talk about the – his throat?'

My breath caught. I hadn't known which details Lillie had been given.

(The wounds; the bruises; a long, blunt object.)

It took me a few moments to realise that I'd left her questions unanswered.

'I don't know what to say.'

'No one does,' she replied.

Before Lillie could escape, I wrapped her in my embrace. She was unmoving, arms hanging by her side. Her hair smelled fresh and fragrant, figs and cut grass.

I didn't have much to be thankful for in that moment, but I was glad of one thing: that Lillie had not been there that night; that she had not found her father's body; that she would not face the detectives' suspicion. I could bear it all if I reminded myself this was for the best – for the burden to fall on me and not her.

'Lillie,' I said, as the question occurred to me, 'why weren't you there that night? Where were you?'

She pulled away.

'I mean, it doesn't matter,' I quickly added, 'but you told me you'd be arriving at the party after visiting your friend, so I just wondered . . .'

Lillie's shoulders fell; there was pain in her eyes. This was the wrong time to be questioning her.

'I'm sorry,' I said. 'Let's— We'll talk another time.'

She returned to her room, left me dawdling with an empty glass.

I rarely saw her that week at all. Under one roof, we lived separate existences. Every now and then, passing her bedroom door, I heard evidence of life: a theme tune or snatch of dialogue from her laptop speakers. I felt like a ghost. It was her space – potted palms and blue ceramics, photographs of friends I had never met. The shower refused to obey my commands. Glasses and plates were never in the first cupboard I opened.

I kept a notepad and pen on the coffee table. But I'd only written one line: the time of my flight to LA, and the time I'd arrived at Richard's. I would do what Scott had asked, I told myself. I would do it later. I would do it tomorrow.

Instead, I watched drug commercials on TV. Ignored my calls and texts. Ate nothing but a bowl of plump, cold blue-berries I discovered in the fridge – two or three at a time – washed them down with a chilled Sauvignon Blanc, past its best. Saw Richard's body, and his fingers, and his neck. Vomited up the blueberries.

Every so often, I would find another task and throw myself into it. Lillie's laundry basket; a stain on the carpet. I cleaned out the fridge-freezer, scrubbed every corner with bleach. I dusted her bookshelves and rearranged cushions – found items that she'd taken from our apartment in New York without having asked me first. A salt pig that had been a wedding present. Silverware, a French press.

There was one area of the house that I tried to avoid: Lillie's living-room wall, covered in framed prints. But I couldn't help myself. I had to straighten them every time I walked past. A fraction to the left, a hair's breadth to the right. They never lined up. And they were always there.

Richard stared at me, a young man in gelatin silver, sandwiched between glass and wood. It was a moody portrait that had accom-panied his first proper magazine profile, his first award season after *The Anatomy of Inquiry* – taken by Leibovitz. Or was that later? But I remembered the reviews well: *A young British direc-tor's ode to the classic New York noir. Elspeth Bell, as Cassandra DiSotta, embodies a female fragility – at once fierce and vulnerable.* The image had been hung next to an original poster from the film: that iconic silhouette of my lips and nose, the silver barrel of a pistol.

I counted four photographs of Richard and Lillie together, chronicling her youth, and there was another, a candid shot, from the set of *Dominus*. Richard was studying papers; Lillie rested her chin on his shoulder. I tilted the frame to the left, the right. Tried to leave it alone. Tried to walk away. Tried to ignore the fact that there was only one photograph of my daughter and me, which had been stolen from one of the albums that sat beneath my coffee table.

Astroland, Coney Island, back when bread pizza had been her favourite meal.

Squeaking chews filled the room.

'Hmm, rubbery,' Charlie said through the flesh. A drop of juice rolled down his chin.

I caught a flash of movement from the tank behind him. Persephone's eight limbs flicked and writhed. I could not imagine this creature dead, no matter how chopped and canned the body.

The heat of bile crept up my throat.

'How is it like?' Sabine hovered over Charlie.

'Fishy. I want to say . . . almost smoky? Briny, for sure.' Charlie over-enunciated, spoke slowly, through his mouthful. He wanted the room to cling to his every word.

'Okay, I will taste,' said Sabine, picking a smaller slice.

Kei looked uncomfortable. 'Really? This seems wrong.'

Sabine held up a hand. 'Frankly, my dear—'

'Don't be such a pathetic killjoy,' Richard said. 'There's nothing wrong with it. They don't hunt them; they just accidentally get stuck in the fishing nets.'

'They could throw them back,' said Kei.

'And it's very good for you. High in protein, low calorie.'

'Delicious and nutritious,' Charlie said, staring at Richard. The actor laughed, loud, like he'd told a witty joke.

I watched him as he realised Richard would not respond, watched him survey the group, a claw for attention. I looked the other way when his gaze swept over me.

Charlie sat back down. Picked up his glass. Pretended to be bored; a little boy, salty with neglect.

Sabine gave her verdict: 'It needs vinegar.'

'All right, all right, pass it here,' said Jerry. 'Come on.'

Tommo asked whether I would try. 'Aren't you curious?'

'Not at all.'

He left my side to join the carnivores.

'Persephone would eat it,' said Richard. He walked to the tank and cooed: 'You would eat it right up, wouldn't you, my sweet? You would hunt your lover without a thought. You would devour every inch and you would suck the beak clean.'

I looked away; I felt sick. Jerry giggled. I could still hear that crunch of shell and flesh as he had torn the lobster apart. Was I imagining it, or did it still linger in the air – the brine, the sweet, fishy odour?

'I swear to fucking god,' Kei was not joking, 'if you feed *that* to *her* in front of me, I will leave.'

'Suit yourself. She can finish the tin later.' Richard passed the can to the nearest waiter, nodded his head towards the kitchen.

Honey muttered something under his breath.

'What videos?' asked Kei.

Persephone was crawling away from us, slipping between two rocks.

'No, no.' Our host shook his head. 'Honey, baby, they don't want to watch that. It's so dull. It's not the time nor the place. Not now.'

'Watch what?' asked Jerry. 'Now, if you're into those sicko tentacle things, I'm telling you, *I'm* getting outta here.'

'It's not that,' Honey began, barely audible, 'it's . . . He films it.'

'The octopus? Doing what?'

Richard did not answer; he looked to Honey. I saw his jaw clench.

Honey stared him back.

'They don't want to see it, baby,' Richard muttered through his teeth.

My throat was tacky. I tried to swallow.

'See what?' asked Sabine. 'Now you must tell.'

Honey turned away from Richard's warning glare and answered her.

'Richard films the octopus.' He pointed to a CCTV camera, red light blinking, in the corner of the room. 'She escapes the tank every night.'

'She escapes *every night*?' said Kei. 'And you film it? Dude, what the fuck.'

'That's messed up,' Miguel said. 'Rich, that is messed up.'

'There's not much I can do about it.' Richard raised his voice over the protestations. 'She escapes through a valve in the water-filtering system.' He took a step towards her. 'But she can't get far; she needs water to breathe. So she squashes herself back – pulls one of the little metal levers through after her to keep the valve open. Clever old bitch.'

'I feel a little nauseated,' said Tommo.

'Oh, she's sentient, yes.' Richard bent down to her level. 'But I find that makes them all the more delicious.'

Persephone had positioned herself in front of him, suckers gripping the glass, velveteen skin rippling slow. I was so engrossed in this swaying, I could have been next to her, submerged in the tank; not a part of the group, but watching from the water.

Then she blinked and I was in my body again – skirt sticking to my thighs.

'. . . but it's not a big deal,' Richard was saying. 'It's just like a dog streaking away when you unclip its leash. It returns because it wants to, because it needs you.'

With a flash of outrage, I heard myself protest. 'It returns because it's suffocating. It should be in the ocean.'

'Calm down, darling, the tank is huge.' Richard batted the criticism away. 'Much bigger than regulation. You should see the boxes they stuff them into at proper aquariums.'

He stood up and stretched his shoulders.

'It's all fine, really. I have a guy, a neuroscience student with aquarium experience, looking for a bit of spare cash. So he comes round to check on her and the tank. He says the escaping is harmless as long as I don't mind it. It's a game for Persephone, something to keep her occupied. Okay, yes, we could seal the filter, but then he wouldn't be able to reach it for cleaning.'

Charlie yawned. 'Are we gonna watch the video or what?'

'If you insist.'

Richard took a remote control from his pocket; the music stopped, the tank whirred and bubbled. Then a screen unrolled from the ceiling with a hum. Tommo nudged me, sniggered. Richard, flicking through his phone, mumbled: 'Aha.'

An image of the atrium fizzed into life from the projector: a collection of pale infrared shapes. In the bottom right-hand corner of the tank, a murky silhouette shifted.

'So that's where the filter is?' said Charlie, pointing at the aquarium beside him, to the corner nearest the seating area.

'It's concealed by a fake rock. She lifts it,' Richard said.

A dark plume of dust puffed from the floor. The silhouette appeared to shrink.

'This is the amazing part – she squeezes herself through the pipes, then unscrews the panel from behind.'

A small object fell from the base of the aquarium. Then another. Miguel whistled, low. The panel flipped open.

There was no sound in the room – then cries of disbelief. I heard Tommo take a short, sharp breath. The enormous creature had begun to squash her body, viscous, through an opening so small it could not be seen on screen. She was materialising before our eyes.

'How?' Charlie exclaimed.

'Like a magician pulling a handkerchief from his fist,' Richard said. 'She's barely solid.'

'Toothpaste,' said Sabine.

'Snot,' said Jerry.

Richard pressed fast forward. We watched the shadow slump across the floor, almost reaching the doorway through which I had just walked. There she sat, motionless, for what appeared to be a minute. Then she crawled back, pulling the flap shut behind her.

'We have to screw those bloody things back every morning.' Richard was switching off the projector. 'And she trails water all over the floor. Yola – our housekeeper – hates it.'

'Will she make the escape tonight?' said Sabine.

We looked to the tank.

'She only tries in the dark, when no one else is around,' Honey answered. 'She can tell when humans are here.'

The opening in the creature's eyelids was thin as a bobby pin. I would have thought them shut, had they not blinked at that moment.

It wasn't until the night before my next interrogation that I began the task Scott had set. He had called after dinner from his hotel, confirmed the time I needed to arrive at the station, and then said: 'And you've made your notes?'

I lied.

'Great,' he replied. 'We want you to feel confident about what you can remember.'

Guilty, I took the notepad to Lillie's kitchen table and opened my laptop, as though a change of medium might jog me to action. I copied the one line I had written into a Word document. My arrival in LA, my arrival at the party. I couldn't type any more – I didn't know how to separate the evening into events. There was the party and then the morning. His body on the couch.

'What are you doing?' asked Lillie, finding herself a plate.

I almost didn't tell her.

'Scott wanted a record of that night,' I said. 'The police are questioning me tomorrow afternoon, remember?'

'Oh, yeah.'

Maybe one day Lillie would want the sequence of events for herself. She hadn't asked me any questions about that night yet. And I had certainly not volunteered the memories.

'I was thinking,' I said, 'after I'm done, I might watch a movie?'

'Sure,' she said. Took some chocolate from the cupboard. 'Do you need me to show you how to—'

'I thought we might watch together.'

'Oh.' She hesitated. Snapped a row of squares from the bar and then put it back. 'Um, no. I don't think – I'm actually in the middle of reading a novel, so . . .'

'What are you reading?'

'*I Capture the Castle.*'

'Is that the beautiful second-hand one you used to have? With the blue cover?' She nodded; I smiled. 'You carried it around everywhere when you were little. Did I buy it for you? Was it for school?'

'No,' she said. 'Dad did.'

Lillie dawdled for a second, like she wanted to leave but wasn't sure how.

'You know you don't have to spend all of your time in your room,' I said. 'It's your home; you can sit in here, or on the couch. And if you want this space on the table, I can move. I don't want you to feel like you have to keep to your bedroom just because I'm staying here.'

'I don't feel like I have to,' she said, then put the row of chocolate onto the plate. 'I prefer it.'

I was left with my screen again. The blank white page. Lillie's bedroom door shut behind her.

What had happened after my arrival at Richard's? The meal, the speech. My conversation with Tommo; then we had watched Persephone. I looked at the blinking cursor. Opened the web browser instead.

It was out of boredom – not curiosity – that I typed the word into the white bar. The first results were brands and PR companies, then the Wikipedia page, then some videos. Lacking concentration, I clicked on the latter.

The documentary opened with dramatic strings, a murky sea. We were beneath an octopus as it pumped itself forwards with all eight limbs – lifting them up, up, slowly into a parachute and then thrusting them down. An ominous voice detailed the alien's anatomy over a montage of prey being hunted, and then, with a climax of thudding drums, we were given the title. I slipped off my shoes. Pulled up my feet to cross them beneath me.

The rest of the documentary was much more sober in approach. We met a marine biologist, heard about his experiments to map out the creature's intelligence, and watched as his test subject slopped herself out of the tank and onto the floor to inspect the laboratory. The octopus was returned to its tank and underwent a series of tests. Mostly they consisted of objects being dropped into the water; her interactions with them were observed. Other experiments, with other octopuses, followed. They seemed to have different personalities: some would tentatively explore objects, with gentle curiosity; others handled them roughly, with flashes of impatient aggression.

Despite my distance from these creatures – they were only images on a screen, after all – I felt a growing unease. There was something very real, something evocative, in the way they moved on screen. How they gripped the glass of their tanks, how their heads dragged like soft sacks.

I lost myself in these movements – jumping when the voiceover man began to talk again. He and his dramatic strings were beginning to grate, so I dragged the volume slider to zero and sat with the images alone. When the first video ended, the player automatically selected another, then another and another. And so I sat there, watching. The cars passing on the road could only be heard faintly, every now and then. I liked this silence – the surreality it lent the videos.

At some point I realised my ankles had grown numb. I was bathed in the blue of the screen. I stretched my arms and stood up – checked the missed calls on my phone, replied to none of the messages. When I brushed my teeth, I noticed red veins webbing my eyeballs.

The creeping unease had remained, deep in my stomach. It was there as I washed my face and smoothed on eye cream. There as I passed Lillie's door, noted the cracks of light at the hinges. It followed me to the bedroom, between the sheets.

I saw them still when I shut my eyes, and they were watching me, and I was watching them. As my breathing steadied, my thoughts tumbled into the obscurity of a dreamer teetering on the brink of subconsciousness, and the tentacles became barbed wire, and Richard was a pile of pebbles, and my fingernails were teeth, and the ocean encroached, and the pebbles turned to emeralds, one by one . . .

I couldn't name my unease until the next morning, after the sun had risen and dazzled me awake. I stretched my legs and buried my face in the pillows. Then it came all at once:

The itch at my arm where it had lain in water; how I had rolled over to dry it off. I'd opened my eyes to the shaft of light. And my arm was cold and wet.

If I had sucked my fingers after feeling for Richard's pulse, would I have tasted salt?

'But what people don't understand is that the industry isn't cyclical. I see it as more of a bicycle wheel: it goes around, sure, but it's always moving *forwards*. And I was thinking . . .'

I regretted taking this seat. *Miguel Montana, Montana Entertainment* – as his business card stated and as he had repeated while pushing it into my hand – had now talked for ten minutes without once asking a question. Why hadn't I left the party altogether? After I was cornered by Miguel, there hadn't been a pause for an excuse.

'So maybe you need to get back into the game. But I would do it sooner rather than later. There's a real craving for the older actress at the moment. Sorry, mature. Gritty, emotional roles. Can't say it does great at the box office, but it's something, right?'

Did this qualify as a question? He did not wait for an answer.

'Look, I'm not going to promise you the world; we can't turn back time and I don't need to tell you that. How old are you? Mid-forties?'

I was only forty-two, but I couldn't be bothered to correct him.

'Mid-forties, we can work with that – you still have an agent, right? You know, I want to look out for you. A friend of Rich, any friend of Rich, is a friend of mine. And I'm all for this feminist stuff . . .'

I winced a little with each 's'. Miguel had one of those wide-cornered mouths that stretched itself to mild speech impediments and exaggerated facial expressions.

'. . . because I can appreciate male actors have longer careers, higher pay. I listen. It's my job to listen. Ask anyone – I'm the biggest cheerleader for actresses. I mean, look at you, you're gorgeous, why can't you get interesting roles too? We've got to do better. I said the same thing to Honey, he needs to put himself out there. Modelling pays fuck all, and I said he should get into the game, there are some solid roles for Black actors right now.'

He smiled conspiratorially, came uncomfortably close. I could see the transition of his hair as it moved from natural wisps at the sides to a grid of transplants.

'And that scene in *Anatomy*. You were—'

'Miguel.' I stood up, flashed the smile I now reserved for the biggest donors at my fundraising events, the smile that had charmed many a producer, journalist, maître d' in the past. 'Miguel, as much as I'd love to sit here basking in your flattery all night, I'm afraid my phone is beckoning. Would you excuse me?'

'Sure.' He grinned. And then, with a wink, 'And I won't tell Rich about your contraband if you promise to come right back to me. I mean it, I think you've got a great career ahead of you.'

I dashed from the room, rummaging in my bag as though I could feel impatient rumblings, until I had turned the corner.

The distant noise of traffic hit me as I crossed the doorway from kitchen to yard, past the little pile of cigarette stubs left by the chefs and waitress. I stared at my phone screen for a few minutes – still no reply from Lillie – in case Miguel was watching, then raised my head. It was lovely to be alone. I would let myself enjoy this moment.

From here I could understand the clever illusion: how the slope of the hill beneath the atrium had been hewn to a straight line, creating the impression of a dramatic drop. Inside, I had thought the house clung to a cliff face. But no: the lawn was a plateau, and as I walked across the pristine grass to its edge I found a five-foot drop before the hill rolled again.

I sat on this smooth-concrete border, a kid dangling legs into the swimming pool. Its coolness pressed through my skirt. Beyond the shadowed trees, I could see string lights hanging over a neighbour's garden – and could just about catch the chatter of another party on the night breeze.

It had been a while since anyone had mentioned my acting career but it still happened every so often, when Richard's fans caught me in coffee shops, when working the small-talk crowds of charity galas and art shows. I had rehearsed my response well: the smile, the modesty. I knew that the most interesting part of my character was my past; I wasn't deluded. But it was still tedious. They were always well-meaning enquirers, but not without pity – that unarticulated thought that it was too late for me, as they insisted: *You were so* beautiful, *such a* shame *you left it all behind.*

These comments weren't malicious. Yet it was difficult to brush aside the mention of my looks, rather than my talent, and the conspicuous past tense. I would smile through aching cheekbones. I would demur, touch the forearm, and think: *You have no idea. My sunkissed life in California soured long before my looks ever did.*

How bizarre – to find myself here once again, swallowed by the sky and hemmed by the hills. The city lights below speckled from the black.

I don't think it was nostalgia that I felt while sitting alone with this view. Maybe instead it was that dislocation that can come with revisiting a place of memory. The thought that I had been there before, and that my self of the past, looking out across the city, would have seen my current self as a stranger – might not even have recognised me. And that made me wonder if I would ever be here in the city again, thinking back to this time as a memory. Maybe I wouldn't even need to be in the city to revisit this moment. Maybe it would come to me, suddenly, sitting in the back of a New York taxi. Maybe I would see it in some other cityscape, or at another lonely party. I was certain I would remember the moment again: if only the dusty smell of the polluted breeze, the city lights, that small but incessant curdling in my stomach.

This had never been a city, or an industry, to which I had

desperately aspired. Chance had led the way. A job at the Douglaston Golf Course, a co-worker – a friend – with ambitious plans: Tanya had wanted to move to LA and I simply wanted to escape. A party we attended so she could meet casting directors. And a charming encounter with a British filmmaker.

But, now – could that be right?

Was I nothing more than a passive creature? Or had I flown to LA with Tanya nursing an unarticulated desire? Had I not taken care over my makeup, my outfit that night? Had I not attended dozens of parties? Had I not been living there for months by the time I met Richard? How many hours had I already wasted listening to men as the ice melted in my glass? How many lines on my pocket mirror to keep myself awake and interested? Maybe it was easier to believe I had never wanted to become an actress – that I had effortlessly slipped into it – than to admit that I had wanted this career, more than anything, and yet had quit, regardless. Maybe it was easier than to fully confront the reason why I had left.

(Lift your head, look over here.)

(I said, *lift your head.*)

But there, on that ledge, I let myself swallow it all: the countless car headlights, the glowing windows, twinkling into the distance.

(Lift your head. Your head.)

Perhaps I could appreciate the beauty, from up there, then.

(No, your chin, upwards.)

(Like this.)

(Can you feel? Good girl. Take it from the top.)

Hearing heeled steps behind me, I stood.

'Don't move by my account.' It was Sabine, taking a black cigarette from her purse. There was no generosity in her voice: she had wanted me to stay in my own world, but we both knew it was too late for me to turn back and ignore her.

I wandered over, arms crossed, unsure of where to pitch our conversation.

'Warm night,' I began.

'For an East Coaster, perhaps.' She struck a flame from a

matchbook, drawing her first smoky breath. 'Wear nothing in June, do as you wish in May.'

I had noticed this affectation, eavesdropping on discussions earlier, how she expressed herself in the poetry of a stranger to a language: mother-tongue idioms that no longer made sense, phrases from movie dialogue, wild metaphors invented in the search for adjectives.

'You're French?' I asked, hoping geography would be easy terrain. 'I was in Paris just last spring.'

'Yes, a piece of me.'

She did not elaborate. I wondered whether I could escape the conversation yet – or whether that would confirm my worthlessness. She was barely acknowledging my presence, her boredom palpable.

I settled into silence, looked beyond Sabine to the atrium. Richard was weaving between conversations; the waiters stood, expressionless; the guests laughed and talked without sound escaping the glass. I imagined the house as an enormous aquarium. A brilliant display in the dark of night. The bright clothes, sparkling jewellery; a tank shelved on the hillside. It was enchanting, if I let it be so.

'How well do you know everyone?' I asked.

Sabine inhaled, exhaled, before answering. 'From *Dominus*, yes. Kei and Charlie, I know the best. Then Honey, I know. Miguel, not so much. Thomas, Jerry, I only meet tonight.'

She turned to the window, watched the others as well. I couldn't tell which figure's path her eyes were tracing.

'And Richard?' I said. 'He's a close friend too?'

Her attendance had been puzzling me all night. Charlie, I understood. As Richard had said, he was at the very start of his career – and I could imagine it was important to maintain his relationship with Richard and Miguel. It was there in his veering from boredom to exhibitionism: he had probably expected a large, star-studded party, as I had; yet he couldn't bring himself to snub Richard; kept trying, sporadically, to impress the birthday boy.

But why would Sabine – *a star, an artist, an icon* – have stayed at this strange, quiet house? Didn't she have other events to attend? More important people to see? She'd been involved in the group conversations all night – charming, measured – but I hadn't seen her interacting with Richard much. They didn't seem to be old friends or particularly close, and why would they have been? She was barely in her mid-twenties.

'He is a friend, yes,' she said, and tapped her ash.

'But you've only worked together on *Dominus*? No other projects?'

'Many questions,' she remarked. 'But no. No other projects with Richard.'

And why had Richard invited Charlie and Sabine, out of all the actors he had worked with? Maybe they were ornaments, his latest pretty things. Or maybe he had invited others, and they had declined. Either way I doubted Richard was really as close to the actors as he had insisted in his speech.

'How did you find working with Richard, on *Dominus*?' I asked.

Sabine said: 'Don't you know from your daughter?'

This silenced me for a few moments. Her question had not been asked with sharpness, but I felt it there: something she didn't want me to prod.

'I'm just curious.' I smiled. 'It's such a small party. I'm fascinated by how everyone knows Richard. Aren't you?'

'I'm not very interested, no,' she said, tired. Opened her mouth as though she was about to say something. Paused, then settled on another thought: 'But I can understand how you are.'

'How I am . . . ?'

'Interested in Richard.'

Sabine let her words sit.

'I thought it was quite admirable,' she said. 'How you stood by your man.'

It sounded almost like a challenge. She drew on her cigarette, eyes thinning.

My cheeks flushed as I grasped her meaning. There were many retorts in my head, but only one settled upon my tongue:

'He's not my man.'

'And yet you still supported him.' She sucked on her teeth with a pink tongue. I couldn't place her tone – was she mocking me? 'Admirable.'

What did she think? That I still loved Richard? That I still felt I had a duty to him?

'My daughter,' I said. 'I did it for my daughter.'

Sabine blew another trail from her pouting, scarlet lips. The stain wrapped the gold filter, the sky was velvet black. And then – I could not tell which – came either American acceptance, or European sarcasm.

'Sure,' she said, blankly. 'Sure.'

I spent that morning on the internet. There were endless videos. Documentaries detailing octopus anatomy and behaviour. Clips of killing prey. CCTV footage of the creatures escaping from tanks in aquariums, boats in the sea, mazes in laboratories. Recordings from experiments: could they see humans, problem-solve, communicate? And, of course, the sensational: wrestling and swallowing six-foot sharks; leaping out of rock pools to devour crabs; dragging seagulls from the surface of the water, down to the rocky depths.

Watching the videos, I realised that it would not have been the bony beak that killed Richard, as I had first thought. They were not long and blunt but sharp, slicing things, made for puncturing prey and driving through hard crab shells. Richard would not have suffocated on such a lethal weapon; rather, bled to death. Bruised, they had told me, not shredded.

I wondered how hard the tentacles were when flexed taut – whether Persephone could have stuffed one, two, or three into Richard's mouth to block the windpipe.

It was unlikely. It was ridiculous. Why would an octopus not use its venom, its toxic ink, or flinty beak? How would it know we breathed through our mouths? But no matter how many times I told myself it was illogical, I could not shake the suspicion.

All morning, I could see it in my mind, captured – as it might have been – on that CCTV camera. How Persephone silently unscrewed the flap. How she forced her body through the opening. How she slipped out onto the floor, viscous. I could see her dark, grainy form in the pale-green infrared scene. Again and again I saw her slugging to Richard, clinging to his face, holding him tight as he struggled, injecting him with venom to slow his movements, and then, as he screamed, pushing a long, fat tentacle between his lips.

I knew this was not possible. The forensic examination would surely have noticed the signs of struggle, round lesions from suction cups; toxicology reports would have discovered the venom, the sea salt.

Then a needling question: what if they were simply looking for the wrong things in the wrong place?

I tried to silence that thought. If I told the cops my theory about the octopus, they would only laugh. I could picture the female detective's face: the confusion, at first, then disbelief, then amusement. An octopus as the murder suspect? I didn't need to draw attention to myself, compromise my credibility, with wild ideas about a vengeful, bloodthirsty creature escaping its tank to suffocate my ex-husband. I didn't need to make Scott's job any harder.

And so, making myself a salad for lunch, I ran over the events of the night as Scott had asked. With each slice through the tomato skin, I weighed down my octopus suspicions with solid facts: eight guests, and then the meal, and then the speech, and then—

Lillie emerged from her room, still in pyjamas.

'Do you want some?' I asked. 'Caprese.'

She nodded and sat at the table.

I drained the mozzarella and tore into it with my bare fingers, letting the soft clumps fall on the tomatoes. A few basil leaves – clapped in my palms to release the flavour – then oil drizzled, salt sprinkled. I found an extra plate for Lillie and set it all down.

'Late night reading?' I said, dropping some salad on my plate. 'You haven't been out of the house, have you? All week? I think you should get some fresh air. That might help.'

I was taking care not to spill olive oil onto my shirt – I'd already changed into smarter clothes.

'You could come with me now – I'm about to leave to go to the police station. I could drop you at a friend's house?'

'It's okay,' she said, 'I can drive myself if I need to.'

'I'm not offering because you need to be driven, Lillie. I just think it might help if you keep busy.'

'I am busy,' she said. 'I've got a friend coming round.'

'Which friend?'

Lillie was chewing each mouthful thoroughly. I'd already nearly finished, and her plate was almost full.

I checked my watch. I needed to leave. 'Look, I'm sorry but I've got to go. Leave the dishes. I'll clear them when I get back.'

As I packed my things into my purse, I said: 'Maybe when all of this is over, the investigation, we could both go back to New York? It might be helpful for you to get some space. Or if you're worried about the media, we could go away? Europe or something. What do you say?'

Lillie swallowed her food. 'I have to be here for Dad's memorial.'

I had forgotten about the memorial. We hadn't spoken about it at all. I didn't even know who would be organising it – whether Lillie would play a role.

'Of course,' I said, quickly. 'After, I meant after.'

'I don't know,' she responded. 'My life's here now, isn't it?'

I kissed her cheek goodbye and tried to quash the guilt. I needed to concentrate on the interrogation; I would ask her about the memorial later.

But as I sat in my car, waiting for her gate to roll open, I couldn't keep my thoughts on the party. Lillie had insisted on picking me up when I touched down at LAX. I could rent a car later, she said; wouldn't I be exhausted from the flight? But I knew her true motivation. She had wanted to carefully orchestrate that moment, when I saw her behind the wheel for the first time. *See*, she had wanted to tell me, with a casual press of her key fob, *I'm not a kid any more*.

As we drove to her house, she let the radio sing. Asked me

about my flight, talked about all the things she wanted to show me. New restaurants, hiking trails. She wore her sunglasses, the window was open – she chatted without looking at me.

'Are you okay?' Lillie asked, mid-sentence. 'You seem quiet. Is it the plane? Are you tired? You might have time for a nap.'

I was not tired; I was overwhelmed. All the ways in which she had changed, all the time since I had last seen her. We had days ahead of us – how would we fill them? And the spectre of Richard's party, that very evening, hanging over my every thought.

'Yes,' I said. 'Exhausted.'

'Aren't you glad I came to pick you up? I mean, maybe you should rethink whether to hire a car at all – I could drive you, you can take taxis. When's the last time you were behind the wheel anyway?'

I looked out the window at the roads, at how much the city had changed, and hadn't, in the ten years I'd been away. 'Please, Lillie. I've been driving longer than you've been out of diapers.'

She threw her head back with laughter.

'Having a licence is not the same as driving,' Lillie said. 'You're so pampered in New York. You'll have to get used to how different it is here. No driver, no doorman.'

I did not remind her that I had lived in LA for much longer than the year and a half she had spent there. I did not want to remind her that this city had been our home, until I dragged her across the country to condensed high-rises and biting winters.

'Speaking of pampered,' she said, checking her rear-view mirror, 'how's Julian?'

'He's . . .' I studied the bumper of the truck ahead of us. 'I don't know. We separated.'

'Wait, what? No. You broke up? When?'

'A few months back. In January.'

Lillie was silent for a few minutes. Then asked: 'Why didn't you tell me?'

I sighed. 'You don't want to hear about my boring life back home. Honestly, it didn't seem that important.'

'You were together for two years, weren't you?' She frowned.

'I thought you were talking about moving in together. I'd say that's pretty—'

'Let's not turn this into an issue, Lillie. I didn't tell you right away because I knew I'd mention it at some point.'

And when was the last time we had spoken on the phone for more than ten minutes?

I clutched my purse, tight, and looked out the window again. The concrete walls bordering the highway were grey and feature-less.

It was unmistakable, the absence of excitement, the silence between us, as we wound up and around the hills to reach her house.

'Well,' she said flatly, while we waited for the gate to open, 'here we are.'

'A barista!' Richard poked Charlie in the stomach. 'Barista.'

'Oh, man, that was a lunch to remember.' Miguel folded his arms, leaning back against the kitchen sink. Directed his next question at me: 'You heard this? So Rich is an *hour* late for our lunch meeting and I'm really pissed. Already ordered for myself, fifteen minutes in, thinking he wouldn't turn up, and I'm just about finishing my second course – the truffle pizza, Soho House, wood-fired, divine, you've got to try it – when he bursts in, sees me, shouts across the room: *Miguel, Miguel, you won't believe this!* So I think somebody's *died*, and I'm out of my seat like, *Which hospital did the ambulance head to?* Because I've never seen Rich like that, I literally think there's been some kind of accident. But he's so into his story he doesn't answer. He says: *I was just served coffee by the quintessential Luke Winters—*'

'Come on, guys, that's not . . .' said Charlie. 'I didn't serve him coffee, did I? I wasn't even working that day. I was dropping off some flyers for—'

'Well, needless to say, I'm relieved,' Miguel steamed on, 'and the the wait staff is too. I mean, we're all on standby. Not that Rich would notice – he's all jumpy, can't talk about anything else. *I've got to have this guy. I've gotta have him for* Dominus.'

'Yes.' Richard was grinning. 'Quintessential.'

'I was like, *Sure, okay, let's see what this barista can do*' – Miguel nudged Richard – '*but can I order dessert first?*' They both fell to laughter.

'You make it sound like you just came into the coffee shop and, like, handed me the job.' Charlie was laughing as he spoke, yet he looked almost pained, shifting from foot to foot. 'But I was already an actor. I had an agent then, and I was Brick in that—'

'Oh my god.' Miguel slapped the counter. 'I forgot that part, I forgot.' He turned to me again. 'Get this: this guy, Charlie here, when Rich offers him the audition, he's like: *I'm sorry, I can't make it. I'm in rehearsal that day.*'

'It wasn't a rehearsal, it was the first matinee,' Charlie said. He was still smiling, but his hurt was hardening his words, now.

Kei added: 'Maybe he didn't want to let people down.'

'Exactly,' Charlie said. 'Plus my agent always told me: go for the role, not the promise.'

'You need a new agent, buddy,' said Miguel.

Richard smirked. 'Changed your mind sharpish when you went home and googled me that night, though, didn't you, Charlie boy?'

Charlie didn't respond.

'Anyway,' Kei was sitting on the counter, beer in hand, frowning, 'it's not really in the spirit of the game to say Charlie would be a barista.'

'But it's true, isn't it?' Richard pounced, eyes shining. 'If he wasn't an actor, that's what he'd be doing.'

Tommo was counting out five glasses. He paused and pointed at me. I was still awkwardly lingering near the door to the yard. 'Want an old-fashioned?'

I hesitated; I really needed to get going.

'They'll taste delicious, darling, have one.'

'Yeah,' Kei was saying, 'but it's like – what would you be doing in a different life.'

'I'm making you one,' Tommo had already grabbed another glass, 'and you can decide if you want to finish it once you've tried the first sip.'

'A life where I hadn't met him?' Richard said. Then he adopted an atrocious American accent, which I recognised well from the days when he'd mimicked me: '*Uhhh . . . is that a grande or a tall? And you wanted a side order of my headshot? No? Well I'll slip you one for free, bro. Can I get, uhhh, your name? To put on the order? How is that spelled, is that uhhh R-I-T-C . . .*'

Miguel clapped him on the back. Charlie tried to laugh along, but he said, too loud: 'I have a college degree, I know how to fucking spell. And I think you'll find it's D-I-C-K.'

'Bit close to the bone, Charlie boy?' said Richard, grinning at his producer.

Miguel added: 'Yeah, what d'you major in anyway? Mochaccinos?'

'Community theatre.' Richard laughed.

'Well, anyway,' Kei cut in, 'I think I would probably be an architect.'

'No,' Richard said, 'you'd be shooting music videos for whiny indie bands.'

The group quietened with a knock at the kitchen door. One of the waitresses poked her head around the corner.

'That's it,' she said to Richard. 'Everything's loaded up. Is there anything else you—'

'No, thank you, Sally, you've been wonderful,' he said. Then to the rest of us: 'Weren't they wonderful? The staff are leaving now.'

Everyone murmured their agreement.

Richard pressed an envelope into the woman's hand. 'For the staff to share.'

'Oh,' she said, 'that's – thank you. Very generous.'

'Please,' said Richard. 'You all deserve it. And if you could remind everyone about discretion . . .'

'Already done, Mr Bryant. Like I said, it's in the contracts.'

'Much appreciated,' said Richard. When the door had closed behind her, he turned to us. 'You know how it can be,' he explained, 'with all these camera phones and gossip blogs and tweets nowadays.'

Tommo nodded at the door. 'She would have been a naval officer. Did you catch her barking commands at the start of the night?'

'What's the game?' I asked.

'It's called alter ego,' he replied, opening the bourbon. He gave it a sniff, then started pouring. 'You have to say what you might be doing if you hadn't ended up where you are today.'

'Which isn't, strictly speaking, the concept of an alter ego,' said Richard.

Kei shot him a sulphurous look. 'The point is it's *not* supposed to be something you've done. It has to be something totally different – but something that would suit you.'

Sabine was coming in from the yard. She sighed at Kei's remark and did not pause as she swanned through to the corridor. 'Always with tedious games. Where is Honey? You bore me.'

'Okay,' said Richard, 'so I'm visualising Tommo sitting on a building site, slobbering over Page Three until he clocks off early for a pint at the local Wetherspoons.'

'Did you understand any of that?' Miguel asked me. 'Is this guy speaking English?'

'He's alluding to my apocryphal working-class background.' Tommo was shaving peel from an orange, unamused. 'All lies. My parents worked in construction, fine, but they were business owners. And if I weren't in finance, I could see myself as . . . I don't know. A mixologist. Maybe have my own bar.'

He paused, tapped the peeler against his palm. 'But that's beside the point, isn't it? Because now Richard has tactfully informed you all that I wasn't born with a silver spoon in my mouth, unlike him.' Tommo resumed his peeling, spoke calmly. 'It's supposed to be some sort of slight. He's forgotten, of course, the endemic magnetism of the American dream – I'm the noble one in this territory. So, now you've clumsily jibed at me, who's your next victim, Dicky?'

Richard was unfazed by Tommo's retort and answered without hesitation: 'Elspeth.'

There was a moment of silence as I was studied.

'I can see Elspeth as a painting, a masterpiece,' Miguel ventured. '*Girl with a Pearl Earring*, or – what's that one where she comes out of the shell?'

'She's a . . .' Charlie tapped the neck of his beer bottle, thinking. I realised what it was, earlier, that had unnerved me. The disconcerting look in his eyes was a result of his stare, which he maintained for an uncomfortably long time. 'I want to say . . . a model. Like an older model? From one of those Patek Philippe ads.'

I raised my eyebrows.

'I don't know what the fuck you're talking about, dude,' said Kei. 'Elspeth is clearly an art dealer.'

'No, no, you're all so unimaginative,' said Richard, finally diverting Charlie's attention from me. 'She's a postwoman.'

'A mailman?' exclaimed Miguel. 'Come on, Rich, she's more interesting than that.'

'She's a little old postwoman in a small neighbourhood,' Richard went on, sizing me up. I kept perfectly still. Tried to relax my expression. 'She reads all the letters. She knows exactly who hasn't paid their bills, who orders items from the naughty catalogues, who gets multiple Valentine's Day cards . . . but she never tells a soul. She doesn't speak to anyone. Not even a wave to the neighbourhood children. She's a little old quiet postwoman, wheeling along her—'

'Fuck,' Kei said, 'that is no way to talk about the mother of your child.'

Tommo was handing around the drinks.

'You should have seen how he spoke to me when we were still married,' I told her.

'It's a joke, it's a joke, she knows what I mean. Don't you, Ellie?'

I did. He knew that I had always been fascinated by mail as a child – I had told him about our class trip to the Queens Processing and Distribution Center. How I had watched the envelopes shuffling past on conveyor belts and had marvelled at the endless stories they contained. I wanted to know everything, about everyone, these strangers and their lives.

But I resented this reminder of how well he knew me. The attempt at closeness, especially in front of his friends.

'He's just being rude again,' I said.

Tommo broke the tension.

'Well, you're all wrong, anyhow,' he said. 'Elspeth is obviously a world-class poker champion. Now can we please go through to the living room? I want to be sitting down and relaxing as I drink this, not soaking my arse in the kitchen sink.'

'Ms Bryant Bell?'

The interrogation hadn't been as challenging as I'd feared – no surprises like the first time I'd sat in this room, when I'd learned of Richard's murder. Scott had told me that we would just be running over the facts, and all I needed to was recount my memories. Which I had done, and it had been straightforward, but after what felt like hours of conversation, I was starting to flag.

On the way in to the station, I'd crossed paths with a small woman, who had looked me up and down – then held my eye with disdain. I was sure we'd never met before, but that face had stuck with me. Beady eyes and a hard little chin.

And the look she had thrown at me: recognition, then disgust. As the questions continued to drum, that look haunted my mind. Like it was a judgement of my performance, punishment for having stayed awake all night thinking of octopuses.

'Ms Bryant Bell,' repeated the female detective, 'you were saying?'

'Well, I was certainly awake,' I said, trying to forget the stranger's stare. 'But I want to state, for the record, that I was probably intoxicated at the time.'

Scott coughed. We had not agreed on any plan of action for the questioning, but I had learned to shut my mouth when he so much as sniffed.

'With alcohol, I mean. Intoxicated as in tipsy. So my memory isn't perfect.'

'Try to think back to that moment,' said the officer. 'Can you recall where everyone was?'

I shut my eyes. Saw the marble coffee table, the couches to each side, the tank bubbling in the background. I pushed

Persephone and the judgemental stranger out of my mind. (Richard pulled his belt through the loops.)

'Richard was sitting on the couch next to the aquarium,' I said. 'Beside him, on the couch, was Charlie and then, next to him, Miguel. Miguel was definitely asleep by that point. As was Jerry – he was asleep on the other couch. I was sitting on the floor, near Richard. Around the corner of the table.'

(The floor chilled my cheek.)

The female cop drew a crude square on the back of a piece of typed paper. Then two crosses. Pointed with her pen.

'Like this? Mr Bryant here, you there?'

I nodded.

'Then Jerry was on the corner of the other couch nearest to me,' I continued. 'And Sabine and Kei were beside each other, next to him. I think Kei was still awake, but she was just smoking, I don't think she was involved . . .'

'In the consumption of heroin?' clarified the male officer.

'No, exactly – she was just smoking cigarettes. And Sabine was asleep, with her head on Kei's lap.'

'Thomas Coates?' he asked.

'He was sitting on the floor. Opposite side of the table from me.'

'And Mr Carlisle?'

I shut my eyes again.

'Honey was on the floor, at Charlie's feet.'

'Was he awake?'

'I don't think so, no,' I said. 'I remember seeing him passed out towards the end of the night. I think he slept through the whole thing.'

'Due to alcohol consumption?' asked the male officer, cocking his head to the side. 'Or drugs?'

'The former, yes.'

'And he had fallen unconscious before you all went to sleep?'

'Apart from Jerry and Miguel, yes. Like I said, they fell asleep quite early.'

'Ms Bryant Bell,' the female cop said, 'do you believe Mr Carlisle may have woken up later on in the night?'

I thought for a few seconds. There he was: I could picture him: lying face down. His arms were cocked at strange angles.

'No, I don't think so. I remember Honey on the floor, and . . . The position of his body . . . I don't think it was just sleeping. I'm sure he had passed out. I'm certain.'

The officers looked at each other.

'And you are absolutely certain, Ms Bryant Bell,' pressed the female cop, 'that there were no other guests that night besides the eight present when police arrived at the scene? Nobody that visited the party after the caterers had left, nobody that was present when Mr Bryant began to—'

'Nobody else came. Only us.'

And an octopus.

'Not even a delivery man, driver, cleaner?'

'Not after the staff left. It was only us nine.'

And an octopus.

The male cop suppressed a cough.

His colleague went on: 'So you were around the table, and you had been consuming a quantity of alcohol, and then what happened? Describe it in your own words.'

I tried to summon the sequence of events, but only blurred impressions arose.

(A rustle; a smack. The floor chilled my cheek.)

'Ms Bryant Bell?'

'Beyond that point,' I said slowly, 'I'm not sure there *is* much I can recall. I was on the floor, and then . . . Then it was morning, and we were all waking up.'

'So you were asleep when Mr Bryant actually took the heroin?' asked the man.

'Or shortly after.'

'Convenient,' muttered the woman. 'You all seem to have been asleep by then.'

'Was it Mark or Luisa heading the production team?' asked Kei, sitting on the couch with Charlie. 'For *One Hundred Years*?'

'Mark,' said Richard.

'But I thought Luisa was pregnant with Daisy when we were shooting. Like I remember her in that big blue coat on set?'

'No, no, no,' Richard replied. 'That wasn't *One Hundred Years*. Because, remember, Mark hated the narration and we scrapped it at the last minute. No, you're getting confused with *The Shewings* because of the period detail. But Mark was definitely on *One Hundred*.' He turned back to Miguel. 'What were you saying?'

'That toast,' he answered. 'The one you gave earlier. Really reminded me of something from—'

'Shakespeare?' said Richard. 'It's *King John*.'

'No, it reminded me of something from my childhood. And it just hit me now, it's this hymn we used to sing: *All glory, laud and honour to thee, redeemer king*.' He recited the words without melody or rhythm, but I recognised it well. '*To whom the* something, something . . .'

'*Lips of children*,' I said. '*Made sweet hosannas ring*.'

His face lit up.

'You know it! Yeah, that's the one.' He clinked his glass against mine. 'Nice. So you're Catholic?'

'Elspeth is a godless heathen,' said Richard.

'I'm not religious,' I told Miguel, ignoring my ex-husband's comment. 'But when I was a kid, my mother occasionally took me to Mass. I remember that hymn, though. It was my favourite one.'

'Mine too,' said Miguel. 'Regal, right?'

'Alas,' said Richard, 'Ellie ran away from home as a teenager.'

Miguel seemed baffled by this remark.

'He thinks he's being funny,' I said, and took a sip of my drink. It had been disappearing faster than planned and was now mostly ice. 'But he's right, I haven't been to church since I left home.'

Miguel struggled to respond. 'I'm sorry to—'

'Since you fled,' Richard talked over him, 'to a city of angels.'

'Hell on earth,' I retorted. My words felt slippy with the bourbon.

And then, politely, to Miguel: 'But no, in answer to your question, I don't think I would describe myself as Catholic. Anyway I'm sure you're bored of my childhood. Tell me about your latest—'

'It's my birthday, we'll discuss what I want to discuss, Ellie,' Richard snapped. Then smooth, charming: 'Miguel, my ex-wife is such a fascinating psychological case study. You see, Elspeth was a troubled child, like me. We never liked our parents, so we both escaped from our prisons – and then we came across each other, two orphans on the run . . .'

'Mate.' Tommo had wandered over to our group. 'I've met your parents many times. If I recall correctly, they remain rosy-cheeked, if estranged.'

'Abandoned, then.'

'And didn't you two meet after you moved to LA? That must have been nearly a decade after school.'

'It was,' I said. 'When Richard graduated high school, I was only a kid. I was eighteen when I first met him.'

'Irrelevant nit-picking.' Richard scowled at his friend.

'But if we're talking about our childhoods,' Tommo said with a smirk, 'I have tales about this one . . .' He nudged Miguel. 'Now, has Dicky ever told you how sumptuous he looks in floor-length gowns?'

I moved to the liquor cabinet. Poured myself a bourbon so I could leave the conversation without drawing attention.

'I swear, he made the most irresistible Desdemona in our Lower Boy play,' Tommo was saying. 'Curves in all the right—'

'Actually, Tommo, buddy,' said Miguel. 'As much as I want to hear that story – and I do, I do – I need a moment to talk alone with Rich here. Do you mind?'

'To what do I owe this honour?' I heard Richard reply.

'Not here,' said Miguel. 'Outside.'

I was looking for my car keys when she confronted me.

'Was it the house?' she called.

I looked up: it was the small woman I had bumped into when entering the station. She was climbing from a parked car, like she'd been watching for me all afternoon.

'Excuse me?'

'The house,' she said. 'Is that what you wanted? The money wasn't enough?'

I found the keys but she was blocking my path, moving closer, arms folded. She had a round, open face, nipped to a little nose in the middle. I was certain now that she was a complete stranger – I would have recognised a face like that.

And so I tried to keep my voice gentle; she had obviously mistaken me for someone else and was possibly a victim, or a criminal.

'I don't know what you're talking about.' I smiled as kindly as I could. 'I'm sorry, I need to get to my—'

'Your divorce money,' she said. Her nostrils flared. 'Didn't get enough in the divorce and – what – the child-support payments have stopped so you needed some other way to keep yourself in' – she looked me up and down with a sneer – 'Chanel sunglasses and blonde highlights?'

'I'm sorry,' I said. 'I think you've mistaken me for someone else.'

'Elspeth,' she spat. 'I know who you are. I recognise your face. You know he kept all your photographs on the wall, after you left?'

I gripped my car keys, held my purse close, but spoke calmly as I asked: 'And who are you?'

The woman ignored my question. Took another step closer.

'What kind of woman,' she said, jabbing a finger, 'doesn't stay by her husband's side when he's going through hell? What kind of woman steals a baby away from its father? What kind of woman bleeds a man dry, takes everything he worked for?' She struggled to contain her voice. It trembled as she went on: 'I always wondered what kind of woman could do that, and now I know. Now I see.'

I tried to push past. She stepped in front of me again.

'You don't know what you're talking about,' I said. 'Excuse me, I need to—'

'Oh, I know you, *Elspeth*. I know you.' She nodded violently with each syllable. 'I picked up the pieces. I looked after the man *you* left behind. I know everything about you, and I know what you've done.'

'I haven't done anything, I'm sorry. You're confused.'

'So it's a coincidence then?' She mirrored my movements as I tried to walk around her. 'You come back to LA and the next day Richard . . .' Her face crinkled as she said his name. 'Richard is . . .'

A black sedan was pulling into a space across the lot.

'I'm sorry,' I repeated, 'you're clearly upset, but you're confused and—'

'I'm not confused!' she shouted, through her tears. 'I'm not upset. I'm—'

A man got out of the sedan and walked towards us.

'You ladies okay here?' he said.

'Fine, thank you,' I told him, and took my chance to push past the woman.

As I unlocked the car door with shaking hands, she called after me: 'They'll find out. They will. I know you, Elspeth Bryant.'

I slammed the door behind me, muffled her venom.

The solitude, the physicality, was true relief – I took a long route back to Lillie's to try to recompose myself, looping around Griffith Park and then meandering through the hills. I got snarled up a couple of times, and lost myself more than once, but it felt good to run my hands over the wheel, to be in control.

I adjusted the mirror to check my lipstick while stopped at some lights. The billboard to the left was advertising shades similar to the ones I was wearing. The frames were a blueish grey, criss-cross stripes embedded; I liked the way you could see the layering of these marks, caught in the resin, as you held them up against a light. They'd made me feel calm when I bought them – you could lose yourself in that texture.

As I looked at my reflection in the mirror now, they didn't have the same effect. All I could see were the large logos on either side of the frame, which the woman must have caught, and added to my sentence.

The house, is that what you wanted? The money wasn't enough?

The smell of garlic butter hit me as I walked through Lillie's door.

'What's that?' I called from the hallway, slipping off my shoes. 'Smells delicious.'

'Pasta. Tagliatelle.' She was sautéing large slices of mushroom. 'In a sage butter sauce.'

'Where did you get the ingredients?'

'I went out. You were right,' she said. 'It was good to leave the house. I don't know why I was so paranoid. I just put on a hat, and obviously no one recognised me.'

I put my arm around her shoulders and gave her a sideways hug. 'As long as you felt comfortable.'

Lillie said: 'It was weird. You know, seeing, like, the moms with their babies, stocking up on, I don't know, diapers and cereal. It felt – I'd kind of forgotten. How everything else would continue.'

As she cooked, Lillie talked me through each step. While the pasta was bubbling, she ladled its starchy water into the frying pan, turning the butter almost to a cream. Then she took the tagliatelle from the pot before it was fully cooked and finished it in the sauce, stirring rapidly.

'You never cooked like this at home,' I said.

We sat at the table, grated the Parmesan straight onto the plates. The curls were so fine, they writhed as they melted.

'Because we always had takeout; I never needed to learn.'

'Have you had lessons since you moved?'

'More like how-to videos online,' she said.

That was when I saw her real smile for the first time in a week and a half – for the first time since Richard's death. It was a weary smile, but a smile nonetheless, and my heart ached with hope.

And then I realised: it truly was just me and Lillie now.

Throughout Lillie's childhood, I'd had to relinquish the reins for her biannual visits to Richard. It was only for a few weeks, at the most, and I loathed her father, but perhaps I could acknowledge, in some deep and painful part of my heart, that Lillie deserved a relationship with him. They adored each other. And

I could only imagine what Richard would have done if I'd cut off their contact entirely. Sue for full custody; reopen old wounds. Who would Lillie have sided with in such a battle? I could not bear the thought.

It wasn't an easy arrangement to accept. Every time she left, it felt like I was making that heart-wrenching choice all over again. I would hand over my little girl to the airline personnel, with her red knapsack and buckled shoes.

I'd keep the wobble from my voice, when she finally called having reached the other end. She was always bursting with happiness, tales of everything Richard had bought her, everything they would do. Already restless to hang up on me, to carry on with their exciting games. I had to keep telling myself that love is endless. It wasn't that for every ounce she gave her father, one would be taken from me.

It was difficult to believe this when she moved to LA to work on *Dominus*, when it became clear she would stay for good.

I twisted the pasta ribbons around my fork. Would my existence in New York feel different when I finally returned? Would I sense Richard's absence, when he had been missing from my life for so long? I wondered whether I would ever grieve for him – whether I could.

We ate our food in silence for a while, then she asked: 'How was everything with the police?'

'It was okay,' I said. 'Long, tiring. They just want the facts. When I arrived at the party, who I talked to, things like that. I've got another session tomorrow.'

Then I added: 'There was one strange thing, actually. This woman, when I came out of the station. She – can you remember, did your father have a relationship with a woman after he and I . . . ?'

'No.' Lillie was horrified. 'I don't know who you – no.'

'I must have been mistaken.' I was about to drop the subject, but the woman's accusations were still with me. 'It was this small lady. Dark hair, tied back from her face. And it was – she was really small, but had this round—'

'Sounds like Yola.'

'Yola?' I felt I'd heard the name before.

'Dad's housekeeper,' explained Lillie. 'She looks like that. Small? Like, really friendly? That's Yola. Why? Where did you say you met her?'

'It doesn't matter.' I stacked our plates, stood up to put them in the dishwasher.

'No, it does,' she said. 'Why did you think that Dad—'

'I was just confused,' I said. But Lillie didn't look as though she would let the subject slide. I sat back down and explained: 'She . . . she was very upset, and she shouted at – I think that she thinks I did something.'

Lillie raised her eyebrows.

'To your father,' I said, 'which is absurd because – I mean . . .'

Lillie took the plates to the sink and started scrubbing them by hand.

After she'd rinsed and stacked them, she turned back to me. Said quietly: 'Well, that doesn't really sound like Yola. I don't think she'd accuse you of something like that. Maybe it was someone else, or maybe you misunderstood.'

'I don't think I did. She told me she'd looked after your father, after the divorce, so I assumed they'd been in a relationship. But if she was his housekeeper, that makes sense.'

'Yola wouldn't say something like that. She's lovely. She used to look after me when I visited Dad and we would always—'

'Like I said, she was upset and confused. It doesn't matter. And the accusation itself is absurd.'

'Is it?'

We looked at each other, from either side of the kitchen table.

'I can't see Yola saying something like that,' Lillie said. 'But I mean, would it be absurd? If people did think that? The police *are* questioning you.'

I took a few seconds to respond. 'Yes, they are – to find out about the others, to ask me about that night.'

Lillie didn't move.

'Yes, it's absurd,' I repeated, louder.

She picked up our glasses and took them to the sink. Before she turned on the tap, she said: 'Just be careful, okay? It wouldn't hurt to be careful. Think about what other people could be thinking.'

As I walked to my room, as I took a hot shower, I kept turning over that warning. Did the police have any reason to believe I could have killed my ex-husband?

I was seeing Scott tomorrow, for my next interrogation. I would call him early, I thought, towelling my hair. We would meet before, talk everything over.

I went to the kitchen for a glass of water. Paused outside Lillie's door to listen for activity. She was playing a movie; I could hear the soundtrack strings. I held up my hand to knock – then stopped myself. Was there anything to say? Maybe Lillie was right to worry.

My phone was vibrating when I returned to my room and for a second I froze – was it Scott? But no: Kirsten from the board of trustees still trying to get through. I waited until it rang itself out, then changed the settings to silent. I would call everyone back at some point. Just, not now.

I opened my laptop, found more underwater videos.

And you are absolutely certain, Ms Bryant Bell, that there were no other guests that night, besides the eight present when police arrived at the scene?

Actually, no, Officer – there was a ninth guest. The alien among us: Three hearts and, some say, nine brains.

Suckers, two by two, which can cling to the roughest edges.

Pigment cells, chromatophores, to camouflage instantly.

Toxic ink to confuse predators.

Venom to still the limbs of struggling prey.

An intelligence we have barely begun to comprehend.

I let the videos play and play, until I reached an old Painlevé film, black and white close-ups of octopus anatomy. Each time the clip ended, I started it again. Let the knobbled skin and rhythmic breaths lull my mind to nothing.

L'œil fermé, the caption said.

L'œil ouvert, très humain.

I tried to spot Miguel and Richard through the window, but they were nowhere to be found. In the far, shadowed corner of the lawn, maybe, or perhaps somewhere more secluded.

Jerry was standing by himself at the other end of the atrium. I decided to give him some company.

'Elsie,' he said. 'So you're still here.'

'I'll leave soon,' I said. 'Maybe one more drink.'

'I thought Lillie was going to swing by?'

'So did I.'

We sipped from our glasses. I needed a refill.

'She got caught up?' Jerry asked. I didn't think it needed an answer and wouldn't have known what excuse to give. He added: 'Well, hey, if she's not coming, you oughta give her this.' He handed me a little slip of paper. 'Like I said, my pal Bob's email.'

I folded the slip and had no idea where to put it – then spotted my purse, discarded, beneath the dining table.

'One second,' I said and made sure the paper was safely tucked away before I could forget.

I checked my cell again – no excuses from Lillie. Then felt for the bottled water. It was gone. How strange. I'd put it in my purse earlier, when Richard told me off. Had he confiscated it, as some kind of punishment? I made a mental note to find some water soon.

'I wanted to tell Lillie,' Jerry said when I returned, 'I thought she was great in *Dominus*. Knocked it out of the park.'

I nodded, smiled. There was nothing I could say on the matter: I still hadn't seen Lillie's debut. I was not invited to the premiere – it was a night for her and Richard – and then it seemed wrong, pathetic, to watch it alone in a New York movie theatre. And besides, she had told me she spoke only six lines, appeared in only one of the scenes. I would have to sit through the entire drawn-out, three-hour romance between a graduate chemist and a Parisian art student, written by my ex-husband, all for six lines. In a movie theatre? Where someone might see me? I was waiting for the DVD release. I thought maybe she and I could watch it together.

And I was adept at changing the topic, whenever the question arose. 'How about you? How's work?'

Jerry rattled the ice around his glass.

'It's not the good old days, you know.' He snickered to himself. 'Remember those? All fast cars and booze and girls with massive tits.'

'I think there may be some incongruity in our two experiences.'

'Don't give me that, Elsie,' he said. 'I still remember the first time I saw you, gliding down Alto's staircase in that glittering gold dress. A vision, a fucking sensation. I was kicking myself that I hadn't met you first. The most beautiful woman I'd ever seen. But as fast as he could, there was Rich, offering you his manhattan. That bastard. You know, I was chasing him because he was fresh out of rehab. And his therapist was clear: no drinks, no nothing.'

'I know,' I said.

'But I didn't need to chase him, did I? Because there he was, offering the glass to you. Bastard lied next time I saw him. Said he never meant to drink it. *I was saving it for the most beautiful woman in the world*, he said. That's why he offered it to you, Elsie.' His words slurred together. 'Beautiful woman in the world.'

'And the rest is history,' I said. Then: 'I don't know if I'd have ever gone for you though. That baggy bird-egg suit you used to wear, pulled up to your belly button. And the glasses.'

'Those goddamn aviators.' Jerry shook his head. Chuckled. 'God, Elsie, we thought we'd never make it past fifty. Immortal. Invincible.'

'Please,' I replied. 'That was you and Richard. I had a young daughter to think about.'

'Later, maybe – but that girl in the gold dress . . .'

That gold dress, the swimming pools, the mirrors – someone else's credit card sculpting lines on the glass staircase.

'Bigger hair,' I mused.

'Smaller waistlines.'

I rapped his forearm.

There was an eruption of laughter from the other side of the room.

'Nicotine Fantastic, how's that?' said Kei.

'Honestly? I love it,' exclaimed Honey. 'I would be . . . Professor B. No wait, Liquid Fire.'

'Why?' Kei said. 'You got a UTI?'

He laughed.

'Do me,' said Charlie.

'Wonderboy,' Kei said. 'Oh, I know what our group name would be—'

'Our *squadron*.'

'We would be the Renegades.'

There was a chorus of agreement.

'And our number one enemy would,' she continued, 'most definitely have to be Richard because of—'

'The accent.'

'Yes, the accent, oh my god.'

'And his name,' said Kei, triumphant, 'is Maverick.'

'Like Mave*Rick*?' asked Charlie. 'As in Richard?'

'Congratulations, Charlie,' Honey patted him on the back, 'you finally understood a joke.'

'Fuck off.'

As the others laughed, Honey looked up, caught me watching. I turned back to the window, tried not to eavesdrop again, but it was difficult with Jerry's silence.

I said quietly: 'Shall we join the others? Or we could go outside.'

Jerry was lost in the view. 'Huh?'

'Never mind,' I told him.

There was another burst of laughter.

'. . . and then Richard was like, *It's not a breed of fish, it's the name of my accountant.*' Honey was echoing Richard's vowels. 'But you should have seen this guy's face, it was hilarious. Literally hilarious.'

The group was quiet for a moment.

Charlie spoke next. 'So, uh, you guys are back together now? Everything's . . .'

'It's cool,' said Honey. 'Yeah, we're cool. I don't—'

Charlie made a noise, as though he was about to speak.

Honey went on: 'I kind of don't want to talk about it, if you don't mind. You know.'

'Sure, man,' said Charlie. 'Yeah, sure. That's cool with me.'

I watched their reflections in the glass. The faces were blurred, but I could imagine Kei staring angrily at Charlie.

Someone was tapping a beer bottle in the group's silence.

'So . . .' said Charlie after a while. 'Pretty nuts about that Thanksgiving thing. You really didn't have it as a kid?'

'And no birthdays,' said Honey. 'No presents, no Halloween.'

'That's crazy, man. Did you – what does your family think about Richard?'

'Charlie,' warned Kei.

'What?'

'Don't push it. He said he didn't want to talk about—'

'No, it's fine,' said Honey. 'It's . . . yeah, I don't really speak to them now.'

'Wow, man. I cannot imagine that. My brother's like my best—'

'Charlie,' said Kei. 'Seriously, dude.'

'What? He is.'

'Yeah, I miss my little brother,' said Honey. 'We were pretty close growing up. But there's this rule in the Church and it's like when you leave, you leave. So he hasn't spoken to me since I was seventeen, and he was . . . I guess, fifteen?'

Charlie said: 'That's fucked up.'

'I'm sorry,' said Kei.

Honey took a long breath. 'You know, I'm not angry with him. It hurt, but I'm not angry.'

The other two waited for him to continue.

'I've tried to reach out to him a couple times over the years. He's still in Minnesota. But he never – one time I even waited outside his house. And he brushed past like he'd never met me.'

Honey dropped his head.

'He thinks it's the right thing to do.' He clasped his hands over his neck. 'They tell you that if you love someone and they leave the Church, you have to shun them. So they'll repent and return, you know? That's what he really believes,' Honey said. He lifted his head. 'That's why I'm not angry. When he ignores me, I know it's coming from love and not hate. Although it didn't feel like that when I was younger, it's . . . it took a lot of time.'

'I can't imagine what that must be like,' said Kei.

'I always think,' Honey said, 'one day, maybe I'll get to him. If I can't speak to him on the street, then . . . not with the modelling but it's like, I don't wanna do that forever. I want to make art, you know? Something my little brother might see and he'll know that I love him and I forgive him. It's all about forgiveness. And love.' He laughed, rubbed his chin. 'I'm sorry, I've been—'

'No,' said Kei. 'Dude. I think that's beautiful.'

'When you were growing up,' Charlie asked, 'did you, like, watch normal TV?'

The sky was a black-orange ember; the glow of the city. Helicopters circled the neighbourhood below.

'Are you feeling okay?' I asked Jerry. 'You don't seem yourself.'

'I'd give anything to go back,' he said. I didn't know whether Jerry was answering my question or talking to himself. 'All the way back to the start.'

He swirled the drink, threw it down in one gulp.

'How did it come to this, Elsie?' Jerry was smiling, but his voice grew hoarse. 'When did we get here?'

'Well,' I offered, ever steady, 'I'd say it's always been getting to this – and the when is the how.'

He propped one arm on the glass, brought his face to the window. Stared through at the peppering lights.

And then I noticed the seam in the glass. It had been foolish to think a pane this large would exist, but I had been duped, regardless. I ran my finger down the groove.

'This place is pretty amazing, huh?' Jerry said. 'Your first time at Sedgwick?'

I nodded.

'Me too. Rich and I – we don't hang out as much any more.'

He attempted another sip from his glass, not noticing it was empty. A drop rolled onto his tongue. 'I was pretty shocked he invited me to this.'

The group on the couches began to sing, something that could have been the theme tune to a kids' TV show.

'We're not his young, cool friends, are we?' I said, smiling. And then: 'I don't know though, I think you're wrong.'

The singing crashed to laughter; it was pounding at my head.

'It would be hell to go back to the start,' I said. 'I wouldn't want to be that naive again.'

Jerry did not reply. Kept looking through the window. His empty glass in his hand, hanging by his side.

'How long have you known Jerry Debrowski?'

'He was there when I met Richard for the first time,' I said. 'But I don't think – I can't remember if I spoke to him that night. It would have been soon after that, though. So almost twenty-five years, I'd say.'

'He's a good friend?'

'He was when I lived here, yes. But we lost touch after the divorce. He was closer to Richard.'

The policewoman paused, rifled through her papers.

I still had not gleaned the names of my interrogators. They'd handed me their business cards at the end of my first interrogation, but I hadn't found them in my purse or pockets – who knew where the cards had ended up between the taxi, the mall, Lillie's house. If I asked for the detectives' names after all this time it might seem rude, might turn them against me. The metal table between us was just about too wide to read their shining badges.

I made a mental note to ask Scott later. He would have kept the cards they'd given him somewhere safe – and he wasn't the type to forget a name.

We had met for coffee an hour before our appointment at the station. Green tea for me – I was already too jittery for caffeine – and a caramel mocha with whipped cream for Scott.

'I have a sweet tooth,' he said, grinning, then: 'You wanted to discuss something?'

I didn't tell him about the confrontation with Yola — she had been distraught, caught up in the moment, and there was no need to involve my lawyer. Instead, I explained that the last interrogation had thrown me: the follow-up questions, the female cop's remark that it was 'convenient' I was falling asleep when Richard took the drugs.

'Scott,' I drew close, even though our corner was deserted, 'do you think I should be worried? About being a suspect?'

He thought for a while. Ate a spoonful of cream.

Before he could speak, I held out my arms, laughed, and added: 'I mean, there's no way I'd be strong enough to do that to someone.'

'Ms Bryant Bell,' Scott said, unsmiling, 'let's be real here. Your ex-husband was probably already unconscious. You wouldn't have needed to be a linebacker to take him out.'

So Lillie had been right to worry. And I'd been naive.

'Look, I'm not trying to worry you,' he went on. 'But let's not get too comfortable. You're a person of interest in this investigation. You were present at the scene. You were the ex. These are just the facts, Elspeth, and you know me, I'm not going to sugarcoat it. The police will be investigating you seriously.'

Had I missed the suspicions behind certain questions?

'However,' Scott scooped more cream, 'let's also not forget the facts in your favour. There were seven other guests that night, who were also close with Richard. You don't have close — or let's say recent — ties to any of the other guests. So I doubt the police are interested in investigating you for conspiracy or as an accomplice. You didn't take anything that night, unlike other guests. If I were a cop, I'd probably see you as one of the more reliable witnesses. And you are a woman, mother of the—'

'Exactly. Lillie. So how could I have done it?'

'Well.' Scott sucked his spoon clean and jabbed it in my direction. 'You still *could* have done it. If we're discussing hypotheticals,

Elspeth. I simply meant that you are a less *likely* suspect if we consider all the facts. But here's the thing: I only know what I know. You'll remember me asking that question when you first called. And you assured me you were innocent.'

He had – but I'd let it slip past. I had been gabbling, apologetic about not calling sooner.

'I should add,' he said, more gently now, 'that I don't think you're being aggressively investigated, not currently. As I mentioned to you in that first conversation . . .' He slowed his speech, like he knew I hadn't listened the first time. 'Should the situation change, my advice would be to bring in a local attorney. A criminal attorney who has experience with jury trials.'

Those last two words slammed through me. Suspicions were one thing – charges entirely another. For Lillie to see that? Unthinkable.

I gripped my mug, let it scorch my palms. 'Is there anything I can do to prevent that kind of . . . development?'

'As I keep saying, record your memories of that night as they come to you,' said Scott. 'Be clear and honest with the police. Directly answer their questions. Do not, *do not*, communicate with the other guests. These are simple things, Elspeth. Straightforward. I don't want to scare you, but let's not lose sight of the situation we're in.'

I ran over those instructions as we walked into the station, returned to the empty interrogation room, that hard plastic chair, the cold table. Repeated them like a mantra as the policewoman rifled through her papers. *Clear, honest, direct.*

'It's funny,' she murmured. 'You say you weren't close to Mr Debrowski. But I've got testimony from one of the waitresses here. She said he immediately approached you when you arrived at the function. Gave you a kiss.'

'Yes. I mean, I guess he did,' I said. 'Yes.'

The detective looked up from her notes. 'You didn't mention that before.'

'You didn't ask,' I said. And then, worried that this might have sounded like a criticism, I explained: 'Like I said, I lost touch with Jerry after the divorce. But when I saw him at the party, I was pleased we'd have a chance to catch up.'

'That's nice,' she said, affecting a smile.

Scott had said the police didn't see me as a conspirator or accomplice, but I was concerned about where their questions were veering. This session was making me jumpy – too many layers behind each word.

The male detective scrutinised me as he asked: 'Was Mr Debrowski acting aggressive at all that night?'

'Not aggressive, no,' I said.

His colleague looked at her notes, like they claimed something else.

'Not that I saw,' I added. 'But he was maybe melancholy. Very drunk. Why? Do you think that he . . . ?'

'We're just trying to establish some facts, Ms Bryant Bell. Do you know why Mr Debrowski was invited to the party?'

'He and Richard have – had been friends for years. And he's Richard's manager, of course.'

The cops looked at each other.

The woman took over: 'Mr Bryant had recently fired Mr Debrowski.'

'Richard fired Jerry? No. Why would—'

'Unfortunately Ms Bryant Bell,' the officer said, 'we cannot give you any further details.'

'But when? Why?'

The conversations I'd had with Jerry replayed in my mind. He must have thought I knew; had I offended him in any way?

'What I believe my client means to say,' Scott interjected smoothly, 'is that she might be able to provide you with more helpful information if she fully understands the situation.'

I fixed on the male officer. 'So much happened that night.' I smiled. 'You know how parties can be – maybe if you fill me in a little, it might jog my memory?'

He gestured to his colleague, and they left the room for a short consultation. When they returned, the female detective gave me the bare bones: there had been stresses and disagreements during the filming of *Dominus*; Richard had fired Jerry.

I could not believe the real story was this straightforward. Jerry and Richard had been working together almost from the beginnings of their careers – and Jerry had stood by my ex-husband through all of his scandals, steadfast, dog-loyal. Only a monumental dispute could have broken them apart. But then, they had seemed perfectly amicable on the night of the party. None of it made sense to me.

This information had scattered my thoughts. I was struggling to reinterpret Jerry's behaviour.

'I have to say,' I said, selecting my words slowly, 'Jerry didn't seem resentful at all. At one point he grew sad; he was drinking a lot, I remember that. But by the end, I think he had thrown himself into the spirit of the party – we all had.'

'Thank you, Ms Bryant Bell,' the male cop said. 'Of course, we know you had been drinking and we don't want to put too much emphasis on impressions, but it's useful – can't really tell what it'll throw up.'

'But these professional concerns aren't restricted to Mr Debrowski,' the female officer cut in. 'Are you aware of the issues surrounding Mr Bryant's latest film?'

'Could you be a little more specific – which guest are we talking about here?'

'All involved: Miguel Montana, Keiko Nakamura, Sabine Selmi, and Charles Pace.'

I drove back to Lillie's as fast as possible. Opened my laptop, ready to flesh out the information the cops had given me with gossip-blog rumours.

I would begin with Jerry. I scrolled, I clicked. I opened every link I could find, right back in time, and there it was: the beginning of the story, two months before the release of *Dominus*.

A slideshow of photos through a long-range lens: fuzzy-grained figures in a stop-motion sequence; two men outside a restaurant. One was facing away from the other, head hung low. The other reached a hand to his companion's shoulder. In the next image the two were facing. And then a blow to the face. One figure turned back towards the photographer, blood dripping from his nose.

It was a shocking red, and I could see – even through grainy pixels – how it dripped thickly down his face. My hand covered my mouth.

Richard was a master at goading others to anger, but I could not imagine what he had said to provoke Jerry – gentle, loyal Jerry – to hit him in the face with such force.

I gathered myself and resumed scrolling. There was no comment from the manager of the establishment, the Tam O'Shanter, but another diner reported shouting and clattering heard throughout the lunch service. I explored the other articles, moved forward in time, rooting out all of the theories. Among the plausible: a personal spat, payment disputes, rumours of difficulties circling *Dominus*. Both men refused interviews.

I opened another article, this one from a month later. Jerry had grown paler in the paparazzi pictures, eye sockets sinking. A 'source close to the manager' claimed to have visited him at a rehab clinic in Culver City. This was fictitious, I was sure: Jerry was not an addict. Jerry, the steadfast friend who had driven Richard to rehabilitation three times.

I opened another page. Jerry's family had given a statement, only two weeks before Richard's party: stage 3 prostate cancer. Jerry had 'retired' to focus his energies on recovering.

Privacy and prayer appreciated at this difficult time.

The front door slammed. I jumped up from my computer; I hadn't even realised Lillie was out.

'Yeah, exactly,' I heard her say, 'we'll put it on the list for tomorrow.'

She was on the phone, waved when she saw me.

'Sure,' she said, continuing her conversation. 'That's what I was thinking too.'

She smiled an apology, went to her room. That was fine, that was good – her friends were reaching out now. And time spent alone could be used for research.

I reopened my computer to those pixelated photos.

The fight, the firing, the cancer: I couldn't slot the pieces of Richard and Jerry's relationship together. Had Richard fired Jerry because of his illness? I knew my ex-husband could be cold-hearted, but he had always kept Jerry close. The friend who knew all his secrets.

I was certain the police knew much more than the bloggers, but I couldn't figure out why they had asked me about Jerry. If he was the first guest they'd enquired about, did this mean he was their primary suspect? Or did they question me about him because of that waitress's comment? Did they really think conversations amounted to conspiracy?

Lillie didn't come back to see me and I was getting tired, so I went to bed early. The pictures were there as I closed my eyes: the two men through a long-range lens. Lillie was right: I needed to be careful, I needed to examine what others, what the police, thought of me. And I needed to re-examine what I thought of them. If a basic internet search had revealed tension between Richard and Jerry, what could I discover about the other guests?

There was a knot in my chest, squeezing tighter. A part of me wanted to contact Jerry. Ask him outright what had happened that day. Ask him about his prognosis. Poor Jerry. Gentle, loyal Jerry – who could draw blood with one blow.

Someone called my name.

'Elspeth.' Tommo sidled up beside me, whispered in my ear: 'There's an awful stain on your hemline.'

I looked down.

'At the back,' he added.

I caught sight of it in the window's reflection – a grey smear across my white skirt.

'Shit, I was sitting on the wall outside. Shit.'

'It's fine, darling, don't fret. I'm sure Richard has some stain remover. I'll find him – you go through to the kitchen.'

By the time Tommo joined me, I'd already discovered Tide pens in the utility closet and was twisting to catch the stain.

'Need a helping hand?' he asked, snatching the stick and crouching low. 'What do I do? Just colour it on?'

'It's probably easier if I take off the skirt.'

'Elspeth, I love you – but not like that.'

There was silence as he concentrated on his task.

'Now what?' Tommo stood to face me. Liquor laced his breath, fruity.

'We wait five minutes, then I'll wash it off in the bathroom.'

'There's a hair-dryer in the one upstairs.'

He put both hands on the kitchen counter and swung himself up. Tapped his hands on his thighs. 'Have to say, I'm glad the staff have left. Keeps me on edge, being watched like that all night. Not really sure why Dicky hired them.'

'It's all part of the theatrics,' I said. 'He needed a supporting cast.'

'Well, I say it's unnatural,' said Tommo. 'Like to pour my own drinks. Can't decide if having waiters is an aristocratic or an LA thing.'

'Oh, both.' I laughed. 'Most definitely both.'

'So,' he said. 'Dish: what do you think of the others?'

'I don't feel like I've gotten to talk to them,' I said. 'Besides catching up with you and Jerry, I spoke to Sabine outside, briefly . . .'

I remembered that I had walked back into the house before her. She must have seen the stain and chosen to say nothing.

'. . . and Miguel.'

'He's a bit of a character, isn't he?'

'I would love to be able to say I hadn't already met dozens of men like him.'

'Oh, I get it, I do. But he seems particularly tedious,' said Tommo, over-enunciating with his gin-and-tonic tongue. 'It doesn't take a psychoanalyst. He was telling me about his brothers – he's the youngest of three, and they all took over the family business when Daddy Warbucks retired. But now he's being edged out, as he was the one who brought Dicky on board.'

'What did Richard do?'

'I don't know all of it. It's not just the box-office numbers; apparently he's been a naughty boy from the start – something to do with messing the studio around. Slipping schedules and bad press and refusing to play along with public engagements, something like that. Anyway, Miguel's getting the rap because Big Brother didn't want to make this movie in the first place, but Miguel can't bring himself to cut his losses with Richard. Thinks he's a bloody *auteur*. And so he can't choose either way – lose *l'artiste*, or lose his power and his money and lose the fucking artist anyway. I think it's an easy decision, but then,' he came close to and stage-whispered, '*what the fuck do I know?* However . . .' He raised his voice and flung his arms out. 'However! It does explain why Dicky invited such a bloody wet blanket to the party. Buttering him up, nice and tasty.'

Tommo jumped down from the counter and sauntered forwards, a sly grin on his face: the very image of Richard.

'*You're a good friend, Miguel, you know you're more than a patron. Without you my art is nothing. Without you I wouldn't be half the man I am today . . .*' He was on his knees, grasping at my ankles, pleading. '*Maestro, master, Lord and Saviour. Mummy, Daddy, buddy, baby.*'

I applauded this perfect impression. Tommo fell backwards – not entirely on purpose – and sat on the floor.

'And so Miguel is torn, he's in *anguish*, Elspeth. It's put him on edge tonight. Well. That's what he's told me four times already – four fucking times and we've only had three conversations – along with giving me his opinion on every single fucking facet of the entertainment industry. I know, I know, he's not a bad person but *god*, do I wish Dicky hadn't sat me next to him at dinner. He won't fucking leave me alone, thinks we're bloody best pals.'

He had risen to a crescendo of rage and was now catching his breath. I empathised with Tommo's predicament – but there was something else in the story that had pricked my ears.

'So Richard's a loss-maker?'

Tommo stared.

'Darling. You can't expect *Dominus* to do well in these circumstances. Too much scandal – and none of it's good. The saying isn't true, you know. All publicity . . .'

Lillie had not mentioned any of this to me: the slipping schedules, the box-office failure. Although that was not unusual. She had only ever divulged her successes – the kind of kid to smuggle away bad report cards, smile through tears after grazing a knee.

But the fact that I had not found out regardless forced me to acknowledge the extent of my mental hermitage, my efficacy in blocking all social media, magazine, TV gossip.

'I hadn't heard.'

'Where have you been hiding away?'

I smiled, said nothing.

'Anyway,' Tommo went on, 'speaking of drama – how are you finding being here at the same time as him?'

'Richard?'

'Honey.'

I had no idea how to answer. Let myself flounder until Tommo specified his question.

'I have no problem with it. He's Richard's partner, so—'

'But do you like him?'

'I don't know him.'

'He's really quite lovely,' said Tommo. 'Charming. One of those thoughtful, creative types. Maybe you should talk to him. I'm sure that once—'

'How could I?'

Tommo closed his mouth.

'Look,' I said. 'These chemicals have been on me for five minutes at least. I should wash them off.'

'Down that corridor, up the stairs, make a U-turn and you'll find the guest bathroom. With a hair-dryer.'

As I walked away he called after me: 'You can't escape that easily, Elspeth. We'll talk later.'

I resolved not to.

★

I made myself a coffee early the next morning, opened my laptop on the kitchen table. Until yesterday I hadn't wanted to think of the other guests as suspects. Two of them were old friends and even if it had been one of the other five, it was nonetheless a terrifying thought: that someone so violent had been present all night; that I had been lying only a foot or so away when they'd taken their chance to kill. But if I was a suspect too, I'd have to live with that idea. I'd have to turn it over in my mind, view the memories from every angle.

Questions had been eating away at me all night. If Jerry, whom I had known for years, was not quite who I thought he was, then what did I know of the other guests? I had been foolish to focus on Persephone. Those mesmerising videos of octopuses had quelled any other suspicions that might have arisen.

By morning, I had reached three conclusions. First, that I should stop fixating on Persephone. I could see my octopus obsession for what it was: a foolish distraction, an easy answer – and one that left Lillie and me vulnerable. Second, that I would stop being passive: I would pay attention during my interrogations, try to follow in the detectives' tracks; I would keep myself guarded and sharp and inquisitive. The third conclusion I had reached was that I knew very little at all.

And so there I sat that morning, with my laptop. I had a few hours before my next appointment with the police. The pictures of Richard and Jerry's fight were still on screen; I clicked away from them. I would explore the other guests, starting with the subject the police had raised yesterday: the filming of *Dominus*. The detectives hadn't told me much, didn't dwell on the 'issues' themselves – they were only interested in my impressions from that night. I'd told them of Tommo's gossip in the kitchen, and the female cop nodded like this wasn't new information. She hadn't made any notes at all.

'But how were they behaving the night of the party?' she had asked. 'Let's start with Charlie Pace.'

There were countless hits online for Sabine and Charlie. As far as I could tell, they hadn't been personally involved in the scandals surrounding *Dominus*, hadn't addressed rumours about Richard's troubles with the studio, kept smiling in interviews and on the red carpet. But their existence was newsworthy enough. Sunbathing on the beach, meeting friends for lunch at the Chateau Marmont: I recognised it all from my own time as a star.

It was the journalism, instead, that had transformed entirely in the ten or so years I had been avoiding it. Once deep into gossip-blog territory, it was difficult to resurface. Websites screamed out, distracting here and there with more links, more videos, more pictures – many more pictures than words now. And how the pictures had altered: three composed selfies to every sly paparazzi shot. I read through the hashtags, somewhat bewildered, and the comments beneath, and the product placements. I could recall the days in which designers would send me soft-leather goods with handwritten notes, but it seemed every aspect of these young people's lives was sponsored now, from their drinks to their teeth, their holidays to their workouts. And people were brands, and corporations were their 'families' and their bodies were lissome, roaming commercials. And they were so, so *thankful* – to the companies, the designers, the hair and makeup artists. Everybody needed their mention.

Sabine kept this under control, with photographs mainly chronicling her red-carpet appearances. She had not given too much of herself away; she knew that true glamour needs some level of mystique.

Snooping through the stories and profiles of her co-star was an altogether different experience. Charlie had his publicists working overtime, or vice versa. I noted the 'M' punctuating his follower count. These millions did not all seem to be fans; there were adoring comments but also hundreds of people trying to lure followers to their own profiles, like some kind of frenzied digital Ponzi scheme. How many followers were even real? Looking at this online version of Charlie, it would appear the failure of *Dominus* had done little to halt his career. He was advertising a product or experience in every photo. But was that

what he wanted to be doing? No new roles had been announced,
I noticed, since the release of his debut.

Nevertheless – or, perhaps, consequently – Charlie Pace partied
harder, laughed louder, in every uploaded image. I had recognised
this in him, the night of Richard's fiftieth. You could see it in his
eyes, beyond the shine and the large black pupils: you could see
the late rehearsals and cancelled runs, the humiliating auditions
and graveyard service shifts. He had tried to kill off that part of
himself, had tried to deaden everything less than perfect behind
a cold, hard stare. But he had not succeeded. The desperation
was still there in his feigned nonchalance, which was swiftly
betrayed by his greed for attention; there in his too-loud voice,
his too-wide smile; there as he spoke to Richard. How palpable,
his hunger.

I shuddered at the memory of him dropping the octopus into
his open mouth . . .

(Now lift your head.)

. . . and recalled his pained laughter in the barista conversation.

(Lift your head, look over here.)

I could see it that night and now with these internet searches
too: he was willing to do anything.

(I said, *lift your head.*)

He was hungry.

(Lift your head. Your head.)

He was starving.

(No, your chin, upwards. Like this. Can you feel?)

I could not begrudge him this determination. I had never hired
a publicist, but we had all sacrificed something. I rubbed my
temples, tried to straighten my posture.

What Charlie lacked in job opportunities, his publicists had
tried to make up for with staged paparazzi shoots. Blogs linked
him to several women: pop stars, actresses, and public personalities of unidentifiable occupation. They emerged from restaurants
and bars together, in the camera glare – holding hands, beneath
baseball caps.

I clicked through a slideshow detailing his red-carpet looks.

And I thought: how fortunate for him – and for Sabine, Kei and Miguel – that the movie was still showing in theatres at the time of Richard's passing. How fortunate that he had appeared in the last-ever creation of a much-loved director. How fortunate that he could be photographed leaving the police station. The headlines were writing themselves.

I closed the tabs of these articles and found Charlie's Twitter account. It was incredibly dull – more sponsorship, more self-promotion – and I almost immediately left the page. But then the 'Likes' section piqued my curiosity and I found myself scrolling down. It didn't seem as though he knew that these likes were collected, could be browsed: this section was, more so than his own tweets, a window into his mind.

And that mind was profoundly egotistical. Most of the likes were for gushing middle-aged women . . .

If this was at my gym, wrote one beneath a shot of him working out, *it would almost be enough to make me actually go!*

. . . and for moviegoers, praising his work in *Dominus*.

Among the latter, a pattern emerged. Charlie had liked dozens of tweets from one specific account. Its picture was, I guessed, a football team logo; the handle was @patriotsforbowl.

Doesn't know what she's talking about, read one of their tweets, with a link to a review. The piece was a take-down of *Dominus* that pinned the film's problems on the miscasting of the male lead. Too handsome, too blunt, was the critic's verdict, to nail the emotional complexity Luke Winters' story required.

Exactly, said another, in reply to a long thread claiming the issues with *Dominus* resided with the director. *How can a movie succeed with all these problems? Doomed from start.*

I agree it was great. Cried in the theatre, another read: a response to a young man who told everyone to *Go see dominus NOW!!!*

My suspicions about the account were confirmed when I clicked through to read the rest of their tweets. It wasn't that every last one was focused on *Dominus*, but the person hiding behind the account had made only a weak attempt to cover their tracks. Each *Dominus* tweet would be preceded by something else

– a proclamation on sports results, or seasonal greetings – but nothing of any substance, no interactions with anyone else on topics other than the film. The account was a shill. And, yes, it could have been a family member or friend, but there was something in the sharp turns of the tweeter's opinions that made me think it was Charlie typing. It reminded me of his behaviour that night: bored until he was centre of attention; best friends with Richard, then sulking when ignored.

Dominus was supposed to be Charlie's break. The lead in a serious, artistic film, but one that was tipped to pull in big money; co-starring with Sabine, already at the top of her game – Pace was poised for a dream debut. I could imagine the sleepless nights he'd enjoyed in the days after he'd won the role. This was it. This would be it.

And then, in the end, it wasn't.

I could see from the tweets that Charlie didn't know who to blame – there was no rational campaign behind them. One day they would vilify Richard, the next they would defend him, defend *Dominus* as an overlooked masterpiece. Charlie was like a small kid: kicking his toys, furious at his father after being scolded, but then arguing with other boys in the schoolyard that his daddy was the strongest, the smartest, the richest-most-handsome. I could almost feel the psychological contortion as he tried to reconcile those tearing emotions: how could Daddy be both hero and villain?

I wondered what that conflict could do to a young person. How it might feel to have your grandest hopes and aspirations puffed up by someone, to feel like you're there, almost there, only to have that dream – not fail, not collapse, but deflate, maybe; dwindle. A failure caused, in part, by the person who'd given the opportunity in the first place. And then to see that someone celebrating their life in their enormous house, seemingly unfazed by the failure, surrounded by their riches, their wealthy friends, their privilege; how would that make you feel? Bitter, confused. Enough to make Charlie drink more as the night wore on, enough to make him consume drugs, behave erratically. And all the while,

Richard continued to jab at him, humiliate him, in front of colleagues, friends and strangers. I could imagine that pushing Charlie to violence: he wasn't capable of regulating his emotions; he couldn't take criticism. He'd been awake with Richard before I fell asleep, hadn't he? What if Richard had taken it too far?

I returned to Charlie's latest Instagram post. There he was, on a red carpet, arm wrapped over Richard's shoulder, head thrown back in laughter. Beneath this image, Charlie told his followers to count their blessings, live every day as though it were the last. He would be taking some time to focus on himself. And he was sending love, and prayers, and thoughts, to all of Richard's friends and family in this most difficult time. Richard was a great man, he wrote, a genius of a man, and he could only be grateful for the short time they'd shared.

The bathroom was easy enough to find. I unzipped myself and slipped out of the skirt, held it under the faucet. It had been reckless to apply the stain remover without checking the label, but the fabric seemed fine. I rummaged for the hair dryer. It wasn't in the cabinet, which was empty – secrets buried elsewhere – but in a wicker box, lying on folded towels. Clinical. I put one arm through the loop of the skirt and held the dryer's nozzle to the wet patch.

Standing in my hem-less, flesh-coloured underwear, I felt the drink settle on me, heavy. I should have left the party already; it was the only way to avoid talking about Honey – or, worse, to him. I remembered his expression, as he caught me watching – it was unreadable, not surprised, not provocative. I wondered whether he'd known I was listening in as he continued to speak. *It's all about forgiveness. And love.*

What did he think of me? I must have seemed unimpressive in person. Old, irrelevant. Did he hate me?

I would have.

I accidentally caught my reflection's eye. She was waning. I imagined Honey standing next to her – how his smooth skin would glow against her dull wrinkles; his crisp shirt against her flouncing blouse. Why I had chosen to wear this, I could not remember. It was not fashionable nor seductive – not even elegant, compared with Sabine's low chignon, her blossoming red lips, the white silk slip gliding over her décolletage. We were all in white: Sabine, Honey and me. How embarrassing. I had chosen the outfit knowing it was Richard's favourite colour on me. Pathetic bride. I stared blankly at my reflection – hating her, hating everything she had done.

Detecting the faint whiff of singed fabric, I realised the patch had dried. No stain. I turned off the hair-dryer and the abrupt silence brought me back. I pulled the skirt over my hips, checked my lipstick one last time. I would make my excuses to Tommo and Jerry and I would call a cab.

As I pushed open the bathroom door, voices echoed up the stairs. I strained to pick out the words.

'. . . that Honey is here, that they're still together. And his ex-*wife* as well?'

It was Kei. I felt uneasiness creep up my spine, as I had during my conversation with Sabine. Of course they all knew, of course they were all judging.

'I know. She's so dull,' a deep voice, Charlie, replied.

'I don't think she's boring,' said Kei. 'I just can't get a read on her, she's so quiet. Like she's been watching us, judging, you know? But that's not what I was talking about, I meant, like, don't you find it weird? This party, the guests. And did you know Honey and Richard were back together? I did *not* expect to walk in and find him here. He's nice, but I've always found it hard to get to know him properly, because of Richard. You know how it is. And now it's even more awkward. Like, are we supposed to pretend that nothing happened?'

'No, he's . . . You heard what Richard said. It's his fiftieth, he wanted to celebrate with us and—'

'I'm not so sure. Like, why is his ex-wife here?' She gave an empty laugh. 'Why would he invite her? Why would she come to this?'

Charlie did not answer.

Kei went on: 'Why are any of us here? Why do any of us keep coming back?'

'I know Richard can be difficult, but—'

'Did you hear what he was like during the museum scene? God, you think he's a perfectionist—'

'Come on, he's a good guy—'

'It's his accent,' said Kei. 'People think he's fucking charming and intelligent because he tells you that you're *rubbish* and not *garbage*.'

There was a pause. My knees were aching. I'd been standing motionless, desperate not to make the smallest scratch of noise.

Kei continued: 'You don't have to defend him. I saw the way he treated you and Sabine.'

'He was fine, he—'

'Dude, you can think that now, but once you've worked on other sets you'll realise things don't have to be this way. You don't have to treat people like shit to make art.'

Charlie's voice grew hostile, accusatory. 'And I saw how you guys were. So why do *you* still work with him?'

Kei sighed.

'I've asked myself that question so many times.'

They fell silent again. I held my breath and closed my eyes, not moving an inch. My fingers were sliding down the bathroom door, sticky with sweat. I wanted to let it swing shut, muffle the whispers downstairs. But if I could hear them, they could hear me.

'Same reason as you, I guess.' Her voice was quiet, weary. 'Before he met me, I was just directing shitty music videos. You know, it's not like other people are lining up to hire me for big projects at the moment. How many people, hell, *women* who look like me do you see doing what I . . . Fuck, I don't know why I'm telling *you* this.' Her voice changed, became stronger, decisive: 'Richard and I, we may not work well together, but I know it's good – the result. It's really fucking good. And he knows I'm good too. I think that's worth something.' Pause. 'Although it doesn't always feel like it is.'

'Do you think he's a genius?' asked Charlie.

Kei snorted.

'I know he's an asshole, that's for sure.'

I did not hear them leave, but when Charlie laughed again it was distant. I peered down the empty staircase, then decided to explore Sedgwick before returning, noticing, as I went to switch off the bathroom light, that my moist handprint still lingered on the door.

The moon peered through the skylight above, but the stars had been erased by the light of the city. It followed me, skylight to window, as I wandered across the darkened rooms.

It was only the next day, switching on the television, that I truly understood the architectural achievement of Sedgwick – when I caught the paparazzi footage, the helicopter panning from above. Only then could I see the structure as a whole, how it clung to the hillside among the trees; a glittering cubic growth. Only then could I appreciate that the glass surfaces, too, were a disguise. With the sun shining fierce, the camera caught nothing but angled façades, throwing back a broken sky.

Charlie's social media accounts had kept me distracted all morning. At some point I'd stopped learning anything new about him – realised I'd been sucked into a rabbit warren of links and comments sections and slideshow arrows.

Of all the guests who had worked on *Dominus*, Charlie Pace seemed the most sinister, the most desperate, the most likely to kill. Yet he wasn't the only one to have benefited from Richard's death. And so I followed the link trail to gossip blogs that had covered other stories surrounding *Dominus*.

They didn't tell me much more than Tommo had recounted at the party: Richard had screwed over the studio; there were questions about whether the project would be dropped. It hadn't been, and Miguel was to thank for that, but it was a bet that hadn't paid off, and Richard was to blame. The box-office failure must have been a disaster for Miguel. Financially, yes, but also personally: Tommo had told me that Miguel was in some kind of power struggle with his brothers. Wouldn't Richard's death have removed the issue? Wouldn't the media attention improve the film's reception?

The situation must have been dire for Richard to have invited Miguel to his intimate birthday – to have flattered and charmed the producer all night. And – was I remembering correctly? – hadn't Miguel pulled Richard away for a private conversation at one point? Maybe he had, in fact, broken the news to Richard: the studio was dropping him. I knew Richard wouldn't have taken that lightly. Could he have retaliated? Threatened Miguel in some way? It was only speculation, but I could see how it might have played out. I knew my ex-husband all too well.

Yet there were three other guests who, I was certain, had recently clashed with Richard: Charlie, Sabine, and Kei. I couldn't know the extent of it – there were no mentions of this online – but I'd heard the acidity in Kei's voice as she whispered with Charlie at the foot of the stairs.

Things don't have to be this way – wasn't that what Kei had said? *You don't have to treat people like shit to make art.*

Why would Kei have attended the party if she hated Richard so much? To take her revenge? I couldn't see it: throughout the night Kei had looked out for the others, had tried to include me. She seemed kind, genuine. But I didn't know Kei, not truly. And I didn't know how far Richard had pushed her during the filming of *Dominus*.

Or the two leading actors.

I had wondered, that night, why Sabine was there. I couldn't see her in the same category as Miguel or Charlie: she was probably less invested in the success of *Dominus*. She had fame, money – what was one dud on her long list of credits? None of the reviews chalked the failure up to her performance, and unlike Charlie, Sabine seemed to still be garnering accolades: two magazine covers, I noted, in the last month alone. So she wouldn't have needed to eliminate Richard for her career, like the men. For a personal vendetta, then, like Kei? Had she attended Richard's party with the intention to kill?

I didn't know. This was flimsy conjecture.

I absentmindedly clicked my way through a slideshow of the *Dominus* red carpet. There were Kei and Richard, smiling together. Then Charlie and his date. Sabine posing alone in an emerald-green dress. Hand on hip, chin over the shoulder; sultry, eyebrow raised. I'd never mastered that look myself.

I closed the webpage and found the last article I had opened, waiting behind. I had not noticed when reading it earlier, but beneath the story of Richard's dispute with Montana Entertainment, other clickbait headlines were listed. My own name nestled within.

I told myself not to click on it. I knew what it contained. There was no need to read what people had written.

My right finger pressed down. I should not have clicked on it—

A door slammed. Lillie's footsteps approached the kitchen. I snapped the laptop shut and stood up as fast as possible. Opened the fridge and pretended to browse.

When I closed it again, Lillie was standing in the middle of the room, staring at me, as though she knew there was something strange in my behaviour but could not quite put her finger on it.

'Are you heading out?' I asked, a little too rushed. She was already dressed – unusual for midday.

'Yep,' she said. Went to the sink to fill a flask with water. 'Another interrogation today?'

'This afternoon.'

Lillie screwed the cap back on. 'I'm going to the station tomorrow. They want to question me too.'

'I'll come with you,' I said. 'You shouldn't be going by yourself.'

'Why not?' she said.

'You might need support, in case . . . You're too young.'

'I'm not a minor.'

'Don't roll your eyes, Lillie. I'm serious, you're barely an adult.'

She zipped up her backpack. 'I think the police would probably rather I went alone. Considering, you know.'

She left it unsaid: that I might be on their list of suspects.

'Okay.' I decided to stay away from that topic too. 'But maybe Scott should go with you.'

'I'm not a suspect,' she said. 'Why would I need a lawyer?'

'You never know what they're going to ask.'

'I do,' Lillie said. 'The cops told me. They just want to ask some questions about Dad and about the filming. Unless you're worried about something else?'

'What would I be worried about?'

We stared at each other.

'What I could say about you, maybe,' she said, pulling on her bag. 'I don't know. You're the one telling me that women have been approaching you in parking lots. Saying they think you—'

'Come on. Don't be ridiculous,' I said. 'If they ask anything about me, tell them the truth. Why wouldn't I want you to do that?'

Lillie shrugged. 'I don't know. I just – I don't think it's going to be a big deal, tomorrow. You don't need to be worried.'

'Right,' I said. 'But you told me to be careful. I'm just saying the same to you, and that's my job, isn't it? I'm supposed to worry. So can we talk about it some more, at least? Let me ask Scott what he thinks later.'

She didn't respond, but she didn't refuse the suggestion either.

'See you later,' she said, and left.

When I opened the laptop, the article was there, waiting. Richard, Honey and me. I could not face it in that moment. I would kill the next few hours with octopus videos, instead.

'. . . absolute muscle, because there are no tendons or bones,' a biologist said to the camera. 'You would not want to be on the wrong side of a giant Pacific. Their suction cups alone are unbelievably strong.

'But what you've got to remember is that these animals are gentle. And if I put my arm in the water like this, see' – her glove dipped in – 'she'll start crawling on up. But all she's gonna wanna do is explore it. She's interested. She's tasting me with her suckers. Tryna work out what's going on.'

The show didn't tell me anything I didn't already know, but it was interesting, watching the creature interact with a human. The octopus on camera, Charlotte, was about the same size as

Persephone, the same brickish-red, and I remained glued to the screen until it ended. The image turned black and white, the text appeared: *Charlotte*, it said, *2010–2014*.

I waited for the next video to load. Found myself reflected in the empty black screen.

I felt the tipsy languor of each step. As it had appeared from below, Sedgwick's rooms slotted over one another, and I wandered lazily over several levels, circling the tasteful sculptures, the furniture in velvets and gold. Brancusi, Bauhaus, Cocteau, and Ernst; Mahdavi furnishings; a Matisse lithograph or two.

I had seen spectacular homes before – above all, in LA. The whimsical, the novel: a home shaped like a shell; a home carved into the earth. The harsh and unforgiving: plateaus jutting from the hill; roofs stretching at great angles. Homes devoid of life and colour; homes bursting with plants and people. And always, without fail, the views below: everything we were trying to escape.

It was not the magnificence of Sedgwick that I found alluring; each home I had visited in the city was an ode to braggadocio. Instead, it was the secrecy, the evasion.

I found my way to the mezzanine hallway.

Deep blue and darkness. My fingers brushed over the concrete wall until they hit a ridge. I peered closer. A small pock smoothed over with cement, almost invisible to the eye.

'I'm glad I caught you.' I looked up, quick, to see Richard emerging from the shadows. Had he noticed my absence? Searched for me among each group of guests? 'Not trying your escape, I hope.'

I shook my head, tongued my words deliberately: 'Not at all – I just needed a quiet moment. But I am thinking of leaving in a few—'

'I won't keep you long, I promise.' He stuck his hands in his pockets. 'But can we talk for a moment? There was something I was trying to tell you earlier, I . . .'

Had this speech, too, been rehearsed?

'I wanted to thank you,' he said.

My skin prickled. He took a step towards me.

'I know it must have been difficult – and if there was any way, anything I could have done to avoid dragging you into it, you know I would have.'

'I know, Richard.' I stood my ground. He came closer still.

'But *Dominus* was released that week and—'

'I know.'

Every inch of my body was screaming to get away from him. 'It would have ruined me. It would have ruined Lillie's debut.'

'I know,' I said, taking a decisive step backwards. 'And *you* know I only helped because Lillie asked. It—'

'Yes, it was breaking her heart to see those lies.'

'No, Richard. I was going to say that it could have harmed her career, her reputation. But it would not have destroyed *her*. God knows you've broken her heart countless times before and she's survived.' Then I repeated: 'I did it because she asked.'

'That doesn't make me any less grateful.' He put a finger to the tank, traced an invisible crescent.

'It was such a mess, Elspeth.' He closed his eyes for a few seconds. 'Just a silly fight, you know how it can be. I said some things I regret, and he did too, but I didn't hurt him. It was just the emotions. You know how it is, with love: all those emotions. He regrets it now. He didn't mean to spread those lies.'

This speech was perhaps the emptiest of all.

I said nothing, left him in the corridor. Alone, with his vacant wall of water.

Lillie was still out when I came back from the police station, and I fell asleep before she returned. But I heard her the next morning – the sound of her engine awoke me. I checked my clock. She wouldn't be going straight to the station at this time. So she'd deliberately left before I could discuss whether Scott could accompany her. Typical; any attempt to convince Lillie to change her mind only resulted in a resolute stubbornness. She'd probably left to spare us both the argument.

I lay under the covers for another fifteen minutes, frustrated with myself for not approaching the subject more gently. It wasn't that I thought she might say anything to incriminate me or that I thought she needed legal protection. It was the thought of her alone in that cold, hard room with the flickering light and two nameless detectives. At least if Scott was with her, she wouldn't be alone. I tried not to let it worry me too much: the questions the police could ask. The things that Lillie might discover about her father.

My own interrogation yesterday had been the most frustrating so far.

'Would you say that of all of the guests, you were closest to Thomas Coates?' the female detective had begun.

I took a moment to answer. After the revelations about Jerry, I had been holding on to Tommo as the only person I couldn't find a reason to suspect. And now that too was lost.

The detectives hadn't given me much, but they spent two and a half hours attempting to link us:

I hadn't seen Mr Coates since the divorce?

But hadn't he just opened an office in New York?

We hadn't even met for a casual drink?

But we had mutual acquaintances – hadn't I heard he was in New York?

Wasn't he my daughter's godfather?

And then came the strangest part: a waitress had seen us 'cuddling' in the kitchen. I would have laughed at this, were it not so infuriating. Each question was an accusation, but I didn't understand why. If I'd known why the police were so interested in Tommo, maybe I'd have felt like it was worth it.

The closest I came to a hint was the question the female detective ended with: 'And what,' she threw in, amid a line of questioning on Lillie's relationship with Tommo, 'was the argument that night between Mr Coates and your ex-husband, about?'

I tried to charm the male cop again, said it might 'jog my memory' if they shared what they already knew. But his colleague put her foot down, and I left the station no wiser. Racked my brains driving home: had Richard and Tommo argued that night? All I could recall was their bickering about school and that alter ego game.

I hauled myself out of bed. At least I had a day off from the interrogation. I would begin by cleaning the house – it could be a nice surprise for Lillie. I scrubbed the fridge again. Straightened the pictures on the wall. Polished the espresso machine.

Lillie had given me a tour of her house when I'd first arrived. It was concise at the start – after our awkward conversation about Julian, driving from the airport, neither of us had felt like lingering to discuss why she had chosen each shade of paint, each cushion and each rug. But by the time we reached the kitchen, she couldn't help but show off. The multi-functioning oven, the expensive espresso machine.

'A gift from Dad,' she said, patting its red-lacquered shell. It stood out among the silver appliances. 'He was horrified when he found out I still had one of those cheap twenty-buck drip machines. Don't tell him,' she dropped her voice to a mock whisper, 'but I never threw it away.'

I laughed.

'But it was very generous,' she added quickly. 'My friends are all impressed.'

'What time are we going to head over?' I asked, happy that our drive had been forgotten. 'I'd like to wash my hair, if we have time.'

Lillie had looked at me apologetically. And then she'd told her lie: she needed to drop in to see a friend; I would arrive at the party alone. But there was time to take me to the car rental that afternoon, if I still had my heart set on driving myself everywhere. I did – I needed the independence. And so she dropped me at the rental, gave me the spare keys to her house so I could go back and get ready, and repeated the lie once more: she would see me at the party in a couple of hours.

What was she actually doing that night? Why did she lie? I'd only heard Richard's side of the story; I hadn't remembered to ask her for the truth since my first clumsy, aborted attempt. But maybe it didn't matter. Maybe it was inconsequential in the face of Richard's death, in the face of the murder inquiry.

I pushed the question out of my mind as I stripped the sheets from my bed for the laundry, then thought: *I should wash Lillie's bedding too.*

Her bedroom was a little more lived-in since I'd seen it last – since I'd left her in its emptiness, with an insect tapping at the window, to go and learn of her father's murder. It was minimal, in keeping with the house. White sheets and pillows, strewn plumped and messy – she had never been one to make the bed. There were photographs on the wall, people I did not recognise. Polaroids, back in style once more. A pile of *Vogue* magazines took the place of a bedside table. On top of them, a glass of water, some earrings, and a velvet scrunchie.

As I lifted the covers, papers tumbled to the floor. I shuffled them to a pile. A script, Lillie's script. Lillie's script from *Dominus*. I placed it on her bureau, took the sheets to the washing machine. The plants needed watering; the furniture needed a polish. I returned with a duster. And that was when I noticed it – a little cardboard tag that must have fallen beneath the bed with the scattered script. I opened it without thinking. *Lilliput*, I read, *I can't tell you how proud I—*

I shut the card. It had a little hole where a ribbon had been attached, perhaps tying it to a bouquet of flowers. I had received one just like it, for my own debut.

(Can you feel that?)

(Good girl.)

(Take it from the top.)

I slipped the card between the pages of the script. Busied my mind with bathroom bleach, then vacuuming.

It was only in the silencing of the vacuum that I noticed the noise – a low thrum of voices from the road. I opened the front door without thinking, and chaos broke loose.

'Elspeth.' 'Elspeth, over here.' 'Hey, Elspeth, was your daughter at her father's birthday party?' 'Elspeth, were you there when your ex-husband died?' 'Elspeth, did you kill your ex-husband?' 'Elspeth, over here.'

They were a horde of crows, cameras snapping, climbing over one another. Ten or fifteen men, maybe, but it was difficult to pick the swarm apart. I froze in the flashes.

'Did you kill Richard Bryant?' 'Do you know Thomas Coates?' 'Did your daughter's godfather kill his best friend?' 'Do you know Honey Carlisle?' 'How's your ex-husband's new boyfriend, Elspeth? D'ya think he did it?' 'What about Jerry Debrowski – isn't he a friend of yours?' 'Why was Jerry at the station?' 'Did you kill your ex-husband, Elspeth?' 'Give us a smile.' 'Give us a smile, sexy.' 'Did you and Thomas kill Richard?' 'Is your daughter a killer, Elspeth?'

I slammed the door shut. Stood, shell-shocked, in the darkness for a few moments, then reached for my cell. Lillie's phone was off – I left a voicemail message. Scott picked up on the first ring.

'They're here,' I said. 'Photographers, at Lillie's. Journalists too, maybe. I – I don't know. They're here.'

'Slow down, Elspeth,' he said. 'Breathe. Are you inside?'

'Yes.'

'Where are they? They didn't follow you onto the property?'

'They're in the street,' I said.

'Can they see the house from the street? No wall or anything?'

'There's a wall, but you can see over it.'

'Ah,' said Scott. 'Unfortunately, if they're not on private property, there's not much we can do. Keep the curtains closed. Stay inside as much as possible. Any reason they'd visit today?'

I closed the front-facing curtains, violently, quickly. Paused to look when I reached the last. The men weren't watching the house anymore. They were checking phones and surveilling the road.

'Lillie,' I replied. 'She has a session with the police.'

'Okay,' Scott said. 'They've probably been staking out the station to see who's being questioned. But it's not like the police would put up with paparazzi on their doorstep – it would interfere with the investigation. So my guess is the photographers wait for the high-profile figures to return home. Try to provoke a response there. I've seen this kind of thing before.'

'It's inhumane.'

'It is,' he said firmly. 'And, quite frankly, they're assholes. But it's not illegal to be an asshole. I'm checking state laws as we speak, and . . . Yeah, I'm sorry, Elspeth, there aren't any options. Watch out for trespassers; obstructing drivers too. Not much you can do beyond that.'

'We can't make them leave before Lillie comes home?'

'No. If it continues, she'll have to get a taller fence. But I don't think it will. They'll get their photos today, and if Lillie lies low for a while, they'll lose interest.'

I thanked Scott and tried to call Lillie again. Her phone was still off. I left another message.

And then I was alone with the faint sound of the men outside, their jeers and taunts and questions still ringing in my mind.

What had they been shouting? It sounded like they knew very little, if they were accusing Lillie of anything. Scott was right, they were only trying to provoke a response – to catch me countering one of their claims or exploding in anger at their allegations. *Did you kill your ex-husband, Elspeth? Give us a smile.*

But they had asked whether I'd been there that night. They'd asked about Jerry, and Honey, and Tommo too. They knew little, but so did I.

I was still questioning everything – every memory, every guest. And the memories were resurfacing, incessantly: Tommo recounting the failure of *Dominus*, Jerry's melancholy mood, Charlie and Kei whispering at the foot of the stairs. *And what was the argument that night between Mr Coates and your ex-husband about? Eight limbs, three hearts, suckers, two by two.*

I had walked into Sedgwick an outsider, believing that each of the guests loved Richard – and that he loved them all in turn. But I knew nothing of their relationships, their histories. What *did* I know? That there had been some kind of friction during the filming of *Dominus* involving Charlie, Sabine, and Kei: Richard had treated them poorly; I'd overheard Kei disparaging him to Charlie for this. And that would have been around the time of Richard's argument with Jerry, the fight, and the firing. And then what? The film had done terribly at the box office, which would have hurt the careers of Kei and the actors – but, more significantly, it affected Miguel. So, there were four guests who had attended Richard's party despite recent trouble with Richard – Jerry, Charlie, Sabine, and Kei – and four guests who could benefit, in money and prestige, from the death of *Dominus*'s director – Miguel, Charlie, Sabine, and Kei.

Was I certain that I could trust Tommo? He had mentioned his schoolboy rivalry, how he had suffered at Richard's hands. I'd seen my ex-husband jibe at him throughout the party, and now I could see them both in my mind: the two schoolboys in caps on a cold winter morning, one shivering in his river-soaked clothes. There must have been a reason for the police to devote an entire session of questioning to our friendship. And for the paparazzi to ask about him – had they seen Tommo entering the station, or was there something else?

And what of Honey? I had seen him lying unconscious that night. Could I entirely rule out the possibility that he had woken up later on? After the rest of us had fallen asleep? I tried to recall the scene. He had been lying face down, and with the position of his limbs, I was certain he hadn't just been sleeping. People don't wake up, sharp and lucid, only an hour or two after collapsing like that. *How's your ex-husband's new boyfriend, Elspeth? D'ya think he did it?*

There was a shout outside, and the crowd exploded again. I ran to the door.

There they were: surrounding her car, scrambling over one another, frenzied, to flash their cameras.

'Get away,' I shouted. 'Let her through.'

I couldn't be heard over the din. Lillie was inching her car through the swarm. The gate rolled open. Her face was flinty beneath sunglasses and a baseball cap, stare fixed straight ahead. The gate closed behind her, but the men continued peering over the wall – the ones at the back of the crowd lifting cameras aloft, snapping and snapping.

'Haven't you got what you wanted?' I shouted. 'Can't you leave her alone?'

But Lillie was opening her car door, and the jeering cries found their target.

'Lillie.' 'Hey, Lillie.' 'Over here.' 'How are the cops doing, Lillie?' 'Did you kill your daddy?' 'D'ya know who did it, Lillie?' 'Hey, hey, Lillie.' 'Who killed your daddy, Lillie?' 'Did you do it?' 'Over here.' 'Was it your co-stars, Lillie? Was it your god-father?' 'Give us a smile.'

Lillie held her jacket across her face.

'Go away,' I said. 'Leave her alone.'

This only fuelled their sneers.

'Running to Mommy?' 'Mommy looking after you?' 'Is Mommy protecting her little murderer?' 'Who killed your daddy, Lillie?'

Then Lillie was pushing past me, and I could shut the men away.

'Lillie,' I said, as the front door muffled the racket. 'I tried to call.'

'I'm fine,' she was saying. 'It's fine.' Her hands were trembling as she removed her glasses and cap.

I began, 'What they were saying—'

'They were just baiting me. I don't listen to it.'

Lillie lay down on the couch, covered her face with her arm.

'You should have stayed inside,' she said. 'I can deal with it. I'm used to it. They'll lose interest soon.'

'You shouldn't have to deal with it,' I said. 'But Scott says there isn't anything we can do. Maybe a taller fence, if it continues.'

'I know.' She shrugged. Then said, 'This is what I was telling you before. About not wanting to go out. Not wanting Scott with me. Can you imagine if I was photographed with a lawyer?'

I sat on the arm of the couch.

'How was it?' I asked. 'The questioning.'

'Fine.'

'What did they ask you about?'

'Like I said,' she was slipping off her shoes, 'they only wanted to ask about Dad and his filming.'

'Was it difficult, talking about him?'

'I told you,' she said. I could hear the exhaustion in her voice. 'It was fine. They were more interested in asking about the cast and crew.'

'The ones at the party?'

'I guess,' she said, and then sat up. 'But, Mom, can we do this another time?'

She started walking to her room. I followed her.

'Could you just tell me what kinds of questions were they asking?'

'I don't really want to talk about it right now.'

I should have dropped it, but the photographers' accusations were still gnawing through. 'It might be useful, Lillie. For me to know. It might help me remember. Did they ask you about Miguel? And what about the other people at the party – the paparazzi were saying things about Jerry, Tommo. Do you know why—'

'What is this? Another interrogation?'

I hung back. Apologised. 'I'm sorry. It's the stress,' I said. 'The investigation must be getting to me. Those photographers.'

'And you don't think I'm stressed too?'

'I'm sorry.'

She opened her door, and said: 'You know, it was hard enough going through those questions once.'

'I'm sorry, Lillie. It's just that you might know something that could help me, especially after you worked—'

'That's right, I worked with those people. How do you think that feels?'

When I didn't answer, she went on: 'To know that your father was murdered and to know that the only suspects are your friends, your colleagues, your godfather, your *mother*. To have it thrown in your face by a bunch of middle-aged men hiding behind cameras.

'How do you think that feels?' she said. 'If I knew anything helpful, then I would have told you and I'd have told the police. I don't want you to go to jail. I don't want any of you to go to jail, but it had to be – what am I supposed—'

Lillie turned away from me, caught her breath.

Then said, in a smaller voice: 'I can't do this now, Mom. Please.'

'I'm sorry,' I said.

She closed her door.

I made myself a coffee and sat with it in silence. No thrum of voices from the road – the swarm had dispersed.

I felt ugly, contaminated by those men and their taunts. Poor Lillie – to face the police, the paparazzi, and now my questions too.

This had always been our problem. We kept things to ourselves; we avoided difficult conversations. We compressed them away. But such things have a way of pushing to the surface – and when they pushed their way between Lillie and me, they always burst into confrontation.

Now she was grieving, I was embroiled in an investigation, and after living apart for more than a year, we were squashed back together. There were always going to be difficulties, arguments, hurt. But I shouldn't have asked her about the other suspects; it wasn't the time.

And yet: when would it be?

Lillie's door slammed. She came into the kitchen, red-cheeked.

'What the fuck, Mom? What the fuck?'

I froze, my lips hovering over the coffee cup. I had no idea what she was talking about.

'My room?' she said. 'What the fuck?'

'I thought it would be a nice—'

'That is not okay. You can't do that. You can't just go into my private space.'

The washing machine in the next room was picking up speed. She shouted over its roar.

'This is *my house*,' she said. 'This is *my* private space. And you touched my things? That is not okay.'

Lillie was about to leave, but she hesitated. When she turned back, she was on the verge of tears. 'I thought I'd lost the card from Dad. Don't do that. Don't touch my stuff.'

'I didn't know,' I said. 'I thought it might be helpful. Your sheets.'

She put her head in her hands. Rubbed her face.

In her silence, a terrible thought struck – the script, the note from Richard; Lillie's friends and colleagues.

'Lillie,' I said, trying to keep my voice composed, 'you haven't been in touch with any of them, have you? Since that night.'

She said nothing.

'Lillie?'

She turned back to me. I could see it in her face.

'Lillie, who has been contacting you?'

'All of them,' she said.

'Did you respond?'

'Only to one,' she said. 'Honey.'

'But what about party scenes? I always think they have so much potential for confrontation, for character development,' said Miguel. 'Romances, mistakes, arguments. I'm always saying that. You gotta have a nice party set piece.'

'Totally,' Kei said. 'And every character has something they want to achieve. It's socially awkward and—'

'Hey,' said Jerry. 'Rude.'

'My favourites are proms,' Honey offered.

'Honey.' Sabine giggled. 'My treasure. You like the crowns and pretty dresses.'

I listened to the conversation in the atrium as I picked my way down, relieved my absence had not inspired more gossip. I could not hear Richard behind me, but he would be there, following. I walked faster to put distance between us.

'Dear god, no.' Tommo pretended to vomit. 'Please. What an awful, tacky trope.'

'I think it's endearing,' said Honey. 'You know, the paper decorations and a wonky corsage. It's like what Miguel said about parties but amplified by all the teenage melodrama. I love that rite-of-passage stuff.'

'But is it a trope when it's a part of life?' Miguel said. 'When it's something people actually experience? The mean girls and jocks and nerds in high school, are they a trope?'

'*American* high schools,' Tommo corrected. 'We had ruggers and readers.'

'Is marriage a trope?' said Jerry.

'No,' said Kei, considering. 'But weddings are.'

'Divorce,' said Richard from the mezzanine. 'That's a trope.'

'No, dude,' Kei said. 'It's a cliché.'

'Along,' I called, 'with love itself.'

Tommo laughed, moving towards me to offer a stabilising hand for the last few steps.

'Are you okay, darling? You don't look well at all,' he whispered.

I nodded, cleared my throat.

'In that case, can I get you another drink?' He squeezed my arm. 'We've moved on to a delicious bottle of vodka.'

I hesitated, with the attention of the room focused on me, and said: 'Depends on the mixer.'

'We don't do mixers here.' Kei laughed. Then shouted at Tommo: 'Pour another round of shots.'

I regarded the group, wondering whom to position myself beside, and caught Charlie studying me, as though measuring whether I was worth conversation. When he saw that I was looking, he quickly turned away, began to talk with Honey. My irrelevance must have appeared contagious.

'Brought the vodka with me.' Miguel had wormed his way next to me. 'You've seen this brand before? Pretty cool, right? It's Crystal Head. Additive free. So, listen, I've been thinking about what we discussed earlier and I'm sorry, I just can't let it go. You just *have* to get back out there. I was telling Nicole at Brian's house last weekend – you know Brian, right? – about this problem we have with casting older women and she was like, *Miguel, honey . . .*'

As Richard came down the stairs, Sabine skipped up to him. I watched her place her hands around my ex-husband's neck, watched them slide down the length of his body. The others were taking turns with the shots – shrieking like teenagers. Kei poured the vodka straight from the skull-shaped bottle into Jerry's open mouth.

'. . . but I don't think Matt's right for the role. What would you say?' Miguel continued. 'I mean, when you think about the character's motivation. He's just lost his job, he's . . .'

'A birthday dance?' Richard said. 'I'm a lucky boy.'

Sabine flipped her hair, slipped a hand into his pocket. I could see her fingers moving beneath the fabric. Miguel was still blathering on, the others were throwing back glasses – had none of them noticed? Sabine giggled, swaying her hips back and forth. And then she pulled out the remote.

'Hey.' Miguel hit the back of his hand, a little too hard, on my arm. 'Thought I lost you for a second there! So anyway, I call up Bruce . . .'

'Devious,' called Richard. 'Minx, harlot!'

She was running away from him, cackling, thumb stabbing the volume button. The beats drowned his insults.

'. . . and it was a DUI, you know, so he couldn't shake it.' Miguel raised his voice. 'Anyway, that's the funny thing, he came by *my* house the night before. But then his wife, who's a jewellery designer . . .'

Honey turned from the liquor cabinet, wiping his mouth, and reached for Sabine's hands. She kicked off each Louboutin – a flash of red sole – as he pulled her onto the coffee table. Her naked tiptoes tapped a perfect rhythm on the marble. His hands rested on her hips.

'Elspeth?' said Miguel. 'You want one?'

Kei was holding out a shot glass.

I should have left then. I could have kissed Tommo and Jerry goodbye and called myself a cab, escaped – far from strange Sedgwick with its shifting floors and haunted name, far from the silent creature, the troubled guests. I could have slipped my fate: the wet 'O' of the mouth, the stare of the eyes, the stench of vomit.

'Well?' asked Kei.

The music pounded. I hesitated. Saw Richard step onto the table, between his darlings. Took the glass, bit back the cold spirit, returned it to Kei for another measure.

Many times throughout the investigation – piecing together the events of that night – I recalled this moment, wondering why, after Richard's ambush in the hallway, I had accepted the glass. Perhaps I was drunk already, to have thrown back the vodka without thought. Perhaps it was fury or hatred; insouciance or fear. Then three shots were finished and I was pushing off my shoes as Tommo took me into the throng.

'Honey found an envelope in Dad's desk,' Lillie said. 'It was labelled *In the Unlikely Event*. Dad's will, those kinds of documents. But also instructions for his memorial. Food, music. Guest list, speeches. So then he messaged me—'

'When?'

'A day or two after Dad died, that's when Honey texted about the memorial. But I didn't really reply until he started calling.'

My heart lurched. 'He called you?'

'Yeah, and then he came to see me. The day that the cops told him what had happened.'

That was right: she'd known before I'd told her. But I had never questioned how.

I frowned. 'He told you that? That was Honey who I saw driving away from your house that day?'

'He was distraught,' she explained. 'He just wanted . . . He thought I was the only person who'd understand. And I did, he was right. I couldn't have gotten through any of this without Honey.'

'Don't you find it suspicious? That he reached out right after your father's death?'

'We need each other,' she said. 'He's the only one who understands what I'm going through.'

'But he's a suspect, Lillie.'

'I know, I know, I just don't think he—'

'Can you trust him? I mean, how long had your father and Honey been back together before the night of your father's death?

If they had broken up before, if things had been bad between them before, don't you think there's a chance—'

'Do you?' Lillie said. 'Do you think he could have done it?'

I didn't think he had done it. I had seen him unconscious, hadn't I? But that was just one paper-thin memory. Would I bet my daughter's safety on that memory?

'Do you honestly think he could have done it?' Lillie repeated. 'You saw them together that night. Tell me.'

When I didn't reply, she went on, 'Honey loves Dad. They were fine, they'd – I don't know exactly what happened between them, I don't know why Dad forgave Honey, but he did. And if Dad could forgive him, then . . .'

I knew she wanted to believe Honey couldn't have done it. I knew she was trying to convince herself.

After a few moments I spoke – deliberately, without anger. 'How many times have you seen him? Was that it? The day he told you about the investigation?'

'Of course not. We've been planning the memorial. There have been loads of things to—'

'How many times have you seen Honey?'

'I don't know. We speak at least once a day. He's dropped by a couple of times.'

I'd seen how she'd been opening up over the past week, how she'd been throwing herself back into the world. Now that I knew it had been with Honey, I felt sick. A nasty, ugly sickness; a terrible dread.

'When I've been out?' I asked. 'At the police station?'

Lillie nodded.

'Don't you think that's suspicious? Why hasn't he visited when I've been here?'

'It's just how it happened.'

'So he just decided to strike up a friendship with you, when I'm not here, right in the middle of a murder investigation?' She flinched. Was I shouting?

Lillie had rarely mentioned Honey in the years before the allegations. He never entered her childhood tales of LA I had assumed that Richard preferred to have quality time with his daughter and that, consequently, Honey had been only a distant figure for her. Had I got this wrong? Had she purposefully omitted him from her stories over the years, knowing it would make me jealous?

'No, I – no,' she said, 'it wasn't out of nowhere. Before Dad and Honey broke up, we were pretty close.'

So this wasn't a new relationship; it was just new to me.

I couldn't say any of this, not now. All I could do was repeat: 'But he is a *suspect*, Lillie.'

'I just . . .' She was quiet, voice straining. 'I guess I don't find it suspicious because it's true. It is. We need each other. Honey's the only other person who loved Dad as much as me, and he knows what it's like to lose family.'

She didn't need me.

I closed my eyes. How had I let this happen?

'Mom,' said Lillie, almost pleading. 'You said you didn't think he did it.'

'No, Lillie, I never said that.'

'I could see it. In your face. I could see.'

'I never said that.'

'Well, *do* you think he did it?'

Again, I couldn't answer.

'Because I don't. And I believe that with my whole heart,' she said. 'But if you have one good reason to think Honey did it, you need to tell me now. If you don't, then I'm not going to stop seeing him, and we're going to keep organising the memorial together. He's my only link to Dad. I need him. Why shouldn't I see him? Give me one good reason.'

*

The night progressed in lulls and spurts. Dancing came and went with the erratic playlist, the room clearing when Miguel chose a song; he did not care, he danced, content, alone. Conversations gathered in strange corners of the house: the kitchen, the hallway, the doorway to a room. Every so often I stepped outside by

myself, watched the group through the glass and resolved to
drink more water, call a cab. Why had I not left yet? I could
never remember.

Only snippets of conversation, isolated scenes, survived my
vodka-steeped memory.

Kei sitting on the lawn, humming to herself as she rolled a
cigarette, telling me it was the taste she liked, the time it took to
create.

Miguel struggling to contain his tears as he played his favourite
childhood song.

'Earlier,' Tommo mumbled, cornering me on the other side of
the octopus tank. 'Earlier, darling, I meant to ask . . . I wanted
to see if you were . . . Because I read about it a few months ago,
and I know we've never talked about it, but I always wondered
whether . . .'

At one point I found Sabine and Charlie in the bathtub, clothes
sticking to their skin like cresting waves.

'There's no swimming pool,' she told me, matter-of-fact, and
Charlie giggled like a kid. As I backed out to find another bathroom, he kicked his legs as hard as he could, slopped water
everywhere.

They emerged some time later, lips lilac, and danced across
the atrium floor, as if they had never left, as if their clothes were
not soaked translucent, their limbs and nipples not prickling with
the cold.

'Excellent – we can corroborate that with the security-camera
footage,' the male officer was saying.

I had thought we'd been over the events of that night enough
times already. But apparently not. The detectives had spent the
morning 'cross-checking' facts, things that they'd presumably
learned elsewhere in the investigation.

The officer was flipping through his papers when the last
comment rang through my thoughts.

'The security cameras, wait.' I sat up, excited. 'There was a
camera in the atrium corner – facing right where we were sitting
– it would have captured everything, the whole night. Richard

used it for . . . Well, it wasn't specifically a security camera so perhaps you haven't yet—'

I had been gabbling so quickly, I had not noticed the female officer holding up her hand to interrupt.

'I'm afraid that isn't possible, Ms Bryant Bell,' she said. 'Or perhaps you knew that already.'

'Knew what already? It's there, it records every night, I'm sure if you check . . .'

Scott adjusted his cufflinks with two sharp movements, so I let my words trail off.

'No usable footage from that camera.' The male cop cracked the bones in his neck. 'There was a screen covering the lens.'

Of course. The projector screen. If they had already questioned me four times in the past couple of weeks, I wondered how many hours they had racked up on this cold table, in this soulless room, with the other guests. I wondered how much the others had revealed. Did the police know about all of the *Dominus* disagreements? Had they reached my conclusions about Jerry, Miguel, Charlie, Sabine and Kei? And what did they know about Tommo? I tried to work out the motives behind each probing question they asked, tried to slot them with my own suspicions.

'Do you recall,' said his colleague, 'why the projector screen was lowered?'

'We watched something early on in the night. Richard rolled it back up afterwards,' I said. Then: 'Wait, yes, sorry – I do remember. Later on, quite late in the evening, it was brought back out again. We watched Richard's movies.'

I could not piece the memories together, yet I knew it had been some time after the dancing – beyond the point at which the night shattered to fragments.

However, I did remember wedging myself between Jerry and Kei. I remembered trying to ignore Richard and Jerry's unrelenting commentary throughout the opening scenes of *Anatomy*. I remembered licking the warm, yellow, salty powder of microwaved popcorn from my fingers, covering my eyes when my former self appeared. Maybe someone was passing around a joint, maybe someone was smoking a cigar; when I pictured my own face projected large, reciting lines to a jeering, slurring audience, it was dreamy, softened by the haze.

'Do you remember who suggested the films?' asked the officer.

I did not, only that they continued rolling in the background. Every so often I would catch glimpses – surreal, displaced, silenced by the return of dance music. They would snatch me away from conversation, pull me back to the story each time.

Sweat behind my knees and swaying alone in the bathroom.

Swells of movie soundtrack, drowning out all else.

The lines that I had spoken in another life. *You gotta believe me, Officer. He took me to the coat check at the club and put his gun right in my mouth. And I could taste the metal, you gotta believe me. It was cold, Officer. So cold.*

Lines my daughter had spoken only a year ago. *And do you love her, Luke?*

The octopus suspended in the water, watching.

Swigs from the bottle.

Unstoppable music.

And through it all, there was one figure my gaze returned to, again and again.

'Okay. And, finally, we have a few follow-up questions on your answers regarding Anton Carlisle – known as Honey,' the male cop said, reading from his notes. 'Now, you mentioned that he was the first individual you saw when you woke up . . .'

'Apart from Richard,' I said. 'Yes.'

'Would, uh . . . do you think he was awake before you?'

'I couldn't say.'

The female officer, hair slicked into a painful-looking bun, leaned forwards and asked: 'Can you recall his behaviour the night before?'

'We didn't talk. We're not really . . . I don't know him.'

'There were fewer than ten guests that night.'

'I know, but we—'

'So you were avoiding him?'

I sighed. 'Yes. You could say that.'

She scribbled in her notebook.

'Officers,' Scott said, amicable, calm, 'we've been here all after-noon. I'm sure my client would appreciate—'

'Just these last few questions.' The male cop stretched his arms. Added, as though with a wink, to me: 'Don't worry, you'll be out of here in the next half-hour.'

Scott glanced at me; I gave a small nod. Better to get it finished today.

He checked his watch and said: 'Half an hour.'

'We appreciate your continued cooperation.' The female officer smiled with her teeth, then turned to me. 'Ms Bryant Bell, is it safe to assume the hostility between yourself and Anton Carlisle stemmed from your recent press statement?'

My heart drummed. I could hear it pulsing in my ears. I real-ised I had not blinked, that I was twisting the bracelet around and around my wrist, that my breathing was uneven, that my throat was sticking, that time had passed and I still had not answered the question, that I had not prepared myself to face this subject, not today, not in this interrogation, not as part of an inquiry into the death of my ex-husband, the father of my child, my first love, my—

When I did not immediately answer, she went on: 'Your state-ment regarding Mr Carlisle's allegations of abuse?'

I wanted to stop watching him, to tear myself away. But it was as impossible as shunning a pernicious thought. I couldn't fail to be drawn to Honey: across the room, through the window, or talking with another group. To analyse the way that he poured himself a drink (timidly, always having first offered one to the nearest person); to note his conversational technique (intimate, intense); to linger over the slope of his high cheekbones and the length of his limbs.

I kept as much distance between us as I could and yet I could not stop watching as Richard moved towards him, slipped an arm around his waist, whispered in his ear. I saw their smiles and I knew they were genuine. I knew that Honey did believe he was happy in that moment.

When Lillie had announced that they were back together, I'd known that I would see this at the party. Of course, I had also thought there would be more people – that I would be able to escape it. That Lillie would be by my side, reminding me that I had made the right decision, that there was someone else to protect.

But Lillie was not with me and I could not escape the sight of Richard beaming triumphantly, as he rested his hand upon Honey's hip. It was more than I could bear. I looked away, left the room, each time Honey smiled. It broke my heart. How many lies had Richard told him? How many had Honey told himself?

Across the room, through the window, over my conversational partner's shoulder, my eyes returned to the long-limbed beauty. His shirt never creased; he fiddled with the back of his right ear when bored. He danced like his entire body was laughing. He was so *young*.

Did I talk to Honey that night?

I did not.

How could I?

'Officer, my client—'

'Your client's cooperation is greatly appreciated, sir,' said the female detective. 'Now, Ms Bryant Bell, your statement describes Mr Bryant's character – you say he was *a wonderful, dependable father to Lillie* and *the best husband I could have asked for*. You do not, however, at any point address rumours discussed in the press – namely, that Mr Bryant may have acted violently towards you. My question is very simple.'

(Now lift your head.)

Her hands lay flat on the table. A glittering engagement ring, bitten nails.

'Did he?'

(Lift your head, look over here.)

'My client would like to—'

'As you know, Ms Bryant Bell, you have the right to refuse to answer our questions,' she interrupted. 'But this would not be in your best interest. We do need an answer going forward.'

(I said, *lift your head.*)

Scott's watch ticked in the silence.

(Lift your head. Your head.)

'It's a very simple question,' she said. 'Was your ex-husband or was he not physically or emotionally abusive during or after your marriage?'

(No, your chin, upwards. Like this. Can you feel?)

The watch ticked.

'No.'

(Good girl. Take it from the top.)

'Could you state that for me in full, Ms Bryant Bell, for the record?'

'No, Richard was not abusive during our marriage. He was the best husband I could have asked for and a wonderful father to our daughter.'

'It can't have been that bad, though. I mean if they're back together.'

I was sitting in the garden, catching some fresh night air, when I heard Charlie enter the kitchen with someone else. I wondered whether to slip away while I had the chance. If the conversation stretched on, there would be no escape, no excuse: I was directly beneath the window.

But I wanted to stay. I had to. This was what had made the party bearable – enjoyable, even. I was apart, I was removed, I was watching. I knew the others in ways they could not imagine, and that power was intoxicating.

I would wait for one more second – see who Charlie was talking to.

Jerry groaned. 'Honestly, I didn't think much of it in the first place.'

His words were sluggish: he'd drunk more since our last conversation. I heard the pop of a liquor-bottle stopper. Then a clink, a glug. I slowed my breath, held myself still: I needed to hear this.

'What do you mean?'

'Think about it,' said Jerry. 'Unknown model, famous director, new film release . . .'

I hugged my arms in tight – the night chill was creeping through my clothes.

'You think it was Montana? A publicity stunt? Fuck off. If anything, it harmed—'

'Tha's not what I mean,' said Jerry. 'All I'm saying is, don't you think it's a little convenient the allegations came out at that time, when there was already maximum attention on Richard? And I don't know what the guy wants, maybe it's the media attention, maybe he was thinking of an out-of-court settlement . . .'

I didn't want to hear this. Not Jerry saying this.

'Did he ask for money?' said Charlie.

My knees were aching, legs crossed.

'No, but listen pal, the evidence was against him.' Jerry had raised his voice. 'Everyone was on Rich's side. Rich is a nice guy, you know he's a nice guy. So okay, he can be demanding sometimes, but come on, he'd never do that. I've known him forever. *You* know him. He wouldn't. And then, what? Three months later they're back together.'

A pause. I was shivering but my face was hot. A nasty, acidic heat.

'I dunno, man,' said Charlie. 'I don't want to say he's lying. But I agree, I can't imagine . . . Maybe it was a misunderstanding? I feel like it was probably an argument. A misunderstanding.'

Jerry gave a hollow laugh.

'I'm jus' saying what we're all thinking, pal.' He was fumbling his words. 'You've got to admit it's sus – suspicious. And now he's a fuckin' household name.'

'But the stuff people were writing about him . . .'

'Gotta break a few to make a few, baby.'

'It would be fucked up, though.'

'What?'

'If it were true,' said Charlie. 'That would be—'

Footsteps.

'Oh, hey. Hey man. Great to see you, man. We were just talking about—'

'Omelettes,' slurred Jerry. 'We were talking about omelettes. You like omelettes, Honey?'

The first time I tried to leave it all behind, I was twenty-three years old, pregnant with Lillie, and desperate for freedom. There was no planning. I took only my purse and travelled to LAX in the clothes I was wearing. I had not booked a ticket. If I had planned at all, Richard would have known. I am certain he kept tabs on every phone call I made, the people who visited the house. Not that I had any friends to help me by that point. And no colleagues either – Richard thought it would be better if I gave up work, from the earliest days of the pregnancy. He earned enough for both of us and was I really going to continue with these kinds of roles once I had a baby to look after? I didn't take this rubbish seriously, did I? It wasn't exactly art, was it? Wasn't the baby more important? The baby, our baby, my baby.

It would bring us together, he said. Had he not wondered whether it might give me reason to escape?

I think he'd known I would leave this time, though he could do nothing beyond locking me in, and there were too many people working in the household then, too many witnesses that day. So he apologised. He knew that would not be enough. I had found a syringe in the bathroom the night before. He had broken his only promise to me – and when confronted, his anger took hold. It always did. But this was different: I wasn't one person then; I wasn't only myself.

And so I moved back to New York City in my maternity clothes, to spend the remaining months of pregnancy weighing my fate.

Richard did not cut off the credit cards, I think as an apology. But, also, he knew that without money I would be forced to live with my parents in Queens. And that was too much for him to bear – his wife and unborn child seeking refuge in that borough. I was thankful for the credit cards. Thankful for my husband's jealousy, snobbishness. I lived at the Pierre. Looked down on everything I had looked up to as a kid across the water.

During those days, as I watched the crawling cars and blinking lights, I had a recurring urge: to knot each pair of corners of my bed sheet together, hook the ties beneath my armpits, jump from the window and let the makeshift parachute cradle my fall to the ground – a fall so slow it could be flying. I would daydream the fall again and again, let the AC kiss my cheeks cold.

I found it hard to discern the outlines of my real life, which, while I was in LA, had always seemed to lie in New York. But this city was not my own. This city was a constellation. I hopped across destinations in my taxi, drawing lines from dot to dot, stepped out like a visitor from a distant planet: to the doctor's office, the baby departments of Fifth Avenue, home. I did not walk the streets. I was untouched.

When Richard checked into rehab, I told myself that this demonstrated his determination – the problem was the addiction, he knew that. And he could fix it. But only with my help. He had apologised one thousand times. He was the father of my unborn child. He loved me, didn't he? And there was something else, our baby, and things could be different now, couldn't they? He would change, wouldn't he? And there was so much – *so* much – to fight for.

These were the things I told myself, booking my ticket so I could return to the West Coast before giving birth. But perhaps they were dishonest. Perhaps the essence of it was: I missed him; I missed the life he'd given me.

'Here's what we're struggling with, Elspeth.' The officer put down her notebook and laid her hands flat on the table between us. It was the first time she had used my name. 'We've spoken to everyone who was at Sedgwick on the night of the murder. We've spoken to your ex-husband's other friends as well, his family in Britain, his colleagues and acquaintances; his housekeeper, his landscaper, even his favourite deli-owner – and by nearly all accounts he was not a particularly nice man.'

I looked to Scott, panicked. She bulldozed on.

'Oh he was charming, yes, and generous and popular. A *talented* man.' She enunciated the word *talented* as one might pronounce *paranormal, necromancer, alchemist*. 'But at the same time, we're having no trouble at all establishing credible motives. He was a man with a temper . . .'

(I said, *lift your head*.)

'– a perfectionist . . .'

(Lift your head. Your head.)

'– with high expectations for everyone around him. He was controlling . . .'

(No, your chin, upwards.)

' – stubborn . . .'

(Like this.)

' – and often selfish. And his struggles with substance abuse, which he grappled with over several decades, only exacerbated these traits. But then you come along and you swear, you are adamant, that he was, and I quote, *he was the best husband I could have asked for*. Can you understand why we're having a hard time believing that?'

'He was never—'

'Look, I'm not saying you're hiding anything on purpose or that you're trying to misdirect this investigation. We just want to build an accurate picture. I want you to know that you can trust us.'

'I meant what I said, he was a wonderful—'

'Was he?'

I avoided her piercing stare. 'I mean, Richard had a temper, yes, but who doesn't? He was a man with a lot of professional stresses, he carried a lot of responsibilities and sometimes he struggled with . . .'

'With substance abuse.'

The male cop was watching us, back and forth: a spectator at a tennis match.

'Yes, and, you know, a lot of people do.'

'Not all addicts become violent, Ms Bryant Bell. They can

push their loved ones away, they can lie and manipulate to get
what they want, what they need. Believe me, Ms Bryant Bell,
we've seen it all in here. However—'

'But that's exactly why I left him, my daughter . . .'

'And how did it feel to see him return to his old habits?'

'I told you, I was asleep. I didn't—'

(I just want to take the edge off, is that so awful?)

Scott tried to interrupt us: 'Officer, I think—'

(I just want to take the edge off.)

'They were still close weren't they? Your daughter and your
ex-husband. How did that feel?'

'He's her father, I couldn't stop—'

'—her spending time with an addict?'

'Okay, Officer, I think you've got all you need.' Scott said.
'Now, we agreed—'

'One more minute, sir,' she answered, then waited for my response.

(One promise. I asked for one promise from you and—)

'Ms Bryant Bell?'

'I didn't let Richard have her until he was clean. She didn't
go stay with him until . . .'

'But he still had a temper, didn't he?'

'Not with Lillie. I mean, not with us, Lillie loves – she loved
him. And I'm sure she's told you what a good father he was.'

'Is that why you were seen in the hallway, that night, arguing
with Mr Bryant about your daughter? He asked Lillie to lie to
you, didn't he? That's what a waitress overheard.'

Of course that argument had been reported. *Of course.*

'And your daughter confirmed it. Do you know where she was
that night?'

'He's a good father. Something came up – a premiere and—'

'She was sitting in a movie theatre, killing time, Ms Bryant Bell.
Not at a premiere or whatever excuse your ex-husband concocted.
You know, Lillie says she actually wanted to attend the party, but
your ex-husband wouldn't let her. Why? I'm not sure. You tell me
why he didn't want her there. What did he want to hide from her?
What might she have heard him saying to you, Ms Bryant Bell?'

'Lillie, the party – that was a misunderstanding.'

'Didn't sound like a misunderstanding to that waitress.'

'Officer.' Scott said. 'Half an hour—'

'He's a good father,' I repeated.

'Oh, I'm not querying his fathering skills, Ms Bryant Bell. I'm just trying to understand *your* relationship with him.'

'Lillie will tell you, he . . .'

The policewoman was not convinced.

I raised my voice. 'I told you the truth. I'm not going to go over this again. Richard was the best husband I could have asked for and a wonderful father to our daughter.'

'Elspeth—'

'No more questions.' Scott stood up, slammed his briefcase on the table. 'My client will not answer any more questions on this matter.'

I had always believed that the next person would be stronger.

And, I reasoned, I left eventually, I escaped finally, despite my weakness. Surely this could not happen again – Richard had changed, Richard was different, Richard was clean – and if it did, nobody else would stay as long as I had. I had stayed for Lillie. I had stayed because I was weak.

Really, it was easier to not think about it at all. I lived on the other side of the country, in comfortable denial. The settlement was swift and generous – with the release of *One Hundred Years*, Richard and his studio were desperate to quell the gossip. It was worth it, he and his lawyers decided, to ensure my mouth stayed shut. They never said that explicitly, but Scott pointed out the clause in the divorce papers. Something about discretion, about avoiding publicity that could negatively affect his takings.

I would not have told, regardless. I could not imagine Lillie growing up, knowing the things that had happened to me. The things that I had worked so hard to keep hidden from her, within the walls of her childhood home. My cowardice, my weakness. And it was still there – the fear. Richard could discredit me, I knew he would: rewrite my words, change their meaning, use them to take my daughter.

I chose a new life, instead, for Lillie and me.

I had enough from the sale of our family house to put down a deposit on a small, Upper East Side apartment. With the leftovers and pay from my early films, I started my investments. Richard wanted to fund Lillie's education, agreed to monthly child support. She made friends; we organised play dates. I went for coffee with the kids' mothers; I joined committees and boards of trustees, organised charity galas and bake sales. With my therapist, I talked over the stresses of playground politics and my strained relationship with my parents, and that was enough. It felt healthy. Everything ran perfectly. Every moment burst with tasks and functions.

When I awoke in the middle of the night – sweating, anxious, gasping for breath – I could tell myself it was a nightmare.

When Lillie visited Richard, I could listen to her voice chirping down the phone line and believe that she was with a different man. Not my ex-husband but her father. And he did care about her, she was safe – in both of those facts I had full faith.

And when Lillie told me about Honey, that he was Richard's new boyfriend, that he seemed nice, she didn't know him well, but yes, the relationship was getting serious and yes, it looked like it might last, I began to scour the internet for pictures of them together, and I found the gleeful, gossipy reports stretching back to their first public appearance – of course the bloggers and journalists had a field day with that one – and it was foolish, I know, I was a fool, but I could reassure myself: Honey looked too strong, they looked too happy, for any of that to happen again. Would I have reached out to Richard's partner if he had been dating a woman? Or would I have made excuses, regardless? If there was another voice inside my head, telling me to say something before it was too late, guilting me towards action, that voice could be drowned out with schedules and appointments. Barre on Wednesdays, Pilates on Thursdays, followed by lunch with Gloria afterwards. Hair with Eduardo on the first Tuesday of the month. Board meetings on the second Saturday.

As Lillie grew older, I even began to enjoy her coast-to-coast trips as time to myself. I met Julian. We were spending long weeks in St Barts eating fresh fruit and grilled fish. He tucked my hair behind my ears every time he bent down for a kiss. He rested his head upon my shoulder. When I woke up in the night, our ankles were locked together and he pressed, warm, against me.

And then Lillie left, and I was not sure that Julian could be enough.

He was not enough when I saw the allegations. Then his warmth beside me, in the middle of the night, was a weight. His gentle concern was a needling dig. There were lies in our silences.

It was easier to face Lillie alone, when she was outraged and asking me:

'Why would Honey say those things? Dad's not like that, is he? Dad wouldn't do those things, would he?'

And I saw the blotchy pink skin and the tears in her eyes, which she had tried to hide from me, and the bravery in her chin betrayed by the fear in her voice, and the way she looked hopeful, nonetheless, and what could I say but:

'Of course not, sweetie.'

And then it became:

'Dad never did any of those things to you, did he? You would know, if he was like that, wouldn't you?'

And how could I reply, except with:

'Of course he didn't. Of course I would know.'

And then the questions became requests and biting my tongue became lying.

And silence was writing a statement.

The female cop snapped her notebook shut, bringing me back to the room. I blinked several times, trying to recall the words that had just fallen from my mouth but they had disappeared. The afternoon was already fading.

'Okay, well,' she said, standing, 'I guess that concludes our questioning.'

Was her skin paler, eye bags deeper, than that first day we had

met? She looked down at me, silent, for a moment, then added:
'And if there's anything – if you change your mind or you
remember something, you have our number.'

'Thank you, Officer,' said Scott, back to his breezy charm,
though she had been speaking to me. For the first time in the
investigation, I felt like I was the one with the power. There was
a helplessness in her forehead furrows, a desperation.

The male detective sniffed loudly.

She went on, back to business: 'If you could, however, remain
in the state while we continue our investigation, that would be
very much appreciated. As your attorney will confirm, this is in
your best interest.'

After everyone had gathered their belongings, we all walked
to the entrance of the station together, through the ringing phones
and shamefaced pickpockets. Both officers shook hands with
Scott, and me, each in turn, and so the four shakes were
completed in an odd and seemingly choreographed fashion. I
noticed, exiting, that there were stars embedded in the sidewalk.
Each featured the name of a police officer, their date of birth
and death. I wondered whether, walking into work each day, the
female detective felt proud to see her fallen colleagues honoured
– or whether she loathed the reminder of her mortality, how
close her occupation took her to it every single shift. I would
have felt as though I were striding over my own grave. I would
have taken the back entrance.

How odd that I had not noticed these stars before. Perhaps I
had always been too focused on the impending interrogations, on
settling the facts in my mind. Often – not just on my way to the
sessions, but while brushing my hair or washing my face – I had
run over the sequence of events. I had repeated my chosen wording
until it was firmly imprinted. And then I could find strength in
those sentences, because I knew them. Recitation was easy enough.

Nobody else came, only us.

We hadn't talked. I don't know him.

*Then the others were waking and I had to tell them what had
happened – that Richard had overdosed in the night.*

He was the best husband I could have asked for.

Unlocking my car door, running over those lines in my head, it occurred to me that I would never repeat them. I would not return. I sat in the driver's seat for a few moments to enjoy this realisation – but it didn't come with elation or even unburdening. It was quite unreal.

I started the engine.

With a low fog drifting, the gargoyle resembled a frozen sailor, hanging from the crow's nest. Only a few seconds later did it make sense, as the plumes dispersed and we plunged to street level, the pigeons of Notre-Dame taking flight.

'It's beautiful,' I said, because it was: the pinks and orange, an early-morning opal.

'Thanks.' Kei smiled, the colours of the projection reflected in the corners of her teeth. 'Although I always say establishing shots are the easiest. There's something inherently beautiful about landscapes, cityscapes, empty rooms. But when you can make humans beautiful, compose the bodies and the busyness – that's true genius. Space is cowardice.'

'Is that what you think about when you work – beauty?'

– and whether or not –

'Depends,' Kei said through a mouthful of popcorn. 'Mostly I like to tell stories.'

– we knew it was over –

The dialogue from *Dominus* rose and fell around us. I'd walked into the room late and only caught the end of the scene in which Lillie appeared. For those five minutes, that one line, I stood at the back of the room, transfixed. I'd seen her act in countless school productions, at drama camp, in the little shows she put on during her play dates, shunting aside my coffee table and rolling up the rug. But this was different: she wasn't herself. She was a young woman, a college student, wearing spectacles, a thick, knitted pullover, and an expression – of concern? of curiosity? – that I'd never seen before.

And then Lillie was gone, and I sat next to Kei, struck up

conversation. I didn't care about the rest of the movie. It would spoil my DVD watch.

  – there was nothing we could do.

'How about you?' she said. 'You seem to have abandoned the other side of the camera.'

'It wasn't for me,' I said.

'Dude, are you fucking kidding? I used to love your work.'

I couldn't help but laugh.

'Seriously, you were phenomenal. You were fucking beautiful.'

Someone handed me a smouldering spliff – I passed it on to Kei.

'Thank you, that's kind,' I said. 'But is it the vodka talking? I was only ever in trash.'

'Don't talk yourself down. *The Anatomy of Inquiry* used to be my favourite film of all time. A masterpiece. I still remember that scene where—'

'Okay, *Anatomy* won awards. The others were terrible though.'

Kei let the smoke escape slowly from her open mouth. Her jaw clicked as it shut.

'I know how it is though.' She inhaled again, keeping the smoke inside her as she spoke the next sentence in a strained, nose-blocked voice: 'You've got to get your face out there, gotta get paid.'

Will you be there tomorrow?

'But you seemed like you were going somewhere, when you gave it up.'

'Maybe.' I rested my head back on the couch, looked up at the vaulted ceiling.

Kei giggled.

'And I know that. I was, like, your biggest fan.'

'Come on . . .'

'No, I was.' Kei passed the joint to Jerry and then rested her head next to mine. 'Cassandra DiSotta, what a fucking character. She was my awakening. She was fucking mesmerising.'

'Now you're making me feel old.'

'Did you always want it?'

I said, don't touch me.

Don't fucking touch—

I had heard Kei's voice but missed the question, distracted by the action unfolding on screen. 'Sorry?'

'The acting, was it what you wanted? Was that your dream career?'

I frowned.

'I don't know. Maybe at one point it might have been, but . . .' I began to say, before starting again. 'It's difficult to remember because it all just happened. I mean, I was very fortunate, but it happened, and then . . . then it became something I didn't want any more, so . . .'

You can't leave, not now.

'And now?' she asked, innocently. Jerry was snoring. His head was falling, falling slowly – he jerked it back up. It started to fall again.

'I'm happy,' I said.

'But what's your dream? What do you picture when you're lying in bed at night?' She caught my smirk. 'No, not like that . . . Like, when I'm lying in bed at night – and this is stupid, I know – but when I'm lying in bed I envisage all the recognition I might get. You know, I don't think I crave the money, and when I say recognition, it's not even that I want awards. I just want people to recognise that I'm good at what I do and that I have something to say. I want people to value my point of view. And maybe then I'll have space to work on things that are just for me.'

We watched the screen.

When Camille left, I was ready to kill myself. I locked my door and I just sat there with my pills, thinking about everything that had happened, everything that she had said. But when the glow of the street lamp hit the curtains, I realised I had made it through the day—

'You're a storyteller,' I told her.

Flake white: lead. Minium: red lead. Realgar: a ruby of arsenic

sulphide. Cadmium red, orange, yellow, green . . . Paris green: copper
acetate and arsenic trioxide. I had been reciting pigment names to
myself, all day. Every poison I could list more splendid, more beau-
tiful, more glorious than the amber prescription bottle that I held in
my fist.

'Yes, I'm a storyteller.' The screen blacked out. We were in
darkness for a moment. Then we cut to another scene. It reflected
in Kei's smile again, but this was a different palette – inky purples,
deep blues and pastel greens. Smears of paint on a canvas. 'But
seriously though, tell me. I can't figure you out.'

I lay my head back again and closed my eyes.

'Perhaps I don't have dreams like that any more. I get by each
day and . . . I don't know. I don't know anything. I can't think
about myself like that.'

'Something tells me that's not true,' Kei said. 'You don't seem
like someone without hope or passion.'

I couldn't think of a response. Thankfully we were interrupted
by a shriek from the other couch.

'It's coming, it's coming,' shouted Charlie, leaping up. 'Where's
Sabine? Sabine!'

Jerry woke up, rubbed his eyes.

Kei murmured to me: 'Now there's someone with hope. Weren't
you ever a Charlie? Weren't you ever hungry like him?'

I sat up to find his face on the screen. His top lip quivered;
his expression was pained. It was a tight shot, so close the screen
cut through his chin. We could see each individual hair in his
stubble, a grey vein beneath his eye. Saliva coated his lips. Sweat
trickled.

'I wanted it,' I whispered, 'yes, but not like that. I was never
that—'

'Desperate?' Kei offered.

Why weren't—

'—you there?' Charlie said along with his character.

'Not that desperate,' I told Kei. 'Like I said, I was very fortunate.'

'I told you I wouldn't be,' Sabine answered, cold, from the
screen, from the door. She walked towards Charlie, dragging each

foot behind her – perfectly synchronised with the figure overhead. 'And I thought I told you not to expect the impossible from me. Remember, you'll only disappoint yourself.'

'I don't think you could ever disappoint me.'

Sabine laughed with her image on the screen. Then paused. Raised an eyebrow. 'And what about you? Are you going to fail me?'

'You know I can't give an answer to that. I could tell you the chemical formula of lapis lazuli. I could bring you ancient Egyptian glass and ruins from Pompeii. I could make you a liquid gold. But predict our future? No, that would be impossible.' Charlie took Sabine into his arms, swung her body low, almost to the floor. His character overhead was walking towards hers. Placed a finger over her lips. 'And if you expect that from me, you'll only disappoint yourself.'

As his character kissed her on screen, he bent his real-world head close to hers. She shut her eyes, expectant. The room watched. His lips moved closer.

Then he had dropped her on the floor, and was walking away with his middle finger raised.

'*Branleur!* You . . . you son of a bastard,' she shouted, and pushed herself up to chase him out of the room. '*Je te chie dans le cou! Je te pisse à la raie!*'

Jerry clapped his hands with delight.

'Richard's talent never lay in writing,' Kei whispered in my ear. Richard was sitting on the other couch, Honey's head in his lap, smoking a cigar. His eyes followed the whooping actors, his free hand played with Honey's top button. 'But it's fucking impossible to refuse him.'

★

The sunlight stretched, golden and buttery; it was getting late. As I climbed farther above the city in my rented car, the houses grew scarcer, the white walls gave way to dry grass and ferns. I passed tourists posing for photographs and dog-walkers and dogs.

Hikers marched in Day-Glo sneakers, pumped their arms, stretched their muscles.

I knew why I did not feel elated, despite the end to my interrogation. Every subject my mind turned to was a nest of thorns, waiting to snag, to scratch and ensnare. There were the painful memories that the police had dredged up: my marriage to Richard, the lies I had told; the part I had played in preventing a young man from making his escape. There were all of my suspicions raised during the investigation, and then there was the knowledge of what I was returning to: Lillie's questions about Honey, my inability to answer.

I could see Honey lying unconscious that night. I had seen it. I had been so sure I had seen it when I told the police. But how could I ignore my unease about him?

When Lillie had asked for one good reason not to trust Honey, there was nothing I could say. How could I confess my lie? And even then, even considering everything I knew about Richard, I wasn't certain that Honey should be suspected. I had been thinking about it all week, in the run-up to my final interrogation session, on Monday. And there were no conclusions. Honey unconscious; the press allegations.

Maybe, I told myself, my unease was just jealousy – that Lillie had chosen Honey, not me, to heal with, confide in. Lillie had kept her relationship with him secret all these years; she had known it would hurt. And it did. It felt like a betrayal: to find out they were close. To have learned that over the past two weeks he had visited multiple times, that she had lied to me – or at least, omitted to mention those visits – multiple times. I could not deny that hurt. And there was guilt, and there was shame, because I had been the one to break them apart. I had lied to Lillie when she asked me about the allegations; I had let her side with a monster. Now this was my punishment: their closeness, my helplessness.

Or maybe this wasn't the origin of my unease. Maybe it was instinct – that something wasn't quite right. I didn't know. How could I forget that Honey, far more than any other guest, had reason to wish Richard dead?

Yet Honey was also the guest who loved Richard the most. And there lay the paradox that could not be ignored. Richard was central to each of our lives and we to his. We probably all had reason to wish Richard dead or gone, just as we all had reason to love him, to want him alive. This was the maddening thought: that if only I could view each guest's love for Richard from the correct angle, the killer's motive would be blindingly obvious.

I felt no closer to understanding than I had been that morning when I found my ex-husband's body, touched my fingers to his cold neck.

My time in LA had begun with a terrible, brutal event. Instead of escaping, I had fallen deeper into chaos. I had been forced to face my dishonesty and I had lied again. I had spent time with my daughter, but she was further from me than she had ever been. I had researched my fellow guests, but this had only led to more questions, to knowledge of my own ignorance.

Everything was futile.

And so, as I drove back to Lillie's, I tried to escape myself. I sped over the crests of the hills. I turned the music up until I couldn't think. I put the roof down so my hair would whip my face. The wind was growing stronger but the air was thick with heat, and so it caressed my bare arms like a bed sheet. Each twist of the road brought a new view and I was climbing higher and there were no more houses – just the sloping rock and dust to one side, far distance on the other.

'Seriously, man – she's been creeping around that corner for the last half-hour,' said Charlie, not taking his eyes from the tank.

'I'm telling you, honestly, she won't escape,' Honey said, stretching out on his back in front of the couch. 'She knows we're still here.'

'She knows we're here, *she knows we're here* – and that's supposed to calm me down?'

The ashtrays were stale, the lights low.

'You're fucking paranoid. Eat something,' said Kei, throwing a bag of chips at Charlie.

It smashed into his chest. Miguel, sitting next to him, woke up, blinked around for a few seconds, then let his head fall back again.

'If we were all still,' Charlie said, 'would she try to escape? Like if we were all asleep?'

Honey thought for a few moments. The music – now a murmur of Ellington – played in his silence. Kei lit a cigarette, perched on the arm of the couch. One leg was cocked – her elbow rested on it, rakish.

'Maybe,' said Honey. 'I don't know how well she can see – I don't know if she can track our movements and position and shit.'

'Fuck,' Charlie said.

Kei walked over to him, took the chips, opened the bag and waved it in his face.

'Eat something.'

Charlie obeyed her order and began mechanically pushing handfuls into his mouth, crunching them to pulp.

'She can't stay outside the tank for long, though.' Honey yawned and stretched his arms, then folded them under his head. His shirt had come untucked – a slip of his stomach visible. 'Needs water to breathe.'

'But, hypothetically, couldn't she, like, keep poking her tentacles in water or something?' Kei said, taking a drag. 'Hop from glass to glass?'

'She can't stay outside the tank for long,' I said. 'They're just full of alcohol.'

'True.'

I was sitting next to a snoozing Jerry, on the couch in front of the aquarium. I stood so I could observe the creature. Charlie was right: Persephone was propelling herself towards the corner and then back again, like a wildcat pacing its cage. It was an unnerving sight. As she pushed herself forwards, her tentacles trailed straight lines behind; she glided over the rock bed like a phantom.

'Besides, she breathes through another part of her body,' Honey was saying. 'Gills or whatever.'

Persephone came to a crawling halt in the filter-flap corner. Her tentacles lifted and snaked. I walked towards her and, as I neared, saw that she was stroking and circling, with two free limbs, the rock that concealed her escape.

'I wonder if she could get further if it was raining,' said Kei. 'Unlucky fuck to end up here.'

I pulled my gaze away from the beast – Tommo had materialised on the other side of the glass. His shirt was half untucked, in one hand was a bottle of champagne, and he was propping himself up on the tank. I joined him. The creature flinched with my movement.

'Of course,' he muttered. 'Of course he wanted to own her.'

She crawled closer, as close as she could get. We watched her and she watched us.

'Why?' I asked. 'What do you mean?'

Tommo looked at me. 'Why do *you* think he wanted to own her?'

'Because she's beautiful? I don't know. Ostentatious? Exotic?'

'Yes,' Tommo said. 'He *loves* to own *lovely* things. But that's not it . . .'

He looked at her through the glass. He seemed to be lost in thought.

'What is it, then?' I prompted.

'He wanted her because she's intelligent and dangerous, and it wouldn't feel thrilling otherwise.' He said it loudly, with a wave of his hand, like I was being dense. 'To look at her trapped like this,' he gestured, 'every day. He can look at her and know he's conquered. And it's not as fun to win over someone less capable. That's all he cares about, Elspeth.' Tommo tapped the tank. 'Winning.'

I didn't completely agree with this analysis yet couldn't be bothered to challenge it.

'Do you think she's lonely?' I asked.

But Tommo was already stumbling away, still talking to himself.

I placed my hand on the aquarium, before the swaying tentacles. Her red-ringed eyes closed. A slip of glass between my forefinger and her suction cups, squashed flat and tight to the tank. It was her hideousness, I thought, that made the creature so beautiful.

When I recalled these late, late-night scenes, as I did many times throughout the investigation, Richard was entirely absent. Kei and I continued talking as she rolled and smoked her cigarettes; Jerry and Miguel were snoring; eventually the films ended and the projector glared blue light. Sabine and Honey whispered in the corner; Charlie stared into the middle distance, with peeled-white eyes. Persephone watched us from her rocky lair. Tommo stumbled in and out, muttering to himself – picking up open champagne bottles by the neck and taking them outside, where he sat on the wall, drinking alone.

I could account for everyone but Richard in those quiet hours past midnight. Was it that my muddled brain had erased him from the record? Perhaps he had simply been silent or elsewhere. Perhaps I was incorrectly placing all of us together in the atrium at the same time.

With each interrogation session, I had strained to recall the slightest scrap of memory. I didn't think Richard and I had spoken again, alone, after the conversation on the mezzanine where he had thanked me and I had backed away. This seemed odd. There were only nine of us at Sedgwick that night and the conversations I could recall surely didn't amount to the hours I'd spent at the party. Maybe dancing whiled the night away – more likely, conversations were lost to glasses and shots.

But I did remember the last thing he told me.

It must have been two or three in the morning, when Richard returned from wherever he'd been. We had hauled a wading pool up from the cellar. After Sabine's incessant whines about swimming, Richard suggested someone venture down and take a look. One could have travelled, he said, from house to house, a relic of our daughter's childhood. Lo, there it was: dust and grime, held aloft by victorious Charlie and Sabine. Jerry and Miguel woke up with the cheers.

The unexpected treasure drew us all into the game. We were kids again: brushing off cobwebs and stretching out the inflatable on the atrium floor. The men took turns blowing it up by lung. It was Sabine's idea to fill it warm; we sloshed stove-boiled pots from the kitchen, back and forth like ants. Kei squirted in dish detergent.

We slipped into the lukewarm foam, fully clothed. Tommo had fetched chilled champagne and we were drinking it from the bottle, not caring when it splashed into the sudsy water. My chiffon blouse ballooned beneath the surface. I remember catching myself staring at it, tumbling, furling.

'We were never well suited, were we, Ellie darling?'

I looked up. Richard had shifted himself beside me. His shirt was undone to the sternum; his hair in wet, boyish curls. I could not think of a reply – no sentence could do justice to our relationship, the pain that lay at the heart of it. And so I didn't answer. My gaze returned to the water; I drifted my hand through the bubbles, each a globe of its own. Richard pinched my chin, lightly, between crooked forefinger and thumb, lifted my face back to him.

Was it the unexpectedness of this gesture, the presence of the others, or old fears that kept me from throwing him off?

(No, your chin, upwards.)

(Like this.)

'You needed someone who—'

'Loved me?' I said.

(Can you feel that? Good girl.)

'Poor darling.' Richard stroked his thumb against my skin.

I veered around the last bend in the road before Lillie's house, and the memories were still with me. How Richard's thumb pressed into my chin; the tumble of my blouse beneath the water. The murderer must have been there, in that lukewarm pool, as we laughed and drank and splashed each other. Was it planned?

Had they known, sitting there, of the crime they would be commit-
ting only a few hours later? Or had they acted on a violent
impulse?

Lillie was not in the house. Was she seeing Honey? I almost
didn't want to know. It was too much to contemplate.

I poured myself a glass of wine. Found the computer.

I scrolled down. There was a new video in the search results:
a British documentary. A fisherman lowered a trap into the ocean:
a cylindrical wire cage with a small opening that crabs could
crawl through. Once inside, escape was impossible for the crus-
taceans, with their under-developed brains. The camera cut to
another part of the ocean: a rocky nook where a giant Pacific
resided. It crawled out, then thrust itself forwards. The octopus
had found the cage.

The creature couldn't reach the crabs through the wire – the
only way to get to them was to enter the trap. It slipped through
easily enough, smashed the crab shells, and devoured them in
seconds. But then it was stuck. The fisherman was hauling up
the trap. The octopus felt around with its arms, trying to understand the shape of the wire cage. The trap was almost at the
surface of the sea.

And then the creature found the opening – escaped seconds
before the fisherman reached the trap. Only two crab shells and
some shards were rattling inside as he lifted it from the water.

I finished my wine. Poured another glass. Waited for the next
video to play itself. It was another clip from the same BBC show.
This time, not a giant Pacific octopus, but a small, brown one,
with polyp-covered, almost leathery skin.

It was resting underwater, and then the camera cut to the land
and I could see: the octopus was in a tide pool. One arm, now
mucous in the air, slithered out of the water. Then another, and
another. The creature was slipping over the rocks, from pool to
pool, in search of a meal. It was disturbing: the slicking, mushing
sound; how the limbs slid, almost fell over one another, like a
bag of wet meat, like entrails.

When the hunter found a crab, the kill was instant. There was a close-up of the octopus's face as the crab shell crunched. It did not blink. The face was unmoving as it slaughtered.

I searched for a phrase: *How far can octopuses crawl on land?*

It was ridiculous, and yet I could not stop thinking: my arm had been wet that morning. A puddle on the floor. The little brown octopus in the documentary had roamed far, because it could use each rocky pool as a human might use pockets of air when trapped in an underwater cave. Had Richard been the one to suggest the pool, knowing that Persephone could use it to walk on land?

I closed my computer. Stood up to rinse my glass. I was being ridiculous. I was exhausted, anxious. I had resolved to put aside my octopus suspicions.

There was something about this wild theory that made perfect sense. If Richard had killed himself in such a spectacular manner then his would be one of the most famous deaths of all time; it would write ten thousand headlines, launch one million tweets. His films would be watched across the globe, would become cult classics even if they later faded to obscurity. It would be redemption, a saving grace from the gossip surrounding *Dominus*.

Could Richard do something so selfish to his daughter? Could he so single-mindedly obsess over his own reputation? Would he value legacy over life?

A phone rang, shrill, somewhere else in the house. Lillie had a landline? Instinctively, I followed the sound, and there it was, in the hallway, by the shoes. I had not registered its existence before – it had been silent all this time. Its ringing seemed absurd, misplaced. I stood there, staring at it, knowing I shouldn't answer but unable to ignore its cries.

Then the answering machine kicked in – the automated message, the beep.

'Lillie' – I knew the voice – 'I hope you received my flowers. You know, I understand if you're not ready to talk to anyone and I'm sorry for your loss, I am, but, listen, I'm calling for your mother, so if you could—'

I picked up the handset.

'Hello?' Miguel said. 'Is someone there?'

'How dare you.' My voice was too quiet – I was trying to catch my breath.

'Elspeth? Is that you?'

'How dare you,' I said, stronger now, 'call my daughter in the middle of the investigation into her father's *murder*. You people. How dare you. Can't you leave her alone?'

'Elspeth, I was just calling to get hold of your number,' he said, smooth. 'I wanted to check in and see how you were doing—'

'I was doing fine before you called.'

'—and I'm sorry for not calling sooner; my lawyers thought it wasn't the best idea. But who's gonna know, it's just a phone call, right? And I was sitting here with a bourbon, thinking of you, because this friend of mine, Brian, was telling me about this neat little rom-com project he's picked up. And he mentioned this role for the mother of the lead and, you know, immediately I thought of you. Immediately.'

'What do you want, Miguel?'

'Elspeth, please.' I could see him, leaning back in his chair, drink in hand. 'I'm calling as a friend. We're friends, aren't we? We were getting friendly that night, remember? I was telling you it might be time for you to get back to work, so maybe my assistant could set up a meeting and—'

'I don't think that would be appropriate.'

'Okay, okay, I understand, another time. But that's not the only reason I'm calling – you know, I get concerned, Elspeth, when I think of you girls all alone in that little house on Cahuenga.'

Panic seized me. My eyes flitted to the door.

'Are you threatening me?' I was gripping the phone.

'Threatening you?' He sounded genuinely taken aback. 'God no, Elspeth, please, I—'

'Good. Because I'm an inch away from hanging up and calling the cops.'

'Elspeth, let's, let's calm down.' Miguel laughed uneasily. 'Come on, it's me, I just wanted to see how you were doing.'

'Like I said, I *was* doing fine.'

'Well, okay. Okay then, but you know you can call me anytime.'

His sweetness was nauseating. I imagined him leaning closer, closer. 'If you're worried about anything, if you wanted to talk over the investigation or, or, you know, anything you remember from that night, you give me a call, okay? I'm always here for you.'

'If I did want to discuss anything,' I said, 'I would do so with my lawyer or my therapist, not another suspect. I suggest you do the same.'

'But, Elspeth, there are things I could tell you,' he said too quickly, dropping his faux concern. 'There are things you should know. Some people can't be trusted and if you—'

I hung up the phone.

'I think we should remove our clothes – it's rude to be fully dressed in the presence of the moon.'

'Sabine, babe, we'd all take off our clothes if we looked as good as you,' said Kei. 'Trust me, I'd be prancing through the fucking Getty in my birthday suit if I had your body. It's a goddamn work of art.'

'Keiko,' giggled Sabine.

'It's not quite an Icelandic hot spring, is it?' said Tommo as he slipped in. 'I thought it would be warmer. Champagne, anyone?'

'Me first, me first.' Charlie took the bottle and slugged it down.

'What is this "birthday suit" anyway?' asked Sabine. 'It is this?' She gestured at Richard's stomach. 'Is this the birthday suit?'

'Now, that would never make it into a gallery,' said Miguel, cackling hoarsely to himself.

Charlie belched.

'Hey, don't be so rude,' said Jerry. 'It's the quintessential Lucian Freud.'

He choked as Richard splashed his face.

'You bastard,' he shouted, kicking back.

'*Fils de pute*.' Sabine, collateral damage, swept a wave towards him. And then we were all kicking and splashing as hard as we could.

'Mind the bottle, mind the bottle,' Tommo cried over the commotion.

'Don't think you'll escape so easily,' said Richard, throwing water in his schoolfriend's face.

The splashes calmed to giggles, and we were resting our heads on the inflated walls, catching our breath.

'You got a little something on your face,' said Jerry, blowing a handful of bubbles as I looked down at my nose.

I laughed. Wiped the suds from my eyes. 'You better not have ruined my mascara.'

'Wow,' said Jerry. 'It can laugh. It can actually enjoy itself.'

'Oh, I do enjoy myself,' I answered. 'But maybe this *is* the first time I've ever laughed at one of *your* jokes.'

'Touché.'

'Hear, hear,' said Tommo, holding the bottle to my mouth. 'To Jerry's shitty humour.'

Our legs were piled in the centre of the pool; we passed the bottle around until our fingers grew wrinkly. I turned to find Richard gazing at me.

Wresting the bottle from Charlie, he took a deep swig, never shifting his eyes from mine. 'To two orphans on the run, Ellie darling. And our perfectly imperfect fit.'

What could I say to that? He put the bottle to my lips. I drank deeply.

Honey watched us, silent, from the other side of the pool.

ACT II

I re-entered the shadow of the concrete mausoleum with Lillie at my side. My black skirt soaked the sun as we walked from car to door – it was a bright day, as it had been on my first visit. But against this afternoon sky the structure seemed less harsh, more forgiving than before. We rang the doorbell. Waited in silence. This time I did not adjust my clothes.

Honey answered the door, and Lillie fell into his embrace.

I stood behind, cheeks burning, awkwardly enduring the moment. He nodded at me over her shoulder. I smiled a paltry smile.

Then Honey held Lillie at arm's length and said: 'You'll make him proud, I know it.'

She took a deep breath. We entered.

And Sedgwick: just as I remembered. The confusion of the slotting levels, the dazzling light and spacious glass. Black-clad ankles peeked from the gaps between adjacent and higher floors. Strappy Jimmy Choos and polished British brogues: guests were exploring Sedgwick, as I had the night of the party. These signs of life only underlined the clinical precision of the architecture – movement exaggerating the still.

Lillie and Honey linked at the elbow, fell into step. I walked behind, silent.

Over the past few weeks, Lillie and I had ground to a silent impasse over Honey. There was no way I could prove, even to myself, whether he was or wasn't guilty. And so I didn't, couldn't, prevent her from organising the memorial with him. Partly, that memory of him lying unconscious reassured me: how could he have done it? But there was another, overwhelming consideration:

Lillie would never forgive me if I stopped her from playing a role in Richard's memorial, especially if Honey's innocence was later proven.

Give me one good reason, she had said that day. Did I have a reason to suspect Honey?

All I could say was: 'I have a feeling.'

Lillie had looked disappointed. Not because she'd hoped that I did have a reason, but because she'd hoped I was better than that. Better than feelings and accusations and baseless suspicions.

As I watched them walk ahead of me, I wasn't sure what that feeling was. It was fear, yes, but was it rooted in jealousy? Was it fear of a murderer or fear of my daughter finding someone else?

The truth was unavoidable: Honey brought something out in her that I could not. I watched them pause ahead of me. He reached down to collect an eyelash from her cheek, and Lillie shut her eyes to make a wish. Blew it from his fingertips as naturally as if they had grown up together. Observing them like this, I knew that even Lillie's admission of their friendship had been understated to spare my feelings.

Before Dad and Honey broke up, we were pretty close, she had said. Pretty close, very close, closer than she and I. Honey said something I couldn't quite hear and she laughed – she laughed with him, even on a day like today.

It raised the hairs on my arms – because he was a murderer, or because he was, simply, someone else?

Event planning had taken up so much of Lillie's time over the past few weeks, I had barely seen her. There were endless phone calls, meetings with Honey. When she emerged from her room she was always speaking into her phone screen, white wires leaking from her ears. I knew she had a lot to arrange, and it was good for her – to have something that she could focus upon, throw herself into wholeheartedly, something to drown out everything else. But I also wondered if she was avoiding me. Every time I saw her I remembered that disappointed look.

I let Lillie and Honey pace ahead, lingering behind to ready myself for the next act in the interior's three-act drama. They vanished around the corner. And then I was alone with the aquarium.

My stomach tumbled as I approached it, though I knew Persephone would not be visible. She would be crawling across the rocks, one floor beneath me. But even the notion of the water, lapping against the glass of the tank, was enough to churn my insides.

I had been dreading the memorial, almost physically, violently. Not just because Richard's notes for the event seemed almost engineered to give him a hold over our daughter, one final attempt to tug her from me – but because the thought of the birthday guests reconvening at Sedgwick was unbearable. I relived the party each night, feverish, as I drifted off on Lillie's couch in the blue light of the laptop. The red-ringed eyes: knowing, watching. The faces of the other guests, one by one. There I was, in the dreams, a distant spectator, but also there, lying on the floor, there at Richard's feet – sleeping oblivious to the silent slaughter.

The police had made no arrests; I had heard nothing since my last questioning. A few times, catching Lillie in her hallway, I'd asked whether the detectives had been in touch, whether there was any progress. She told me nothing had happened, and each time she'd looked so increasingly despairing, I had stopped asking. It wasn't fair to remind her.

Both of us were all too aware of what this meant: that the murderer would be at Sedgwick today too. Lillie couldn't have disinvited any one from his last night, not when they featured at the top of Richard's 'In the Unlikely Event' guest list. I worried about how she would handle this, amid the pressure of hosting. But when I'd raised it on the drive over, she brushed off my concern.

'I can't talk about that now,' she'd said. 'I need to run over the speech again.'

Then she put her earbuds back in – she'd always learned lines like this. Recorded herself reading them aloud, played them back, paused after each sentence, repeated each word. At home, in the run-up to school productions, I'd catch her in the kitchen having a conversation with her character.

And so I let her mutter the speech, undisturbed. Concentrated on the road. I was nervous about seeing the other guests myself. All the unknowns. Would we even talk to one another?

Miguel had not called Lillie's landline again. After hanging up on him, I'd listened to our conversation, recorded on the answering machine, before deleting it. My voice sounded cold and defensive. Too cold, I thought, upon hearing it again. There had been no threat in Miguel's voice – just a bourbon slur. He'd probably mentioned Lillie's address without thinking. He'd probably called because he was lonely, or scared – or wanted to compare thoughts on the investigation. And maybe I would have been more curious had he not caught me as my mind ran wild with images of Richard's death, the octopus hunting, the crunch of shell.

Regardless, whatever Miguel had been trying to do, whatever he'd tried to tell me, I didn't regret warning him away. It was best to keep my distance. I didn't know him; I couldn't trust him.

I hadn't heard from any other guests. Not even Jerry, Tommo. I was certain now that we'd all received the same legal advice: stay far from the others. But maybe we would have to talk to one another at this event – maybe avoidance would be more unnatural, raise more suspicion. I told myself it would be an opportunity. I could look each of them in the eye. I could ask them directly about the things I had discovered during the interrogation.

I told myself this – but I was having a difficult time holding on to it. I was sick with the thought that the murderer would be there. That I might have to talk with them.

That they might be waiting beneath the water.

I slowed my steps, placed one foot in front of the other. Would I perceive the creature's guilt once it was floating right before me? Would it recognise me? As I greeted old acquaintances, would I be able to scrape the fevered scenes from my mind?

(The dark, grainy form in infrared: slipping from the filter, slipping across the floor, slipping between the lips.)

But the corridor was curiously light . . .

(The fingers, the eyes, the sharp stench of vomit.)

. . . and as I neared, I saw: the aqueous glow on the mezzanine had gone. Persephone's tank was now empty, a glass wall encasing air.

I stared into the depths of nothing. The light caught the slow-waltzing dust. I tucked my hair behind my ears, then I was ready to enter the atrium.

Girls huddled over my glass table with credit cards and plastic baggies. The bass pounded – waves of nausea. Too many people, not enough space, and I knew none of the guests in my own home.

How long did I have to stay before heading upstairs to sleep? Would Richard mind if I left before midnight? What time was the sitter returning Lillie tomorrow? Everywhere I turned, glimmering bodies bounced to the beat. I slipped off my heels and kicked them beneath a table.

Two emaciated girls were slumped against the wall beside me – one draped her arms around her friend's neck, the other was spitting out words as fast as she could, her pupils black-mooned.

'. . . andthenhetoldmethatitwasntwhathewantedbutIwaslike—'

'Mrs Bryant?'

The caterer was wringing a dish towel between her hands. Wisps of hair poked out of her hat, stuck to her face. She looked as wretched as I felt – I'd been drinking in the sun since late afternoon and my mind was sluggish, my skin burned pink.

'Mrs Bryant?' She raised her voice over the music. 'I know you wanted the cake at midnight, but none of us have seen Mr Bryant for a while, so we're wondering whether we should bring it out?'

I brushed the back of my hand across my forehead: sweat.

'Because we don't want to light the candles – if he's not around, I mean. Forty candles, well, that's a fire hazard if we let them burn. We want to make sure he'll be there to blow them out. And the cake's pretty heavy. It's a four-man job. Big cake, just like you asked. With the meringue and the cream and berries.'

I struggled to hold onto her words.

'Unless you've seen him recently?' The caterer flipped the towel over her shoulder and crossed her arms.

Had I seen Richard recently? The crowds were doubling in my vision after four martinis. The birthday boy had vanished into their masses.

'Your husband, Mrs Bryant,' shouted the caterer, slowly, 'do you know where he is?'

'No,' my tongue stumbled. 'I don't . . . I haven't seen him.'

A woman had climbed onto my table in Lucite platforms, thighs jiggling as she danced. She needed to get down from there: the glass would not hold.

'. . . and it's getting late. We only covered staff till midnight in the budget, but I don't want to ask the waiters to work overtime because they're getting tired and, well, it was all in the contract, Mrs Bryant. Till midnight, it said. We've cleared everything else away.'

A middle-aged man in tight white underwear joined the dancer, pumped his fists into the air. My table – where was Richard?

'That's what I'm asking you, Mrs Bryant.'

I tried to recall our conversation. 'The cake?'

'We'll just put it out for you with some plates and then get out of your hair. People can help themselves. No candles, but we'll leave them to the side in case your husband turns up and you want to put them in his slice or something.'

I smiled – this was an easy solution – and tried to thank the caterer, but she was already gone.

Something knocked into my elbow. My vision clouded with white feathers. A golden Adonis with great stretching wings was backing into me. I was hypnotised, mesmerised by this angelic sight – until he stood on my toes.

'Hey, you better watch yourself,' he called, bashing his feathers into my face when he turned. 'Can't see a fucking thing over these fucking things.'

His cigarette hung out of his mouth, burned up a long snake of ashes. I wanted to ask where he had materialised from – what he was doing in my house – but I was silenced by three events in quick succession:

First, the ashes dropped from his cigarette to the floor.

Second, there was an almighty crash of glass.

And then the girl beside me vomited over the wall. It splashed onto my white mini-dress in a deep, disgusting purple.

Jazz Rolling Stones covers floated over conversation; titters and clips of English accents cut through the noise. They were there in their hundreds: all those aunties and uncles and schoolfriends – second-rate copies of Tommo – that had attended our wedding, then faded back to their rainy isle. From the mezzanine, I tried to identify them. Their pallor and static were conspicuous amid bronze limbs and blowouts. I noticed expressions of disgust cross their faces as the musicians picked up tempo, and other guests began to dance. This was unlike any memorial service I had attended before, but it would be entirely alien for Richard's compatriots.

I imagined he had anticipated this reaction when including them on the guest list. It was so like Richard to curate an experience that would make people uncomfortable, thrust them into a new world, force intimacy upon strangers. All the bodies were packed in tight, spilling out to the lawn, the corridors, the crevices of the house.

Another mourner had joined me on the mezzanine, so I hung back to watch him descend. A young man in sunglasses, carrying a matte-black box tied with a thick white ribbon. Were we to bring gifts to this party? A few moments later, I watched him below, weaving his way to the far corner – and then I saw what he was heading towards.

A floral shrine, a tower of black boxes bursting with the delicate, the colourful, the blooming. I wondered whether this cornucopia had been detailed in Richard's notes and suggested in guests' invitations, or whether, simply, bouquets were obsolete in the industry these days. The young man removed his sunglasses.

It was Charlie, pink eyes and only half himself. He had shaved his head. He was gaunt, spectral. Was it guilt or grief that haunted him?

Charlie untied the ribbon, then lifted the lid. Nearly fifty white chrysanthemums were lined up inside. He removed a box at the front of the table, hid it on the floor. Then placed his own centre stage. Took the phone from his breast pocket. Snapped a picture. Moved swiftly on. Another mourner was approaching, with yet another box.

It was time to descend. As I picked my way down the spiral staircase, I heard an elderly Bryant enquire about the tank.

'Ah yes, the invisible exhibition,' Tommo replied. 'Richard wanted to display a cubic foot of air from every country he visited during filming.'

'How marvellous,' exclaimed the lady.

I giggled, in spite of myself.

'I've given different stories to each Aunt Edna,' he whispered, hugging me tight. 'I told one it was waiting for a Hirst and another that Richard wanted to display himself like Bentham.'

I laughed again, stopping when I noticed the surrounding English stares.

It was good to see an old friend. Something about Tommo – perhaps the familiarity of his smile, his earnest eyes – was unchanged by that night, untainted. He was tired, yes, a little harrowed, but still himself. Still Richard's Tommo. He couldn't have killed his best friend, could he? I watched his face for any nervousness, any hint of a lie.

'Do you think,' I said quietly, 'we should be talking?'

'More suspicious if we don't,' he muttered, 'but let's not dwell on the subject.' He thrust his hands into his pockets, raised his voice. 'So, here we are. It doesn't seem real, does it?'

'These things never do,' I answered.

'Naturally, a memorial organised by Dicky would have a surreal air to it,' he said. 'But some of these guests are quite incredible.'

'It's the party of the month.'

'And Dicky wouldn't have settled for anything less.' Tommo looked around. 'Lillie's giving a speech, then, is she?'

'It'll be lovely if her line-learning is anything to go by – she's been reciting it all week.'

'Good sport,' Tommo said, watching her. 'Like father, like daughter.'

Lillie and Honey were still together, moving from group to group like polite newlyweds. I saw the way Richard's lemon-lipped relatives recoiled as their darling's brazenly beautiful partner walked among them. Lillie rested her head on his shoulder every now and then, territorial.

I tried to quell my jealousy. Tried to pry my mind away from everything I had done, before Richard's death, that had kept Lillie and Honey apart. The silence, the statement to the press. The things I could have said differently; the truths I could have told.

'Sir, ma'am,' a waiter said, offering a tray of champagne coupes. Was there something familiar about him? 'The speeches will begin on the lawn shortly.'

I looked up from the vomit on my dress to where the glass table had stood only seconds before. It was nothing but a metal frame, which the dancers hopped over to escape.

'Why were you dancing on the table?' I shouted after them. 'It was *glass*.'

A man on the couch called over the girl in his lap: 'Chill out, it's just a table. They were having fun.'

'It was an expensive table.' Fury sharpened my tongue. 'They shouldn't have been standing on an expensive. Fucking. Glass. Table.'

And the shards might not clean out of the rug – what if Lillie stepped on one? The underwear man was trailing scarlet footprints across my white-marble floor.

'Hey.' I tried to get his attention over the thudding dance music. 'Hey, you!'

'Leave him alone,' said the man on the couch. 'What's your problem?'

'My problem,' I said, crouching to collect glass, careful not to step on the pieces, 'is that *this* fucking idiot just broke my table.'

'Oh my god.' Glee dawned on his face. 'Are you Rich's wife?'

I dropped the shards. There was nowhere to put them. The cleaners could deal with it tomorrow; the guests could slice their feet.

'Fuck.' The man laughed. 'I heard he had a wife locked away somewhere.'

'Don't be silly.' The woman sitting on him batted his arm. 'Isn't Rich—'

'Elsie.' Jerry tapped my shoulder. 'Elsie, the caterers want to know where to put the cake.'

Four men were carrying the platter on their shoulders, like pallbearers.

'We were told the table in here,' one of them said, 'but . . .'

I looked back to the shattered glass, the empty table frame.

'I don't know how much longer I can hold this,' a muffled voice called.

'Should they take it back to the kitchen?' asked Jerry.

'No, please.'

'It's too heavy to—'

'Anywhere, I don't care.' I sighed. 'Just put it down anywhere.'

The men shuffled over to a leather armchair, lowered the cake. Icing smushed on my upholstery; the strawberries would stain.

'Great party.' Jerry was still beside me.

'When I agreed to host the birthday party,' I could hear the slurring in my voice, 'at the same time as the *One Hundred* wrap, I didn't quite think . . .'

'It would get out of hand like this?' Jerry laughed. 'Can't remember the last event I went to that wasn't just quiet schmoozing. Take the compliment, Elsie – it's a fucking great party. People want to let go.'

A tall brunette was lifting Jerry's hand into the air. 'Can we dance?'

He cooed: 'One second, I'm talking to a friend.'

She pouted.

'Why don't you dance over there,' he said, 'and I'll watch you from here.'

'You're such a voyeur, babe.'

His eyes followed her – the long legs, the tiny black dress – as she disappeared into the crowd.

I raised an eyebrow. 'Letting go, right, is that what you call it? Isn't your wife here tonight?'

Jerry rolled his eyes. 'She can go fuck herself as far as I'm concerned.'

'You two aren't fighting again?'

'Judy was furious when I said we had to come because it's her sister's birthday. But it's a work gig, what are we going to do? Miss the wrap party?'

'And the little black dress?'

'If my wife wants to ignore me all night,' Jerry said, 'let's see how she likes it when I find company elsewhere. Hey, have you seen her at all?'

'I don't think so.' I narrowed my eyes. 'Have you seen my husband?'

Jerry shook his head. Over his shoulder, I could see guests crowding the cake. They ignored the plates and forks that the caterer had placed beside the armchair and were shoving fistfuls into each other's mouths, sucking cream from fingers.

'What's that smell?' Jerry scrunched his nose.

And then the stench reached my nostrils too. I had forgotten about the vomit seeping through my dress.

I caught Kei's eye across the scattered crowd. She was dressed in a suit, black shirt and tie, the edges of her torso tattoos just about creeping over the collar line. She looked away immediately, squinted into the fierce sun.

It seemed my thoughts about the other guests were right: there was an unspoken agreement between us eight. The press had still not found a source to detail the guest list of that night. Naturally, none of us had broken our silence, but it was miraculous that none of our friends, relatives, or staff had done so, nor had the caterers from that night. Some of us had been spotted entering the police station with our lawyers, ambushed by paparazzi on the way home, but was it so incredible that the cops would want to speak with Richard's oldest friends, his ex-wife, colleagues? And others, who had not attended the party, were also interviewed by the police repeatedly, were pictured in the press. I noted, with strange satisfaction, that my name never popped up. Richard's ex-wife would be questioned after his death, yes, but would she have been invited to the most talked-about party in Hollywood? A has-been actress? Don't be ridiculous.

And so we birthday guests stayed far from one another at the memorial – save those among us already acquainted before that fateful night. I noticed Kei clinking her glass against Miguel's at the toast, Sabine air-kissing Charlie, and I spoke with Jerry when the crowd listening to the speech dissolved to conversations and canapés on trays. Were the others wary, like me? Were they judging one another too?

But all of us avoided the guests I had spotted paying their respects to Lillie just before her speech: our two police detectives. They watched through the crowds as Jerry began to talk.

'Great speech, huh?' he said, nudging me from behind. 'Would have thought Rich wrote it himself, it was that . . .'

'Fastidious?' I offered, resolving to ignore the nameless spies. Their attendance made me feel no safer. It was simply a reminder that the murderer was here too. Perhaps in the crowd, perhaps standing right before me.

'You got it.'

'I think he did write parts of it, actually,' I said. 'Richard left notes for Lillie. She's been locked away in her room for weeks, studying them.'

'Ha, of course he wrote the speech too. Yeah, I heard about his notes for the day. Classic Rich. Always over-prepared.'

'So I was trying to guess which parts were his. I imagine the Auden poem would have been his suggestion. Richard always used to talk about that boy falling out of the sky. He recited it to me on our honeymoon, when we were in Paris.'

I could feel the cops watching as I said, quieter now: 'I wanted to give you a call, Jerry. But my lawyer advised me to keep to myself.'

'Oh yup,' he said. 'They'll do that to you.'

The weeks since Richard's birthday had deflated Jerry. He was naturally a chubby man, but now the fat had shrunk to wrinkles. Without his trademark chuckle, I would not have recognised him. Even the eyes, the facial expressions, were different. Exhausted, dull. But there was no way of telling how much this change was due to illness, how much to something more sinister: remorse, shame, the stress of resisting discovery.

For a moment, though, I quashed my suspicions. This was Jerry, whom I had known for years; the only thing I could be sure of was his illness, his suffering.

'I want to apologise, Jerry,' I said. His face fell a little, so I lowered my voice further: 'That night, I didn't . . . I hadn't heard about your diagnosis, or your disagreements with Richard, and I wish I could have called to say—'

'Cops have loose lips, huh?'

When I opened my mouth to apologise again, he jumped in: 'Look, don't worry about it. Kinda guessed you didn't know. And yeah, sure, the cops told you about everything. Heard my fair share of your marital problems.'

A pang of curiosity in my stomach. The notion had not occurred to me – if I had learned of the other guests' relationships to Richard, what had they been asked about me? More importantly, what had they told?

I remembered that conversation I'd overheard at the party: Jerry and Charlie, whispering in the kitchen about Honey's allegations. Jerry had been drunk, but he'd meant what he said – these were thoughts that had been festering since the allegations. He believed Richard over everyone else. And so, though he felt like an old friend of mine, I knew: if Jerry had any reason to doubt me, he would not hesitate.

'It's funny, you know,' said Jerry, 'this reminds me of your wedding.'

'It's the relatives, isn't it? Another transatlantic affair.'

'The accents, yeah, sure. But also, I don't know, maybe the feeling that Rich is here.' Jerry looked around him. 'Yeah, really reminds me of your wedding. He always did throw the best parties.'

'He did.' I tried to keep my voice normal, my eye contact steady. But I was studying Jerry's body language, waiting for a chance to bring up the murder and watch his response.

There was no need.

'I know we're not supposed to be talking about it,' Jerry said, 'but don't you find it strange that we're all here? I've counted every one of us, all eight. And that means the killer's here too. Can't believe they haven't caught him yet. Freaks me out.'

'Unless it wasn't one of us,' I said. 'The eight.'

I found myself peering behind Jerry, through the atrium windows to where the empty octopus tank stood. But it was too sunny – I was only met with the blurred reflection of the crowds on the lawn.

'You think someone else came in the night?' asked Jerry. 'Didn't they rule that out early?'

I watched his face as he said this – was it a genuine question?

'Jesus Christ,' he went on, 'I really thought Rich would outlive me. Despite his problems. And not that night, with all of us there, it's . . . You know, I got him sober four times now? And kept him sober between. I thought he might have been thinking about it again, recently, with everything in the press. I just knew – I just knew that those kinds of situations triggered him. And I tried to bring it up over one of our lobster lunches, but it didn't end well. You know he fired me, right?'

I nodded. The pictures – so that had been the reason for the punch: Jerry was trying to keep Richard sober and had been fired as a result. Was the punch for the dismissal? Or for something Richard had said?

'Sure you do. Everyone does now. Well, that's why. But I think he wanted to reconcile when he heard about the illness, and I thought he would be safer, you know, if I was with him on his birthday. So now I just keep thinking, if I'd been – if I had stayed awake I could have . . . But I was so tired, Elsie; I shouldn't have been there at all.'

Jerry's story made sense, but I couldn't stop thinking about those paparazzi pictures. The man before me seemed so gentle, so concerned about his friend. But that punch had been violent. Blood dripping thick down Richard's face.

'Ma'am?' A waitress held out a green bottle.

'Thank you,' I said. 'But only an inch more, please. I'm driving.'

'Of course,' she said.

'No thanks, sweetie,' Jerry declined, keeping a hand over the top of his glass. It was full of orange juice.

When she left, I fell to a whisper again. 'Do you recognise that waitress? She was there that night, wasn't she?'

'Huh? Oh yeah,' he said. 'The blonde, right? Amelia. Great gal. Chatted with her earlier – apparently Richard said in those memorial notes that he wanted the same catering company for this event. And Amelia's boss doubled the fees because they were already overbooked today. That's what she told me. Honey paid it anyway. Totally nuts. I find it pretty morbid, you know, planning those details. But that was Rich, wasn't it? What did you say? Fastidious.'

I spotted two familiar figures behind Jerry. Yola was approaching Lillie. She swaddled her in a tight embrace. A tall man in an oversized suit hovered beside them – Yola's husband? When Yola pulled away, Lillie turned to him, received a kiss on her forehead.

Jerry noticed my distraction and smiled.

'Yola's such an angel,' he said. 'She's been dropping by to see me and Judy at least once a week. I mean, she went through it all with Samuel, so she really gets it. Have you tried her *tres leches*? No? Oh my god, it's heavenly. I always say to her, I always say: Yola, if it gets to the point where I'm not eating the entire dish in one sitting, you'll know that's when the cancer's really got to me. That's when it's got me.'

He chuckled. Looked down at his orange juice as though to drink it – and then did not.

'I don't really know her,' I said. Yola was resting a hand on Lillie's arm. 'But she seems . . . nice. Devoted to Richard.'

'Devoted?' said Jerry. 'Huh. No, I don't think I'd use that word.

Yola loved Richard, sure, she was the closest thing he had to family for a while. But devoted? Makes it sound like she blindly worshipped him or something. Hell no. Yola calls bullshit when she sees it and you know Rich. He was full of it. What made you say that?'

'Nothing, nothing.'

Yola was wiping tears from the corner of her eyes with her fingertips as she spoke to Lillie. Her husband offered a tissue.

'Come on, Elsie.'

'She just – she said something to me, that's all. About our divorce. She clearly doesn't think much of me.'

Jerry laughed. 'Your divorce? That was a lifetime ago.'

'I know,' I said. 'That's why I said she was devoted to Richard. It was a long time ago, so I don't get why she has it in for me. Especially about a divorce that, as you know, was mutual.'

'Was it?'

I turned to look at him. 'Yes.'

He raised his eyebrows, pursed his lips.

We turned back to watch Yola and Lillie. I thought that maybe Jerry would drop the subject, but he never had been one to back down.

After a few seconds of silence, he made a kind of drawn-out wincing sound. 'Ehh,' he said, 'well . . . I know how it is – two sides to every story. But as I recall, you were the one who left.'

'That doesn't mean Richard wanted me to stay.' I had spoken too quickly, each word a flint.

'Look, I know that when a marriage has its problems, usually everyone is to blame. But I was there, Elsie, and Rich was a mess. He wanted you to stay. Whatever he had done to make you leave, I know he regretted it. More than anything.'

Richard couldn't bear the thought of losing me, that was true. But not because he loved me. Not because he felt he'd made a terrible mistake. I said nothing to Jerry.

'You have to understand what it was like when you and Lillie left,' Jerry said. 'You know, that's when Yola started working for Rich. After he got out of rehab that last time. And he was cut up, Elsie, that was the worst I've ever seen him. I couldn't leave him alone. So I was the one who hired Yola to cook and clean, and she was a godsend. She would throw open the curtains every day, push him into the shower. He needed that.

'But that's what I was trying to say – if anything, it was Rich that was devoted to Yola. He noticed, after she'd been working there for a few months, that she was taking these naps halfway through the day. She was mortified, but then he got it out of her – she'd been working a night shift cleaning offices downtown. You know what Rich does? He says if it's not enough pay, he'll double it. He insists that she can't do her job if she's exhausted. Same thing happened again a couple of years later. She got this flu, but she kept working. No insurance, of course. Rich sorts it out, puts Samuel on her insurance too. And, you know, that probably saved Samuel's life. Leukemia, but the doctors caught it early. Wouldn't surprise me if Rich had left them a nice lump in his will.'

I didn't doubt this – it sounded exactly like Richard. A grand surge of generosity. It wasn't just that he wanted to make people happy, improve their lives; it wasn't even that he wanted to ensure loyalty. He simply liked how it felt: the gratitude. He was a king, extending his arm, permitting paupers to crawl close and kiss each jewelled finger.

Jerry threw back his orange juice with a satisfied grunt, then exhaled loudly. 'Anyway. All I'm saying is that I'd understand if Yola still remembers the divorce. She's not a bad person, she's just – it was a bad time. For all of us.'

'Jerry.' I frowned. 'I never said she was a bad person.'

'You didn't need to. I could see it in your face.'

Honey was approaching the group. He put his arm around Yola, and they stood there like that, half hugging, listening to Lillie. It looked almost comical – Yola only reached Honey's elbow height. I wondered what she had thought of his public accusations. I wondered what things she had overheard in the hallways of this house. Maybe Jerry was right: maybe Yola wasn't devoted to Richard. She certainly hadn't reserved for Honey any of the malice she felt towards me. Yola's husband said something, and they all laughed.

I think it was only at that moment, watching the four of them laugh together while I stood alone, that I truly understood: Lillie had another family, and it was one that included neither Richard nor me.

Jerry was looking at me with a strange expression on his face. 'You know, sometimes, Elsie, I feel like I've known you my whole life. And sometimes I don't think I ever knew you at all.'

That made two of us.

A group of women nearby brayed with laughter.

'. . . but Fee and Cressie couldn't *drag* him in,' one of them was saying. 'Dicky sat there, scowling in the summer house, wearing a woolly jumper and trousers in the middle of August.'

Jerry and I exchanged glances.

'I gotta say,' he murmured, 'I don't remember this many of them attending your wedding. Have they multiplied?'

I noticed Judy locking on to us; she began snaking through the crowd.

'Jerry, I'm so sorry, can we continue in a moment? I wouldn't mind finding a bathroom.'

'Elspeth.' He gave me a look. 'I can tell you just saw Judy coming over. You don't need to make excuses: I hate my wife's yakking as much as the next person. I swear to god, she's been eyeing up the caterers; keeps saying' – he raised his pitch – '*Babe, we need to find out the price. We want something classy for your do, and this is real nice, real nice.* She yanked a waiter at one point – literally, grabbed him by the collar – *What's your hourly rate?* Imagine, some poor guy working for less than minimum wage, rushed off his feet, and she's trying to book him for her husband's funeral. *I'm so sorry to hear of his passing,* he says. *Oh, he's not passed, babe. Oh, how cute, you're such a doll. Here's my hubby, right here.*'

There was a flash of the old Jerry in this impression.

'But, no, I jest,' he went on. 'She's been great the past few months. Looking after me, taking me to hospital appointments, the police. Even stopped threatening divorce. What's the point when she'll get it all in the – Babe! So lovely of you to join us.

But you'll have to catch Elspeth later, she just said she wants to find a bathroom.'

Judy's mouth twitched sour.

'Such a shame.' She leaned in close; her perfume clogged my nostrils. 'You've been avoiding me for years, hon. I'll have to track you down later.'

I caught myself in the bathroom mirror. The dress stain was smaller in the reflection than it looked from above, but vomit was the least of my problems. Everything else was a mess.

My lipstick had worn away, leaving only a heavy outline, bleeding into my skin. I wouldn't be able to fix it – I couldn't remember where I'd left this particular shade. Another bathroom, in another part of the house. Or maybe hidden from the party guests on a bookshelf somewhere, stashed for reapplication. My sober self was too well organised. She knew that Richard would be furious if he saw me in this state.

I sat on the toilet lid and gripped my temples. Richard had disappeared and I needed to find him. Or did I need to find him? The cake. The cake had been eaten. And somebody had thrown up on my dress. Did I need to find Richard to tell him I was going to bed?

My eyes were closing, slowly closing. Somebody rattled the handle. I called out: 'Just a minute.'

Richard never complimented me, not any more. He only mentioned my appearance if there was something to criticise – as if perfection was in the job description for *wife* and anything less was intolerable. But I couldn't make too much effort, I couldn't be too charming or too friendly at social events. If Richard was in a difficult mood, that would tip him over the edge. He would pull me close, in a crowd, after I had made someone else laugh. Whisper through his teeth: *Who are you trying to impress?*

I learned to be a beautiful, forgettable ornament.

It was like high school again. I had always been beautiful – although only adults used that word when I was younger; to other students I was 'cute' or 'pretty' – and at that time it was a liability.

Guys in grades above would follow me home; one of my algebra teachers kept trying to get me to stay behind for 'private tutoring'. I hated the attention. With kids my age, I'd learned, envy only led to bullying. I kept my head down, shoulders hunched. Smoothed my conspicuous 'Elspeth' – a musty cast-off from some Scottish great-aunt – to a quick, unobtrusive 'Elle'. Hung around the peripheries of friendship groups, blandly. Desperately avoiding being seen.

If anyone had looked closer they'd have noticed the clothes I was wearing. The strange assortment of hand-me-downs from a male cousin and my mother. It wasn't that we were much poorer than other families in the area. Just that my parents seemed to care less about how presentable I was. Other girls had their ears pierced. They had matching socks and moms who did their hair. They smelled of fresh powdered detergent and they shared their flavoured Maybelline lip glosses with one another. Sometimes, on days when I'd done the laundry too late and it hadn't dried on the line, I'd have to go to school in one of my mother's old shirts from the grocery store where she worked. I'd pick off the embroidered logo badge. Prayed nobody would notice the tell-tale circle of needle-punches.

As soon as I hit sixteen, I started waitressing every evening at a neighbourhood pizza place. It was a miracle, having my own money, although I never used it to hang out with my friends, or buy cooler clothes. What was the point? A new T-shirt every month would never change my life. My socks still wouldn't match. Makeup would only make it seem like I wanted to be noticed. So I saved it up for luxurious things – beautiful for their own sake. Pearlescent nail polish that I wore only on my toes; a silk eye mask that cost six months' pay, and that I kept hidden from my mother because she would have died if she knew. I took the F-train into the city on the first Saturday of each month, just to buy *Vogue* magazines. They sold them at the bodega near my school as well, but that wasn't the point. Once I even went to Bergdorf Goodman for a jar of face cream aimed at women three times my age. I didn't care. It smelled like jasmine and came in a ribboned box – even the tiny, sample-sized version.

I lingered at the counters, listening to the women with their husbands, their assistants, their daughters. I watched them remove their leather gloves to massage in the tester creams. I copied their vowels, their movements, their stony indifference, as I handed my money to the saleswoman and thanked her.

'Is this for your mom, sweetie?' the saleswoman had asked, placing the box in a lavender bag. A gorgeous, glamorous lavender bag. I'd have spent a week's pay on that paper bag alone. It stood proudly on my dresser until I moved out.

To be honest, the money wasn't the only reason I waitressed. I just liked the routine of shifts. I liked falling into bed exhausted, asleep before I could think. I liked having tasks – even if that meant spending a dead hour scrubbing mould from the back of the freezer because the health-department inspector was making rounds. That job was my escape from my parents' bickering. From the fact that I was the only teenager in Queens doing nothing on a Friday night.

That's why, when my mother found out about the job at Douglaston Golf Course, I jumped at the opportunity. Weekends working on reception fit in with my waitressing shifts. Throughout senior year I very happily had no free time at all.

And that's where I met my best friend Tanya. It had been her dream, this life of mine. A white mini-dress and a house full of famous guests, a glass table topped with dancers – this loneliness would have been worth it, for her.

'. . . was the attention to detail that made him such a genius.' 'Idaho?' 'Terrible tragedy. But I thought the daughter did well with her speech, didn't you?'

I was trying to reach the upstairs bathroom without being seen by any mourners I knew, but it was difficult to keep my head down while carrying champagne and navigating the rabble. The band had taken a break – they were drinking beers and chain-smoking outside – and so I caught snippets of chatter, in a plethora of accents, as I went.

'Is that the wife? The *ex*-wife, I mean?' 'I can't do next Friday. Tuesday?' '*Sí, el cineasta llegó a Nueva York, pero* . . .'

'Oh, I thought I recognised her.' '. . . to Cambridge, but you see, he's never been much of a scholar.'

'Should we offer our condolences? What's the etiquette?' '. . . a massive boost. Miguel was telling me . . .'

'No, I think it's more of a "congratulations" situation.'

I kept my head down, walked on. It pained me to swim through the gossip. Not the sly comments about me – I'd had decades of thickening skin – but knowing what Lillie would hear. About her, about Richard, his death, his relationships. I could not spot her figure in the crowds. Wherever she was in Sedgwick, the whispers would be following her too.

'It was all totally fictitious, you know what the media's . . .' 'February.' 'Oh, Dicky always was made of tough stuff but you would have to be to survive in *that* family.'

'I know, I know. I just think, come on, how could anyone who's ever met Richard—'

'Even if he did, it's . . . it's irrelevant, isn't it?'

I tried to keep my expression neutral, push past groups without drawing attention to myself. There was Charlie, holding out his glass for another refill. Our eyes met. His gaze was as empty as it had been the night of Richard's death.

If it had not been Persephone stuffing Richard's throat, of all the guests I could readily imagine Charlie having the requisite ruthlessness. Those eyes. I tried to escape them as quickly as possible.

'Sure, I found the pigment stuff as self-indulgent as the next guy, but now I think, wait, this film was made by an artist in love with his craft.'

'Exactly. It was never about romance between the leads. This is a film about despair.'

'And mistakes and obsession.'

'With perfection. Exactly. Yes.'

I had heard it in the gossip around me all afternoon: *Dominus* was still in theatres, was being watched more than ever. Even the critical tide was turning, with tastemakers reanalysing the film they had previously panned as the director's final manifesto. How fortunate, I kept thinking. How fortunate for those guests who had worked on the film.

'. . . charming little chalet in Val d'Isère so we'll be taking the cousins.'

'Were you there that night? Come on, I won't tell.' 'Unrivalled. He'll be up there with the greats.'

I slipped by Miguel, who was muttering into a well-known actress's ear. He flashed me an odd look, perhaps a warning not to approach. The actress smiled. He brushed back her hair and bent down to speak again. But I could not catch his words – they were drowned by surrounding conversation.

'Put it this way: I'm not going to tell you I *wasn't* there.'

And then the empty tank. Blurred black silhouettes: through glass, the boundaries between each individual were indistinct, a mass of limbs and bobbing heads.

'Such a fucking Gemini.' 'Apparently Lucia told James and Pippa but there was no response, absolutely none. And I know they haven't seen each other for a while, but who doesn't mourn the death of their only child?'

I reached the staircase.

'Ghana?' '. . . a muted eggshell.'

'Sierra Leone.'

And that was when I heard the voice – an urgent whisper: 'Elspeth.'

I began to climb. I might not have heard.

'. . . still remember that first feature I wrote on him back when I was at *Vani*—'

'Elspeth,' the whisper called again. I resolved to ignore it.

'What happened to the music anyway?' said a woman sitting on the stairs. I stepped over her legs, tried to avoid looking down.

'Hey, Elspeth,' said my caller.

But I was reaching the mezzanine, and he was still stuck at the bottom. I climbed faster. My heel missed a step. As I fell forwards, I glimpsed him through the stairs. Couldn't he see the attention he was drawing? In what world would we have known each other? In what world would he have wanted to speak to me? Unless, of course, we had both attended Richard's birthday.

The woman I had climbed over watched for my reaction. I lifted my head. Three more steps.

Reckless, foolish Miguel. Why was he so desperate – to catch me then, there, in a room full of spectators?

'Hello? Hello?'

The thumping on the door was as relentless as the dance music. I wondered whether I could hide in the bathroom all night – wait until the hideous guests had removed themselves from my house and only then slip out. By now, I had been in the bathroom too long to leave. Nobody would notice my absence. Not the guests, not Richard. Beloved birthday boy.

My bare feet were cold on the tiles. Where had I left my shoes?

'Anyone in there? Hello?'

I breathed in through my nose, out through my mouth. Tried to control the waves of nausea. Just one moment more.

I wondered what Tanya would think of me now, hiding from everything she had always wanted. I wondered what she was doing, whether she was happy. Whether knowing my truth she would still envy me.

Tanya was a year older than me; we worked the golf club reception desk together, two Queens girls, teenagers. That was where she told me about her aunt who lived in LA and her plan to move across the country, 'make it big'. Tanya used the phrase unironically; she spoke in idioms, tattooed them on her shoulder and lower back. I thought she was the best person I had ever met.

She had ideas and she was clever, but most of all she was magnetic. Confident, but not in the tough way that girls at school were. Tanya was never covering up insecurities; she was totally self-assured, she didn't care how I looked or that I rarely had anything to say. She would talk for us both. And at one point, I couldn't say when, her first-person subjects became plurals.

'Step one: we save up for a few more months, for the travel and starting money,' she would say, chewing gum, walking her fingers across the desk. 'Step two: we get there, we find jobs in retail. That'll be easy, my aunt knows some stores who always need extra hands. Three: we save money living with her and we take acting classes. Four: we find the best parties. We fake it till we make it.'

We went ahead with the first part of the plan, and by the time I'd finished school we were ready to leave. We never quite reached the third step, though. It was cheap living with Tanya's aunt – both squashed onto a pull-out couch in the front room with no AC – but we paid our share of rent and bills, and living in LA was hard on the wallet.

The fourth part of Tanya's plan, however, was more than cost-effective. Almost every night after closing, we would get ready in the Food 4 Less staff bathroom, layering our mascara with all the care of interns knotting neckties for their first interviews. Then we'd hang around with Joe, an older guy who stocked shelves, getting just about high enough that we could arrive wherever we were going docile and giggly. Just enough that we could laugh along with the bad jokes. Just enough to quell our nerves.

Tanya knew I needed to be confident. Tanya knew all the tricks. She befriended bouncers and chauffeurs, PAs and nannies, all the club promoters. And once she heard about the most exclusive parties, there was no way we weren't getting in.

Knocking on limo doors a few yards from the house, so we could make the perfect entrance. *Our car broke down and these heels are killing, would you be a sweetheart and take us up the last part of the hill?*

Making small talk with a recognisable star, so the doormen assumed we were plus ones. *Sorry to interrupt, but do you have the time?*

Or simply marching right in. *How are you? Tanya and Elle. Yeah, we're on the list.*

Tanya wanted to be an actress desperately, painfully. Afterwards, whenever I thought back to that time, I had a feeling she only dragged me to LA so she could have a partner in crime: one who was younger, shyer, easy to eclipse. After making it past the door, we could tell – from who was speaking, how many people were listening – who our targets would be. And at that point, it was every woman for herself. Maybe I was prettier than Tanya, but she knew how to turn it on in a way that I did not. When to talk and when to shut up, how to flatter and how to flirt. Mostly, I watched and learned. Tried to imitate.

We managed to make a few connections with this modus operandi – some invites to audition; Tanya got two callbacks, some dates with execs. But we were young and naive and there were hundreds of girls like us. Our résumés were fictitious and bare. Our headshots had been taken by one of Joe's pervy friends, in the parking lot behind Food 4 Less. It never quite worked out.

Until Alto's party. Until I borrowed Tanya's gold dress. Until I walked down a staircase at just the right moment and a young, handsome British man was waiting for me at the bottom, manhattan in hand.

Sometimes I wondered – sometimes I still do – whether everything might have been different. If only it had been Tanya in that dress, on those stairs, and not me.

I had thought the upstairs bathroom might be more secluded – as, ironically, had others. The door was unlocked but there were two mourners inside, caught in a comforting kiss. They leapt apart. Sabine dashed past.

And there was Kei, holding open the door.

'I'm sorry, I had no idea there were people in . . .' I blathered. 'I didn't mean . . .'

'Dude, it's fine. At least you're not an undercover reporter.'

'Scout's honour.' I crossed my heart.

She smiled and hugged me.

'It's good to see you without having to ignore you,' she said over my shoulder. 'Want to talk in here?'

'Is that always your opening line?'

'Fuck off,' she said, laughing, as she shut and locked the door.

It was difficult not to warm to Kei; she seemed so friendly, genuine. On the other hand, I could not forget her difficulties with Richard. And she was undoubtedly benefiting from his death now: from the new *Dominus* audiences, from its critical re-evaluation. What had she told me that night? *When I'm lying in bed I envisage all the recognition I might get.*

'So.' I set down my glass and rested against the sink. 'I didn't realise you two were – but it makes sense, thinking back. I guess I was too wrapped up in my own drama to notice that evening.'

'Yeah.' Kei shrugged. 'We've been together since the *Dominus* wrap party.' She rolled her eyes. 'Cliché, I know. We're keeping it on the down-low. Better box-office figures if fans can fantasise about Sabine. Buy her posters, gossip about who she is or isn't dating. Her manager says we can be more open when she reaches ten million Instagram followers.' I couldn't tell whether this was a joke. 'Whatever, I don't care, it's good. Especially this last month – I couldn't have got through any of it without her.'

'Cops went hard on you too?'

'I meant the whole thing, to be honest. The body, Richard.'

I smiled my empathy.

'Sorry, sorry,' she said. 'My therapist tells me I need to put the brakes on this guilt. What did you ask? No, the cops didn't go hard. Well, not on me. They asked about problems during production. Richard was always a bitch to me, and everyone on set knew it. But no matter how shitty he was, he was also supportive. Professionally. My biggest fan, you know. I could never . . . But Sabine got it really bad.'

'What do you mean?' The officers had not asked me about Sabine at all.

Kei ran her fingers through her hair.

'It was fucking awful. The cops had this theory she was sleeping with him, that she was jealous that he wouldn't leave Honey. Or that he had tried to coerce her into, you know, and she'd had enough of . . . They had no evidence, other than the fact that she's gorgeous and he was directing her sex scenes. But they took her phone and laptop and read every message as a flirt. They logged records of meetings. I mean, of course she and Richard met up with each other, they were working together. I don't think the cops understood, though. How the industry works. How it's different in . . . I don't need to tell you.'

This was an interesting theory, which had not crossed my mind. And it made sense: why Sabine would have attended such a small event, why she threw herself into the party. Her white dress, her cold shoulder.

'I'm sorry to hear that,' I said. 'It must have been awful, unable to say anything in her defence.'

'I know. Her fucking manager wouldn't . . . Yeah, it was a nightmare.'

'But they dropped it?'

'They had to. There was no evidence.'

I sucked in my lips.

'Look,' I said, 'I don't want to create any problems for you guys, but I feel I should mention, I saw Richard and Sabine at the party . . .'

'Flirting?'

I nodded, expecting Kei to press me for details, but she only laughed.

'It's fine, I saw it too. Nothing's ever happened between them. I mean, sure, Sabine is bi, and she does get pretty extroverted after a snort, but that's just her messing around, joking. She's loyal as fuck. She would *never* do that to me. Especially not with Richard; she finds him creepy. I mean, found. She found him creepy. And he knows we're together – it's why we were both invited to the party. Knew. *Fuck.*'

Maybe this was true. But it did not mean Sabine was innocent. She was still involved in the disagreements surrounding *Dominus*; she too had benefited from the box-office surge following his death. And could I trust a defence that came from Kei, who was, quite clearly, enamoured?

'I'm sorry I said anything,' I said. 'I wasn't trying to – I just didn't want to see you get hurt.'

'I know,' she said. 'I get it, I get what you'd think of Sabine. She was so cold when we first met, but I found out later it was nerves. You know, she really admires you. She told me. She does.

But I think the European air makes her seem snooty. Then you see her dancing around after a few drinks, and you think, great, so it was me, she definitely hates me. But that's not her at all. She just loosens up with alcohol.'

'Loosens up? She was dancing on the table and swimming in the bath.'

We laughed together, then stopped abruptly.

In the quiet, Kei spoke.

'Feels weird to be talking about that night, doesn't it?'

I wrapped my arms around myself.

'You're so lucky. To have Sabine. You know, I haven't spoken about anything that happened that night, except with cops and lawyers.'

'Any thoughts on who did it?'

'None at all,' I said. 'I want to think it was all just an accident.'

'Me too, but I have my suspicions.'

'Who?' I said. 'Honey was passed out. Then Jerry, Sabine and Miguel were asleep. I mean, I guess they could have woken up but—'

'Honey passed out? Okay, he fell asleep later. But passed out? Who told you that?'

I froze for a second – then remembered. He had been lying face down, arms cocked at strange angles.

'I saw him passed out,' I said. 'I definitely remember – he was gone before Richard even got the gear out.'

'No way.' Kei looked at me, odd, folded her arms. 'Don't you remember him telling Richard not to do it? He hates dope, always has. He's pretty straight-edge when it comes to that. I think it's his upbringing – like he's reserved in certain ways. Passed out? Nah, dude, he's not a big drinker.'

It made no sense. Seeing my confusion, Kei unfolded her arms and came to hug me.

'It doesn't matter anyway. Richard's gone; that's what we need to focus on today. Let's meet up, when all of this has blown over?'

'I'd like that.'

She pulled away.

'I'll leave now, you must be desperate. Sorry for keeping you so long.'

As I watched Kei leave, it was there again: that chill creeping up my spine. It was so easy to trust her, a rare confidante. To think that, because of the ordeal we had been through, we were somehow bonded together.

I saw the way he treated you and Sabine, Kei had whispered to Charlie, at the bottom of the stairs.

And he shot back: *So why do you still work with him?*

I've asked myself that question so many times.

Part of me wanted to forget this. They had all attended Richard's party; it couldn't have been *that* unpleasant, filming *Dominus*. None of the rumours online, of problems surrounding the film, had involved Kei, Sabine, or Charlie. But another part of me could not forget it. Because I'd heard the hatred, the hurt in her voice. And I knew what Richard was capable of. I knew what he had done to me while filming *Anatomy*.

Things don't have to be this way, Kei had said.

I locked myself in and was alone.

I suppose the fact that Richard was charming helped put me at ease when I first met him, at Alto's party. I never thought he might be important – he was younger than most of the other men, though nonetheless secure in himself, in the crowds. He was funny, and educated, and his blue eyes caught the light, and for the first time since arriving in LA, I had found somebody who was interested in me and my opinions. *Golden girl*, he called me, gesturing at my sparkling dress.

Nevertheless, I left the conversation after a few minutes with the manhattan in my hand and a sinking heart. Tanya was beckoning me. I thought she was going to scold me, maybe point out our next target: yet another grey-haired man in a black polo shirt with overly whitened teeth. But instead she hissed, 'Richard *Bryant*? You're trying to keep him to yourself? Introduce me, introduce me – don't bogart him, you skank.'

Apparently Richard had been profiled that month in a *Vanity*

Fair feature on upcoming talent – he had won some award for an indie film. Not quite a box-office hit, but fresh and original. All the hallmarks of a future great.

'And he's *handsome* and *British*, Elle, you've *got* to introduce me.' Tanya bushed up her hair. 'Won't even have to fake it.'

But when we went back inside, he was nowhere to be found. Tanya scowled her pink-frosted lips.

I saw Richard again later, by the pool, when the crowd had grown and the sky had darkened. I was sitting on a lounger, enjoying a solitary cigarette and studying the scene, when his face appeared in the space between two strangers. He had been watching me, watching the crowds. Neither of us smiled. The pool, the distance, prevented any conversation. We simply looked at each other.

And then I knew what I wanted. I wanted to mesmerise him; I wanted to pull him in.

I could hear my pulse in my ears. I stood, still meeting his eye. Then I did the one thing I had never done at one of these parties before: I turned and walked away.

A taxi was dropping a guest outside the house. I waved at the driver, threw myself onto the back seat.

'Where to?' he asked.

I told him to wait a second, a friend would be joining me. He tapped the meter. 'Your dime, princess.'

It wasn't. I didn't have the money for it; I was down to my last ten dollars. But some part of me was certain Richard would follow. I could wait until the meter hit five dollars, and if he hadn't arrived by then, I'd leave. Catch a ride with Tanya and her latest mark.

And so I waited. My heart was hammering. I tidied my hair, picked my nails. I avoided looking back at the house, maybe superstitiously, and fixed my eyes, instead on the meter. It crept to four dollars. Four dollars twenty. Four forty. Four sixty. I felt sick. I watched it hit five. I caught the driver's eye in the rear-view mirror. He was watching to see if I would bolt.

I told myself Richard was just saying goodbye to the hosts. I told myself he would only be another minute. I told myself he probably hadn't understood he was supposed to follow; I could go back and find him. The meter reached five fifty. Then I told myself that if he wasn't following me, Richard wasn't worth pursuing anyway. I unclipped my seatbelt and leaned forwards to tell the driver. There were footsteps outside.

The taxi door clicked open.

'You waited,' said Richard.

I nodded, cool, but my heart was beating fast. He looked at me strangely – eyes narrowed, a measuring glance – then turned to the driver and gave his address.

As we pulled onto the road, Richard sat back. The driver turned up his radio.

'How far is it?' I asked, suddenly aware of his knee, warm, against mine. My legs were crossed, pressing tight together – my dress had ridden up my thighs.

'Fifteen minutes,' he said. 'Aren't we lucky?'

I almost couldn't think about it: what would happen when we arrived.

'So,' he continued. 'The golden girl. Just before your friend dragged you away, I'd given you my name and I believe you were about to tell me yours.'

'Elspeth Bell.'

'Elspeth . . . Good god. Where did you get an old Scots name like that?'

I shrugged, nonchalant. 'It's a family name.'

'Is that right? I never thought I'd meet an Elspeth in Shangri-LA.' He rubbed his chin with his hand. 'And you're an actress, is that right, Elspeth?'

He was shockingly handsome, I realised. Not as a sum of parts, though those parts were beautiful – the cheekbones, the stubble, the eyes, the suit – but handsome as a person. The way he sat, the way he watched me, how quick he was to laugh. It was difficult to look at him, alone, in such close proximity. To hear the depth of his voice.

'Correct,' I said, pulling down the hem of my dress. 'And you're a filmmaker.'

We passed a row of street lamps and the cab was illuminated. He raised an eyebrow. 'Interesting. As I recall, we hadn't quite broached that subject yet. An educated guess?'

'My friend, Tanya, told me. She knows everything about everyone – she's like that.'

'But you aren't,' he said.

'No, you're right. I'm not.'

'You like getting to know people in a different way,' said Richard slowly, as if considering this for the first time. 'You prefer to observe them surreptitiously, like when I caught you by the pool.'

'Maybe,' I said, calm, though his diagnosis had shaken me. I had never been scrutinised like this before. It felt like he had seen every inch of my body.

'I think that's your technique, Elspeth. And I think you're quite right to do so. You'll learn much more that way. Is your friend an actress as well?'

I nodded.

'Well, of the two of you, Elspeth, I'd say your methods are far superior . . .' He caught my smile. 'Wait – are you laughing at me?'

I hadn't been, but the question tipped me over the edge. I let myself giggle, relaxed into it.

'You are, you're laughing at me. What's so funny?'

'How you use my name,' I explained. 'It's ridiculous. Only politicians and prostitutes use people's names like that.'

'Like what?'

'Like a sales tactic, *Richard*.'

I was enjoying the moment. I was feeling clever. The tension between us – the unbearable anticipation – had weakened its hold.

He laughed. 'A sales tactic. Okay.' He rested his arm on the back of the seat. Turned to face me fully. Then asked with a grin: 'Is it working?'

'No.' I laughed. 'Like I said, *Richard*, it's too unnatural.'

He gave me the measuring glance again. Shrugged. 'Well, I like it – laugh at me all you want. I like hearing you say my name.'

Could he see the goosebumps on my arms?

Thinking back to that drive, fourteen years later, while I sat, abandoned, in the home we had made together, I knew what my mistake had been. I was young and inexperienced, but I had thought I held the power. Of course I did; Tanya and I had always seen ourselves as the manipulators, playing a game to get our way. I thought I was the magnetic one. I thought that *he* could not resist. And that misconception had taken root, as our relationship blossomed. It became the lie that we both tried to maintain.

Richard was stronger, Richard was clever, but it was *me* who made *him* weak.

I could not see, in those early days, how he would twist this lie around – use it to justify his actions.

(Good girl.)

Of course, Tanya was furious when I saw her the next day. Even more so when I moved in with Richard, when I started working for him. It was never supposed to be me who made it. She was supposed to win a role first, walk the carpets, grace those glossies – and then, maybe then, she would find me some bit part, put me in touch with her contacts. The problem with Tanya was that she wanted success more than almost anything – almost. Just not enough to swallow her pride and envy. After I got the *Anatomy* role, every time we spoke, she would go on and on about a fictitious 'project in the pipeline'. She refused any offers of help. Tanya and I saw each other less and less, then not at all.

I was a teenager, living in a strange city with no friends, no family. I was inexperienced – professionally, generally. I relied upon Richard for my home, my job, my entire social life.

Now here I was, years later, alone in a house full of his guests, nothing of my own. A white mini-dress stained with a stranger's vomit.

Another surge of nausea.

I waited for it to ebb, then stood up from the toilet. Accidentally caught my reflection again. What would Richard say if he saw me like this on his birthday? In front of his friends, his colleagues? I tried to blot away the smudged lipstick. And the vomit: the vomit. I lifted my dress and tried to stretch it to the sink, but it was too short, too tight. Fuck it. I would be upstairs, locked in the safety of my bedroom, soon enough. I could throw the dress away.

The handle rattled as I was washing my hands.

'Ah, so you had the same plan as me – I'd no idea I was so distinctly unoriginal.'

I had answered the door to a beaming Tommo. The memorial jazz, the scent of lilies, floated up the stairs.

'Neither did I,' I said. 'Kei and Sabine were here before me. Maybe this should be the rendezvous point for us birthday guests; maybe you'll have the fortune of bumping into Mig—'

Tommo placed a finger over my lips and ushered me back inside. The sudden movement, his strength, alarmed me.

I told myself there was no need to worry – even if Tommo was dangerous, he wouldn't do anything to me, would he? And not here, with guests exploring the house?

He locked the door. I watched him carefully.

But then he turned and smiled at me and said: 'Sorry, darling, but careless talk costs lives. Now we can chat freely.' And I knew, with that smile, that my skittishness was unfounded. It was the house, my paranoia. There was nothing to fear.

'Want me to turn on the faucets as well, Mr Bond?'

'Very funny, Elspeth, but that's actually not a bad idea. There are cops and reporters everywhere, and I wouldn't put bugging past them. The bastards can't even leave us to mourn in peace.'

He lowered the lid of the toilet and sat down, rubbing his head.

'Tell me,' he said, 'are you enjoying the celebrations?'

'Well,' I said, 'I've managed to spend my entire time here either listening to speeches or hiding in this bathroom, so I'd say it was going fairly well.'

'I bet you've missed all of these Ednas and Tommos.'

'Dearly.'

He looked at me with weary eyes.

'How are you doing, Tommo?' I asked. 'Have you been in LA all this time?'

He groaned.

'It's been a bloody nightmare, Elspeth. I've moved to the New York office so I can still get stuff done, but London's been up my arse about returning, and the police kept asking me into the station at a moment's notice. I feel I've been in the air more than I've been on *terra firma*. If I don't have deep-vein thrombosis by now, I'll eat my next boarding pass.'

'Work troubles?'

'An understatement.' Tommo sighed. 'I've had a lot on my plate; another client's left me. I don't suppose you're looking to diversify your portfolio?'

'It's tacky to talk business at a memorial.'

'Of course. Just a joke, dear. And how about you – have you been handcuffed and shaken under a bright lamp as well?'

'I've had my fair share of questioning,' I said. 'But nothing too serious. I think they mostly wanted to find out about the others.'

Including Tommo.

He said: 'You don't think you were a suspect?'

And maybe he had been asked about me. My concern must have shown on my face, because his voice softened as he added: 'Well, no need to worry if the police weren't interested in you.'

'Were they interested in you?' I asked, curious.

'My god, it was a farce. They were dragging up the most bizarre stories. Our rivalry in school, his becoming Head Boy. The time Dicky almost got me kicked out of Cambridge. Money I had lent him for his first film equipment, which he never paid back. They even tried to tell me I'd been in love with you.'

My mouth dropped open. I'd been questioned about our close-ness – the waitress reporting us 'cuddling' – but not love. Nothing as serious as that. Maybe Tommo had been questioned before me, had put the more outlandish suspicions to rest.

'I know, I know, ridiculous. They wanted to construct some kind of Cain and Abel narrative, a continual struggle between us. I was the scholarship boy, I'd worked hard my whole life, whereas it had all come easy to Dicky, and now he was the famous one. I told them to take a look at my bank account if they didn't believe I was successful enough, but then they pointed to my lack of partner, lack of children, lack of aristocratic ancestry. A bloody farce. What kind of forty-year friendship doesn't have a history of disagreement?'

I shook my head.

'Apparently Charlie told them he'd overheard Dicky and me arguing, which is fucking ludicrous. I'll wager that pretty boy pointed his finger to distract from all the illegal substances he consumed – and his own bloody tumultuous relationship with Dicky. Doesn't have a fucking clue who he's messing with. Because – I'll be honest, Elspeth – Dicky and I barely spoke to each other that night. I can't remember seeing him much at all between about one and three in the morning.'

'Neither can I.'

'Wouldn't trust that Charlie twatting Pace as far as I could throw him.'

'How awful,' I said, 'to lie about something so serious.'

I remembered the young actor's cold stare. The red-raw eyes.

'Anyway,' Tommo went on, 'they couldn't make any of it stick and then told me at the end of an interrogation session that they didn't need any more information; I was free to return to London. Not that I could, because this had been scheduled by then – so I've been hiding in my hotel room in back-to-back conference calls for the past few days.'

'You poor thing,' I said, remembering my own computer-filled weeks. 'So do you think they have another theory? If they were leaving you alone?'

'Well, I've been trying to find out.' Tommo rested one ankle on the other knee. His foot was jiggling up and down. 'It seems Honey was initially their main suspect; he was the partner, and lord knows you Americans love to arrest Black men. But apparently he's been cleared.'

'Well, he couldn't have done it, could he? He was passed out before Richard—'

'Passed out?' Tommo cocked his head.

'Yes,' I said. 'Don't you remember him lying on the floor? He'd drunk way too much; he was entirely unconscious.'

'I distinctly remember Honey being awake,' said Tommo. 'He was arguing with Dicky about the smack.'

'It's so strange,' I said. 'Kei told me exactly the same thing earlier, but I was adamant I saw him passed out.'

'Well, maybe that's why he's been cleared. I could be wrong; I'd been smoking a little earlier on so perhaps my timings are confused.'

'Maybe.' I frowned.

'Anyway,' Tommo continued, 'my lawyer thinks the whole thing's going to be dropped. He's been asking around – old-school LA, knows people at the DA's office. They have their doubts about some of us but not a strong enough case on any one account. No evidence of a conspiracy, no murder weapon, so what choice do they have? It would fall apart in court, especially with our pedigree of defence lawyers. They'll probably write it up as an overdose. Dicky choked, but it could have been on his own vomit.'

'What about the bruises?'

'It could have been anything,' said Tommo. 'Who's to say they weren't from earlier in the night? Don't you remember when we passed round the bottle in the paddling pool and people were seeing how deep they could push the neck into their mouths?'

'I don't quite remember that,' I said, 'but I can see some of the others doing it after a few drinks. Richard, though?'

'Elspeth, he was wankered.' Tommo laughed. 'But, you know, not like when he had his problems. He was having fun. I hadn't seen him like that since uni.'

'He was, wasn't he?'

'He had a happy last night.'

We were silent for a few seconds.

'I remembered something odd from that morning,' I said. Tommo looked up, eyes narrowed. 'My arm was wet and I wondered . . . This will probably sound ridiculous, but it made me think of Persephone.'

(A long, fat tentacle slipping between Richard's lips.)

'The octopus?' Tommo was horrified – not at the disturbing nature of my theory, it seemed, but at my stupidity. I regretted saying a thing.

'I keep thinking of those videos, the escape,' I spoke quickly, 'how Richard had passed out right next to the filter flap. You don't think she could have . . . ?'

'Darling.' Tommo had decided to smile. 'Are you getting enough sleep?'

'I know, I know.' I shut my eyes, pinched my sinuses. 'I've already told myself it's nonsense, but – if she had put her tentacles down Richard's – then maybe . . .'

Strong arms cradled my body. Tommo pulled me in close, stroked my hair. Warmed me with his clean-linen scent.

'Darling, I understand. It's easier to imagine that creature killing Richard than to face any of the alternatives.'

The alternatives: had Tommo also considered whether Richard deliberately overdosed? What did he think of the other guests? And could I even trust him?

His chest was hard; I counted its rises and falls. I would not cry. I would not cry *now*.

I took a deep breath and pulled away.

'I should get back,' I said. 'I ought to find Lillie.'

'Will you be returning to New York after this? Maybe we can talk about your investments.'

'I'll hang around for as long as Lillie needs me.'

'Of course.'

'But let me know when you're next in town for work. I'm sure I'll be back in Manhattan soon.'

'Let me give you my business card,' he said. 'The number's changed, but you can reach me by email. And do sing my praises to any interested friends – as I said, taking on new clients.'

I brushed his arm, and said as I left, 'Look after yourself, Tommo.'

'I always do.' He grinned, then locked the door.

Two men were cackling outside the bathroom. One had stuffed birthday candles into his nostrils, ears, and mouth, and his friend was lighting them one by one. Anger flared in my chest, some maternal reaction to misbehaviour, but it subsided as I realised there was nothing to fear. Let them singe their facial hair. Let them melt the smiles from their faces. Let the house burn down to the ground.

Soon I would sleep; soon Richard's party would end. I picked my way across the crowd in my bare feet, hid the dress stain with a hand.

Through oiled limbs and sequins, Judy appeared. She clouded me in a fragrant embrace.

'. . . must come over for dinner some time – Jerry and I are dying to host you in the new house,' she said, kissing my cheeks. 'Well, I am – Jerry's a lousy host, but I don't need to tell you that. So, forty, can you believe it? Getting old. And this party, quite the occasion.'

The one redeeming feature of conversation with Judy was the entire lack of effort needed on my part. She was a verbal riptide, and I was happy to be dragged away.

'But you've got to tell me, where *have* you been hiding? What've you been doing? It's been a million years, hon, a *million*.'

'Oh, not much. Just looking after Lillie,' I slurred. 'Can I get you anything to drink?'

'*Hon*, come *on*. This is why we hire the waiters.' She flapped her hand at me. 'You just relax and enjoy yourself, you deserve a night off from the kids.' Judy was gabbling faster than usual; I was having a hard time keeping up. 'God, yes, so how old is she now anyway – what was her name, Milly? You know, I don't think I've seen you since—'

'Lillie's nine years old n—'

'*Nine?* Oh, my, god, time absolutely *flies* by. Because you didn't come to the house-warming barbecue, did you? I know Jerry's been missing you, he was asking Rich where you were, but I was like, leave the poor man alone, we all know you've harboured a little crush on Elsie for a while, and it's getting embarrassing for everyone. Speaking of which . . .'

The angel-winged man bustled past us. Feathers in my face again.

Judy was tapping the manicured nails of one hand against the wall. I had missed the question she had presumably just asked.

'Sorry?' I said.

'Jerry. Have you seen him around?' Judy looked like she was about to cry. I tried to pat her on the arm and missed. She tossed her hair. 'It's not – it's nothing, hon. It's just . . . He's such a big kid sometimes. I give him my opinion and he thinks I want to start a fight, but . . .'

I could see Jerry over her shoulder, bustling past my broken table, onto the dance floor with his slinky new friend. He took her by the hand and spun her around, shaking his head out of sync with the beat.

Judy cleared her throat.

'Well, the problem with the contractor, let me tell you, is a *nightmare* – don't approach Jimmy Lint and his lousy-ass sons within a ten-mile radius . . .'

My gaze darted from face to face, searching for my husband, returning every now and then to Judy, to keep up the illusion of concentration. This was unnecessary: she had found her reflection in the window behind me and was slicking on lipstick – somehow nevertheless able to maintain her verbal stream.

'. . . not that Jerry understands at all. For *once*, I wish he'd help me out. But you know what Jerry's like . . .'

My eyes swept the crowd, halting on each brown-haired man. They were never Richard. And if he was nowhere to be found, then he was also not here to see me leaving. He was probably lazing in the pool with models or drinking with studio execs. Richard was not thinking of me at all.

I steadied myself on the bannister.

'. . . so I told him,' Judy went on, '*I told him*, if you want me to get the attorneys involved I can and I will . . .'

I had taken Lillie to New York while Richard was filming *One Hundred Years*; he had barely noticed. He had been staying at home less and less frequently, no longer calling each day to check in. He had not spoken to me once since the guests arrived. He would not notice if I disappeared upstairs.

And yet he was there, lodged in my head – chastising me for letting him down, embarrassing him.

'. . . and would you believe it, Jimmy *Lint's* got the *balls* to call *me* a—'

'Judy, I'm sorry,' I interrupted. 'I'm going to have to catch up later – I . . .'

I walked away without finishing my sentence.

I returned to the memorial the long way, retracing my steps from that night – up and over the staggered floors, touching statues and vases as I went. Perhaps Lillie would inherit some of the artwork. I wanted nothing. I had taken my fair share of memories in the divorce settlement.

And then the darkened corridor again, this time a little lighter, this time without the dancing water. I wondered whether Honey would remain at Sedgwick. I wondered where Persephone had ended up. Maybe the ocean, maybe a lab or aquarium. Perhaps I would find her again in an online video. A burst of sunlight illuminated the tank – an invisible exhibition – and I smiled, remembering Tommo's stories.

The mezzanine was empty; I could survey the crowds in peace. There was Richard's nanny, Edith, wheeled along by a nurse. Miguel, swirling cognac and talking with two smug-looking clones who I assumed were his brothers. Honey, collecting a glass of champagne from a waitress, handing it to Yola. And there was Lillie, swanning across the room in her floor-length Versace. Nobody mourns quite like the Italians.

I tried to visualise how Kei would frame the scene. A close-up of a tear beneath a black gossamer veil? Wide-angled shot to catch the waltz of mingling mourners? Or the view beyond the crowds: the slopes and the city, so distant one could imagine them clean of human interaction?

It was a strange materialisation of the party I had imagined over one month ago, as I stood in the shadow of Sedgwick, nerves thrumming. The crowds I had thought I would find. Ex-colleagues, Richard's cronies. Only one person was absent.

(And what a fabulous present you are.)

Although Lillie's speech had been a success, it saddened me that Richard had forced his way into her words. A chance to hear what a daughter thought of her father, and we were treated instead to one final bout of egomania. He had always enjoyed speaking through other people.

At least she had spun Richard's notes into something more beautiful. She was an intelligent girl, self-possessed. The very opposite of me. Lillie was fluent in that other language: literature and history, philosophy and film. Laughed when I missed the reference, misunderstood a joke. Not meaning it to hurt – she was not her father – but laughing because it was unimaginable to her that someone might not know who Miss Havisham was. Laughing because I had mistakenly tried to correct her use of 'nauseous' or 'you and me'.

It was frustrating that she had decided to shun college.

'Why are you looking at me like that?' Lillie had said, after slipping it into conversation. We'd just returned from her high-school production of *Macbeth*; she had played the Lady. 'I never said I wanted to go to college.'

'You never said it,' I began, 'but I assumed—'

'That I'd do what everyone else is doing? I thought you hated that.'

She was still wearing her stage makeup – a heavy, draconian look; clownish on a teenager, in our living-room light.

'I don't care whether everyone else does or doesn't go to college,' I said, 'I care whether my daughter – my bright, academic daughter – squanders her opportunity to—'

'Oh, here we go again.' She raised her voice. 'I'm wasting my education, I'm wasting all the chances you never got. Is that it? You can't hold that over me forever, Mom. I'm not some, I'm not some *vessel* you can live vicariously—'

'No, you're my daughter, who is too young to make such an important decision—'

'Alone? Well, I can,' Lillie snapped. 'Because it's my life.'

She threw herself on the couch, folded her arms.

'So hastily, I was going to say. You're smart.'

'And I've had such a good education, yada, yada, yada. Come on, get to the point where you call me ungrateful or naive.'

I sighed. Rubbed my eyes.

'That's not what I was trying to say,' I told her. 'But since you brought it up: yes. I think it's a waste of opportunities and a waste of a good education.'

'An education you didn't pay for,' Lillie muttered.

'Excuse me?'

She did not answer.

'I just think,' I said, measured, 'that you shouldn't dismiss college so quickly. I always regretted that I missed out on it. It's a life experience.'

Lillie did not speak.

'Maybe you can start working on applications,' I went on, 'and then you'll have the option of whether to submit them or not. And even if you do submit them, it doesn't mean you have to go. I think you need to keep the possibility open.'

'You don't understand,' she said. 'It's not just a form. It's a lot of work. And I *know* I don't want to go.'

'How? How can you know? You haven't even visited—'

'I want to be an actress.'

I sat down next to her.

'I know you do, and you're very good at it,' I said, gently. 'You were wonderful tonight.'

'But?'

'But you can learn more about it at college, while trying other subjects. Or what about acting school? That could be a good compromise.'

'I don't need to,' she said, meeting my eye, challenging. 'Dad offered me a role.'

Of course. I took a slow breath.

Before I could give my thoughts, she pleaded, quickly: 'Just listen, Mom. I'll learn more working with him than I ever would in a lecture hall. And I know it might look nepotistic, but it's a small role; it'll be good experience.'

My mouth was a tight, thin line.

'I've thought about it a lot,' she continued. So this was not a recent development. 'I even talked to my teachers and they agree.'

'I don't think it's a good idea, Lillie,' I said.

'Why?'

'Because.'

'Because it didn't work for you?' She pulled away from me. 'Is that it?'

What could I say? I said nothing.

She laughed.

'It is, isn't it? Oh my god, you do this all the time.'

It had always been hard to shake Lillie's suspicion that my motives were selfish. For the first two years of the separation, before Richard was allowed to see her, that had been the conviction.

'But *why* can't I see Daddy?' she would ask, through tears.

And it was exactly the same when she was fourteen and I told her she couldn't spend a month with him. Her schoolwork would suffer.

'Just admit it's the truth,' she had yelled. 'You want to keep me away from Dad!'

It was. I did. But I could never tell her why.

I said: 'It's not about that, Lillie. It's your education.'

'I'm not having this argument again.' She walked towards the door. Turned back to me and said: 'You know, just because you became some washed-up actress doing fuck all with her life, doesn't mean that I will.'

We had both regretted that line.

I watched Lillie converse with a guest. That angry teenager in a hoodie, with her waxy, Elizabethan makeup, was long gone. She was greeting colleagues and family, politely chatting with strangers. All of her father's charm, none of his calculated cruelty.

We had been awkward with each other the day after the argument, but she was the first to apologise. I knew she had never meant to hurt me – she had been tired from her performance, frustrated with my lack of justification. I also knew there would be little I could say to change her mind. My criticism would push her away. Richard would turn her against me. So I let her go.

And there she was in the crowd below – my self-possessed adult daughter in her floor-length mourning gown. Nodding solemnly, smiling warmly. Standing inches from where I had found her father's body.

Judy was stunned by my sudden departure, barely had time to call out my name before I turned the corner. I was away.

I clung to the bannister, clambered over couples on the stairs, piles of birthday cake mashed into my carpet, and bottles lying on their sides. I paused to breathe, to rub my forehead, when nausea overwhelmed. The sun and martinis were drowning my brain. Was it possible to foster a hangover while drunk?

And Richard . . . Richard had disappeared. But that was good. If he was busy with his guests, he wouldn't notice. This was his night. And I was invisible.

I needed sleep; I needed quiet.

But upstairs the revellers were no less hellish. Two women in flamingo-pink mini-skirts emerged from a bathroom, wiping their noses – a man pushed past to scream vomit into the toilet. I hopped over abandoned shoes, items of clothing.

Another person I did not recognise was curled up against the corridor wall, being comforted by a friend.

'Why?' he cried out, mucus smeared across his face. 'How could she?'

The friend held him tight but said nothing.

'Why?' the man said again. 'It's too many, too many, not enough, I . . .'

His incomprehensible wails echoed behind me as I turned the corner.

I paused for a moment, nausea catching up with me. Music pulsed through the floor; conversations muffled. I reached my bedroom door. I opened it.

And there was Richard, sitting on the bed, unbuckling his belt.

I had no idea what to do with myself once I abandoned the mezzanine, joined the black-clad guests below. I couldn't stomach conversation with Richard's colleagues and relatives, didn't feel ready to seek out any of the other murder suspects. But appearing occupied was near impossible. I longed for something to hold – a glass or cigarette – something to consume, to keep me company. I had neither. And so, cast adrift among the sea of mourners, I found myself gravitating to the floral shrine. A rainbow beacon amid the charcoal, onyx, jet.

Delicate petals spilled out of the boxes so invitingly, I had to stroke them – the freesias, the hibiscus and irises. I read the messages on tags and cards, took note of various names. A box of chunky, unfolding peonies was tied with a blue ribbon and a small tag. There was no message but I recognised it well: Richard's name on one side in spidery inky-blue letters; the universe on the other, a black and sparkling-silver sky. *Space*, it declared at its centre. When I let it fall from my hand I found another card looped to the ribbon: *Honey*, it said; *Earth*, vined and leafy.

The tag on the box beside it also intrigued me. Attached to otherworldly blood-red orchids, it had no name. Only a phrase, cryptically repeated in dark green, cursive:

Willow trees, willow trees.

'They are beautiful, no?'

Sabine was beside me, pinching the petal of a rose between forefinger and thumb. She plucked it off and, with eyes closed, pressed it against her nose to inhale.

'A glorious tribute,' I said. 'The messages are very touching.'

She nodded, tears in her eyes.

We were turned away from the crowd – no onlookers to wonder how we knew each other, whether we had been guests and murderers. No flouting of the pacts we had made with our lawyers.

Sabine whispered, quite earnestly: 'It is death that persuades us to live.'

She allowed herself to look up at me for one second; her eyes were lifeless. Then she picked up a branch of orange blossom, breathed its scent, placed it back. 'Are these flowers already dying? Or not yet. *Presque*. I dream about his body every night. I hear the cries that we did not listen. And I go to his side. I hold his hand.'

'I see him too,' I said.

(The fingers, the eyes, the sharp stench of vomit.)

'Yes, I think we will always see him,' she murmured. 'And this is our judgement. There must be a suffering.'

We looked again to the flowers.

(The wounds; the bruises; a long, blunt object.)

'Sabine,' I said, 'do you have your cigarettes with you?'

Our silent agreement could be damned.

Richard stood to grab my wrist. I was already out of the doorway.

'It's not what it looks like,' he said, following me to the corridor.

'No, Richard.' I tugged my arm away, stepped backwards onto a piece of cake. 'No, I can't do this.'

'I wasn't going to—'

'Why were you taking off your belt, then? Why are you up here, in our bedroom, hiding from your guests?'

I had never seen him speechless before. The dance music downstairs was picking up tempo. His silence made me strong.

'Give me any excuse,' I said. 'Tell me, Richard. Someone spilled a drink on your pants and you had to change? You wanted to put on your swim shorts to—'

'Elspeth, please, you're drunk. You're embarrassing yourself.'

'No.' The anger had taken hold. 'Don't, don't do that. Don't – I can be – I'm allowed to be angry, Richard. One promise. I asked for one promise from you and – who was that in the room with you? Your dealer?'

A woman tottered up to us.

'Bathroom's that way,' I hissed, then turned back to my husband. 'It's ridiculous. It's laughable. You know, even after everything we've been through, I thought you could do this one thing for me. For our family. I thought you were strong enough to—'

'I was.' He raised his voice, then looked around and lowered it. 'I *was*,' he whispered, gripping my wrist again, 'and I've kept sober for nearly a decade, Elspeth, but . . .'

'What?' I said. 'Is it my fault, Richard? Tell me how it's my fault. Tell me how it's my fault you can't control yourself. Tell me how it's my fault you're weak. Tell me how it's my fault that your daughter—'

Richard gritted his teeth, tightened his hold. 'Shut up. Shut *up*. My birthday guests – there are journalists here. Control yourself.'

'Let go,' I said.

He leaned in closer. His face twitched. 'I'm an adult.'

'I asked you to let go, Richard.'

'And I can make my own decisions. I don't have to answer to you. Look at you. You're a fucking embarrassment.'

'I said, *let go*.'

'Trying to cause a scene at my birthday, my wrap party. What, are you jealous? Because it's not all about you for once?'

'You're hurting me.' I raised my voice. Surely someone would hear. 'Let me go!'

'So you have a few martinis, is that right? Let your hair down. Now look at you. Sunburnt. Purple puke down your slutty dress and face like an old hag. Is it any wonder that I try to escape you, when you're such an embarrassment? You look just like your mother when you're drunk. It all comes out. Sweaty, common . . .'

I was shouting now: 'Let me go, let me go, Richard, *let me*—'

He threw my wrist down. It smacked into the bannister.

Neither of us spoke.

I waited for someone to come up the stairs, emerge from one of the rooms, but there was no one. Just Richard and me, staring at each other, catching our breath over the beat of the music.

My voice lowered, trembling, as I said: 'I will not raise my daughter with an addict.'

'Our daughter, Elspeth.' He thinned his eyes. Face full of disgust. 'Don't give me that. You knew what you were getting yourself into.'

'If you go back into the bedroom,' I said, 'there are no more chances. You made a promise.'

The music thudded below. Conversation; shrieks of laughter.

'Don't give me ultimatums,' Richard said. 'You chose this life. Look around you, Elspeth. Who pays for this house? Who pays for your clothes and your car? Who feeds Lillie? Who gives her everything she wants?'

I did not answer.

'You'll do well to remember that next time you feel like telling me what to do. You'll do well to remind yourself where you'd be without me.'

He was smiling strangely.

'Our daughter, Elspeth,' Richard said. '*Our* daughter.'

I turned away from him, so he would not see the tears. And then I heard the bedroom door open again. I heard it close. I heard the click of the latch. And I was alone.

Sabine and I made our way to the far corner of the lawn, far from the other memorial guests. Stood at the precipice, looking across the cityscape, as we had that fateful night. The first draw on the cigarette rushed to my head. I steadied my feet. Giddy with the nicotine, dizzy with the height.

'Where are you from?' said Sabine, after a while.

I was studying the gradient of the sky, how pollution faded the buildings away in layers, like stage scenery.

'My parents always said we lived in Floral Park, Hempstead, Long Island. But really we lived the other side of Jamaica Ave, in Queens.'

'You should be proud of your home,' Sabine said. 'I could say that I am from Paris, but every time I do an interview I tell them Clichy-sous-Bois. Clichy-sous-Bois: I want them to know.'

She extended her arm to tap ashes over the drop.

'This area, this is a suburb,' she explained. 'But the *banlieue* is not the same as American suburb, it's not so good. People are very poor, there are no jobs, and too many police, watching, questioning, violent. Clichy-sous-Bois, we are mostly known for the *émeutes*, which is . . . I can't remember the word. Like rebellion, but stealing, smashing, cars on fire . . .'

'Riots?'

'A riot, yes. I was only a child and I remember, it scared me. But still, you understand why. Growing up, there is not so much there. So now I like to say Clichy-sous-Bois in the magazines. I like everyone to know how it makes me.'

'And now you live in LA.'

'Mostly,' she said. 'But I go home often and I see my mother.'

'She must be proud of you,' I said.

My parents had been proud of me too, in the beginning, even though they had no right to be. They had laughed when I told them I was moving to LA to become an actress because sure, I had the face, but I'd always kept to myself and I did know that actresses were required to speak, didn't I? After I left, they didn't call, not once, not even on my birthday – not until they heard about my part in *Anatomy*. By that time it had already been showing for weeks; an old classmate's mother had informed them I was in it. My parents did not believe her. Not till they saw it for themselves. They recounted this gleefully over the phone. Like it was a hilarious tale.

They were coming to visit. I told them the timing wasn't great, but they had already booked the tickets and hotel. And they were *so expensive*, my mother repeated, until I offered to cover it. That was how I found myself with blisters on my feet, walking up and down Hollywood Boulevard in mid-July, taking photos of my parents pointing at every star, listening to them bicker over who had appeared in which movies. Richard insisted on treating us all to lunch, and my parents jumped at the chance to meet him – a real-life celebrity – and did I think that he had ever met Farrah Fawcett? I told my mother to ask him herself and immediately regretted it.

Of course, the meal went terribly. My father complained about the food: the plates were not big enough, not *at these prices*. Was Richard really going to pay the check? *At these prices?* My mother ignored all of Richard's polite questions, only remarking on his accent.

As soon as we had dropped my parents back at their hotel, Richard was scoffing. He couldn't believe it – I was so different from them. And it was true, I was, but he had no idea that the girl sitting beside him had been carefully constructed. All those weekends copying gloved ladies at Bergdorf's. All those nights watching women at Hollywood parties. How they smiled and laughed and tossed their hair. How the most magnetic were also the quietest. How easy it is to pretend you understand the conversation when you say absolutely nothing at all. I didn't defend my parents. I couldn't. Not when I had tried so hard to distance myself from them. Not when it was true, Richard was right – they were ignorant, they were rude, they *had* been ungrateful and selfish.

I felt awful the next day, when I took a taxi with them to the airport. They were waiting for me on the kerb, carrying their own bags. Sweaty and sunburnt, wearing Studio Tour T-shirts. My mother told me how much they had liked Richard, how proud they were of me.

As she said that, I felt an intense disappointment.

I could not put my finger on it until I had waved goodbye to them at security. It was Richard. I hadn't wanted them to like him. I had wanted my mother to tell me it was wrong – to be seeing a man almost a decade older than me. I had wanted my father to call him a snob – to see through the expensive meal and the flashy car. I had never thought they would be impressed. I had thought they would see it: how lonely I was. I wanted them to tell me to come home.

My cigarette was finished – I had burnt it up too quickly. I flicked the stub down the hill.

'Do you – do you see Lillie a lot?' I asked Sabine. 'I mean, do you spend time together outside of work?'

'A couple of times, but not so much.' She shrugged and took a final sip of smoke. 'I think her friends are younger, but I prefer calm. I know she sees Honey, though. When we were filming, he came to the studio with them. Lillie, Richard, Honey. A little three together. Little family.' She dropped her stub nonchalantly, then turned to look at me. 'You don't see her?'

'Not much since she moved,' I admitted, then cleared my throat. It hurt at the pit where it met my heart. 'We've never been best friends, not like some mothers and daughters. But we were always together. And I've missed her since she left – neither of us is much of a talker on the phone.'

I folded my arms. Went on: 'When I came to visit for Richard's birthday, I thought it would be nice to spend time together. Of course, his death swallowed everything.'

Sabine did not reply.

'And she's finding it very difficult,' I said. 'We both are. Lillie's getting closer to Honey. And she's pushing me away.'

I caught my breath. The confessions had spilled from my mouth too fast. I barely knew this woman. And Kei had said so herself – the cops suspected Sabine of murder.

'I don't think so,' Sabine said carefully. 'I think Lillie is only sad and you are blaming yourself. But I know. I understand you.'

She scuffed her shoe on the concrete border, back and forth like a tap dancer.

'The police,' she continued, 'they ask me: *are you guilty?* And what can I say but yes? Yes, we are all guilty. Not one among us can say he is innocent.'

I spent the night in the guest bedroom. Lay on the bed in my vomit-stained dress, with the door locked, barely sleeping. A few times the handle rattled – drunkards looking for a bed, Richard wanting to talk, I wasn't sure, I didn't care. I lay there, frozen, unanswering. The music continued to thud; my head ached and churned. It took hours for my anger to ebb away. And when it did, a determination was left in its wake.

Dawn was breaking and I felt sober enough to leave. I snuck back into the bedroom to pack myself a suitcase.

Richard had not locked the door. He was lying on the bed, comatose.

It was fusty – the AC was off and the sun was heating the blinds – and there he was, lying there, comatose and stripped to his underwear. His belt was curled on the floor, the buckle beneath his hand. There was a young man beside him. One of his user friends, face down, white boxers. A thread of silver sparkling around the back of his neck. His arms were cocked at strange angles; the palm of one hand was up and open. But it was Richard who lay closest to me, to the door. His head was turned away. The hair on his calves was so familiar. And then his belt, inches below limp fingers.

I found the strength. I looked away.

Holding my breath, I dashed to the walk-in closet as quickly and quietly as I could. Rummaged through my shoe boxes to find the one containing my passport, the secret credit cards. After my last escape to New York, nearly ten years earlier, I knew I could not be too careful – I had opened new accounts, saved money, little by little. It would be enough to get us started. I stuffed everything into my gym bag, along with some clothes, leaving room for Lillie's belongings. She would want her teddy and some books, and did I need to pack some schoolwork as well? My breath caught in my throat. I sat down for a second.

With every inhalation, exhalation, I gave myself a sentence:

You know what you saw.

He tried to lie to you.

A lie cannot overwrite the truth.

He broke his promise.

You are leaving for Lillie.

You know what you saw.

I found Lillie at the centre of the atrium crowds, comforting a sobbing woman. Even across the room, her exhaustion was visible. Couldn't these people leave her alone? She had been on her feet for hours, making small talk with strangers, directing the caterers and musicians; for weeks she had been organising. It was too much responsibility for a young woman, an only child.

A hand touched my back. I suppressed a flinch.

'It's lovely to see you,' said the man. 'Although, I should say, terrible given the circumstances.'

'Hello,' I said, scanning his features – no recollection of a name, but the awkward stance and accent gave him away as a school friend.

'It's David,' he said. 'I'm sorry, you haven't met me since the wedding, so I'm sure you've forgotten the face. It's certainly changed over the years.'

'No, David, yes, I do remember, you went to school with Richard.' I could place him now. The hair had been a blaze of red at the wedding; with its greying, David was unrecognisable. 'Tell me, what are you up to these days?'

'Journalist.' His shoulders hunched inward – an absurd attempt to shrink his lanky form. 'Transport correspondent. Anyway, I just wanted to say, it's lovely to see you. Your daughter gave a beautiful speech.'

'She did, didn't she?'

Behind David, Charlie was approaching Lillie's cluster. As he said his goodbyes, kissed her cheeks, there was no hesitation, no hint of uncertainty on her face. Each of the suspects must have spoken to Lillie that afternoon – anything less would have seemed suspicious.

'It's remarkable, isn't it,' David said, 'how much you can learn about a loved one at events like these? I had no idea Richard played the cello.'

Lillie must have stifled her emotions, buried them below, to have faced the suspects like this. To smile, to thank them for coming, thank them for their sympathy, as she wondered: *Was it you? Did you kill my father?*

'Elspeth?' David was looking concerned. 'Are you all right? You seem a little bit—'

'A long day,' I said quickly. 'There's a lot on my mind. What were we . . . ? Yes, the cello, yes. So it wasn't a childhood hobby?'

'Not one he ever displayed in school. Funny how you think you know someone.'

A waitress held out a tray of champagne glasses.

'No, thank you,' I said, then turned back. 'If you went to school with Richard, you must know Tommo – what were they like back then? Tommo told me this absurd story about the two of them and the river—'

'The river?' David stared at me.

'Yes, when Richard pushed Tommo into the river? You must have heard that one. I'm sure you have hundreds of stories like that.'

David frowned. 'Not really.'

'Well,' I said with a laugh, 'perhaps it was a secret, along with the cello.'

I caught a few bars of 'Silver Train' drifting over the chatter.

'No, I mean, something *did* happen at the river, but Richard didn't push Tommo. Certainly not,' David said. 'I was there, I watched – in fact, we all did.'

He paused for a moment and then found his starting place: 'There used to be three of them, you know. In a little group. Richard, Tommo, and another scholarship boy – Freddie Staines. Richard took them both under his wing, protected them from the snobbery and bullying. But I never quite understood their friendship. They were always jibing one another, pulling pranks – usually Richard, pitting the other two against each other. Pouring water into one of their beds so the sleeper would think they'd wet themselves, running a toothbrush inside the toilet basin. Schoolboy stuff, but even back then I could see there was something nasty about it. Why would you treat your so-called friends like that?'

'I've never met this Freddie,' I said.

'Well,' said David, 'you wouldn't have done. Freddie died in our second year of school. Anaphylactic shock.'

For a moment I forgot my present concerns. 'That's terrible. I'm, I'm sorry to hear it.'

David hesitated, then went on. 'Freddie was deathly allergic

to strawberries,' he said. 'Everyone knew it. The school knew too
– Freddie was always missing out on pudding, and if there was
ever any question about whether a dish contained strawberries,
he'd double-check himself. Richard and Tommo, naturally, teased
him about it. If there was gravy and mash: *Does this contain
strawberries, sir?* And when strawberries were on the menu, they
wouldn't shut up about how delicious they were. Richard didn't
seem to believe Freddie was actually allergic. *Go on*, he'd say.
Have a taste, you'll love it.'

I could almost hear Richard's voice in those words – always
certain that he knew best.

'And then it happened,' David said. 'On his birthday. The
cooks made Freddie a cake, and after taking a bite, his tongue
swelled up. He couldn't breathe. Hives. The teachers tried to give
him his EpiPen, or whatever it was, but they didn't reach him in
time. Neither did the ambulance. We all saw him faint. Turn blue.
He died right before our eyes, on his fifteenth birthday.'

'How awful,' I said. 'And in front of you all.'

'It was. It was horrific. Tragic. I still remember Freddie's father
coming into school to collect his belongings. The first time I saw
a grown man cry . . .'

David seemed lost in the memory.

'Anyway,' he continued, 'it caused a huge scandal. The cooks
were fired. They claimed they hadn't put strawberries in, or even
near, the cake. We'd had jam at tea the day before, though, so
the school chalked it up to accidental contamination. Massive
lawsuit from the parents. But among us boys, there was this
rumour that Richard and Tommo had, well, not deliberately
poisoned Freddie but had maybe tried to test him. Maybe they'd
saved a little jam from tea, maybe they'd added it to his cake. I
remember one of the other boys whispering about it that night:
Richard had been telling everyone he had a *little surprise* for
Freddie's birthday.

'I don't know. It was just a rumour. But you can see how a
mistake like that could easily happen. Foolish schoolboys. I don't
think we knew as much about allergies back then. And, well, yes,

it *was* just a rumour, but everyone could see something strange was going on with Richard and Tommo. Maybe they were grieving, but after Freddie's death something seemed off. They stopped speaking to each other, completely withdrew.

'A few weeks later, a fight broke out between them, as we were walking back from the playing fields, along the river. They were wrestling with each other, both so determined to gain the upper hand that they barely noticed when they rolled right in. But they didn't stop fighting even in the water, each pushing the other's head under the surface. Bloody dramatic stuff. All the boys were yelling, chanting, on the banks, and Richard and Tommo just wouldn't stop. Every so often it looked like the current would sweep their bodies clean away.'

'My god, that's barbaric.'

'It truly was. We thought they were going to kill each other, and they could have done – I saw the blood and bruises after-wards. They only survived because a couple of teachers dived in and dragged them apart.

'We all suspected it might have something to do with Freddie's death. I don't know what the teachers thought – schoolboy scuf-fles, probably – but they had no tolerance for it. And Tommo and Richard should have both been suspended – I mean, anyone who saw that fight could tell both were at fault. But Tommo would have lost his scholarship, see. So Richard took the fall. He was sent home for the rest of the year, if I recall correctly. Two terms. We were all surprised he wasn't expelled, but as an adult I can see that Richard wasn't the kind of student you could expel. You know, all the men in his family attended our school. His grandfather was chummy with the provost.'

'Why would Richard take all the blame if they both hated each other so much they almost drowned?'

'Quite,' said David. 'My theory was that Richard took the fall so he had something to hold over Tommo. Because when Richard returned, the two were as thick as thieves. Ready to conquer the world.' David finished his glass and passed it to a waiter. 'So Tommo told you Richard pushed him in?'

'Yes, he did, I . . . Perhaps I misunderstood.' I tried to laugh it off, but David's eyebrows were knotted firm.

'Perhaps Tommo lied – those two were always trying to get one up on the other, even when they were best of pals.'

'It's a wonder they kept friends like you,' I said.

What had Tommo told me? That the police had focused on their rivalry. Maybe they'd heard many stories like David's.

'Quite frankly, yes, it is.' David was rolling up the programme in his hands, twisting it one way then back the other. 'They were terrible bullies, and after that whole episode, they turned their attention outwards – onto the rest of us. I only really became friends with them when I had supervisions with Richard at Cambridge. I think they had learned by that point that schoolboy pranks don't take you very far in the real world.'

'I can't imagine Tommo hurting a fly. Richard, maybe – he had a terrible temper.'

I had never considered this before – that Richard's friends hadn't all been manipulated by him. That some of them might have given as good as they got.

'Look,' David glanced around him, 'I don't want to speak ill of Richard, not now, but those two made my childhood a living hell. They say boys will be boys, but our school – it was cut-throat sometimes. And I've forgiven them, I have, but it took a lot of work and it doesn't mean I've forgotten . . .'

David cleared his throat and straightened his back.

'I'm sorry, this isn't the time – I should never have . . . You—'

I held his hand. He clutched the programme in the other.

'Please don't apologise.' I squeezed his fingers.

He struggled to control his breathing.

'Thankfully we fostered a different kind of relationship,' David had composed himself, 'and I can leave those things in the past. But it doesn't surprise me to hear that Tommo's lying about Richard now, twisting history when there's no one else to defend the truth. *Vivere est vincere*, as they say.'

'Elsie,' a sing-song voice called. 'I told you I'd track you down again, hon.'

Judy was standing right behind me, unavoidable. I was about to ask her to wait for my conversation to end, but when I turned back to David, he was already pushing through the crowd, hurrying towards the door.

I resigned myself to my fate. Asked, with as much warmth as I could muster, 'How are you, Judy?'

'Hon, I am *not good.*' She flapped her manicured hands with each syllable. 'Everything with Jerry has been a nightmare. The police, you know. And the oncologist's been so unhelpful lately but he's the best money can buy and god *knows* we paid for the best. So I'm dealing with that now and all these insurers. But it's been a real eye-opener, you know, you get to find out who your real friends are—'

'Judy,' I interrupted, 'I wanted to apologise for not getting in touch, about Jerry, his illness . . .'

Her lips tightened.

'And I was heartbroken when I found out, knowing what you'd been going through. I *am* sorry. I had no idea, not even on the night of Richard's . . . party, I—'

'Well, of course you didn't know, hon.' Her words snapped. 'How would you? We haven't heard a word from you in, what, a decade?'

I opened my mouth but she leapt in again. 'And that's what happens when you cut your friends off. You're not around when they go through something life-changing. Decade or so and you don't say a thing to me or Jerry.' Her voice wobbled. 'How can you end a friendship like that?'

'I was struggling, Judy. Everything was such a blur with the divorce, moving and I—'

And Jerry and Judy had been Richard's friends, not mine. I could never have confided in them. That conversation I'd over-heard at Richard's party – the things Jerry had said about Honey – had confirmed it.

'I know, hon, but you let your friends in on the problem, that's what you do.' Her voice lost its spike, exasperated. 'You don't just leave everyone behind, trying to figure out what they did wrong.'

I could not believe she had truly mourned the loss of our friendship. What had it ever amounted to anyway? A friendship of circumstance: awkward wife-talk during our husbands' lunch-time meetings. I didn't feel guilty. And yet a splinter of shame pushed through. It was true: the Debrowskis were going through hell, and I had been none the wiser.

Some physical manifestation of this shame must have reached my face because Judy decided to drop the matter.

'Look, things aren't great with Jerry, and that's just reality. It's non-stop, it is. It's like half my time in the hospital, half my time at the police station, half my time at home, and now these lousy insurers . . .' She sighed. 'But anyway, today's about Rich; it's not Jerry's time yet. So, tell me, how are you doing?'

'I'm doing okay, thank you for—'

'Because you're looking stunning, really. Is that a new shade of blonde?' She fanned herself with the memorial programme: a tasteful black booklet of photographs, the schedule of the afternoon. Richard's filmography graced the back page. 'Your colouring's all different, it's fresh and young and I love it. Stunning. And did a little birdie tell me somebody's seeing one of the Schwarz brothers? Brava, hon, *bra-va*.'

I folded my arms. 'Actually, Julian and I didn't work out, so—'

'Oh, I am sorry. Last I heard, you were jetting all over the world together, but I guess that's what happens when you don't keep up with a friend's life, it's like, what's Elsie doing these days? Who's she seeing? I was chatting to Jerry earlier and I was trying to figure out the last time I saw you, and, you know, it's been a while.'

'It has, Judy, and I meant it when I said I was sorry.'

'And I was thinking,' she bulldozed on, 'it's probably not since Rich's *fortieth*, can you believe it? Ten years and the time *flies* by, it flies. I saw Lillie earlier and my god, she's a woman! I said: *Lillie, you're a woman now!* But hon, you gotta tell me how you're doing. How are you doing?'

Poor Lillie. I would apologise to her later.

'Wonderful, thank you, Judy,' I said weakly, losing track of the times I had already answered this question.

'That's great to hear,' she stage-whispered, 'because I was a little worried, you know, wondering whether you'd turn up at all, with whatshisface, Sugar or something . . .'

'Honey Carlisle?'

'That's the one. You know, it takes *balls* and I am in *awe*, you've put on such a brave face. If I were you I'd be staying a mile—'

'Yes, Richard's death has taken a toll on all—'

'Oh, hon, no, not that.' She swatted her hand. 'Husbands, you know – you love 'em, you leave 'em. Or they leave you, you know; that's what I mean – it's so *brave* of you to be here with that Sugar here, but I know you've got to support your daughter.'

'Because Honey's Richard's partner?' I tried to grasp what she was saying. 'It's no problem at all, Judy – we're all perfectly amicable. He's family.'

Was she talking about the press statement? I did not want to give her the satisfaction of bringing it up myself. If that was the nasty gossip she wanted to shove in my face – at my ex-husband's memorial, of all places – then let her be explicit.

'Oh you *are*? Oh, how *sweet*.'

I could see her little mind recalibrating; she knew I was not going to play. A conversational pause with Judy Debrowski was a home run.

'Because, you know, I haven't seen him since Richard's fortieth either – isn't it funny how these events bring people back together again? But then, when I saw you both here, I was just thinking, *poor* Elsie, how *difficult* it must be . . .'

'Richard's fortieth?' I eyed Judy as she ploughed on, oblivious. She obviously had no idea what she was talking about. Honey wasn't at Richard's birthday a decade ago. Where would she even have heard that? Were the tabloids reporting this?

'. . . seeing the young man her husband left her for in a place of honour at his funeral. When they were only together for a fraction of the time that you were married. It's a scandal, hon, honestly.'

'I'm not sure what you're trying to insinuate, Judy, but Richard and I did not break up over Honey.' I was finished with affability, but I laughed as I went on. 'He would have been, what, seventeen at the time? Richard and I had many other problems.' I widened my courteous smile. 'And you, of all people, know how marriages can become strained over the years.'

It was such an odd and unnecessary tale for Judy to concoct. Was she punishing me for ending our friendship?

Perhaps Richard had stopped caring towards the end, but that was nothing to mourn. It was the unlocking of my door to freedom.

Judy's eyelids flickered.

'Yes, my marriage has been strained recently, what with Jerry's *illness*,' she said. 'But, *hon*, you know I'm only looking out for you. And that Honey boy was most definitely at Richard's fortieth. Don't you remember? He came with that group of young models – I can't remember who brought them, one of the cast members, maybe; it was a wrap party, right? And the models were flouncing around by the swimming pool all night looking pretty. Apart from when Honey disappeared upstairs . . . I guess, hon, I keep forgetting how *out of the loop* you've been, I mean, you positively *disappeared* back to New York, so no wonder you missed all the gossip, but it was scandalous, how *quickly* they got together after the party. I mean, we all just *assumed* that he'd cheated, and can you blame us?'

I could. Richard and Honey had started seeing each other only five or so years ago, hardly a swift transition. Lillie had grown into a teenager in that time.

'It's such a shame,' I said, my voice still light as champagne, 'how swiftly people turn to gossip, isn't it? But I suppose everyone has to fill their mundane lives with some form of entertainment. I only wish it wasn't at the expense of my family, my daughter. You remember Lillie was only nine at the time of the divorce, Judy?'

Nine years old and swept away to the other side of the country: school in Manhattan with Mother; red carpets with Daddy. Speculation about the divorce on every newsstand.

'But it's probably difficult for you to remember that when you were so busy with your . . .' I counted on my fingers. 'What was it? Your third separation from Jerry?'

For once, Judy was shocked into silence. I wondered if I had overstepped the line.

'Anyway, *hon*,' I went on, sickly sweet, 'let me put it all straight now.' I rested my hand on her forearm. 'Richard and I had our own problems, and they were most certainly not caused by a third party. Now I'm going to go and find my daughter. She's had a hard time dealing with her *father's death*.'

'Hon,' Judy said between air kisses, 'think what*ever* you want. I just thought it might be a stressful situation, seeing Honey here. But Richard's gone now, rest his soul, so it doesn't matter, does it?'

'No.' My cheeks ached. 'It doesn't.'

For years, addiction had been the anvil Richard held over my head. When I first met him at Alto's party, clad in that glittering gold dress, he had just left rehab for the second time. He confessed this to me on our very first night. Told me how he'd struggled with alcohol and drugs, ever since his last year of school. Told me the reason why: his childhood, his parents. Told me that somehow he had continued to function, with the help of his manager. Admitted there were still terrible patches, still dark times, and that he had not yet found a way to keep them at bay. He could throw himself into work for a while – become obsessive, controlling, disciplined for his art – but ultimately there would be a period of inactivity and the rot would creep back in.

'I'm waiting for the answer,' Richard told me, our legs twisted together.

We had reached the odd hours of the morning, just before dawn, and I could pick out his features in the speckled, murky light. They seemed to change, second by second, like his face was an unknowable thing.

'I'm certain it's somewhere. That's why I haven't given up hope.' He stroked my shoulder blades, kissed my nose.

That evening, at the bottom of Alto's stairs, Richard had given me the manhattan he was about to drink himself. I had kept him sober. I would keep him sober, I decided in that bed, as he whispered his confessions, ran his tongue along my collarbone.

'Beautiful,' he murmured. 'My angel.'

I could not know, as I lay with him then, what would become of this unspoken promise. I could not know that it would become an unspoken threat. That it would be one of many.

There, in the closet, I drowned out those memories with my own sentences:

You know what you saw.

He tried to lie to you.

A lie cannot overwrite the truth.

I changed out of the clinging, dirty dress, slicked to my body with the sweat, the vomit. Jeans, a linen shirt, and large, dark shades; ankle boots, matching purse, shaking hands.

He broke his promise.

You are leaving for Lillie.

You know what you saw.

I left the bedroom without turning back. The addicts did not wake. As I walked away from our home, I was trembling.

The old Richard would not have let me leave so easily, would have tried to coax me back with sweet lies, would have locked the doors. But this Richard did not really, truly want me any more. This Richard would let me take our child to the other side of the country and build her a new life. This Richard would not dispute the custody and settlement my lawyers proposed. He would not even try to contact me. It would only be a year later, once he had been to rehab and undergone regular drug tests, that I would speak to him again.

And when I eventually saw him face-to-face, at the threshold of a fortress, the man who stood there would be a stranger to me – and that was exactly what I wanted.

Adrenaline surged through my veins as I paced away from Judy. I pushed past mourners, turned my head before they could open their mouths. Tommo, laughing with a group of sharp-suited men, reached for me. I threw off his hand. There were no waiters in the kitchen. Disregarding the stares, I rinsed out an empty champagne glass. Drank the water fresh from the faucet, ignored its mineral bite.

I needed space, I needed to think. But looking out to the lawn, across the room, everywhere, every cubic foot, was occupied with black-clad bodies. Someone tapped on my shoulder – another guest, unrecognisable, trying to ignite conversation. I flashed a fake smile, mouth full, and shook my head.

I had won the conversation with Judy. A group of models by the pool, a seventeen-year-old boy . . . It was ridiculous. It was laughable. I could not have let Judy's sniping go unchallenged.

(It was scandalous.)

What an odd way to get back at me. Or was I supposed to be grateful that she was imparting her precious gossip? Was I to throw my arms around her, to weep with gratitude, kiss her orange cheeks and apologise for my coldness all those years ago because yes, yes, yes, she was such a marvellous friend, yes, yes, yes, such a kind and caring soul, and oh Lord, oh god, how *ever* could I have let her go, how *ever* could she forgive me?

(How *quickly* they got together.)

Richard had almost certainly cheated on me before. I was no fool. He spent months away from home. He had barely given me a second look in our last few years together, unless to criticise. But that was not what had happened the night of his fortieth birthday. I had found him unbuckling his belt, and in the morning, he was passed out next to whichever idiot he'd convinced to shoot up with him.

(Scandalous.)

Or had I just assumed? Richard had told me, early in our relationship, that he was attracted to men as well as women, and while bisexuality wasn't something people discussed as openly back then, of course I accepted and loved him for who he was. But acceptance is not the same as understanding, and perhaps, in that fusty morning room, I had only seen what I thought I would find.

I needed space, I needed silence. This godforsaken place.

'Elspeth.' Honey's hand was on my arm. 'Can we talk for a minute?' And then when he saw my flustered face: 'You look . . . Are you okay? Do you want to sit down?'

'I'm . . .' I almost did ask for help. But then I paused. It was jarring – his materialisation, solid and real, just as I had been thinking about him.

I tried to pull myself together. We were talking, alone, for the very first time. What did he want? I answered, more collected: 'No. I'm fine, thank you.'

'It's about Lillie,' Honey said. 'I know – she told me you're not okay with us spending time together and I just wanted to find you and say now that the memorial is over, I can step away. If that's what you want, I'll understand. Honestly, it'll be hard for me if that's the case because I missed her when Richard and I separated and – I don't have much family left, so Lillie's really important to me. But she's your daughter and I understand that. I don't want to come between you.'

'You're not coming between us,' I said. What right did he have to diagnose my relationship with my daughter?

'No,' he said, 'I'm sorry, that came out wrong. I meant, like, if you felt uncomfortable. About that night.'

A waiter brushed past us with a tray of glasses.

Honey continued, in a lowered voice: 'I know how it is. I've felt weird today too, seeing the others, and all I want to say is that I totally understand if you don't feel ready to trust me.'

If I didn't feel *ready* to trust him? As though I could ever trust him – the murder suspect befriending my daughter? I knew nothing about him, I realised suddenly.

'I don't know what you're talking about,' I said, cold.

The look Honey gave me was not dissimilar from the one Lillie had given me weeks ago, when I'd told her I had no reason to doubt Honey but doubted him nonetheless. There was hurt, disappointment. A shrug of his shoulders. 'Cool. Okay. Well, I just thought

I should offer. She's your daughter, I know. I don't want to cause you any problems.'

I could have said something then, but for some reason it seemed more important to keep myself gathered and nonchalant.

'You haven't,' I said. 'We're fine.' Then added, as though I really had no problem with him: 'In fact, I was just looking for Lillie. Have you seen her recently?'

'Sure.' Honey nodded, took me by the arm.

The crowds parted so we could swim with ease. There was the space – the beautiful, clear, unoccupied floor. When we reached the kitchen doorway, he uncoupled our elbows. We passed through in single file; Honey led the way. And at his neck glinted a delicate, thin silver necklace.

I drew back my arm.

(He was lying face down, a thread of silver sparkling around the back of his neck.)

I had seen him passed out. I had.

It was crisp in my mind. He had been sprawled face down, a thread of silver sparkling around his neck – that same necklace he was wearing today, beneath his formal shirt.

Yet Kei and Tommo – what of their recollections? They were absolutely certain Honey had not been unconscious on the night of Richard's death.

And I was certain I had seen it.

(His arms were cocked at strange angles.)

I tried to replay the last moments of Richard's fiftieth, but I no longer saw where each of us was sitting. I no longer saw Honey lying asleep on the floor beside me, although I remembered everything I had said to the police. It was not a memory – it was a monologue in dead print. Only the rest of the night seemed real: the house, the dancing, the movies, and the pool.

Was Judy telling the truth?

(A thread of silver.)

I had to know.

Honey turned to check I was still behind him. Frowned as he caught my expression.

'Honey, when did you meet Richard?' I asked.

Honey did not answer.

'It was you, wasn't it?' I said. 'That night. At Richard's birthday.'

'Elspeth, are you feeling all right?'

'Not his fiftieth. I mean ten years ago. The wrap party, Richard's fortieth. You were there.'

For a moment it seemed as though Honey would not answer. Guests bustled past us; the band played. At the heart of the crowd, we faced each other.

Then he nodded. 'Ten years ago, that's when we met.'

Was Judy right? I felt sick.

'My god, you were,' my hand covered my mouth, 'you were only seventeen.'

Honey's expression hardened. 'With all due respect, Elspeth, you don't know me. At all. So if you think that you can judge—'

'You were seventeen.' I felt myself sway on my feet.

'Elspeth, I didn't even know he was married—'

'No.' I shook my head. So Richard *had* cheated on me with Honey. Judy was right. But the infidelity wasn't what sickened me. 'You were telling the truth. About Richard. I know you were.'

All those rationalisations over the years – that I could leave my life behind and never look back, that the next person would be stronger . . . The next person had been a seventeen-year-old boy, estranged from his family, whom I should have protected. Whom I failed again, almost a decade later, when I lied to the world, when I chose to protect our tormentor instead.

We held each other's gaze – as we had that fateful morning, when I stroked Richard's stony neck for a pulse, found none, gave the nod – and then Honey looked away. Smiled bitterly. I couldn't tell whether it was a smile of disgust, disappointment, or vindication.

'Of course you knew,' he said.

'But Lillie asked—'

'Spare me the liberal guilt. It's too late now.'
And Honey walked away.

Lillie was surrounded by elderly relatives in the atrium, hands clasped by a great-aunt. I stood a few feet behind the gaggle, alone among the mourners, waiting for her to finish so we could leave this house, with its cursed names, with its cursed crowds, for good.

Standing there among grieving relatives, I became certain. I knew: Honey had been the man strewn across my husband's bed on his fortieth birthday, and I had conjured that image to my memories of the fiftieth, that night of champagne and vodka and secondhand smoke.

Had this, my mis-memory, cleared an otherwise-guilty man's name in the eyes of the police? I didn't think so – the other guests, including Honey himself, must have counteracted my testimony. But it changed everything for my own suspicions. Now there was no reason to be sure of Honey's innocence. On the contrary, I knew he had every reason to want Richard dead. The tentacles, the tentacles . . . Occupied with conspiracies, I had failed to examine my own memories.

There was a tap at my elbow. Yola.

'Please don't make a scene here,' I said, tired. There was too much already to juggle: stories with only an ounce of truth, memories bleeding together.

'I won't make a scene.' Yola was wearing her overcoat, holding her black purse close.

'What do you want? I don't – this really isn't the time.'

She smiled. Her husband was coming towards us.

'I just wanted to tell you,' she said, 'they found it.'

If Honey had killed Richard, did that make me complicit? It was my fault they were still together. If only the world had believed Honey when he told the truth about Richard – perhaps he could have believed it himself and found the strength to never return. Was this why I had held on to the memory of Honey lying unconscious, why I had clung to the possibility of his innocence? If I blamed Honey, I could only blame myself.

'Hello?' Yola was still standing there. 'Did you hear me? I said, *they found it.*'

'I have no idea what you're talking about. Please, can we do this some other time?'

There was a smattering of applause as the jazz band finished the last song and began packing away their instruments. The room was emptying, yet Lillie's admirers continued to grow in number, lining up to say their farewells. Few had tried to speak with me. I was not the widow.

I looked for my ex-husband's lover in the crowds, spotted his long legs ascending the spiral staircase.

'Lie to yourself,' Yola said, smiling, 'but you can't lie to me. They found it. In that octopus filter, last week. When they were taking her away. I was there.'

'Sorry, found what?' I asked.

'I called the police. And they know. They have it now.' Yola's husband took her arm. 'One minute,' she told him. Turned back to me, smug: 'I told you they would find out and now they have. I hope you get everything you deserve.'

They left before I could respond, made their way towards my daughter. I puzzled over Yola's comments: had I left something behind at the party, something that seemed, to her, incriminating? I could think of nothing – chalked it up to her paranoia and hatred. If the police *had* found something incriminating, I would have been called in to the station. I would not be standing at my ex-husband's memorial, with the officers in attendance.

There were more important things to worry about.

I watched the staircase for Honey's return.

Should I inform the police about my faltering memory? The silver necklace, a young man's sprawling limbs. If there was any chance I was still a suspect, as Yola believed, I needed to come clean as soon as possible. What if the police thought I'd deliberately lied about Honey? What if they thought I had been trying to protect him?

'Beautiful day, beautiful,' Miguel said, from a few feet away.

Then moved closer: 'I've spoken to almost everyone here, so don't worry about people seeing us together, okay? That's why you ignored me earlier, isn't it?'

He spoke a little slower than the night of the party but still did not let me answer his question, fiddled with the tail of his tie as he went on.

'Figured most people have left anyway, so it doesn't matter.' He was avoiding my eye. 'No one will hear – well, anyway, my brothers told me to stay away from you all, but they don't know who was at the party, so fuck that, I'll speak to who I want.'

I noticed his two lookalikes standing by the window, checking their phones.

'You shouldn't have called me,' I said. 'You shouldn't have been calling Lillie's number.'

'I know, I know, I'm sorry. Look, I probably had one too many, but it was coming from a place of concern, Elspeth. How are you . . .' He cleared his throat. 'How do you . . . How have you been?'

I weighed whether it was worth trying to push him away. But, no, it would make more of a scene.

'It's been difficult,' I said, resigning myself to the conversation. 'But I've been looking after Lillie, so I've had something to focus on. Something more important.'

His eyes were darting wildly as he waited for me to finish. He sniffed.

'I keep seeing – I keep remembering what he looked like. And his body, I just . . . Fuck. Everything. I can't believe – I mean, no one deserves that. Not even Richard. Not even Richard, god rest his soul.'

He looked around as if Richard were somewhere in the room. I moved away from Lillie, conscious she might hear. Miguel duly crept closer.

'And coming here again, I mean, you must feel it. You notice all the furniture's gone? I'm glad I don't have to see that gold fucking velvet couch again.'

He came closer still. I could smell the smoked salmon on his breath.

'But the thing that's really fucking me up is knowing that he's here. The guy that did it. Somewhere here with us, and it's fucked up, it's so fucked up . . .'

'I don't think we should be speaking about this, Miguel.'

The police officers were on the other side of the empty glass tank, in heated conversation. I wondered whether I should approach them once Miguel had left. Ask for a conversation somewhere private. Apologise. Tell them I had got it all wrong.

I tapped my foot, desperate for Miguel to finish. I needed to think everything through. I needed time.

Then why did I feel I needed to act urgently?

'The walls have ears, the walls have ears, I get it,' he said, gripping my shoulder tight. 'But this is what I needed to say earlier: you've got to be careful, he can be dangerous.'

'Sorry, who?'

'Honey,' said Miguel, perplexed at my question. 'Come on, tell me you don't see it? The way he's been acting today?'

I held my hands together so no one could see them tremble.

'It's suspicious, isn't it? I don't get it. Why haven't they arrested him already? I mean, we all saw it, didn't we? We all saw how he was looking at Richard that night. All I'm saying is, who's getting the house? Who's getting all this artwork? I'm sure as fuck not going to see all the money Richard lost me.'

My palms were sweating. I scanned the room for Honey, but he was still absent, hiding in the depths of Sedgwick.

A thought occurred: if Judy knew about Richard and Honey on the night of his fortieth, did others?

'Do you know when they met?' I said. 'Richard and Honey?'

For the first time, Miguel carefully chose his words. 'I mean,' he said slowly, 'I don't know exactly, but it was a while ago, right?'

The answer was there in his squirming. A seventeen-year-old boy, whom I should have protected. Possibly a killer that *I* had created.

'Elspeth, I'm sorry.' Miguel leaned closer still. His aftershave was acrid, and he had drunk too much of something – not champagne; vodka, maybe. 'I know I shouldn't have brought it up, because the cops haven't, you know, but earlier I saw Lillie with him, so I had to give you my advice, and, look, this is what I was trying to tell you when I called: You need to keep your daughter far away from Honey.'

An icy plunge of terror.

'Because she shouldn't – look, Elspeth, please, Honey can't be trusted. *He cannot be trusted.* That night, I saw—'

A beep and crackle of radio cut over his next few words, and with that the two police officers, beyond the glass, sprinted up the staircase.

Lillie was at the centre of the room, unreachable, stock-still. Yola and her husband were huddled around her. Miguel had stopped fiddling with his tie, was gripping it in a red fist. Even his brothers had paused their conversation, were looking up from their phone screens – looking, with everyone else, to the mezzanine. The room, though full of wait staff and musicians and the last of the guests, felt strangely motionless.

It was my fault Honey had returned to Richard. If I had not lied, if I had not written my statement, if I had not turned the world against him, perhaps he would have made his escape. But he had returned. He had believed it would all be different. And it was not – he was pushed too far.

Honey had killed my ex-husband, my daughter's father, and it was my fault, all my fault.

I looked to Lillie, I looked back at the mezzanine. My heart pounded.

And I could see it in the space only a few steps away, where the couch should have stood, where we danced and talked and drank: the splayed fingers, the eyes, the sharp stench of vomit; the lips opening to a wet 'O', the pink-splattered cotton; the wounds, the bruises, a long, blunt object. And the bodies together, comatose on my marital bed. And how I had stalled the investigation with my weak memory. How I had let a murderer befriend my teenage daughter. How I should have trusted my instincts. And the tentacles, the eyes, the sharp stench of vomit . . .

The room, suspended. Footsteps echoed from the corridor above. Blurred shapes beyond the reflections of an empty tank. Lillie turned to look at me in horror.

And there, on the mezzanine, flanked by the cops, was Tommo.

'Please.'

'Honey, sweetie, baby,' Richard said. 'We talked about this. It's my birthday present, remember?'

'But it's not – can't you just—'

'We discussed it. We decided together. It's disrespectful to bring it up now, in front of my guests.'

'It's not a good idea,' said Honey. 'I'm asking you. Please. For me.'

Richard sighed. 'Don't play that card. Remember what you said? I'll be safer, here, with you. I waited until now *for you*.'

I was cross-legged on the floor, groggy, wishing I had already left. It took me a moment to figure out what they were discussing. When I did, I resolved to stay out of it.

'Remember?' repeated Richard. 'It was you that suggested it. *Why don't you wait until—*'

'That's not what I meant.' Honey raised his voice in frustration. 'You know that's not what I meant.'

Richard shook his head, disgusted. I knew that look.

'Don't contradict me in front of my friends, baby – you know full well what you meant. Don't lie.'

Honey looked like he was going to be sick.

Richard turned away from him.

'Please,' repeated Honey, desperate. '*Please*, Richard.'

'Richard, you don't have to do it,' Kei was saying, from the other couch. 'Come on, it's not like anyone else is into it.'

'I'll give it a try,' said Charlie.

'See,' Richard shot Kei an acidic look, 'you don't know what you're talking about, darling.'

Kei's jaws clenched; her temple throbbed.

'Whatever.' She took out a cigarette, lit it, and turned her head away. One hand was combing through a snoozing Sabine's hair.

Richard pulled his belt through the loops, then stood to lift the couch cushion, humming himself a happy birthday under his breath.

Honey, Tommo, and Kei looked at one another, as though deciding who should speak. I averted my eyes. This was not my battle.

It was Tommo, bloodshot-eyed, who stepped up to the plate: 'Mate, perhaps it's not such a good idea.'

'Mate, mate, *mate*, perhaps you should mind your own fucking business.' Richard turned around, cushion in hand, to face him. I flinched with each syllable. 'Have I not been an excellent fucking host tonight? Have you not had an excellent fucking time? What more do you want from me, mate? What more do the rest of you want? After everything? After everything I've done for you?'

He threw down the cushion and picked up a glass. I inched away. Surely he would not smash it – not now, not with us watching—

He splashed its contents over Tommo's face with one quick jab. 'Drink the champagne I provided for you and mind your own fucking business.'

Tommo had not flinched. He did not wipe his face. He stared at Richard, droplets running down his cheek.

Honey and Kei looked at each other; Charlie looked down at the floor.

The silence stretched out, bloated.

'I'm sorry.' Richard put the cushion back, ran his hand down his face, and sat. 'Look, the stress has really gotten to me lately. I just want to take the edge off, is that so awful? I just want to take the edge off.'

Nobody replied.

He went on: 'It's just that I kept clean for decades, and my promise to myself was that I'd enjoy this on my fiftieth birthday. It's been keeping me going these past few months, keeping me from doing it when I was alone. What – would you rather I waited till you're all gone? Should I book myself a room in a seedy motel? Don't you want to keep me safe?'

I held my breath. Made myself as small as possible. This was not my battle.

'I'm sorry,' Tommo said slowly, a serrated edge to his words. Water dripped from his chin to the floor. 'I shouldn't judge.'

'You're right, we want to keep you safe,' said Honey.

Charlie piped up: 'Exactly. If he wants to—'

'But letting you do this to yourself isn't keeping you safe,' said Kei. 'Guys,' she looked around the group, desperate, 'come on, are you really going along with this?' Her eyes fell upon the actor, her voice hardened. 'Charlie, trust me, you don't want to get into it.'

'Richard, mate,' Tommo spoke up again, 'I just think that if you take this one step, you're undoing years of—'

Richard spoke quietly, wearily, but through gritted teeth. 'Did you not fucking hear me? This is the *only way* I kept myself clean.'

Nobody seemed convinced, but no one challenged him either.

Richard laughed. 'Hey, let's lighten up! It is my fucking birthday after all. Don't end it like this. Tommo? Charlie boy?'

But the room was silent. Charlie avoided Kei's glare. Honey adjusted his cufflinks. Tommo rubbed his jaw, jiggled his knee. The puddle beneath him was seeping into the concrete.

Lillie flashed through my mind and I considered intervening on her behalf. But I knew nothing could dissuade Richard, not even his daughter; protests would only strengthen his resolve. I was tired. My mouth was sealed. My body was exhausted. And this was not my battle.

Richard stood up again, rummaged under the couch cushion. As he drew out a package, he began to mutter:

'*I look into my glass, and view my wasting skin . . .*'

I folded myself onto the floor, rested heavy head on elbows. It was surprisingly comfortable, this concrete.

'. . . *and say, "Would God it came to pass, my heart had shrunk as thin!"* Remember, Tommo? Recite with me. Schoolboy memory never fades, does it, Tommo?'

His friend was silent, wet.

'No? *For then, I, undistrest . . .*'

He rolled his 'r's and sang his vowels. I could not see what he was doing with his hands, only his melodramatic face, mouth twisting out each line. The package rustled. A clatter, a smack.

'. . . *by hearts grown cold to me, could lonely wait my endless rest with equanimity.*'

His voice rose, thespian.

'*But time, to make me grieve, part steals, lets part abide; and shakes this fragile frame at eve . . .*'

I let my eyes fall shut as Richard spoke the last line. The floor was chilling my cheek. The aquarium filter murmured.

'. . . *with throbbings of noontide.*'

ACT III

A colossal whale floated overhead – fibreglass suspended above the shrieking, laughing crowds, but somehow still stately, still dignified. Silent and unmoving, a world apart. Lillie and I strung lanyards around our necks. It had been her idea – to visit the aquarium on the day the jury's decision would be read. Better to hide from the press; better to miss our carefully worded statement, read aloud by Scott on the steps of the courthouse. Better to escape to Long Beach and visit an old friend.

'Do you think she'll recognise us?' I asked, as we entered the blue. Lillie shrugged.

The shock of Tommo's arrest, our uncertainty, the questions – it was all too much.

I had whisked a stunned, shaking Lillie away from the memorial – away from the frantic guests, cell-phone cameras flashing. Journalists or opportunists, I didn't care. Either way, we needed to escape. I watched Sedgwick in my rear-view mirror. Waited until it was submerged in trees, until it could have been any patch of forest, and only then tore my eyes away to look at the road.

I didn't speak until we returned home, and then only to ask Lillie what she wanted to eat. To my surprise, she had answered: pizza. We turned on the television halfway through *Bringing Up Baby*. Ate in front of it silently. And that was how we had existed during the months of the court case: in a numbness, purposeless.

It was as if we had decided to act as normally as possible. Breakfast, lunch, dinner, and sleep, up in the mornings like clockwork. I kept myself busy. I ran. I even got in touch with Jerry, took him to a few of his chemotherapy appointments.

Maybe we could forge our own friendship, I thought, without Richard. Maybe with his death we could all become ourselves, fully.

And it felt right to spend time with someone who had been there that night, even if we didn't discuss it in depth. As we sat on those vinyl waiting-room chairs, Jerry would say something like: 'Heard they've got Charlie Pace on the stand today.'

He never asked me the question I'd been asking myself: did I really think Tommo had done it? Did I think he was capable? Jerry kept his own thoughts close, as well.

Heard the DNA expert is in next week,' he'd say, and that would be that from both of us.

But it was closer to a conversation than Lillie and I ever got.

Once, a few days after the trial began, I thought we might talk. 'What do I do now?' she had asked me.

I was about to say: *There's nothing to do. We just wait and we listen and we wait. That's all.*

But then she added: 'I mean, what do I do while I'm waiting?'

'Could you start thinking about work again?' I asked. 'It might be hard at first. A reminder of . . . But maybe a distraction would help. Some scripts to read? Or you could come with me to see Jerry if you want to get out of the house?'

And then I remembered the piece of paper he had given me that night, months ago. It was there, in my purse, slipped into the lining pocket. There was no reason it wouldn't be, but it nonetheless seemed out of place. A relic, anachronistic.

'Thanks,' Lillie said when I gave it to her, although she didn't seem particularly pleased.

The contact details of Jerry's friend didn't prompt any change in her behaviour. She didn't throw herself into phone calls and meetings and scripts as I'd hoped. She carried on as before: pale and lost. Only leaving the house every few days, to go and see Honey. I wondered if she had even sent the email. Not that I could really blame her.

Mostly, at home, we wasted time, browsing the internet side by side. We spoke to each other, about the mundane. What would we make for dinner? Did we need to buy more bread, milk? The more we approached ordinary life, the more it was exposed as a pretence.

There was nothing real or necessary or true to say. Neither of us wanted to be the first to bring up Richard, Sedgwick, Tommo's arrest. We didn't even talk about Honey – my misgivings about him before the memorial; the arguments. Every time Lillie slipped out to meet him, all she said was: 'I'll be back before dinner.' I knew where she was going, and she knew that I knew. But how could we broach that subject when it was so tangled with the rest?

We could only wait, refresh our newsfeeds. Side by side on the couch.

In the end it had been me who spoke first, inadvertently. During a commercial break, some time towards the end of the trial, I absentmindedly asked out loud: 'What happened to Persephone?'

Lillie blinked blankly.

'The octopus.'

'Honey found instructions in Dad's notes,' she'd said, lifting a lock of hair to search for split ends. 'He wanted it to go to the public aquarium.'

Schools of yellow fish were following as we strolled. Sharks above our heads; coral at our sides.

'Oh my god, Mom, look,' said Lillie. Even amid everything, she couldn't help but be awed. 'They're unreal.'

We slowed to a standstill in front of a jellyfish tank. They were unreal, she was right. Their tendrils were oddly fluffy, drifting through the water as they swam over one another. A mass, a plume of smoke.

'Get yourself to makeup and wardrobe,' someone scolded. 'You were supposed to be here over an hour ago.'

He was the first person to address me since I had walked into chaos.

'I thought I was early,' I said. 'I was told—'

'I'm sorry, I don't have time for this. Grab Petra or—'

The sentence was lost with the buzz of his walkie-talkie. I had no idea who Petra was.

Richard had told me there was nothing to worry about. Someone with a walkie-talkie would point me in the right direction. I still did not understand why we'd had to arrive separately. So he needed to get to the studio three hours before me, couldn't I arrive early and just hang around? Couldn't he introduce me to everyone, show me the set?

'You're sweet.' Richard had laughed. 'The new girl in school. Trust me, everyone'll respect you more if you walk in like a professional. You wouldn't want them to think I cast you because we're sleeping together, would you?'

I strode towards a group of young men. I would not be nervous, I told myself. In only a few hours, I would be performing in front of these people.

'Hi,' I said, flashing my best impression of Tanya. 'It's my first day – do you know where I need to be?'

'Don't ask Craig questions like that,' one of them said. 'He barely knows his 10-4 from his 10-2.'

They roared with laughter. I kept my grin plastered.

'Cast?' asked another, when they had finished. He looked me up and down. 'Find an AD.'

'Someone with a walkie-talkie,' his friend added, patronising.

'Sure,' I said, still smiling, 'I know what I'm doing, I just don't know where I'm going. You guys must know where makeup is?'

Makeup was no less frenzied, every seat occupied. A woman with a clipboard approached. 'Do they need you for the club scene as well?'

I told her I was not an extra.

She shouted over her shoulder: 'No, she's not.'

'Thank the Lord above,' cried a woman brandishing a palette. The man in her chair flinched. 'Who is she, then?'

'Name?' asked Clipboard.

'Elspeth Bell.'

'Oh,' said Clipboard. 'Oh.' Then shouted again: 'She's Cassandra.'

'Mine,' said the other woman. I was shepherded into her chair.

'Cassandra DiSotta,' she swaddled me in a black bib, 'I've been waiting to get my hands on you. First day on set, right?'

Something about the environment – the women, the perfume, the familiarity of a salon – encouraged me to drop my pretences.

'First day on set ever,' I said.

'Wow, okay. Big day. Make sure you enjoy every moment. You only get one first day. Before you know it, you'll be a battle-scarred veteran like me.'

I laughed. Yes, I would enjoy every moment – here I was, with a professional makeup artist, and I was being paid for the priv-ilege. If Tanya, if my parents, could see me now.

'Okay,' she pulled my hair into a bun, 'there's still a back-up in hair and wardrobe, so let's get your face done while we've got a second.' She blew her fringe off her forehead. 'You picked the wrong day to start, girl.'

'Sam,' someone called, 'Casey wants to know where the Mastix should go.'

'Ask Lucy,' Sam said, and then to me: 'It's the extras. Their agency fucked up so they all arrived an hour late. Right, let me get your folder.'

She rummaged through a box. Found my character's name.

'You're much younger than I expected,' she said, looking at my casting Polaroids. 'Don't know what it is – some people are younger in person, aren't they? And this is your first set. Well, that's exciting for you. But you should know now, it's mostly hanging around. It'll flash by so quickly, your time in front of the cameras. Okay, here we go.'

I held as still as I could while she dabbed at my face. When she stood back, I could study my reflection. Heavily outlined lips, thin brows – just like the girls back home.

Strangers across the country, maybe even around the world, would watch this face, would lose themselves in my character's story. In mine and Richard's creation. How many couples could point to an artwork and tell the world: *Look, here, this is our love?*

'Let me find the camera,' Sam said. 'Continuity.'

A few minutes after she had left, a woman sat in the chair next to mine. 'I don't think we've met, have we?'

'Elspeth.' I put out a hand to shake. 'It's my first day.'

'Of course it is.' She smiled.

'Sorry, I don't think I caught your name?'

'Joan. Joan Tucker. I play Kim.'

'So we have some scenes together,' I said. 'When do we rehearse?'

She took a sip of her coffee. 'I thought we weren't filming those till next week.'

'But don't we rehearse before?'

Sam returned with her camera and Joan stood to hug her. They gossiped while Sam captured my face, fanned the Polaroids in the air to dry.

'And you've met Elspeth here?' Sam eventually asked. 'First day on set. Ever.'

Joan smirked. 'I gathered. She was asking when we would *rehearse.*'

'Oh, no,' said Sam, trying not to laugh, 'there's no rehearsal like that. You'll walk through the scene a couple times before shooting . . .'

'But that's for everyone else,' said Joan, inspecting her nails. 'Camera set-ups, blocking.'

'When do we get direction?' I asked.

'Richard might give notes right before shooting, but that's not usual. He'll only tell you what to do when you're doing it wrong.'

'So how do I know—'

'Just do what you did during casting,' she stated. 'I mean, you did go through the audition process, didn't you? They chose you for a reason.'

Joan was unblinking.

I felt myself blush. I had been through auditions, screen tests, but I could see the judgement in her eyes. She knew about my relationship with Richard.

'You'll be fine.' Sam smiled. 'Don't overthink it. Lucy will take you to wardrobe and hair. Lucy?'

As clipboard woman led me away, I heard Joan snigger.

'I don't want to be mean,' she whispered. 'But her? That's the arm candy?'

'I know.' Sam sighed. 'They get younger and younger, don't they?'

In the next exhibit, the jellyfish moved with tiny, rhythmic pumps, as though we were watching a tape in fast forward. I was mesmerised by the slow, stringy pink ones in the case after that, but Lillie preferred the creatures beside them, the violet ghosts. Our favourites, however, were the same: the umbrella jellyfish. They were perfectly transparent, catching light on the lines of their strange anatomy. They would swim and swim, then suddenly pause – as though waiting for something – before moving forwards again.

I could have watched their mushrooming forms for hours, but Lillie pulled me on.

We had avoided most of the trial drama – I followed reports online instead. Tommo's arrest at the memorial had come with an unexpected breakthrough. After weeks of rifling through and testing the mess of that night, police had finally located what they believed to be the murder weapon. As Yola boasted at the memorial, the aquarium handlers had discovered, wedged behind the octopus flap, one champagne bottle. As slender and green as the others, but the only one containing traces of Richard's vomit. The shape matched the wounds; the fingerprints matched Tommo's. It seemed he had pushed it down Richard's throat while he lay unconscious, inducing the bile that had choked him to death.

The motive was equally straightforward. Tommo had not, as he'd told me, lent Richard money for his first film equipment. Of course he hadn't – I didn't know why I'd never questioned this. Richard had always been wealthy, the beneficiary of a generous trust from his grandfather. In fact, as it emerged in court, Richard had invested heavily in Tommo's nascent hedge fund and had, with the catastrophe of *Dominus*, been looking for an out. But his boyhood friend was reluctant to grant him one – given his failure to retain other clients, given his overly ambitious plan to span the Atlantic – and so Tommo had attended the birthday party with the aim of persuading Richard to stay. Tommo had not succeeded. Tommo had been humiliated. And then – went the prosecutor's argument – Tommo had seen his opportunity, as Richard fell from consciousness. If Richard was no longer a loyal friend and did not want to invest in him, perhaps his heir would.

'Nearly there,' said Lillie. Her voice echoed from the glass tanks. 'I think she's in the next room.'

I had shuddered reading the prosecutor's closing remarks, thinking back to the way Tommo's eyes had followed my daughter's path at the memorial. Far worse was the growing dread as I scrolled through reports of character witnesses. Stories of Tommo and Richard tormenting younger boys in school, tales of their disagreements and physical fights; the strawberries and the river incident, it transpired, was only a taste of the truth.

Tommo's lawyers requested me as a character witness for the defence, but I instructed Scott to make clear my hostility. It was not the champagne bottle that had shaken my affection for the tufty-haired boy I'd met all those years ago. It was the dishonesty. How could I provide any kind of testimony when I barely knew the man? How many of his lies had obscured my vision? And so I was not subpoenaed. I imagine the lawyers knew it would not play out well before the jury – hounding the pathetic mother of Richard's innocent daughter.

The defence argued that Richard had acquired the throat wounds earlier in the night – and that the traces of vomit could well be cross-contamination from the investigation or lab. As I read this, I recalled my conversation with Tommo, in the bathroom at the memorial.

What about the bruises? I had asked.

It could have been anything.

Who's to say they weren't from earlier in the night?

Don't you remember when we passed round the bottle in the paddling pool and people were seeing how deep they could push the neck into their mouths?

Tommo's lawyers laid the blame for Richard's death with the other guests. He had overdosed, they said. He had choked on his vomit, they said. Somebody must have heard this, they said, and decided to let him die.

Tommo maintained that when he began to fall asleep, Kei, Honey and Charlie were still awake with Richard. As they took to the stand, one by one, each faced the aggressive questions of Tommo's defence team, who painted a picture of Richard and how each of us had reason to kill him.

'Any of them could have done it,' one of the lawyers told a gaggle of journalists outside the courthouse. 'And it's the responsibility of the prosecution to ensure, beyond reasonable doubt, that they have the correct suspect. It is implausible that anyone could have murdered Richard Bryant while his guests slept soundly only inches away. But equally implausible is the notion that nobody woke as he accidentally choked to death. My client is adamant that one of the other guests must have heard something and decided not to act.'

In aqueous light, my daughter's face traced the shape of Richard. He was in her brow, in the hollow of her eyes, even the curve of her lips. But the chin was mine.

'There,' she said, pointing.

And there it was – a silhouette clarifying as it moved towards us, creeping over the rocks. An alien from a deep and unknowable realm.

'Cut,' shouted Richard. 'For fuck's sake, who the fuck is the fucking fuckwit lingering by the fucking door? You're in the back of the shot, you . . .'

It was only at that moment that we both realised he was talking to me.

'. . . imbecile.'

I froze with the attention of the room. Everyone had stopped mid-task to stare.

'Well?' Richard said, like he had no clue who I was. 'Are you going to move out of the fucking shot, or what?'

I tried to mumble an apology. Felt the gush of shame. Frantically searched for an exit.

It was strange, emerging to evening light. Like I had accidentally slept all day, woken after dinner. I sat on the kerb. Held my head. Found a cigarette in my pocket.

My mistakes had been monumental and I had not yet filmed a scene. I had accidentally touched a piece of equipment and received a tirade from the key grip. I had spilled soda on my white dress, provoking a flurry of wardrobe damage control. And then I had ruined a take by hanging around in the wrong place. I was useless. An embarrassment to Richard.

I leafed through my script again. Mouthed my lines in cigarette smoke.

'Elspeth Bell?' called a man, from the warehouse door. 'Elspeth Bell? They're ready for you.'

I threw down my stub and followed him to the set.

Her bright red was dulled by the turquoise of the water, but Persephone was undeniably herself: the tumbling tentacles, suckers two by two. We watched in awe. And then she was drifting away, squeezing through a crack in the rock. Only one tentacle remained, lifting and falling, as if writing out words in the water.

'So she came out to say hello.' A woman approached. 'Well, you must be Mrs Bryant.'

'Please,' I said, shaking her hand, 'call me Elspeth.'

'And you must be Lillie,' she continued in the sing-song voice of someone who spends their time with children. 'Jim's sorry he couldn't make it today, but he wanted me to thank you for everything on behalf of the aquarium. Persephone, the donation – it's all so generous. And he said you were interested in hearing how we'll use your donation, is that right?'

'Yes, but my mother and I were mostly interested in coming to see Persephone,' Lillie said.

'Excellent. Well let me introduce myself real quick. My name is Monice, and I'm the education co-ordinator here at the aquarium. So I'm not directly involved in looking after our animals, but it's my job to know what's going on and explain it to the public.'

We looked to Persephone's writhing arm. Her skin swayed with the water.

'Let me tell you,' Monice raised her voice as a gaggle of boisterous kids ran past, 'we've got big plans for this one. Gosh, we were so excited when we got your call, Lillie. Because we've got a male giant Pacific, his name is Alfonso – I know, I know, we let the kids vote on names – and both he and Persephone are about the right age for mating. So we'll be introducing them to each other pretty soon, and fingers crossed they mate. Our researchers could not be more thrilled.'

The children's footsteps echoed down a tunnel as they ran away.

'Although,' said Monice, 'if it's successful, unfortunately Persephone won't live for long.'

'She won't?' asked Lillie.

'No. Both the male and the female GPO die after breeding. The male normally dies a few months afterwards. Out in the wild, a predator would probably kill Alfonso – males drift around in the open a lot. Here, he'll die of starvation or maybe an infection. We call this period "senescence" but that's basically a technical term for old age. The octopuses enter this kind of dementia-like state where they don't hunt, don't forage, don't eat; their bodies start consuming themselves for energy; wounds on their skin no longer heal.'

'And Persephone?' Lillie looked uneasily to the tank. The creature was crawling out from her crevice once more, carefully placing all eight limbs.

'Persephone stores the sperm in her body until she wants to lay her eggs and there'll be a lot of them, a *lot*, like tens of thousands, maybe hundreds of thousands,' Monice explained. 'They're about the size of a grain of rice, though, absolutely tiny. And Persephone will attach them to the wall of her den, her rocky nook, and they hang down, kind of like grapes. Then she spends the rest of her days tending to them. Stroking them, blowing water over them to get rid of algae and fungi and other junk.

'And she doesn't leave their sides, not even to hunt. So she wastes away, turns a pale grey. Her skin grows lesions, like the male, as she watches over her eggs. That's for around maybe half a year. And when they hatch she blows them right out into the ocean. Shortly after that, or sometimes even while blowing the hatchlings free, she'll float away from the den and stop breathing.'

The aquarium had grown oddly silent – perhaps it was closing time. Of course, with my countless hours of research, I already knew everything Monice was telling us. But listening to the fate of this gentle, vibrant creature, as her limbs danced before me, felt too poignant, too unfair.

I could see that Lillie was getting upset as well. I placed a hand on her shoulder. Squeezed.

'That's just how it is,' Monice said gently. 'That's their natural life cycle. But you know, even without breeding, Persephone wouldn't live much past the age of five, and that's long for an octopus, really long. And because you, and your late father, have kindly donated her and the funds, we can look after Persephone. We can try to fertilise her eggs, and her DNA will live on. I think that's kind of beautiful.'

Persephone inflated, deflated her siphon, from one side to the other.

'Lift your head, look over here.'

I was so cold.

'I said, *lift your head.*'

And my neck was aching. It was taking every ounce of energy to hold the position without trembling.

'Lift your head. Your head.' Richard raised his voice. 'Come on, we're all waiting.'

The first day of filming, there were only three lines to master, spoken while sitting at a bar. But on the second day I was immediately plunged into my most important scene. I knew the lines well: they had been my audition piece. It was the positioning, my interactions with the co-star, Tyler, that I kept getting wrong. I was sitting on the floor in my underwear when he walked into the scene, and as he began to speak, I needed to turn around – just so. This was the fourth take and I could not get it right. It was impossible.

Richard had paused filming to position me exactly as he wanted.

'No, your chin, upwards. Please, Elspeth, for god's sake, listen.' He walked towards me, hissed into my face. 'You *can* hear me? You *can* understand basic English? So follow the fucking instructions. *Lift.*'

My cheeks seared. My neck was aching.

He pinched my chin.

'Like this.'

Threw it upwards.

'Can you feel?'

I did not dare answer him. Did not dare move.

'Can you feel? Like this.'

He pushed it back to its original position, then up. Repeated the action, again and again.

'Will you remember it this time?'

He threw my head back.

'Will you?'

'Yes,' I whispered.

Everyone watched. I knew what they were thinking. I had seen it in their eyes when I messed up the third take. I was the silly little girlfriend. Arm candy. I had no idea what I was doing. They asked themselves how I had won the role. They knew how I had won the role.

'Good girl,' said Richard, walking away. 'Take it from the top.'

'Roll sound,' called someone.

'Rolling.' 'Sound speeds.'

'Roll cameras.'

'Camera speeds.' 'Rolling.'

'Action.'

I tried not to flinch at the clack of the slate.

Tyler slammed the door behind him.

'Where the fuck have you been?'

I turned my head, sharp. Richard did not cut. I tried not to celebrate this success.

'I said,' Tyler grabbed my hair, pulled it back, 'where the fuck have you been?'

'I was here, Brent, I—'

'Tell me the truth, Cassie. Don't I deserve the truth?' He pulled my hair tighter. It was only supposed to be a stunt – we were meant to move in synchronisation. Me before him so the pull would not hurt. But now he was tugging harder and the tears in my eyes were real. His spittle hit my face. 'Answer me, slut.'

Our car turned from the aquarium directly into rush-hour traffic.

I wondered whether to turn on the radio – let it mask our silence as it had on the drive down – but my finger hesitated over the button. The verdict might have been read by now, and I had no idea whether it could warrant a flash bulletin, hit us without warning. Lillie and I could wait. Seek out the news from the privacy of her home.

'Persephone seemed content,' I said.

There was no response from Lillie, staring out the window, legs folded on the seat. I didn't blame her. My comment was banal, entirely without basis. Who was I to say whether the octopus was content in captivity, with only death before it?

The car in front rolled to a standstill. I sighed. It was a dull stretch of the freeway – utility poles, grass verge. I pulled the sunglasses over my eyes. The world was blue again.

'He never should have kept her in the first place,' I said. Then bit my lip. 'Sorry, I don't mean to—'

'It's okay,' Lillie said, looking straight ahead, to the road. 'I always told him I hated seeing her imprisoned like that.'

Her chin was delicate and hard. This was, perhaps, the very first time I had heard her criticise Richard.

My gold bracelet graced her forearm, hung loose where it clung to my own. I had not noticed it earlier; she hadn't asked to borrow it.

'Did he ever show you those videos of Persephone?' I asked.

'Which videos?'

'She used to escape,' I explained, 'from the filter. She would unscrew the flap that covered it and slip through. Every night. Then she'd crawl back when she couldn't breathe. We watched the videos. They're such intelligent creatures.'

Lillie frowned. 'He never told me that. He said she liked the tank. He said it was spacious.'

She reached for the gold band, ran a finger beneath it.

'Probably because he knew you'd have hated it,' I said.

'And then he would have had to give her away. I would've complained till he caved in.'

'He never could say no to you.'

'The ear-piercing,' said Lillie.

I shook my head, laughed. 'The ear-piercing.'

The driver ahead rolled forwards a few inches. I pulled up behind.

'And Dad filmed it?' Lillie asked. 'Persephone escaping?'

I nodded.

'Of course he did,' she said.

I smiled at her, and she smiled back.

There was a pause, like Lillie was considering whether to say something. She did: 'You know that email address Jerry gave you?'

'Yes,' I said. 'Did you hear back? Who was it – a manager? A casting director?'

The traffic was finally flowing – we were off.

'Neither,' she said. 'He's on the faculty at USC. Before Dad – before everything, I was thinking about film school, and Jerry said he had a friend who could answer some questions. I didn't really enjoy it, you know, the acting. It was talking to Dad about what he was doing, that's what I liked more. I haven't looked for any roles since *Dominus*.'

She paused. Then added: 'I haven't sent the email, not yet. But I'm going to.'

'I think that's a great idea,' I said.

'Yeah,' Lillie said, 'Honey was telling me that—'

She stopped herself, perhaps embarrassed at having brought him up. Before the silence could suffocate us once more, I decided to take my chance.

'Do you understand why I was so concerned about your friendship with Honey? It wasn't about him, it was – I wouldn't have wanted you to spend time with any of them.'

'Yeah,' she said, deliberately picking each word. 'I get that, I do.' There was an air of something else – scepticism at my claim, I thought, until she added, 'I think I wanted to ignore it because I didn't want to recognise the possibility that he could have done it. When they arrested Tommo, I was so relieved. I don't think I realised until then that I'd been holding my breath. The question was always there, at the back of my mind. I never really thought it was Honey, but the question was there.'

'Did you ever question me?'

'Never,' she said emphatically.

Until that moment, I hadn't wanted to admit to myself that this question had been sitting, quietly unacknowledged, between us.

'I never knew,' I said, 'that Honey was such a big part of your life, growing up.'

'You never wanted to hear about it,' said Lillie. 'When I was younger, every time I spoke to you about Dad, about my visits to him, you stopped listening. I could see it in your face – you just didn't want to know. So I learned to keep everything separate. I thought that was what you wanted?'

I let that stay unanswered.

Our half-truths and silences always seemed to lead back to Richard and me. The things I had never told our daughter, the lies, the cold silences that had taken their place. Would I have to explain everything eventually?

'I never knew you felt like that,' I told her. 'I would never want you to have to hide things from me. But yes,' I took a turn off the freeway, 'yes, you know, it probably was painful to hear about your father. And I'm sorry you were stifled by that.'

My words were more clipped and defensive than I had intended them to sound. I was falling back into that old role – chastising, hardening to cover the hurt.

This time it was Lillie who spoke before the opportunity slipped away.

'I lied to you,' she said.

It was quiet, I could have missed it. I waited for her to continue.

'I lied to you about Dad's party.'

'I know,' I said. 'Your father told me. He said you cancelled because something had come up and that he'd asked you not to tell me, so that I wouldn't cancel as well.'

'No,' she said. 'I lied about ever going. I lied from the beginning. Some of it was true. It was true that I didn't want to go to the party and see Honey and Dad back together again.'

'You said you needed my support.'

'I wanted to see you,' she said. 'So I didn't think there would be any harm. I wanted you to stay with me.'

'Lillie,' I said, 'you never need a reason to ask me to visit. I would have come just to see you – I would have booked a ticket the minute you asked. In fact, I did. That's what I did.'

'I didn't know that. We weren't talking much. I thought you disapproved of me moving. I mean,' she narrowed her eyes, 'you never told me about Julian.'

'Sure, I didn't think moving was the best idea. I thought you were too young. That's not why we lost touch, though. I didn't want to intrude on your independence. And you always seemed so busy when I called.'

'You moved when you were my age.'

So we were back to our old arguments.

'Yes,' I stressed. 'And that's exactly why I thought you were too young. But,' I said slowly, reeling us back from the precipice, 'I'll admit I was wrong. You've been doing well since you moved.'

'None of that matters anymore,' she said, empty.

I thought of the verdict, the news awaiting us at her house.

'Well, I would have come to stay, party or not. But is that the only reason you lied?'

Lillie studied her hands. 'Dad and I were arguing about Honey,' she explained. 'I didn't like that they were back together, and I didn't understand why Dad had forgiven him. I guess I was being protective. I said I wouldn't put up with it. I wasn't going to be civil to Honey and pretend everything was fine at Dad's party, because it wasn't. Dad got really upset. He said he was heartbroken, but he understood.

'And,' she took a deep breath, then continued, 'and he told me he was also disappointed because he was hoping I would bring you. He had this idea of a big reconciliation. So he asked if I could persuade you to attend anyway. It would be a birthday present from me to him, and that's all he wanted – to apologise to you. To reconcile with you. I always wanted you two to get along. I felt terrible about lying to you, but Dad said you would forgive me because you'd have a good time and you'd see your old friends.

'Still, though, I couldn't get rid of that guilt and, you know, after I picked you up from the airport that day, I called Dad to tell him I would come along. Lying to you, missing the party, just because of an argument between Honey and Dad that was now resolved – it felt petty and ridiculous and I regretted all of it. But Dad said I couldn't. He was so weird about it. He refused. He said it was too late – he'd planned out everything for the people who were coming, and he couldn't fit in anyone else. I wish I hadn't listened to him. Who knows what would have happened if I'd been there that night?' She looked up at me. 'I'm sorry, though, Mom. I am. I know I shouldn't have lied.'

'I understand,' I said, although in that instant I didn't wholly. It was difficult to untangle everything – to fit her explanation to Richard's lies. But I was certain of one thing: this was all my ex-husband's fault. Lillie could not be blamed for her father's manipulation. It broke my heart to think of the guilt he had piled upon her – making her responsible for our reconciliation. And now this guilt too.

'All this time, you've been carrying that around, haven't you?' I said. 'But if you had gone to the party, your father would have probably turned you away. Come on, you know that. You know how stubborn he can – he could be. I know it's easier said than done, but you cannot blame yourself.'

Lillie didn't answer, so I said, 'The ear-piercing?'

And then she smiled – a little distant, a little sad, but it was there. 'The ear-piercing.'

She hugged her knees to her chest, rested her chin on them.

'Hey, Mom,' Lillie said after a while. 'I missed you.'

'I missed you too.'

And it should have been a beautiful moment, but that was the ugly paradox I had constructed for myself. The more honesty between us, the bigger my lies. The closer we grew, the further I felt. The more I realised I would need to tell Lillie the truth about her father, the more certain I became that I could not.

And onward we drove – to the house, to the verdict.

I whimpered.

Tyler let go. I rubbed my scalp without thinking, realised a moment too late. But that was fine, that was realistic. I went on with the scene. Lifted my head, slow. Watched him circle the room.

'I've been hearing stories about you from the guys at the club. They say—'

'It's not true, Brent.' I knelt up, like Richard had told me. Held on to Tyler's leg.

He kicked me down. That was not in the script, not in the walk-through. My head smacked the floor. I tried to sit up again. His boot on my chest. The cameras were rolling.

'You'll listen when I'm talking.'

I had a line to speak, but I was struggling with the pressure from his boot. I choked out a sound. What was happening? Where was Richard? Why had nobody stopped the cameras?

Tyler removed his boot. Paced the room again. I sat up, gasped for air. Followed his movements with fear in my eyes.

'Carl told me,' he said. 'He told me, and I couldn't believe it. Because why would you do that to me? It wouldn't make sense. None of it. Doesn't fucking make sense.'

He hit his fist against the sink. Shook his head. Looked at me in the mirror. Looked away.

'Fuck,' he said. There were tears in his eyes. 'Why the fuck did you have to go and do that?'

He hung his head. Shoulders juddering with the sobs.

And then a sniff: that was my cue. I pushed myself up from the floor and moved slowly towards him.

'Brent,' I said softly. I wrapped my arms around his waist. 'Please, baby—'

He whipped his body around, grabbed me by the wrists.

'No,' Tyler roared. He trembled with fury, neck veins throbbing. 'No. You listen to me. Listen to me.'

He threw me onto the bed.

'You think I'm fucking around?' He pulled out his prop pistol. 'Does it look like I'm fucking around?'

'No, Brent, it doesn't, I'll—'

Tyler fell on top of me, crushed my face with his free hand to break off my words. His elbow was digging, hard, into my ribs. I could smell the doughnuts and coffee on his breath. He was heavy.

'Didn't you hear me?' he said.

The tears, hot, trickled down my face.

'I asked you to shut the fuck up when I talk.'

He took the pistol. Traced it across my cheek. It was metal; I flinched with the cold. Down my neck, my body. And then I felt it, cold, against my thigh, and he was using it to push my underwear to the side and the cameras were rolling and Richard was watching and this was not scripted, none of it, not where it was, not there, not in there.

As we wound up the road to Lillie's home, I could feel our nerves mounting. Lillie kept hugging her legs. The car was slowing –

whether because I was lessening my pressure on the pedal, or because gravity was dragging us back down the hill, I didn't know. But we were slowing and slowing, like the tyres were submerged in water. At one point I asked myself if we would ever get back. If we could remain ignorant forever instead.

I wasn't sure I wanted to know. Part of me was desperate to have an answer, an end to the torment so that Lillie and I could move on. And the only verdict that would have felt final was the absolute verdict: a concrete guilty verdict. A different, less certain, part of me didn't want an ending. This was a part that – despite the stories that had emerged in court, of Tommo as a cruel child, of Tommo as a ruthless, cut-throat businessman – hoped against everything that it was not true. This was a part convinced by the arguments of the defence, because when I asked myself the question, as I lay in bed at night, I didn't know the answer: could Tommo have done what they were saying?

This part of me didn't crave an ending, because without the absolute I could still ask questions. Without an answer, none of it felt real.

Lillie and I reached her house. I couldn't tell which half of me would win out, but I would know, in the moment, what I had truly been wishing for. I would know when I felt either disappointment or relief.

We went straight to the living room. Turned on the news. Didn't even sit on the couch – just stood, holding hands, a few feet from the screen. It took us a while to understand the scrolling text, the images. When we did, I drew Lillie close.

Tommo had been found not guilty.

Someone was covering me with a dressing gown, leading me off the set. Nobody said anything about what had just happened. Had they seen what Tyler did to me? But they had seen the way Richard moved my face. They had seen the kick. They had seen Tyler's boot, pinning me to the floor. Perhaps it was all improvisation. Perhaps I had no right to complain. I did not know. I could not think. The pistol was supposed to stay above the fabric. It was supposed to stay above. Above.

There were bruises budding, already, on my wrists. The ache where my head hit the floor. A numbness from the cold of the metal barrel.

As I was wiping my makeup, someone congratulated me on the performance.

'You were amazing,' she said. 'We were blown away.'

I could not thank her. I tried to smile.

When I got home that night, I resolved not to speak to Richard – it would be easier that way. He would come home later than me. I could pretend to sleep.

But he flicked on the bedroom lights as he entered, asking with cheer: 'How was your first proper scene, my love? You're a star. An absolute star.'

I did not want to reply. I kept my eyes squeezed shut.

'Elspeth, I can tell you're awake.'

I was motionless.

'Come on, you're not that good at pretending.' He laughed to himself. I heard him unbuckling his belt, removing his clothes. My weight shifted sideways as he climbed into the bed.

His hand slid over my stomach. His mouth on my ear.

'Did you like the little surprise we arranged for you?'

It had been his idea.

The cold of the gun.

I kept my breath steady, my eyes squeezed shut.

'Elspeth?'

He rolled me onto my back. I could not open my eyes. I could not do it.

'What is this? A game? Talk to me,' he said. 'Stop being childish.'

I kept my body stiff.

'Elspeth?'

He gripped me with both hands. Shook my body. I let it flop. I did not open my eyes.

'Okay,' he said. Then laughed. 'Stubborn child. If you want to play a game of statues, let's play.'

He lifted my nightdress.

'Can you feel that? Good girl,' he murmured. 'Good girl.'

I won the game. I did not move until he was finished. Until he had turned off the lights.

We stood before the screen, waiting for an explanation. An anchorwoman described what she believed had been the decisive factor:

The lab that had tested for Richard's vomit hadn't followed proper procedure, and Tommo's defence had sown doubt among the jury with talk of cross-contamination. As for the fingerprints – we'd all seen Tommo passing around the bottle, pouring champagne into mouths – they were circumstantial. The character assassinations, the financial trail, meant nothing without hard, persuasive evidence.

'Let's switch channels,' I said to Lillie, when the anchorwoman started repeating herself. 'Let's turn off our phones and watch a film together.'

We changed into our pyjamas. Piled bedding high on the couch, like I used to when Lillie was sick. She fell asleep twenty minutes into the movie, curled up, resting her head on my shoulder. I stroked her hair from her face. Turned the TV volume low. The picture kept playing, but I was losing focus, until the sequence of images meant nothing to me. Their flickering colours illuminated the room.

I had thought that if only I could get through the investigation, through the memorial, and then through the court case, maybe I could finally move on. But the memories still came at me, screaming, clawing for space.

When I'd understood the verdict, I felt neither disappointment nor relief. I realised, then, that I wouldn't have found certainty no matter the outcome. All I thought, standing in front of the television, was: *That makes sense.* Doubt and indecision and scepticism – it was a familiar land.

The film blacked out for a second; I realised I'd been forgetting to blink.

When the room lit up again, I took my phone – not pen and paper, I was loath to wake Lillie – and began. If I laid it all out, from start to finish, maybe then I could see clearly. How one thing had led to another. The day I met Richard; the terrible experience of filming *Anatomy*; everything that I had hidden from our daughter during our years of marriage; the lies I told thereafter. I tapped it out, there on the couch.

I didn't send it to Lillie, although on a whim, I'd addressed it to her. Instead, I emailed it to myself for safe-keeping. It shouldn't have alleviated my anxieties, sitting inert in my inbox. But it did. It was there: a record. Out of my mind and on the device.

After I sent it, I lifted my head, found that the credits had ended.

I must have fallen asleep with the phone in my hand, because its buzzing woke me up. It was a text message from an unknown number: *We need to talk*, it said, *now the trial is over. Can we meet?*

For a terrible moment, I thought it might be Tommo. And then the second text arrived: *This is Kei. I need to tell you something.*

The next day, Richard presented me with a bouquet of flowers.

'They were supposed to arrive yesterday.' He smiled, sheepish. 'I wanted you to know – I'm so proud.'

I did not take the flowers. He laid them beside me, on the bed. A card was attached. I did not read it.

I waited for Richard to leave the room. Then dressed myself, numb. Found him waiting by the front door.

'I thought we could drive in together,' he said, 'now you've found your feet.'

In the car, I did not speak. As we neared the studio, Richard found this increasingly irritating. Chastised me for 'sulking' – I was behaving like a child. I would have to get used to direction if I wanted to go anywhere in the industry.

'And after the mess on your first day . . .' He shook his head, troubled. 'Honestly, Elspeth, I didn't know whether you'd be able to perform the argument scene. Can you imagine how embarrassing it would have been, for both of us, if I'd had to replace you with someone else? Someone more experienced?'

I said nothing.

'I'm sorry I had to surprise you like that, darling, I am. But would you want that? Would you want your scenes to end up on the cutting-room floor? Did you want to disappoint me?'

Together we had made something truly authentic, he told me. The critics would love it. Was that not what I had wanted? Was that not what I had longed for?

On set, the praise continued. I became everyone's best friend. More than a rookie now, more than the director's arm candy. It was difficult to hold on to my belief that what had happened was wrong. Because what Richard had said made absolute sense. I had not been acting well, not until Tyler went off-script. And now . . .

How could I have felt that it was wrong, when everyone else behaved as though it were nothing? When Tyler joked around like we were schoolmates? When Joan apologised for being rude on my first day?

And so my hurt became a sting of shame. It had been my fault. I was talentless. Richard was right. It was his job to make difficult decisions like that.

I did not really understand what Richard had been doing, not until I saw the final cut of *Anatomy*, not until I read the reviews. *Elspeth Bell, as Cassandra DiSotta, embodies a female fragility*, they wrote. *Fierce vulnerability*. He had wanted my fear as Tyler threw me around, but he had also wanted the determination as I soldiered through the scene. He'd wanted my embarrassment, the tears in my eyes, but he had wanted pride and outrage as well. He had known that even as a prop gun violated me before a room of spectators, I would continue.

Maybe it was that same pride that carried me through the viewing, through all of the praise that followed.

'Such sparkling talent,' Richard said, in bed, the night after we watched the final cut. He kissed my shoulder. 'A world-class talent. I knew you would be when I first saw you. The gold dress, the manhattan . . . Do you remember our first conversation?'

'I remember, *Richard.*' It was still our joke – he would smile, without fail, every time I used his name.

He traced his finger up and down my arm.

'When I saw you sitting by the pool, alone,' he said, 'I knew we were the same. Neither of us was loved as a child, were we? But it didn't break us – that's how we became resilient. And I could see it in your eyes, when I found you at that party. It was like looking into a mirror.'

I raised my eyebrows, sceptical. 'I don't remember that. You seemed so confident. You came right up to me, with that drink in your hand.'

'That was the game,' said Richard. 'Bravado. And you were playing it too. The little trick you pulled with the cab?'

'I almost bankrupted myself with that clever trick.' I laughed.

'That's what I mean. We were both so strong, so confident – and it was all a charade. But later, as we talked, we could reveal our true selves to each other, we could be vulnerable together. Do you remember? I told you everything, my darkest secrets. You told me your hopes and fears. That's why we need each other: because we're both so strong, we can only be vulnerable together. I need you, darling, and you need me too.' Richard propped himself up on his elbow, to look down at me, beneath him. 'I think, perhaps, you're the only true friend I've ever had.'

I stroked his arm. It was warmer, more solid than mine.

'I never had a best friend, growing up,' I said. 'I was always fascinated by those friendships of two halves fitting together. But I don't think I recognised that in you at first. I didn't know you were my person then.'

'No,' said Richard, 'neither did I. That would've been too much to hope for. There was something, though. Something I found in you, something of myself in that girl sitting alone, watching the crowds. But, tell me, when did you know?'

My hand found the nape of his neck, my fingers laced through his hair.

'That you were mine? I'm not sure,' I said. 'Maybe you're

right. Maybe it was later that night, or maybe the next morning, when the sun rose and we still hadn't slept.'

Richard closed his eyes. 'I've never opened up every part of myself to anyone before. My heart, my work, my life.' Then he looked at me and said, as though realising for the first time: 'If you ever abandoned me, there would be nothing left at all.'

He stroked my cheek. 'My angel, my Cassandra.'

'My *Richard*,' I said, and he grimaced. Reached for my stomach to blow a raspberry.

I could not see, in those early days, that his love was a tool. That Richard was the craftsman and people were his materials. Not inanimate objects to hack at and stick together – he was far too clever for that. Rather, he appreciated the fact that we were human; he used it against us. Like a carpenter understands that pine is more pliable than oak, Richard knew us: our fears, our desires; our secrets and the masks we wore to hide them. He selected the perfect tools for each manipulation. This was how he possessed.

He charmed Miguel so the insecure little brother would idolise him. He poked fun at Charlie to make the proud boy prove himself. He competed with Tommo until his schoolfriend went too far; he knew Tommo would self-sabotage.

And with me and Honey, he alternated his methods. Humiliation one day, glory the next. I did not forget that terrible day of filming, not ever, but neither did I forget the months, the years of acclaim that followed. I did not forget his reasoning – it became my own. I did not forget his love, which could not be doubted. Not when he held my hand on every red carpet; not when he proposed, one month into the publicity circuit; not when he had given me everything, everything, every part of my life.

I had replied to Kei's message almost immediately – *Of course, I was hoping you'd get in touch* – but received nothing back.

Where do you want to meet? I texted, to remind her a few days later. Still nothing.

I told myself it was not worth worrying about – Kei would

answer when she was ready. But it was ominous, and I remembered it every now and then, found myself re-reading the text.

This is Kei. I need to tell you something.

Another unanswered question, another nasty hangover from the trial.

Lillie and I were doing our best to move on from such questions. We went for long walks at dawn, watched cooking shows – tried to recreate the elaborate dishes ourselves. We visited galleries in sunglasses and baseball caps, just before closing time, when they were at their emptiest. I took Lillie to a grief therapist; we both attended a support group for families affected by addiction. And she met Jerry's friend for coffee. Came back talking as fast as she could: they had sound stages and post-production suites, and there were screening rooms that could fit hundreds, although maybe she should look at some other programmes at other colleges too, but she didn't know what she would major in – writing or production – and would I go to a campus information session with her next month?

We explored the USC website, watched students' showreels. At one point I asked whether she was certain she wanted to stay on the West Coast.

'I guess it hasn't been great living here,' she said. 'I thought I would be busy with work and I'd meet new people, but I haven't really, not like I thought. I spent a lot of time on set, when I didn't need to be there. And when I wasn't on set or busy with publicity after the release, I was kind of lost. My friends from when I was younger, and I stayed with Dad – most of them have moved away for college, or they're here but they have their own thing.'

'I hadn't realised.'

'I didn't want to tell you,' Lillie admitted. 'Because you were so sure it wasn't the right thing to do.'

She was clicking through the website as she talked, flipping through testimonials of former students without reading.

'Maybe it was a good idea, though,' I said. 'It helped you realise what you wanted to do, didn't it? If you'd gone to college and studied something else, you might still have thought that acting was for you.'

'That's true,' she said. 'And I wouldn't change anything. I needed that time with Dad.'

We fell asleep together, watching films on the couch, each night. It was almost everything I had hoped for when I stepped off the plane, six months, and one death, ago. I knew I should start to think about leaving, what life would be like on my return to New York.

October had turned to November, November went on, and I was still living with Lillie, accidentally dozing on the couch one evening when the buzzer awoke me. I dragged myself up to check the monitor, expecting to find Lillie on screen, perhaps having misplaced her keys I was startled by the sight of someone else.

The figure at the gate was unrecognisable in the evening light. Was it the paparazzi again? A delivery? The person wasn't carrying anything. Their body language was odd. Agitated – shifting from one foot to the other. My finger hesitated over the speaker button. Lillie would have told me if she was expecting someone. Then the visitor lifted their head and pressed the buzzer again. I caught the face on the monitor: Kei.

'I wasn't sure whether you'd ever reply to me,' I called from the doorway as she crunched across the gravel. 'Thought you'd dropped off the face of the earth.'

As she got closer, I could see she wasn't smiling.

'It's good to see you,' I went on. It was, despite her ominous text, despite the unexpectedness of her visit. I didn't care that I was dressed in sweatpants, hair scraped into a ponytail. 'I think there are a couple of beers in the fridge, we could—'

'Would you mind if we didn't?' Kei was hanging back from the door. 'My Jeep's still outside.'

'Bring it in.'

'You want to go for a ride?'

There was a pause as I tried to think it through, sluggish from my nap.

'Okay. Sure. Let me leave a note for Lillie and change my shoes.'

When I came back, Kei had returned to her car. She was sitting at the wheel, engine running, rolling a half-made cigarette between her fingers, over and over. Her hands trembled. I buckled up. Kei scrunched her creation into a ball, tossed it behind.

'Wasn't perfect,' she muttered, pulling onto the road.

No music, no radio. We did not speak.

It was dark now; the roads were good, but Kei would make sharp turns and sudden stops, like she was driving through rush hour with a flight to catch. Jogged her knee up and down at each red light, kept clearing her throat, until I was twitchy with nerves as well – her anxiety was infectious.

Kei didn't need any more distractions; I waited until we had finally cleared the city, cruising north on the highway, before speaking.

'How are you?' I asked.

Kei shook her head.

'Why didn't you come to see me sooner?'

She kept her eyes on the road, ignored my second question, said: 'I'm not good, dude, I'm not good. I didn't know if I could. There's, uh – there's something I need to tell you.'

'About Richard?' I asked, tentative.

'Yeah,' she said. 'About Richard.'

Richard was lying on the bed in a fluffy white bathrobe.

'I don't understand why you went behind my back like that,' he said.

I was on the couch. The curtain was illuminated as a car drove down the street below.

'It was supposed to be a surprise,' I said. 'I wasn't lying, it—'

'But you were lying, weren't you? This whole time. You know, your honesty was one of the things that made me fall in love with you.'

Richard watched me as he said this, waiting for the flinch of pain to cross my face. I tried to keep my expression neutral, but my eyes were stinging and I felt sick. I could not meet his eye.

'You knew about my childhood,' he said. 'You knew how

painful those memories are. I don't understand why you would do this.'

'Because you always talk about your summers at Sedgwick. Like those were your happiest days.'

'Happiest days,' he spat. 'It's all relative, Ellie. I wouldn't expect you to understand.'

I closed my eyes.

'Sedgwick?' he said. 'Fucking Sedgwick?'

I had booked us train tickets to Norfolk, for the penultimate day of our honeymoon. Richard had planned our entire trip around Europe, paid for everything, and I could never afford to treat him as he had me. I poured my heart into this small surprise instead. My little wedding gift.

The estate had new owners now, the Mortons, a middle-aged couple; I'd liaised with them extensively from hotel lobbies as Richard and I travelled. The gardens were closed to the public on Saturdays, but they had been so generous, agreeing to let us roam freely. They knew what it would mean to Richard and to me. The staff at Claridge's – where we'd been staying that week – were in on the secret too. They prepared a little hamper for me to collect in the morning, had researched our route, even weather reports.

'Scorcher,' confirmed the concierge, when I called him from our room the night before, as Richard showered. 'I'd take a hat if I were you, miss.'

And so that's what I was wearing that morning: a large straw hat; a white cotton sundress. The concierge presented me with the hamper, from the chefs, with a wink.

At Liverpool Street, I ordered Richard to ignore the announcement boards, although I hadn't realised the routes only went eastward; our surprise destination was not so well concealed.

'To the Norfolk seaside?' he asked. 'Or am I not to guess? God, I could murder some fish and chips. Doused in vinegar. Is it the seaside, Ellie? Is it?'

I kept my mouth firmly shut. Pleased with myself, gleeful as we boarded the train and he still hadn't guessed – not even as we sliced out of London, through towns, through countryside, past marshland and tractors. And then we changed at Norwich to a local bus service, and he realised.

At the time I had thought Richard might be travel sick, but looking back, I could tell: he withdrew because he'd worked it out. He stopped talking and laughing, let go of my hand. He turned away from the window – eyes fixed on the back of the seat in front. By the time we reached our stop, he was pale and paralysed.

'This is us,' I said tentatively. He did not move. 'Our stop, Richard.'

The couple across the aisle were staring. The bus driver was about to pull away again.

'Wait. Please,' I called out. Then turned back to my husband. 'Richard,' I said. 'Our stop.'

He looked at me with hate in his eyes. And that's when I knew I had made an awful mistake, even if I wasn't certain then, what that mistake had been.

Sedgwick was beautiful. Surrounded by a thicket, the house was hidden until the very last moment, and then there it was: red-brick and cobbled; ivy and wisteria; the most chimneys I'd ever seen on one building. Swans on the river – or was it a moat? The water was calm, layered with lilies; the grass was vibrant with sun. We trudged, unspeaking.

'Elspeth, hello! And Richard too, lovely to meet you. Lovely.' I couldn't tell where the voice was coming from. 'How was the surprise? One second, let me – there.'

Mrs Morton emerged from the bushes beside us.

'Gooseberries,' she said, removing a twig from her fringe. It took a while for me to understand what she had said. *Ghuz-bleece*. 'I'm always picking gooseberries at this time of year. Couldn't stop them growing even if we wanted to. Endless jams, endless. I don't suppose you're fans?'

She removed her gardening gloves to shake our hands.

'But, then, you already know that, don't you?' she asked Richard. 'You must have fattened up on gooseberries every year.' And when he didn't respond: 'Well, I can only imagine how wonderful summers here must have been for you as a boy.'

'Yes,' he half answered.

Mrs Morton looked from Richard to me and back again. 'Can I offer you tea? A biscuit, perhaps?'

'No,' said Richard. 'Thank you.'

I tried to make an excuse: 'It's a kind offer, but we're tired from the journey, actually, and we've brought' – I held it up – 'this picnic. Would you mind if we stayed outside?'

'Of course,' she said. 'I'll leave you to it. You'll want to sit on the lawn, won't you? Well, I'm going that way too.'

As we crossed a little bridge towards the house, Mrs Morton chitchatted on. I winced with each question, with Richard's short answers.

'How are Penelope and James?' she said. '*Such* a shame they couldn't keep up the estate with James's condition. Have to say I don't know them very well, but they seemed such lovely people when we met them during the sale. How are they? How is James? They're in London full-time now?'

'I wouldn't know,' said Richard. He was staring at his feet.

'Richard and I live in California,' I explained. And then, didn't quite lie, but obscured the truth: 'He doesn't get to see his parents much.'

'Ah yes, yes. I do remember, you said. And you've been travelling around Europe, is that right?'

When she finally left us, I felt exhausted, on the verge of tears.

I had envisioned Richard and I strolling through the grounds. We would lie in the grass and I would feed him strawberries as he recounted his boyhood adventures. I thought there might have been a river and we might have removed our clothes, cooled our bodies in the dark green depths. Abandoned our carefulness in the tempered English wild.

Instead, our picnic had a strange formality. I unpacked the hamper. Laid out the cloth, the plates, the cutlery – deliberately, as though pouring myself into the small task would change anything.

I didn't speak. I didn't know how to begin. If I didn't begin, I couldn't say the wrong thing.

Richard sat picking grass.

The kitchen, the concierge, had packed a perfect picnic, had even printed a menu card in miniature: cheeses tied in wax paper, a small seeded loaf, two glass bottles of apple juice, and a Cromer crab and asparagus salad dressed in mustard vinaigrette; to finish, two cream buns and a punnet of strawberries.

Richard ate none of it. I wasn't hungry either, but I felt I couldn't leave everything untouched. I nibbled the asparagus. Felt immediately sick.

We left only half an hour or so after we'd arrived. Richard stood on the bridge whilst I went back to the house, knocked on the door to give Mrs Morton our thanks and goodbyes.

'Are you sure?' she said. 'You came all that way . . .'

I made an excuse: I was feeling under the weather. I felt ugly as I said it, certain she would see through me. But she didn't, and that was worse. She told me to hang on, dashed back inside the house. Returned with a bottle of homemade lemonade that she pressed into my arms.

'Thank you,' I said.

Those were the last words I had spoken until we reached London, till we were back in our hotel room. Richard had undressed, showered, returned to the bedroom in silence. I felt like it was possible: that maybe both of us would wait for the other to talk, and we'd be waiting forever, and maybe I would die before I knew exactly what I'd done wrong.

Then Richard voiced his first accusation, cold: 'I don't understand why you went behind my back like that.'

'It was supposed to be a surprise,' I said.

Kei gripped the wheel, stared at the road, as though searching for a way to begin.

'I know you and Richard had disagreements,' I ventured. 'I overheard you at the party, talking with Charlie.'

'Disagreements.' She snorted. 'That's what the prosecution had me say on the witness stand. But no – that's not the word for what he did to me.'

I pulled my cardigan tight around myself.

'Some of it came out in court,' she said. 'But not all. I answered their questions, told the truth. The defence wanted to show that our professional relationship was volatile. That I hated Richard so much I could . . . so the prosecutors, they were downplaying it. Of course I went along with them. I didn't want anyone to think I was – I didn't. I didn't murder him.'

I let out my breath as quietly as I could. Although I hadn't wanted to acknowledge the thought, it had been there as Kei screeched us out of the city.

'And it worked.' She shook her head. 'Did you see the press? Twitter? *Let's not jump to conclusions. We don't know the whole story.* People who I'd worked with before, saying I was exaggerating, when I was doing the exact opposite. *Richard was meticulous, but that's just the industry. He was a nice guy.*'

'I've been trying not to go online lately,' I said carefully. 'But I can imagine.'

(A wonderful, dependable father.)

(The best husband I could have asked for.)

'Some of that's people covering their asses,' Kei explained. 'Like, they knew Richard was more than "meticulous". But others waded in without knowing. And I get it, I do. You wouldn't want to think someone is capable of – I mean, when the stuff about Honey came out, I didn't want to believe it. I knew how evil Richard could be and I still didn't want to believe it. But even then, I would never – why do people defend monsters like him?'

I could answer that question, but I did not.

I held my breath. Looked out the window – the clusters of houses growing further apart until they were gone altogether.

'The thing is, the lawyers didn't know everything,' Kei continued after a while. 'And I wasn't going to bring it up – I didn't want to make myself look guilty. Now I feel sick. Sickened. Because the story that came out in court isn't the whole truth. That's not who Richard was. And the more news reports I've read about Richard and the trial, the more people defending him online, the more my anger has been building up. And now . . .

'I haven't told Sabine. I haven't even answered her calls the past few days. She – I mean, she knows about this. She always kind of suspected; she saw some stuff on set. You know, Richard didn't treat her and the rest of the cast too well either. But then the whole story came out when we were driving to Richard's party – I told her everything, and she didn't understand why I was making us go to the party. That's why she was being so weird that night. She was like, *if you're making me celebrate this monster then fucking watch me, aren't I having such a great time . . .*'

This made sense. I had never quite been able to understand Sabine's behaviour at the party.

Kei caught me frowning. 'Yeah, I lied at the memorial, when you mentioned her dancing with Richard on his birthday. They never usually flirted. She did it to piss me off because we had another argument and – yeah, I was pissed off. But we were fine by the end of the night.'

Kei had been gabbling fast. Stopped abruptly when she realised she'd talked herself off track. And then remembered what she'd wanted to say.

'Sabine knows about this,' she continued, 'but what she doesn't know is that I'm ready to come forward. I don't know what she'd say about that, there are . . . But I had to make the decision by myself. I wanted to know I was doing it for the right reasons and that it was the right thing to do for me. I'm sorry, Elspeth, I know I'm not making any fucking sense.'

I waited for Kei to gather her thoughts.

'And I've decided,' she said. 'I think I've got to come forward. Who knows – who knows how many people—'

'Kei,' I said calmly, although I could hear the beat in my chest. 'I think you need to start from the beginning.'

I tried to explain: 'I wanted to recreate – I wanted to get to know—'

'I can't do this.' Richard reached for the phone. 'I'm calling room service. I need a drink.'

'Please.' It came out shrill. I lowered my voice. 'Please don't, Richard. Don't . . .'

He paused for a moment, fingers hovering over the buttons. Then slammed the handset. Lay back and stared at the ceiling.

'I thought you would enjoy the trip,' I said, hoarse, after a silence. 'I thought—'

'*You* thought, *you* thought – this is exactly my point, Elspeth. You don't think about how your decisions affect *me*.'

I bit my tongue.

Richard shut his eyes, as though pained. 'Yes, you *think* you did this for me, but if you'd thought about it properly, you'd have realised that I'd never, *never* want this. A reminder of my fucking childhood?'

'You always talk about the gardens,' I said. 'The medieval fishing ponds and the lily pads and how you'd spend hours—'

'—by myself. Yes, because the gardens were my refuge, Elspeth. I spent hours hiding in the trees when Father was in one of his moods. I picked gooseberries straight from the bush when I was starving because my mother had drunk too much sherry to remember lunch. I invented worlds and games and I explored the grounds because I was lonely.

'Do you remember when I told you about the time I fell asleep in the potato patch and a gardener found me? He found me in the morning – no one had noticed I wasn't sleeping in my bed. Remember when I told you about the time my cousins came to stay with us and we swam in the moat? And I told you I insisted on remaining fully dressed in a jumper and trousers in the height of summer? It was because I couldn't show them the scars on my back from my father's . . . I was too ashamed. Until I went to boarding school, Elspeth, Sedgwick was my refuge. There were places to hide. But you should have known that. You knew about my childhood; you should have thought about what I was hiding from.'

I should have known. He was right. I was heartless.

He went on: 'You always do this. You daydream some romantic scenario. And I'm supposed to play the grateful role, aren't I? Well, I won't do it, Elspeth, I can't.'

It was so difficult not to cry. I pressed my eyeballs hard.

'I just don't get it.' Richard sighed. 'I bring you to this fabulous hotel and I spend my money on exquisite meals and we plan, together, to spend a few days enjoying London – one of the best cities in the world, by the way – but now I find out that this whole time you've wanted to go somewhere else. It's so . . . it's so ungrateful.'

He sat up on the edge of the bed.

'And it's typical of you.' He raised his voice. 'Always so fucking nonchalant. I take you to the most wonderful places in the world and you shrug your shoulders like I'm showing you a motel. A bloody 7-Eleven. *Reminds me of New York*, you say on the streets of Paris. *Just like South Street Seaport*. Fucking hell.' He flung down a pillow. Thumped it with a fist. 'Would it kill you to be a little more enthusiastic? I give you everything. I give you *everything*.'

But I had been amazed by it all. I could not believe my surroundings – afternoon tea in Tiffany-blue china; the antique elevator. Chandeliers and a shining, chessboard floor; the wide and winding staircase. And the weeks before: the food, museums; cobbled streets and cathedrals.

How was I supposed to show my wonder? He had plucked me from closing shifts at Food 4 Less and thrown me into a fantasy. I didn't want to seem immature, sheltered, uncouth – I thought I was supposed to act like I belonged there. Like I had always belonged there.

I was crying. I was pathetic.

Richard picked up the receiver again.

'No,' I tried to say. A moan between sobs. 'No, Richard, don't.'

His eyes were resolute.

'I'm not listening to you crying like a child all night,' he muttered, lifting the phone to his ear. 'You're giving me a fucking headache.'

'Richard, don't throw it away. Years of sobriety, your years of hard work—'

'Hello.' He smiled with his teeth, like the concierge was in the room. But his eyes were unchanged: flinty and cold.

'Richard.' I pushed myself up from the floor, walked towards him. I could not stop crying. 'Richard.'

'I'd like to order room service, please. Yes, thank you. I'll take—'

I grabbed the handset away from him. We struggled over it for a few seconds. I was pulling with both of my hands, all of my strength. I could hear the muffled tones of the concierge, asking Richard if everything was all right, and then in one swipe Richard had regained control, had ripped it from my grasp.

He slammed it down on the receiver. Picked it up. Swung his arm back. I could hear the dial tone, see the sweat on his brow. And then he struck me across the face.

I fell against the wall. Held my cheekbone in both shaking hands.

'Sorry,' I heard Richard say, 'I believe we just lost connection.'

The telephone was plastic, but it had felt like a metal bat. The pain throbbed through my skull.

He laughed. 'No, no, I didn't want to order anything, I was just wondering whether there are any plasters in the room? Oh, there's a . . . ? Perfect. Yes, a shaving nick. Okay, brilliant, thanks. Thank you, you too. Goodnight.'

He opened the bedside drawer, found a first-aid kit. Tossed it towards me. Not violently – a schoolboy throw, like he wanted me to catch it. I held still. Let it hit me on the leg and fall to the floor.

Richard sighed.

'I don't appreciate you telling me what to do, Elspeth.'

He stood up, retied his bathrobe.

'And I don't appreciate you crying. Trying to make it all about you. *I'm* the hurt one. Sedgwick. Fucking hell, Elspeth.' Richard shook his head, then walked towards the bathroom. Before he reached the door, he turned to say: 'Don't make me regret this.'

'Regret what?' I asked, in spite of myself.

'What do you think? The wedding, this whole fucking thing. Please, don't make me regret it.'

'I know I seem laid-back,' Kei said, 'but when I started it was tough. Racist, sexist shit. You're sent to costume on your first day. People don't want you carrying equipment. Some guy, your junior, explaining video codecs to you. So you work twice as hard to prove yourself. And when you finally get the respect, the jobs you deserve, you have to be twice as thankful.'

My chest was tightening. I opened the window to inhale the night air. We had driven through the town of Mojave, and now there was nothing but flat on either side of the road – the expansive, blackening sky.

'That's how it was when I started working with Richard. Twice as grateful. It was the first time someone thought I could lead, my first feature as DP. And it was so exciting. Here was the guy who had directed *Anatomy*, one of my all-time favourites. Someone who worked across a range of genres, who *defied* genres. A risk-taker. An artist. *One Hundred Years* was my dream job.'

Kei told me they had worked well in the beginning. Occasional clashes but nothing unusual – they were a team. When an argument escalated, she reassured herself: it could lead to unexpected results, better work.

'But *Dominus* was different, Elspeth,' Kei said. 'I thought I was going to quit. Not just the film but everything. My career.'

She paused while we overtook a freight train on the tracks beside us, waited for its roar to fall behind.

'I don't know what it was,' she said. 'Richard got more erratic, controlling. On the first day shooting the museum scene, he refused to break for lunch. Seven hours in, the cast was exhausted so I told him we needed to stop. *Not till it's done properly*, he said. Production didn't bat an eyelid. But the crew had already worked two hours before shooting; it was ridiculous. So I put my foot down. And we argued. Suddenly he said, *Okay, then – break*. I was about to head over with the others when he yanked me, literally, grabbed my shoulder. *Not you.*'

Kei cleared her throat.

'He said we'd had to shoot for so long because of my mistakes. Not true, by the way.' She looked at me. 'And I told him that. So he started pulling crew members. Asked them to critique me. Cam ops, ACs, right down to the fucking PAs. The way he did it – it's like they'd be fired if they didn't do what he said. And they knew Richard could make sure I was never hired again.

That if they stuck with me, they'd be on a sinking ship. Just like that,' she clicked her fingers, 'Richard tipped the balance. One by one, my crew tore me apart.' Her voice split. 'And it broke me, I'm broken. To have heard those things from my team . . .'

She recomposed herself.

'I was their boss.' Kei smacked her wheel. '*I* was the one who hired them. *I* was the one beside them in the trenches, day after day. I can't explain it, but – in my job, loyalty is crucial. I worked hard to build that, my whole career. And he smashed it down in one hit. Done. I couldn't bear to be on that set. Every morning, I wasn't sure if I would make it in. I'd sit outside in my car till the last minute.'

I did not know what to say. We sat with her words, the sound of the asphalt.

She eventually asked: 'Do you mind if I smoke in here?'

'Not at all,' I said. 'Do you want me to—'

'Nah.' Kei cracked a smile, took a rolled cigarette from her shirt pocket and lit it.

It went on, she told me, her voice emotionless. Again, in the dailies, Richard tore her down. The same thing happened the next day, and the next. Her anxiety slowly consumed her: she stopped sleeping, eating, her hair fell out. Richard knew how to belittle. He made an example of her.

'You know all the cast and crew signed NDAs on his last two films?' Kei laughed, hollow. 'He always told agents it was to protect his "creative process". Bullshit.'

She paused and hunched over the wheel to relight her stub. Sat back again.

'Funny thing is, it would have gone without saying. He would sue. Spread rumours. Yeah, I'd heard of careers he'd ended before. Richard joked about it constantly, even before *Dominus*. Whenever we argued. *Get it right, Kei. Don't make me regret hiring you.*'

She threw her cigarette out the window. Placed another cigarette between her lips. Immediately took it out again to talk. 'He was . . . he . . . I cannot tell you how much I loathe him.'

Kei sighed. Lit the cigarette. Shook her head.

'I hate myself more. I should've quit. When I think about that party . . . I felt like I had to go. I made Sabine come with me because I was a coward. I was always a fucking coward, and he knew how to – and I was smiling. I joked with him. I held up my glass and I toasted his health. But he was always like that. After the project was done, he'd become my best fucking friend. And I would stand next to him in the press photos and I would smile, I would . . .

'It became this joke. *Richard, oh yeah, he can be difficult.* Like it's normal to scream at a colleague. Like it's normal to keep someone up all night with meetings. Like it's normal to shut down an entire set because the DP didn't get the shot he wanted. Like it's a work habit. A character quirk. Artistic process.'

The car picked up speed.

'Fuck that,' Kei said. 'Fuck them. Fuck him.'

Richard and I spent the night in tormenting, cyclical arguments, our silences stretching longer between. Some time after the sun had risen, I finally heard his breathing deepen. I went to the bathroom. I stuffed a towel into my mouth. I sat on the marble floor, let it chill my legs. And I sobbed and sobbed, until I could return to bed empty.

There were silver trays awaiting when I woke later that morning.

'I didn't know what you wanted,' Richard said, 'so I ordered everything. Full English, Continental, berries and yoghurt. All the juices; take your pick. But I ordered a pot of coffee instead of tea – that much I knew.'

He smiled lovingly. Dragged two armchairs to the food trolley, began to arrange the silverware.

'I'm sorry,' I told him. The Band-Aid was itching my cheek.

He dropped a teaspoon, paused.

'It was inconsiderate,' I said. 'I know, and I shouldn't have taken you there.' I did not dare repeat the name: Sedgwick.

Richard was still motionless.

And so I added: 'I'm looking forward to our last day in London.'

He picked up the spoon. 'Forget it, darling. Your food's getting cold. Orange or grapefruit?'

The Wallace Collection, Liberty; I was careful that day. I marvelled at it all, just as he had wanted. My diligent husband – my best performance. Sumptuous oil paintings, sparkling jewels. I was surrounded by beauty and sickened by everything he had given me: the world I did not deserve.

Guilty as he buttered a croissant for me, layered it with jam.

Guilty as he held open doors for me, took me by the hand.

Guilty as he led me to fine jewellery, latched a necklace to my throat.

We had been driving for nearly two hours – I had no idea where we were. My eyes were peeled open and I could feel goosebumps prickling both arms. I was past fatigue. At some point Kei had taken a left off the highway and we were alone, slicing through the land, road barely visible. Nothing but the stars and shadows, a ship in the night.

When I first arrived in LA with Tanya, I couldn't drive. And so a when I got my *Anatomy* pay cheque, the very first things I wanted were driving lessons, a licence, and a car. I had always dreamed of that freedom. But Richard did not understand. *Why would you want to waste that money? Just use the driver. You know I'll take you anywhere you want to go.* It took me years to change his mind, to grant me that small victory.

I had barely said a word since Kei began her story.

As the night cold crept into my limbs, she explained her reason for coming to me. She had an interview scheduled with a journalist in a few days' time. She wanted to speak to me first because she felt like we had become friends, but also, Kei said, she had a favour to ask. Could I tell Lillie? Kei knew that Richard had been careful around his daughter. She admitted that sometimes, shooting *Dominus*, she had brought up difficulties and objections in front of Lillie, because she knew Richard would control himself.

'But Lillie needs to know before the interview is published,'

Kei said. 'I want to give her time to deal with it, before I go forward. Can you – would you be the person to tell her?'

Her voice was small and anxious; I think my decisiveness took us both aback.

'Yes,' I said. 'Yes.'

Kei exhaled shakily. 'I didn't – I thought you would be hostile. That you wouldn't believe me. Maybe you'd try to talk me down to protect Lillie.'

But I was not the same woman who had written that press statement all those months ago. Nor was Lillie the same girl.

I did not say this aloud. I slid my hands beneath my thighs to warm them. Watched a solitary house glide by in the distance: porch lights, curtains closed.

'When I was at my worst,' Kei said, 'I told myself: just get through it.' She sniffed. 'The shooting stretched on, we went way over schedule, and every day I woke up and said to myself: get through it. End with Richard happy. Then you can move on. Finish this project and you can find another.'

I thought about the scenes I filmed for *Anatomy*, the strength it took to return to that set. Every day, numb; every night, paralysed.

I thought about that second escape from LA, my gym bag and the credit cards. That push driving each step forwards, each step away from the house. Lillie beside me in the taxi, only concerned with her choice of candy for the flight – it had always been her treat, whenever we travelled together. She hadn't known it would be the last flight for a while. She hadn't known that on her return, two years later, she would be travelling alone. Little red knapsack and buckled shoes.

'But I've realised something.' Kei spoke slowly, as though thinking it through for the first time. I watched her hands on the wheel, the muscles in her forearms. 'I don't know what would have happened if Richard was still alive. Maybe having broken my spine, made me passive, he'd want to keep me around. I mean, if he did want me for his next project and I refused, maybe he'd have spread rumours – and with that NDA, I couldn't have contradicted them. I don't know. I don't know that *Dominus* would have been the end of it.'

Dad wouldn't do those things, would he?

You would know if he was like that, wouldn't you?

Dad never did any of those things to you, did he?

'It's not about the fact that he's gone,' Kei interrupted my thoughts. 'I think Montana Entertainment might have been involved in the NDAs, and, look, I'm not stupid, I know that telling this story will make me look suspicious, even if I didn't outright lie during the investigation.'

We glanced at each other. Then back at the road, the nothing.

'What it's about, Elspeth,' Kei said firmly, 'is everything I went through. It was hell. And I'm not content to have gone through hell without changing something. No. I look back now at how he treated me in the beginning, and I can see that even those smaller threats, the arguments, were unacceptable.'

Richard's disappointment, my never-ending guilt.

'I can see that the way he treated other crew members, the cast, I can see it for what it was. It was wrong.'

The prop pistol, the game.

(Can you feel?)

(Good girl.)

'And people need to know that. They need to see him for who he was. He was manipulative. He was abusive. He—'

And that was when I said: 'I know.'

I had spoken those two words louder than intended. They lingered in the car, killed everything else. I held my breath, waited for the probing questions, but when I looked over to Kei – how tired and sad she was at the wheel – I knew there would be none.

She nodded once, and then again. She understood.

I didn't feel lighter, having unburdened, but I did feel softer somehow. As though I had been bracing every muscle for years, preparing for an unknown impact. And it had not come, and I had realised it would not come, and I could rest at last. Part of me wondered whether this was the time to go on – let all the memories loose. Another part still cradled the shame. In the end, neither compelled me. Kei had heard the crack in my voice. She didn't require a detailed retelling; she didn't need to hear my justifications for staying with Richard, my guilt for not leaving earlier, or my excuses for keeping silent. She had heard it all in that hairline fracture of the second vowel. She would know what it meant, and that felt like enough for me, for now.

As we drove on, I let my mind drift to the party: that conversation Kei and I had shared on the couch. Was it Richard's murder that had changed everything, or was it all in motion already that night?

I rested my head back and drank the dark air: crisp, sweet. The earth and dust were lifting to life, almost herbal with the brush.

'He always enjoyed throwing people together,' I said, as the thought unfolded. 'I think he wanted to know what they – what we – were made of.'

I smudged my finger along the rubber groove under the window.

'Like how, when you hold two familiar colours against each other, they seem different, unexpected. Richard wanted that. The clashing, complementary, but I think . . . I don't think he ever wanted this. He would have hated this. Us talking, together. Our honesty. He preferred it when people were pretending not to be themselves. Yet here we are. Despite everything.'

I smiled at Kei.

'No,' she said. 'I'm sorry, I can't do this.'

We pulled off the road. The rocks crunched beneath us; Kei cut the engine. My eardrums rang for a few seconds.

'If you don't want to talk about him,' I said, 'that's fine. I just thought, I was just thinking that—'

Kei covered her eyes, shook her head.

'Is it the interview?' I asked. 'Are you nervous?'

She didn't answer.

'I can drive if you want.'

'Elspeth, please, give me a second.'

I waited, listening to her staggered breaths, unable to diagnose my mistake.

Kei lifted her head. 'I'm going to stretch my legs. I'll just be five minutes.'

'Is that safe? Should you leave the car?'

'Five minutes.'

She walked into the night till she was the size of my thumb.

I didn't understand how everything had changed so quickly. Maybe the emotions were just catching up with her. Maybe it was only with my confession that she had truly realised what her interview would mean: the other people she would be carrying.

I watched as Kei took her hands out of her pockets. Crouched down. Covered her face again.

The winds were whipping across the flatlands, rolling gently, then lashing out. It created a strange sound, a whistling, but not against anything – there were no buildings, no mountains, not even rock formations, for miles. Just currents of air, smashing against one another like waves, occasionally rushing through my window. They died down for a moment, and I could hear a lonely bird, calling in the distance. Then Kei's overshirt flapped as the wind lifted again – she stood up and wrapped it tight around her, walked back to the car.

I rolled the window closed. Kei shut her door, and we were sealed from the world.

'I don't want to go back,' she said.

She turned the key.

'But I'm going back and I'm going to drive us. I need to do it myself; I can't be a passenger. It's my decision – do you understand?'

She stared at me, intense.

I didn't understand what she was saying nor the sharpness in her voice, but I said: 'Yes, of course.'

Kei nodded, then hauled the car around.

Again we sat in silence, with only the sound of the road. But this was different from the drive here: there was something ugly between us. I held myself stiff.

'I wasn't planning to say anything about this,' Kei began. I struggled to hear her over the engine. 'They would – I don't know what they'd do to me if they knew. But it always felt wrong to lie to you.'

'About what? About Richard? The filming?' I asked.

'Not that.'

'Then what?'

'I lied and I lied for such a long time, Elspeth. And now I want to tell the truth about Richard and me, but – fuck. This is not right at all. This is not how it's supposed to go at all. I wasn't going to—'

'Whatever it is,' I said, 'you don't have to tell me. If you don't want—'

'I do,' she said. She hit the wheel, nodded violently as she said: 'No, I do, I do. I need to tell someone. If I don't tell you now then I don't know if I can – I thought maybe coming forward about the filming might make me feel better, like it might make me feel like I'm brave and I'm doing something good, but now it's this ugliness and I can't control it. I'm a coward, I'm a fucking coward.'

'You're not a coward, Kei.'

'You don't know that,' she said. 'You don't know.'

'Whatever it is, I'm sure—'

'You don't know that we killed him.'

For a moment I couldn't talk.

And then she said it again: 'We killed him, Elspeth. We all killed Richard.'

'You told me you didn't,' I said. For some reason, that was my first thought. 'You told me you didn't.'

'I know.'

'When you got in the car, you told me—'

'I know, Elspeth. I lied.'

'What do you mean you lied? You killed him?'

She didn't say anything.

'*You* killed Richard?'

She kept driving.

'Who's "we", Kei? Who killed Richard?' I was shouting now. 'Kei, what do you—'

'Let me talk, let me talk, give me a second, okay?'

We had reached the highway and she was going fast. I clung to the grab handle as she swerved around a car.

'I had fallen asleep,' she said. Her voice was eerily calm, even as the vehicle picked up speed. I kept clutching the handle, my other hand holding on to my seat. 'There was the argument with Richard about whether he'd take the dope, remember? I can remember that. And then I think I must have fallen asleep because the next thing I remember is different. It was quieter – like everyone else had fallen asleep – and the aquarium was bubbling. And that's when I heard it. This choking noise.'

(The wounds; the bruises; a long, blunt object.)

'I think that's what woke me up.' She was speaking without emotion, eyes wide, dazed. Like she was reciting a story that had happened to someone else. 'At first I tried to ignore it. I kept my eyes closed. I think because I'd just woken up and maybe I could tell myself it was nothing. But then it happened again, the choking noise, and it was – it was disgusting. I wanted to – I needed to stop hearing it. It was this cough, retching and coughing, and then this gurgling sound. This gurgling cry.'

(The wet 'O' of the mouth, the stare of the eyes, the stench of vomit.)

'That's when I opened my eyes. He was twitching. His legs were twitching. His chest. It was this shuddering, Elspeth. I was frozen. I was horrified. I keep seeing how he was shuddering.'

I was confused. 'But he was already choking when you woke up? So you didn't kill him?'

'He was still alive, Elspeth. He was alive when I woke up. And then I looked around the room to see if anyone else had heard, and—'

'Did you see someone there? Was it Tommo?'

'Everyone was right where they had been before. The first person I remember seeing was Tommo. And he just looked at me and I looked at him and it was like I was asking a question and he shook his head, just a fraction; he shook his head. And then I could see that Charlie was awake as well. He looked at me. His eyes were enormous, he was horrified. And then Miguel and then Jerry. All five of us were watching each other. And then—'

A sob caught in Kei's throat. She went on, her voice climbed higher, got quieter: 'And then I felt Sabine waking up and I just held her still and Richard was choking and I heard the vomit splatter it was going everywhere and Sabine sat up like she wanted to go to him but then it was like she felt me holding her and she turned and she looked at me and that was it I had made the decision for us – I don't know why I made that decision. We were looking at each other when Richard was dying. It was everyone, it was all of us looking at each other while he lay there shuddering and jerking and the vomit—'

'But you said you killed him, Kei. It wasn't – are you saying he was already dying when you woke up?'

'He was alive, Elspeth. We killed him. We just sat there while he was dying, and I think – I know if just one of us had moved we could have saved him.'

'You don't know that.'

'I do. I know it for a fact. I have to live with my decision. I decided in that moment not to let him live. I killed him, Elspeth.'

'You didn't kill him.' I didn't want to believe it.

'Stop trying to defend me,' she shouted. We were going faster, faster. 'Don't justify what we did. We made that decision. I sat there, listening, while a man lay dying, and I decided not to move. I heard him, I heard him. Don't defend me.'

I kept quiet.

Kei released the pedal, slowed us down a little.

When she spoke again, there was something poisonous in her voice: 'You know, we did it on purpose. In the morning, I was awake – I was awake all night – but I kept lying there until someone else discovered him. I think the others did too. That's why you found him, and Honey too. Don't defend me. We did that to you.'

(The flesh was cold to the touch.)

'I saw Lillie at the memorial,' she went on. We were picking up speed again. 'I saw what this did to her. It was wrong, I know it was wrong. It doesn't matter how much I hated Richard or the things he did to me. I made a decision and now I have to live with it.'

'Kei . . .'

'Don't try to talk me down.' She was crying. How could she see the road?

'Kei.'

'Shut up.'

There was a car up ahead, Kei swung into the oncoming lane to pass. The headlights of an approaching truck were growing.

'Kei,' I shouted, clinging to the handle.

'I did it,' she sobbed, 'I did it. We killed him, Elspeth.'

As we paced down the corridor, it took every ounce of discipline not to adjust the collar of my shirt or to tidy stray wisps of hair. I clutched my papers in both hands, held them tight to my chest. The sound of the crowd grew louder – and then the door was in front of us.

'Wait,' I said. 'One minute.'

We paused so I could catch my breath. I looked to the floor. The carpet was a nondescript colour: not quite blue, not quite grey; not textured but not smooth. I studied its fibres. I took my time. Then I raised my head and gave the nod.

The room fell silent as we entered. Somebody coughed. Someone shuffled in their seat.

I settled my papers on the podium and cleared my throat. Ready to address the crowd, the lenses, the microphones.

The cameras snapped.

The night of the party, as we moved from kitchen to atrium, we continued to play alter ego. Miguel was the next victim.

'Billionaire entrepreneur,' said Richard.

'I thought the game was what you could be in another life?' asked Jerry.

'It is,' said Kei, 'but Richard here seems unable—'

Richard held up a hand. 'He owns a publishing empire. Fashion magazines, literary journals. A real patron of the—'

'Incredibly unimaginative,' said Kei.

'All right,' Richard said, 'if you're so good at it, tell me: what am I?'

'A disgraced politician,' offered Tommo half-heartedly, in

Kei's silence. 'You've been fiddling your expenses *and* your secretary.'

'An artist,' said Miguel.

'A *con* artist,' corrected Jerry.

'Please,' said Richard.

We waited for the next suggestion, which came, after a few seconds, from Charlie. 'I think you could have, like, run for Congress.'

'Very astute, mate,' said Tommo.

'What about you, Ellie?' Richard said. 'Tell me, what do you think?'

'A chef,' I said. 'A ship's cook.'

No one reacted, so I explained: 'You're ruthless and exacting, maybe missing a front tooth. You insult the rest of the kitchen. The sous chef can't get it right. And if you don't fire the busboy within a week, he'll have left, in tears, of his own accord.'

Honey and Sabine joined the group.

'But you criticise yourself too,' I added quickly. 'And the dishes are always perfect.'

Richard ignored me, turned to Kei. 'Still no suggestions from you.'

'Don't worry, dude,' she said, unbothered. 'I know what you are.'

'Enlighten us, then.'

'You're a puppeteer.'

Richard gave his sharp laugh. 'Excellent. Fantastic. So that was the nugget of gold we were all waiting for. Sounds like the beginning of a bad joke, doesn't it? *What did the politician say to the puppeteer?* Well, I'd take a puppeteer over a builder, a barista, a postwoman' – he pointed at Tommo, Charlie and me in turn – 'or an unemployed music-video director' – Kei frowned – 'any day of the week. Who does that leave? Jerry . . .'

His old friend grinned.

'Jerry, the heavyweight champ.'

The joke evaded me. Jerry laughed along, punched Richard's arm lightly, but I could sense his unease.

'And Sabine, the starlet who would do *anything*.'

'Leave her alone,' said Kei, too quiet.

'What did you say?'

'I said leave her alone. It's not funny.'

Richard narrowed his eyes. 'She can talk for herself, darling, no need to get involved.'

Sabine took a sip of her champagne, watched him over the rim of her glass.

Honey shook his head, rubbed his jaw. 'Kei's right, you take it too far.'

'And what are you, my love?' Richard turned to Honey, stroked a thumb across his cheek.

Honey shrugged it off. 'Come on, this is bullshit. Let's talk about something else.'

'What is he?' Richard looked around the group. 'No suggestions? None? Surely someone can think of an occupation for a high-school drop-out who left home at—'

'Shut up,' said Honey. 'Seriously, *shut up*. Nobody wants to hear this.'

'No? I thought that's what this game was about. Brutal honesty.'

The music paused between songs – and then continued.

Honey sighed. 'I'm going outside. You can be as honest as you want without me. Sabine?'

Richard watched them leave. 'A fucking puppeteer. A con artist, a cook. So you're allowed to take the piss out of me, but I can't give it back?'

When there was no answer, Richard laughed. 'It's a joke,' he said. 'It's a joke.'

Nobody else laughed.

'But you want to know what a real joke is?' Richard continued. 'This game. Fucking hell, who plays parlour games at parties in this century?'

'I'll get the Monopoly board out,' said Jerry. 'Anyone else want another drink? Okay, I'll just help myself.'

Kei whispered something to Charlie.

Richard sniffed, turned to me. Raised his eyebrows as though he might find a friend.

I looked down at my drink, ready to make my excuses and leave. But a thought occurred – and that was when I asked him, genuinely curious: 'What could Lillie have been?'

'Ellie,' he said, a quiet warning.

But I pushed harder, repeated the question. It suddenly seemed vital to know – what did he think of our daughter?

'I don't know, Ellie,' Richard said wearily. 'She's an actress, through and through. I don't know.'

'You're wrong.' I shook my head. 'She could have been anything.'

He looked at me. 'Yes, she's a clever girl. Very determined.'

'No, that's not what I meant,' I said. 'You don't understand.'

But when Richard asked what it was that he could not grasp, I struggled to explain myself. Could only repeat weakly: 'You don't understand.'

The cameras snapped. The words on the paper.

Kei was not with me as I stood at the podium.

The night of her confession, I had made her pull over. I swapped seats with her and drove us back. She chain-smoked the entire way. When we reached Lillie's house, she got out of the car to return to the driver's seat, but before she opened the door she paused to ask: 'Are you going to tell Lillie? Will you tell the police?'

'I don't know,' I said. It was the best I could do. Kei nodded a few times, defeated.

I had gone to bed numb that night.

I looked at my words on the paper. Swallowed my saliva. My fingers felt sticky.

The cameras snapped.

Kei had postponed her interview, she told me the next day. I called her early, before Lillie woke up, relieved when she picked up the phone. The way Kei had driven, I had worried she wouldn't make it through the night. We arranged to meet for breakfast. I had too many questions – and Kei was the only one who could answer them. I ordered myself a black coffee; she asked for a flat white with a shot of espresso on the side. She looked terrible. She hadn't slept.

'Have you decided?' she asked.

I hadn't.

The waitress set our coffees on the table, asked if we wanted anything else.

'No. Thanks,' said Kei. Waited until the waitress had left to continue: 'So I called Sabine last night. She thinks I'm crazy to even think about going public. And she thought I was crazy to tell you everything.' Kei poured sugar into her coffee. The crystals dented the foam. 'But it's weird, I don't regret it. Telling you. Can I ask something, though?'

I didn't nod, but she went on, meeting my eye: 'If you decide to tell the police, can you just, like, not mention Sabine? It wasn't her choice. I stopped her. The others made the decision for themselves, but she didn't.'

'Why do you think the others let Richard die?' I asked, cradling the heat of my coffee mug.

She sighed, stirred her coffee. 'I couldn't say for sure.'

Then: 'I have my thoughts, though. The stuff about Tommo from the court case – I bet that's accurate. Jerry, I don't know, but he and Richard were in a bad place. Same with Miguel. He told me about this big fight they had that night, something about funding – Richard was threatening to tell Miguel's wife about an affair. And Charlie . . . I honestly think Charlie was just scared. A scared little boy. He was sitting there, terrified. I saw it in his face.'

I didn't understand. 'But you'd be okay for me to mention Charlie to the police?'

'Sometimes I want to protect him,' said Kei. 'But he's not a kid. And, yeah, he was scared – scared about calling an ambulance, being there with the drugs. You heard him panicking about his manager the next morning. It was self-preservation.

'No, Charlie made his bed. We all did. Apart from Sabine – I really believe I stopped her from saving Richard. She's been racked with guilt. The only reason she didn't confess during the investigation, and especially when Tommo was arrested, was for me. Both of us, actually, we wanted to protect each other.'

Kei drank her flat white in one go. Wiped her mouth with the napkin. 'Well, no, that's not quite true. I probably would have given myself up in the trial. I felt bad for one person taking the rap when all of us were guilty. But then Tommo pulled that shit.'

'His defence?' I hadn't thought of the trial once overnight – I'd been too preoccupied with the night of the murder. With imagining what had happened in Richard's last moments, as I slept, just feet away.

'He dropped me and Charlie in it. But that's not what pissed me off. It was – there was no need to bring in Honey. He was innocent, like you. And I know you're friends with Tommo, Elspeth, but you should know he's a nasty piece of work. He knew Honey was innocent, but he wanted to pin it on him because he thought he could get away with that. A Black man; a gay, Black man. Young – and poor when he met Richard. Dirt poor. He knew that Honey wouldn't play well with the jury. So why should I have stepped in to help out Tommo? He's trash. A real piece of shit. He and Richard deserved each other.'

'And Miguel and Jerry?'

'They had no loyalties to Tommo. Miguel looks after number one, and Jerry – can you blame him? With his treatment, not knowing which way it'll go . . . I wouldn't want to spend my last days in jail either.'

I remembered Miguel calling the house, then approaching me at the memorial to point the finger at Honey.

I gulped my coffee. It was still scorching hot. And then I asked Kei the question that had gnawed at me all night.

'Are you sure,' I said, 'that Richard wasn't murdered? The throat bruises – is there any way that someone could have done it just before you woke up?'

'I've thought about that,' she replied. 'I mean, I guess it's possible. But I don't think it would change how I feel about everything. I still feel like I should have helped Richard.

Kei paused on this thought. Then swirled her espresso a few times, threw it back.

'There was something else, though,' she added. 'Have you finished your coffee? Let's go for a walk before this place gets packed.'

We turned off Melrose, up towards Santa Monica Boulevard, snaked our way left then right then left and left, so we could stick to the emptier avenues – the neighbourhoods, with their fruiting date palms and dappled sidewalks, guard-dog signs, parents taking kids to school.

'This is going to sound insane,' Kei said. 'But there is one thing I keep thinking. Tell me it's crazy, Elspeth.'

I waited. 'Go on.'

'I go over every detail, and it doesn't make sense, does it? Why did Richard invite just us? Why did he play those games all night? And the things he said, the speeches, the food. You know he gave each of us a different arrival time?'

I could see myself reflected in her shades. I answered her question with another question. 'What are you saying, Kei?'

'It's just . . . why wasn't Lillie there? That's the thing that . . . I know she would have been there if it had been a normal party. She adored Richard and he adored her. She's the only person who knows all of us, and wouldn't she have wanted to be there?'

A commuter scooted past us on the sidewalk.

'Lillie did want to be there,' I said. 'At first she wasn't going to come – she didn't want to see Honey and Richard back together after the allegations and the media attention. Then she changed her mind, but Richard told her it was too late.'

'Of course he told her not to come.' Kei shook her head at this new information. 'And you know, maybe Lillie *thinks* it was her idea to not attend because of Honey, but can't you just hear him? *I'm sorry, darling, but Honey's organising my birthday. You don't have to come, though. I know you don't want to see him right now. We can celebrate together some other time.*'

I could well imagine he had planted that seed. But it could have been for any number of reasons. 'Maybe he wanted to drink and, you know, he'd bought the heroin. Richard wouldn't have wanted her to see him like that.'

'I know that, I do. But I can't help thinking . . . What if his death was meant to be a test?'

I stared at her. A test?

Watching me, Kei shrugged. 'Yeah, Sabine never wants to hear it. She thinks I'm trying to justify what we did. But whether or not Richard deliberately overdosed, I still regret leaving him to die. I'll always carry that guilt. I'll always be sorry for doing that to Lillie. To you, letting you find his body.'

We walked in silence for a while. Then I said: 'A deliberate overdose. When Richard died, that's what I thought. Until the police told me about his throat. I thought he'd either killed himself or maybe, if it wasn't totally on purpose, maybe he'd been kind of reckless. Because of how *Dominus* had performed and then him being dropped by the studio. He's always struggled with himself.' I thought for a moment. Then added, 'But the throat wounds, Kei. I just don't know.'

'Yeah, I get that. I do.' Kei was slowing her pace, watching each step. She continued: 'I guess I was kind of persuaded by what Tommo's defence said. I wondered that myself – whether he already had the bruises before he died. And then when they found the bottle. That's when I really felt like the test made sense.'

'Because?'

'They found it in the filter, right? I'm certain, I'm *certain,* no one could have had time to push a bottle down his throat, remove it, hide it in the filter, then sit back down like nothing had happened. I would have heard the filter flap. And it's not – why would you kill someone like that? It's weird, right?'

'They could have hidden the bottle later. The next morning.'

'No,' said Kei. 'No, one of us would have seen. We were all there. And you would wipe your prints off too, if you were covering your tracks.' She hesitated. Started again: 'You know, I think back to before the party, and Richard was in this hopeless situation, wasn't he?'

I nodded. I had thought the same when I'd learned of his

death. And I'd only known the half of it then. Richard had slipped the film's schedule with endless takes, with his incessant perfectionism. The studio started to muscle in. He took his frustrations out on the cast, on everyone. At home, he had probably grown more controlling over Honey. Richard was ready to seek comfort in his addiction. Jerry tried to stop him, which had resulted in the fight, the firing. And when Honey came forward with his accusations, right before the film's release, everything collapsed.

But then, Kei went on, Richard turned things around. Somehow, despite his addiction, he went on. I knew that was out of character. Richard would always use in situations like that – when he was at his most frustrated, when he'd lost control.

And the forgiveness that followed Richard's downfall too – as he made amends with Honey, apologised to Kei, Sabine, Charlie, Jerry, Miguel, thanked me at the party. None of that had been genuine, I knew. He had wanted us back in his sway.

Kei thought it was more than that. That he had wanted to test our resolves that night, our love for him, and if it all went wrong – if he couldn't claw his way back into our lives, back to success – then he would conduct the ultimate test. Would we save his life? At least?

'I think he thought that one of us would,' she said. 'I think that's why you were there. You loved Lillie too much to let anything happen to him. I don't think he really believed he would die. But also, like you said you thought initially, I don't think he was scared of death.

'If things went wrong, Richard had insurance. He would take us with him, like a pharaoh buried with his servants and pets. That's why he hid the bottle, with Tommo's fingerprints.'

'You think he did that to himself?' Even as I asked this, I knew that if Richard had set his mind to such a plan, injuring himself in that fashion would have been no challenge for him. He had hurt himself before, to make me feel guilty. Throughout our marriage he'd done countless reckless things.

'I know, it's far-fetched. I know. Sabine thinks it's ridiculous too. I mean, she says that, but there was this one thing . . . You remember those bright-blue candlesticks on the dinner table? When Sabine was talking to Charlie at the party, Richard came over to them with a couple of those candlesticks to show off their "craftsmanship" – Murano glass, or whatever. He *insisted* on giving them to Sabine and Charlie – something about how the pair complemented each other, like the actors had in *Dominus*. It was kind of awkward, Sabine said, so they had to accept. And Richard put the candlesticks in the closet so they wouldn't forget them. Sabine found hers in her purse the next day. Placed it in a drawer and forgot about it, didn't even tell me – until I started wondering about the bottle with Tommo's prints. This idea of Richard taking us all down with him. And then I started wondering whether there was a murder weapon for each of us, waiting to be found. And whichever one the police managed to find first – that person would go down with him. If none of them were found, well, there were still the throat wounds, right?

'Sabine says she doesn't think it was a test – she *says* that, but she let me smash up the candlestick with a rolling pin. We drove to Santa Monica at dawn the next day, threw the shards off the pier into the sea.'

The purse, the glass candlesticks, the champagne bottle – something about this part of the theory was bothering me, but I couldn't quite pinpoint what.

'And *Dominus* has done better in movie theatres since then, hasn't it?' I asked.

'That's a fucking understatement,' said Kei. 'Everyone's re-reviewing it. Rooting out subtexts, like it was his farewell manifesto. And the story surrounding his death? The investigation? It'll be a Hollywood legend. He'll be immortalised. I think the only thing he wouldn't have foreseen is that none of us were named until the court case. He would have wanted more drama, more attention around the investigation. That's why I think he hired staff, so there would be spies that night, leaks to the media, you know?'

'But there weren't leaks, because he had specified—'

'Come on, dude,' Kei said. 'Any one of them could have made

a year's pay by selling their story to the media. We were just lucky. Fucking lucky. If Richard hadn't wanted leaks, he wouldn't have hired any staff. And the memorial too? There were journalists – you saw how quickly the cameras started flashing when the cops arrested Tommo. And did you see that some of the *same* waiters were there as well? That was all part of it. He wanted us to remember that night. He wanted to haunt us. He thought of everything. And it worked – every time I cry, every time I wake up in the night, I see him laughing.'

I could picture it myself.

There was something believable in her theory, I had to admit. I thought of the envelope Honey had found in Richard's desk – *In the Unlikely Event*. His detailed plans for the memorial.

We circled back to the coffee shop to collect our cars as I tried to pick apart Kei's theory. But she had an answer to each of my questions. Was this because it was true or because, like all conspiracy theories, it was flavoured with fact, obscured with minute details and unverifiable conjecture?

As I drove home, I ran over the facts: Richard's envelope, the champagne bottle, a candlestick in Sabine's purse. And then I remembered. That night I had a bottle of water in my purse – until I didn't. Acqua Panna, medium-sized. I'd found its disappearance odd at the time, but had it been taken as 'insurance' for his death? It was just the right shape.

A long, blunt object.

I wished Kei had not told me her theory. It only left me with more questions, more confusion. I didn't know what to think. Not even when I returned to my daughter.

'Are you okay?' Lillie asked. 'You look kinda sick.'

She was carrying her backpack, ready to leave the house. Lillie had found a job as a runner on a reality show, was getting as much experience in production as she could, without her father's connections.

I told her I was fine; she hugged me goodbye. And then I knew, as I waved to her from the front door, that I would never tell her, or the police, about Kei's confession. How Richard's guests had watched him die. She had been tortured enough when the murder investigation began, at the thought of one of her friends, family, colleagues, killing her father. What would it do to her to know the truth: that six of them had let him die?

And if the real story went public, it would never be forgotten. Kei's words were echoing through my mind as I watched Lillie drive away that day. *It'll be a Hollywood legend. He'll be immortalised.* Already Richard's death was legendary; it would be even more so, I thought, if the truth ever emerged. If the public learned that six guests had been guilty, Sedgwick would become a photo op on an open-bus tour for evermore. I couldn't ruin Lillie's life like that. I couldn't let Richard's death chase her, chase her career.

The next time I saw Kei, I let her know my decision. She didn't seem relieved. She just nodded solemnly. I never told her about my missing bottled water – I didn't want to add more fuel to her theorising. Kei deserved to escape. And that's what she did: she and Sabine moved to Paris. I followed their new life on social media. They sat in cafés: with chairs and tables sprawled across cobbled streets, arms around each other, smiling. Sabine holding bunches of flowers; Kei with a hand-rolled cigarette behind the ear.

I kept an eye on the others too. Charlie was doing well for himself. Of course he was, the industry always gave men like him second chances. When I learned that he'd won the lead in a new superhero movie, I couldn't believe I'd ever thought *Dominus* would be his end. As for Miguel, I never read about him in the media, but I assumed he was still making money, that his wife had never discovered the affair. Jerry was still married to Judy, who was nursing him through his chemo. Tommo had disappeared.

After the jury's verdict, Scott asked Lillie if she wanted to file a civil lawsuit against Tommo, venture into battle again. She decided the media attention wouldn't be worth it. Ultimately, as Tommo had predicted, Richard's death would come to be remembered as an overdose, the throat wounds an uncomfortable question raised by the coroner's report, which some were happy to forget, others not.

Honey had retreated as well. In the months that followed the memorial, as the court case rose to front pages and feeds, he shrank from the gaze of the media. He refused them the shortest statement, even when the verdict was read, and suspended his social media accounts. He insisted that Lillie take the money from the sale of Sedgwick. He auctioned off the artwork.

While Honey and I would never grow close – it was too late for that – hearing Kei's account of Richard's last moments had laid any lingering suspicions about him to rest. I would follow his journey over the years, with pride and, maybe, with distant love. Only five years later, he would rise to creative director of an artistic glossy, destined – as whispers had it – for editorship. I would be pleased for him, pleased again a decade later, when I saw the photographs of his wedding: the peonies, the rays of sunlight, the big band and the beach. His hair would be a powder pink, matching the silk of Lillie's bridesmaid dress. And I would wonder if Honey was thinking of Richard, the life he could have lived if it had all been different.

It was Richard that I was thinking of as I took to the podium. As the cameras began to snap.

I gripped the podium to steady myself.

Over the past few weeks, I had slowly unspooled Lillie's life. We began late one night when she returned from work. I read Lillie the email; I gave her space to think it over. The next day, she asked questions and I answered them. Just like that, we unpicked memories, we frayed beliefs.

The time Lillie had missed a birthday party because we spent the afternoon in the emergency room: Richard had broken my wrist. The time security guards had looked after her, let her play with their office supplies: I had fainted in a store, starving – Richard thought I'd been putting on weight. The time Lillie missed pre-school for three days straight: Richard was convinced I was seeing a former co-star, had hidden the car keys, locked the gates of our home, and taken my purse. He had not unplugged the phone line – he never went that far – and I wondered whether it was a test of my love: to taunt me with freedom. But who would I have called? What would

I have said? I told myself that I would only call for help if Lillie and I ran out of food.

We came close. Three days passed – three days of distracting my daughter. Blanket forts in the living room. Bread pizza for every meal. We used up all the toppings, till only beef jerky was left.

The cameras snapped.

I asked myself whether I would have found the courage to stand there, before the journalists, were Richard still alive. I remembered the lies he had told, after Honey's accusations, and the lies I had told as well.

But this was only for one brief moment.

Lillie placed her hand over mine. She did not let go when I started to read my statement – first drafted months ago, as she slept soundly on my shoulder.

'Almost a year has passed,' I began, 'since I read a statement to the press. I told you that Richard Bryant was a wonderful, dependable father to my daughter. The best husband I could have asked for.'

I exhaled a shuddering breath. Cleared my throat again. Continued: 'That statement contained lies, misdirection, and omissions.'

Someone scraped their chair on the floor. I could feel it: the room, listening. I could feel the sweat on my palms. I inhaled, then exhaled. Pictured myself beneath the water. Those tumbling limbs, the suede-like skin. The opening in the creature's eyelids: as thin as a bobby pin.

Lillie had received an email, only a few days before the press conference: Persephone was now a mother. There was a video attached, filmed through a narrow crevice. I could just make out Persephone's limbs beyond the hanging eggs, drifting like willow branches in the wind. Still large and suckered, but withered, whiter than before. Persephone was a ghost of herself, jetting water over the eggs with every last breath.

I was watching the video alone: Lillie had forwarded it to me while she was out at work. I closed my laptop before it ended; it didn't feel like a scene that should be watched.

ACKNOWLEDGEMENTS

Thank you to Carrie, without whom this story would not have become a novel; to Emma and Elana, without whom this novel would not have become a book, and without whom a great many of these words would not have found their way onto these pages; to Josie, Kate, Amy, Steven, Lily, Amber, Maddy, and everyone else at Hodder who has worked on *The Ninth Guest*, without whom this book would not be *this* book, and would not have found readers; to all of the friends, family, colleagues, and writing group members who read and commented on various iterations of this story, without whom I would have had neither the feedback to craft it, nor the confidence to pursue its publication; to my grandparents, without whom I would not have heard as many stories; to Jonah and Maili, without whom I would not have told as many stories; to my parents, for all of the novels and notebooks over the years, without which I might not have found my love of writing; and to Hasan, without whom I would not be myself.